The Death Game

Chris Longmuir

B&J

Published by Barker & Jansen

Copyright © Chris Longmuir, 2014

Cover design by Cathy Helms www.avalongraphics.org

ISBN: 978-0-9574153-3-1

This book is dedicated to the memory of Dundee's first policewoman, Jean Forsyth Thomson.

ACKNOWLEDGMENTS

The inspiration for this novel was generated by my research into the origins of women police after reading Joan Lock's informative book 'The British Policewoman: Her Story'. During further research I came across Mrs Jean Forsyth Thomson, Dundee's first policewoman who worked alongside Dundee City Police from 1918 to 1921. My character, Kirsty Campbell, bears no resemblance to Jean Forsyth Thomson, and is purely a fictional character, the product of my over-active imagination. However, Mrs Thomson did provide the inspiration that allowed Kirsty to step into the world through the pages of this book.

I would like to thank Willie MacFarlane, the honorary curator of Dundee Police Museum, for allowing me access to the museum and providing much valuable source material in respect of the Dundee Police Force in 1919. This gave me valuable insight into working conditions during this period. Without his help I would have been feeling my way in the dark.

My editors, Liz and Betty, have done their usual excellent job in editing and proofing the book, and Cathy Helms of Avalon Graphics has worked her miracle on the cover.

Prologue

Friday, 31 October 1919

She presses herself into the wall when she hears the scrape of the key in the lock. Which one will it be? And which game will she have to play.

So many men. So many games. She does not want to play their games, but she has to. She has to show them whatever they want. Fear. Sorrow. Anger. Gratitude. And above all she has to show them how much pleasure they give her.

The door opens, and light spills into the dark, windowless room. Her ankle chain clinks as she tries to push herself even further into the wall. The silhouetted shape moves towards her, and she clutches her arms around her body in an attempt to protect herself. All the time knowing she will have to do whatever he asks.

The shape reaches her and sits on the edge of her bed. He turns to face her, so his face is faintly illuminated.

'Oh, it's you.' She sighs with relief.

'Yes, child. I have come to take you away, but we must be quiet.'

'I can't go,' she says.

'Why not?'

'Because if I go they will make Cissy take my place.'

'I have arranged for Cissy to come as well. No one will be able to hurt her, and you will not have to do this anymore.'

'Where will we go? We have nowhere but here.'

'Trust me. I have it all arranged. You will both be safe and no one will be able to hurt you again.'

She feels the chain fall from her leg when he unlocks it. Standing up, she takes the hand held out to her.

She hesitates before walking through the door. 'You are sure we will be safe?' A trace of fear sounds in her voice. 'They

1

won't be able to come after us and make me play the games again?'

'Of course you will be safe. There is nothing for you to be afraid of. But we have to be quiet, and you have to be brave. Think of this as another game. The biggest game of all.'

1

One month earlier

Kirsty Campbell entered Ixworth Place Section House slamming the door behind her, shutting out the fog which cloaked everything in a clammy grey shroud. Lately, London never seemed to be free from fog. It crept into every corner, chilling the blood and numbing fingers and toes, even on the warmest of days.

In the gloom of the wood-panelled entrance hall she fumbled to unfasten her belt and unbutton her jacket. Her shoulders, stiff from maintaining a military posture, relaxed, and she wondered if there would be hot water for a bath. Maybe she would be lucky.

The sound of voices leaked through the common room door which hung ajar. Her night shift patrol in Hyde Park had been exasperating and she craved company, so she pushed the door open and flopped into a chair beside Gertie and Ethel.

'Thank goodness my shift is over,' she moaned. 'My feet are killing me.' Bending, she unlaced her knee-high boots.

'I heard a rumour,' Gertie said, watching her, 'our boots are land army ones that were rejected because the leather is too stiff.'

'I'm not surprised.' Kirsty massaged her toes. 'I wouldn't put it past Sir Nevil to have supplied them simply to torture us.'

'He certainly didn't want us to look attractive,' Ethel said, 'otherwise he would not have agreed to the Harrods' design for the uniforms.'

'I didn't join the police force to be attractive.' Kirsty removed her bowl-shaped hat, placed it on the floor, and fingered her short auburn hair away from her neck. Although she was her best friend, Ethel's need for male approval annoyed her.

3

'Heavy day was it?' Ethel refused to rise to the bait.

Kirsty nodded. 'I had Constable Dillon following me today, but he was hopeless. I rousted two men out of the bushes with their trousers round their ankles, and he refused to arrest them because they looked like gentlemen. I wish we had powers of arrest and then we wouldn't need to rely on silly idiots like him.'

'Oh, I don't know, he's not so bad.'

Kirsty raised her eyebrows. 'You don't mean to say . . .'

'He's quite good-looking.' Ethel flushed.

'I suppose so, if what attracts you is muscle rather than brain cells. You know as well as I do, constables aren't chosen for their intelligence.'

'Maybe they should be.' Gertie looked thoughtful.

'Constable Campbell!'

Kirsty, aware of her dishevelled uniform and unlaced boots, pushed herself out of the chair and stood to attention. None of them had heard the sergeant enter the room.

'Superintendent Stanley sent me to fetch you,' Sergeant Wyles said.

'Yes, ma'am.' Kirsty's fingers were already busy fastening her buttons.

They hardly attracted any attention as they marched through the streets to Scotland Yard. Londoners had become used to seeing policewomen in their military-style dark-blue serge uniforms. It had not always been that way, and when the women first wore them, Kirsty, along with the others, had been the subject of rude comments and jokes. But, despite that, she felt comfortable wearing her tunic with its hard stand-up collar, six polished buttons with her whistle on the end of a chain attached to the third one down, wide leather belt that pulled the waist of the jacket in allowing the bottom to flare out below her hips and leaving room for the capacious pockets, the only place to keep personal possessions. Her calf-length skirt was plainer, slightly flared and covered the top of her knee-high lace-up boots.

On arrival at The Yard, they walked through a stone arch and crossed the cobbled courtyard to the main door. Inside was a confusing warren of gloomy corridors, but Kirsty was familiar with the building and knew her way. Wondering what she had done to warrant a summons, she climbed the stairs and walked along the corridor to Superintendent Stanley's office.

'I will leave you here,' Lilian Wyles said when they reached the superintendent's door. 'If you want to talk to me when you come out I will be in my office.'

'Oh,' Kirsty said. She had been expecting Sergeant Wyles to accompany her inside.

A strange smile flickered over Lilian Wyles' lips. 'You will be all right, there is nothing to worry about.'

Kirsty watched until the sergeant entered an office further up the corridor. Feeling bereft, she took a deep breath, straightened her uniform, and knocked on the door.

'Come in.'

The superintendent stood, looking out the window, with hands clasped loosely behind her back. She was a tall woman with square shoulders and a long face. Her hair was cut so short it could not be seen beneath her military-style cap which looked like an inverted soup plate. Her uniform was immaculate while her belt and shoes had been polished until they gleamed. Yet she still managed to look feminine.

Kirsty stood to attention, even though her boots pinched her toes and the ache in her legs and feet was unbearable. She shifted her weight from foot to foot and wondered whether she should cough to announce herself.

The loud ticking of the grandfather clock, standing to the right of the massive oak desk, emphasized the silence in the room. Superintendent Stanley, engrossed in what was happening outside, ignored her presence.

At last, the superintendent said, 'I am proud of my policewomen. Are you proud of your calling, Miss Campbell?' She turned, fixing Kirsty with a penetrating stare.

When Mrs Stanley had been appointed last year, by the Metropolitan Police, as the first superintendent of an official women's police service, Kirsty had thought it a strange choice. She could not understand why her own chief, Margaret Damer Dawson, had been overlooked. Particularly as Commandant Dawson had four years experience running the voluntary

Women's Police Service. But the police commissioner, Sir Nevil Macready, had been unable to forget the suffragette background of Margaret Damer Dawson's voluntary body of women police, and preferred to appoint Mrs Stanley to lead the newly formed, Metropolitan Women Police Patrols. However, he did not have it all his own way because many of the Women's Police Service members joined his new force. Kirsty was one of them.

Despite her initial misgivings, Superintendent Stanley had impressed Kirsty with her professionalism, and she soon forgot her earlier resentment. Now, Kirsty's uniform was every bit as immaculate as the one worn by her mentor, and she always tried to behave in a fitting manner, one that would win the respect of the woman in front of her. Kirsty even had her long auburn hair cropped, although it still curled around her ears in an exasperating feminine manner.

Kirsty straightened, lifting her chin and squaring her shoulders. 'Yes, ma'am.'

Superintendent Stanley studied her for a moment before nodding as if confirming something to herself.

Kirsty squirmed under the superintendent's scrutiny, her stomach did somersaults, and heat spread through her body.

'I understand the Dundee City Police Force is considering the appointment of a woman.' Superintendent Stanley's gaze lingered on Kirsty's face as if waiting for a response. 'Chief Constable Carmichael has approached me for advice, and I have agreed to consider his request to transfer one of my staff. The position will initially be a temporary one but if it is successful it could become permanent.'

Kirsty shifted uncomfortably under the superintendent's stare.

'It is my understanding you have connections with Dundee, so I thought you might be interested. Besides, up to now Scotland only has one policewoman, Miss Emily Miller in Glasgow. It would be beneficial for the policewomen's cause if more women could be introduced to Scottish police forces. It would also be good for your career.'

The unexpectedness of the offer left Kirsty speechless

because she had not been aware Superintendent Stanley knew she was Scottish. She had never had the strong Dundonian brogue with the long drawn-out vowels, so it hadn't been too difficult to lose the remnants of her accent after she came to London.

A lump rose in the back of her throat threatening to choke her, and she had trouble breathing.

When she left Scotland, ten years ago, she had been determined never to return and believed she had come to terms with this. Kirsty had not thought of Dundee as home for such a long time, so the upsurge of homesickness surprised her. Suddenly, she realized she wanted to go home. She wanted to see her mother and father again. And, of course, Ailsa, one of the reasons for the estrangement from her parents.

'I have arranged a meeting for you with Chief Constable Carmichael in this room, at two o'clock, tomorrow.'

It was evident Superintendent Stanley was not anticipating a refusal.

'You do realize,' she continued, 'there is talk of a committee to be set up to examine the role of women police. The police authorities in Scotland are somewhat backward in respect of women providing a police service, but Mr Carmichael is one of the more forward looking chief constables. He likes it to be seen that he is keeping up with the times. I would think he is anxious to employ a woman in his force before the committee produces its report.'

Kirsty nodded her agreement. Afterwards, she wondered if she had been foolish to accept the offer so quickly, and doubts filled her mind. The more she thought about it, the more she felt it was not a good idea.

Her meeting with Chief Constable Carmichael was pleasant. He was a tall, middle-aged man with a perpetual twinkle in his eye. Kirsty liked him. She liked his humour, his appearance, and his ability to put her at ease. She thought he was a man she could trust and respect. Her doubts dispersed, and she relaxed.

'I will not be there when you take up your post, Miss

Campbell,' Chief Constable Carmichael told her as he gave her a letter to present to the assistant chief constable.

The full impact of her decision did not hit her until the next day. She was in the middle of knotting her tie, and making sure it sat neatly under her stiff collar, when she looked in the mirror and met the eyes of her friend who was doing the same thing. Ethel turned from the mirror, but not before Kirsty saw her own misery reflected in Ethel's eyes.

'Oh, Ethel. What have I done?'

Ethel and Kirsty had met when they became members of The Women's Freedom League. They had been suffragettes together, first in Dundee and then in London. When the two main suffragette organizations formed The Women's Police Volunteers, among the first women to join had been Kirsty and Ethel. They had shared their lodgings, their lives, and their secrets.

'How can I face my parents again? How can I face Ailsa?'

'It will be all right.' Ethel laid her hand on Kirsty's arm. 'It's the opportunity of a lifetime, you'd be a fool to miss it.'

'But I've never worked as part of a male police force up to now. My colleagues and superiors have always been women. It's going to be difficult to fit in. There have never been women police in Dundee, and you know what policemen can be like. They will never accept me.'

'Do you remember why we became policewomen?' Ethel stared at the reflection of Kirsty in the mirror and her voice became thoughtful. 'Anyone who knew us then would have thought it a strange job for a pair of suffragettes, especially when so many of us had suffered at the hands of the police.'

'Not all of us suffered as much as others,' Kirsty murmured. 'I was never in prison or force-fed like some of them.'

'That doesn't mean you wouldn't have gone through the same if you'd had to.'

'But so many of the women we marched and worked with underwent more than I did. Even Sub-Commandant, Mary Allen, was imprisoned three times.' Kirsty always felt guilty her suffering had been so much less than that of many of her friends.

'Yes, and we hated the police.' Ethel paused for breath. 'We joined the force because we thought the constant fighting and protesting was getting us nowhere, and we would have a better chance of changing things from the inside. Besides, lots of women have fallen foul of the law and suffered at the hands of policemen. Think of the girls forced into prostitution in order to make a living. Why should they be treated the way they are because they're poor? And what about the victims, the girls who were raped or abused. What kind of justice did they ever get from the police or the courts?'

Kirsty remembered her own rape and her reluctance to tell anyone about it. 'You are right,' she said. 'But we were so idealistic thinking we could change the police force by becoming policewomen.'

Ethel smiled. 'It hasn't all been failure though. Maybe we haven't changed the attitude of the policemen at the top. What was it Sir Nevil Macready called us, "suffragettes and lesbians"? As if being one meant you were also the other.' She laughed derisively.

Kirsty smiled at the idea of flirtatious Ethel being a lesbian. Nothing could be more ridiculous.

'But,' she continued, 'we do help women who come into contact with the police, and we have to keep on working towards acceptance. That's what you can do in Dundee. Make them respect you. Make them recognize women have a place in the police force.'

'But how can I do that? I'll be one woman on my own.' Kirsty paused. 'And I won't have you.' Her voice was barely audible.

'Nonsense,' Ethel said. 'We'll write and if it doesn't work out you will come back. Mrs Stanley would not refuse you.'

'I suppose not, but it would be admitting defeat and I hate giving up on anything. It's not only that, I'll be living and working so close to my parents. What if they refuse to acknowledge me? After all, it's been ten years since I had contact with them after that last horrible argument when my father gave me the choice of giving up the suffragette cause or leaving his house forever. I couldn't give up the cause, Ethel.'

She sighed. 'I accepted his rejection at the time, but it's been hard.' Kirsty paused, struggling to maintain her composure. 'And then, there's Ailsa.'

Ethel's hand tightened on her arm. 'You'll be fine. In a month or so you'll have forgotten London.' She grinned. 'Think about the London beaks and how they treat us. Remember how Mr Mead refused to hear our evidence and threw us out of court last week? "Ladies have no place in a court of law, such evidence is not for their ears".' Ethel mimicked his deep voice. 'It didn't matter the evidence wasn't heard because we were the ones supposed to give it. Do you remember the jujitsu holds we were taught during our training? I was tempted to use one on him.'

Ethel's eyes gleamed with mirth and Kirsty laughed at the thought of Mr Mead being thrown to the floor by Ethel.

'Surely it can't be any worse in Dundee,' Ethel added.

Kirsty nodded. She pulled her belt firmly around her middle and decided she had no option but to get on with it.

Kirsty lived through the next three weeks in a daze and left London in a whirl of activity. Ethel helped her pack, checked nothing was forgotten, and arranged for a motor cab to call at the section house. But even then, Kirsty almost missed the train after a dray horse collapsed in the road overturning its cart, and scattering beer barrels all over the cobbled street.

The cabby was in a foul mood when they arrived at the station and, after grabbing the money for his fare, dumped Kirsty's luggage on the pavement at her feet before driving off.

Kirsty smiled ruefully at Ethel and looked around for a porter. After a few moments, she hefted her portmanteau onto a nearby trolley and pushed it into the gloomy railway station which, in the aftermath of the railway strike, seemed busier than usual.

The smell of smoke, grime and sweaty bodies caught at her throat, and it took all her willpower to battle through the crowds to where the train was getting up steam in preparation to leave.

Kirsty heaved her belongings into a carriage and jumped in.

The door slammed with a finality which made her shudder. She grabbed the leather window strap and pulled it, allowing the window to thud down. Leaning out, she grasped the door handle, but Ethel's hand restrained her and she loosened her hold.

'I'm going to miss you,' Ethel said, her eyes bright with tears.

A cloud of smoke belched from the engine, and the train started to move. Ethel's mouth opened and closed, but the piercing noise of the train's whistle drowned her words.

Kirsty continued to lean out of the window, while she watched her friend becoming smaller and further away. Grasping the leather strap she closed the sash window with a slam and sank into her seat.

All her doubts resurfaced and she would have given anything to be back on the station platform saying to Ethel, 'I'm not going. I've decided to stay in London.' But now, as she listened to the rhythmic sound of the train wheels on the track, she knew it was far too late to change her mind.

2

Kirsty emerged from the station into a dark, dismal, drizzly Dundee evening.

The forecourt was deserted, with no cabs or motor taxis in sight. Already she was missing the bustle of London, the heaving mass of bodies in every public place, the smells, even the London fog swirling up from the Thames.

Shivering, she set her suitcase on the ground, pulled her coat tighter and turned the collar up. There was nothing else for it, she would have to walk.

Her footsteps resounded eerily as she tramped along the deserted street, but it did not worry her. She had walked in far more isolated and dangerous places than Dundee's Union Street during her years in the Women's Police Service. And no matter what Dundee had in store for her it could never match up to the back alleys of Soho, or the munitions towns where she had learned how to deal with all sorts of extreme behaviour from both men and women.

A tram rumbled past as she turned the corner into the Nethergate. Momentarily she thought of hailing it but did not because she was enjoying the walk after the cramped conditions on the train. Although, by the time she pushed through the front door of the Queens Hotel, her arm was aching with the weight of the case.

Depositing it in front of the reception desk she massaged her shoulder and waited for someone to come.

When no one appeared she pressed the bell with the palm of her hand.

A scurrying sound and the faint click of a door lock was the only indication of another presence, although the sensation of being watched was strong.

She hit the bell again.

The curtain behind the reception desk twitched, and a tall, bony, immaculately dressed man sidled round it.

'Can I help you?' His pencil-thin moustache twitched as he spoke. His eyes refused to meet hers, and he seemed to be watching the door.

'May I have a room, please?' Kirsty tried her utmost to be pleasant to this shifty-eyed man who made her feel as if she were dirty.

'I see. You are waiting for your husband perhaps?' His eyes flicked over her ring-free fingers.

'I am alone.'

She stared into his eyes, forcing him to look at her. She had met his type before and was getting ready to put him in his place.

'I am afraid we have no vacancies.'

He did not have to say – for the likes of you – but she could see it in his eyes and the contemptuous way he looked at her.

'I am not a prostitute.' Kirsty had considered using milder language, but she wanted to shock him.

He spluttered, his moustache twitched and his eyes frantically examined the roof. 'I never suggested . . .'

She placed both hands on the reception desk and glared at him. 'I am a policewoman,' she hissed. 'I have had a long journey from London, and I am not in the mood for your snide remarks. If you do not find me a room immediately, I will make sure Chief Constable Carmichael hears how you have treated me.'

He pulled his shoulders back, tugged at the bottom of his jacket, patted his hair and, with a twitch of his moustache, said, 'The only thing available is an attic room. We do not usually rent it out, but in the circumstances . . .' His conscience apparently salved, he rang the bell.

A small, monkey-like man materialized from the rear of the room, the curiosity in his eyes making it obvious he had been listening.

With an almost imperceptible expression of distaste, the manager's eyes flicked over Kirsty's scuffed, leather suitcase which was held shut by a belt. Removing a key from one of the hooks on the wall behind the reception desk, he tossed it to the porter, saying, 'Take the lady's suitcase up to her room.' Turning his back on them, he vanished behind the curtain.

'You fairly put him in his place,' the porter said once they had climbed the first set of stairs and were out of earshot of the lobby.

Kirsty smiled at him. 'Do you think so?'

He grinned back at her.

'It's time someone sorted him out,' he said, with relish. 'Thinks he's God Almighty that one.'

A laugh bubbled up from somewhere inside Kirsty, and her tension eased. This tiny, wizened man hefted her suitcase as easily as if it were filled with feathers, and obviously did not think it strange a woman should be on her own. But then, she was in Dundee where women were the workers and men stayed at home and became what was known as kettle boilers. She had never been anywhere else where women were the dominant sex. Working in Dundee might not be so terrible after all.

'What's your name?'

'Nobody's ever asked me before. I'm just the porter, you see. But it's Sammy Trotter, miss, although when they want me, most folks just shout – hey you.'

'Well, Sammy Trotter, you are the cheeriest person I've met since I got on the train in London.'

'Just doing my job, miss.'

He scampered up a final flight of stairs and unlocked the door of the third room along the corridor. It was dark inside, but he produced a box of matches from one of his capacious pockets and lit the wick of the oil lamp.

'This room is smaller than the other ones and doesn't have electric lighting, but it's cosier and not so airy because it's not got a high ceiling. And, during the day, you get a good view of the river from here.'

'Thanks, Sammy.'

Though she could ill afford it she rummaged in her pocket for a penny to give him.

'Breakfast's in the dining room, from 7 o'clock to 9

o'clock.' He grinned at her as he pocketed the coin. 'Old stiff-arse won't give you the time of day, so let me know if you need anything.'

Kirsty's sleep was peppered with dreams of home. When she woke the next morning the sensation of her mother's arms round her was strong, bringing back bitter sweet memories of an earlier life.

Darkness shrouded the room, and for a moment she wondered where she was, but realization quickly set in, and the comfort of her mother's arms faded.

The feather bed held her in a warm cocoon, but despite this she rose. Pouring water from the jug into the earthenware bowl she washed her face and her upper body. The cold water tightened her pores and made her skin tingle, but she had not even considered pulling the bell rope to have hot water brought to the room. She much preferred the cold.

There had never been much privacy in the cubicles of the police section house where she had lived for the past year, and dressing hurriedly had become second nature. In less than five minutes she was neatly clothed in a calf length, bottle-green skirt, into which she had tucked a green striped blouse. When she surveyed herself in the mirror she frowned with dissatisfaction. She had become so accustomed to wearing her uniform she always felt ill at ease in civilian clothes. Sighing, she rummaged in the tallboy drawer for a silk scarf. Selecting the light green one she tucked it under her collar and knotted it in the front like a cravat. At least it felt more like a shirt and collar now.

The dining room was quiet, and Kirsty slipped into a window seat with the minimum of fuss.

A waitress approached and slid a bowl of porridge and a jug of milk onto the table.

'Will I bring your tea and toast now, miss, or would you prefer it after you've eaten?'

'I'll have it now, if you don't mind.'

The waitress, not quite managing to hide the curiosity in her eyes, scurried off.

Kirsty started to eat. She had not eaten porridge for breakfast since she left Dundee ten years ago and she had forgotten how much she enjoyed it.

Back then, breakfast at home had always started with oatmeal porridge. Cook never risked her father's ill-temper, and the tureen and ladle waited for the family in the breakfast room when they rose.

Her father was never in the best of spirits in the morning, but once he had eaten, and read his daily newspaper, his mood improved. Nostalgia threatened to swamp Kirsty when she thought of how he spoiled and teased her when she was little, and she regretted the arguments that had raged through the house when she left to become a suffragette.

It was to be expected, she supposed. The struggle for women's equality went against everything he believed in. His world was one where the man looked after the women in his family. She had been naive to think he would accept the loss of his little girl to the militant lifestyle of the suffragettes.

She stared out of the window. The Nethergate had not changed much, although she doubted if the Women's Freedom League still had their shop. How exciting it had been back then, haranguing crowds, chalking pavements, sticking posters on any available surface, and some not so available, and avoiding the police. Who would have thought she and Ethel would become policewomen after all their lawbreaking escapades.

A sudden memory of Martha, the unruly Women's Freedom League organizer who had pulled her and Ethel into the suffragette movement, popped into her mind. How Kirsty missed her. Martha was being wrestled out of Winston Churchill's meeting in the Kinnaird Hall the first time Kirsty saw her, and she remembered how horrified she had been. She had never seen a woman rough handled before, although after that she saw plenty.

'You're sure you don't want anything else?' The waitress placed the silver teapot and water jug on the table. 'The kidneys are nice this morning.'

'I'm fine, thank you,' Kirsty said. 'I never eat too much in the morning.'

Firmly, she pushed thoughts of the past away and turned her attention to the tea and toast.

Kirsty sat on the grass at the top of the Law Hill, hugging her knees and shivering in the chill wind. Dundee lay before her with its smoking factory chimneys, tenements, and fancy houses. A distant train, belching smoke and sparks, chugged across the Tay Bridge, and further down the river the Fifie ferry boat was coming in to dock.

Her feet ached from tramping the streets, but she had not wanted to take a tram or a cab, she had wanted to familiarize herself with Dundee again before she started work. She had wanted to get a feel of the place, rub shoulders with the people and savour the sights and smells.

The walk up the Law Hill had been longer than she remembered, but now she was here she reflected on how little Dundee had changed in the ten years she had been away.

The shops were the same, the streets were the same, even the people had not changed. She wondered if the same could be said of her family. The urge to find out was strong but combined with that was a resistance. She found it difficult to admit to the fear that had tormented her over the years. Fear they might reject her in the same way she rejected them ten years ago.

It was no more than she deserved.

Sighing, she struggled to her feet, brushed loose grass from her coat and started to walk downhill to Dundee.

Tomorrow was going to be a big day, and she wanted to be at her best for the interview with the assistant chief constable.

3

Thursday, 30 October 1919

Kirsty woke early the next morning, completed her ablutions, and pulled on her uniform. She pulled her belt tight after giving the buckle a final rub with a soft handkerchief, then buffed her boots, although they did not need it.

She had to look her best today, because first impressions were important.

Declining breakfast, she set out for her interview and arrived at police headquarters in ample time for her appointment.

The desk sergeant grunted when she gave her name and handed him the letter for the assistant chief constable.

'Sit there,' he instructed, pointing to a polished wooden bench stretching the length of the room.

Kirsty sat.

The desk sergeant turned his attention back to the massive ledger on his desk. He wrote laboriously, pausing now and again to dip his pen in the inkwell and sneak a look at her.

Kirsty pressed her knees together and loosely clasped her hands in her lap. She had already become aware her appearance in uniform was a novelty in Dundee. That had been apparent when she walked through the streets to the police station. Men and women gaped at her, and young boys followed her with catcalls. She ignored them all.

The minutes ticked past slowly, and the waiting became unbearable.

'Excuse me,' she said. 'The assistant chief constable is expecting me, and I would not want to keep him waiting.'

The sergeant laid his pen in the groove on his desk and, with a theatrical sigh, lifted the flap at the end of the counter. He opened a door and bawled, 'Duty constable report to the charge room.' He returned to his desk behind the counter, glared at

Kirsty with an expression on his face that seemed to say, 'pleased now?' and lifted his pen to resume writing.

The constable marched in front of her through a warren of narrow corridors. At last he stopped before a door, looked at her with a pitying glance, and ushered her inside.

In contrast to what she had seen already, everything was large. The oak-panelled room, the polished desk, the man sitting behind it frowning at the letter in his hand. He was silhouetted by the light from the window at his back, so his face was partly in shadow. But Kirsty detected unwelcoming vibes.

She halted in front of the desk and stood to attention.

Slowly, he raised his head, placed his hands flat on the desk's leather-inlaid surface, and looked her up and down. She sensed his disapproval and contempt which was accentuated by a silence that seemed to last forever.

Eventually, he spoke. 'I think I should make something clear from the start, Miss Campbell. I did not ask for a woman.' The assistant chief constable pulled his moustache as he looked at her from under heavy brows that met in the middle.

All Kirsty's doubts resurfaced. Dundee was no place for her, she should have remained in London where the respect of her colleagues and superiors made the men's resentment less important.

Struggling to pull herself together, she clenched her hands and stiffened her spine. She must not let his bullying tactics rob her of belief in herself. But, along with that, she knew she would have to remain respectful. Her future in Dundee depended on it.

'I understand Chief Constable Carmichael arranged for you to . . . temporarily . . . join the force.' He tapped the letter in front of him. 'However,' he glared at her, 'as this will be the usual three months probationary period. I would advise you not to get too settled.'

She tightened her lips to hold back the retort that trembled there. He was doing his best to make her feel small and insignificant, and he was succeeding. Knowing she would break down if she looked at him, she studied the top of the too-tidy mahogany desk. She must not lose her composure.

'While you are here, Miss Campbell,' he continued, 'we will try to find something that will be suitable for a woman to do. Meantime, you will stay away from my constables and refrain from causing trouble. I will not have trouble within the police force. You understand this?'

'Yes, sir,' she murmured, in what she hoped was a meek tone of voice because she knew she could not allow the heat of her anger to surface.

'Despite the experience you claim to have had in London you are not to consider yourself a woman police officer.' He glanced contemptuously at her uniform. 'You are a statement taker and nothing else. You understand this?'

'Yes, sir.' Kirsty bit her lip so hard she could taste salt from the abrasion.

'You will be stationed here at Central Office and will take your orders from Inspector Brewster. If he has any problems with you, he has instructions to report back to me. You understand this?'

Kirsty unclamped her teeth. 'Yes, sir.'

'You will report to Inspector Brewster on Monday morning at 9 am sharp.' He picked up a paper from his desk. 'That will be all,' he said, without looking up.

'Yes, sir.' She turned and marched towards the door.

After the door closed she slumped against the corridor wall. If he had said 'you understand this' one more time, she would have screamed.

Tension seeped out of her body and the rigidity of her posture relaxed. She wanted to cry and scream and beat her hands on the wall, but all she did was blink hard to prevent the tears escaping.

Her doubts, about the wisdom of accepting the position of the first policewoman in Dundee, intensified. Although, remembering what the assistant chief constable had said, she was not even that. She was to be a statement taker and nothing else. She would never have come to Dundee if Chief Constable Carmichael had been honest with her. But he had given her the impression he wanted a policewoman.

'What on earth have I got myself into?' she muttered, before pulling herself together and trying to find her way back to the charge room.

The desk sergeant did not raise his eyes from the ledger when she marched past him and out of the office.

'Damn him,' she muttered, 'I've faced worse.'

The newsvendor stared at Kirsty when he handed over copies of the Courier and the Dundee Advertiser. 'What kind of uniform is that?'

'It's a policewoman's uniform.' Kirsty always felt a surge of satisfaction every time she was asked to explain.

'Humph,' he said, 'there's no such thing.'

Kirsty bit her lip, suppressed the retort that hovered there, smiled sweetly, and said, 'Oh yes, there is.' She handed over her tuppence, tucked the two newspapers under her arm and walked on, leaving the newsvendor scratching his head. Maybe Dundee men had never seen a policewoman before, but that would soon change.

Ignoring curious looks and sniggering children, Kirsty hurried to the hotel, thrust her way through the front door and up the stairs to the sanctuary of her room. Her feet were aching and she tugged her boots off, wriggling her toes once they were free of the hard leather. After she placed the boots under the chair at the side of her bed, she slipped her skirt and jacket off, hung them on hangers, and then sprawled across the bed wearing only her petticoat.

She spread the newspapers in front of her and scrutinized the property columns. Ignoring the for sale adverts, although she would have had enough money left over from Granny's trust fund to buy a cottage, providing the price did not go much over the advertised £230, she circled the rented properties with her pencil. The time to think about buying would be after her probationary period was over and she had made her mind up to stay in Dundee. In the meantime, she would look for a rented room with a cheap rent.

She rolled over onto her back. Tomorrow she would start looking at properties.

The next day Kirsty went to look at the properties she had seen advertised in the local newspaper but by the time she had inspected all but one of the places on her list she was thoroughly discouraged.

The first place she looked at had been a two-roomed flat at the top of a tenement. The toilet was shared by six flats on the top landing and another six on the landing below, and stank. The door hung off its hinges, and the wooden seat was split into three parts. The flat was no better. The lock did not work, there were holes in the floor, and the bedroom reeked like the toilet on the stairs.

The next three places were in a similar condition, so her expectations were now as low as her spirits.

The landlord of the last place lived on the ground floor in the tenement next door. He looked at her with a gleam in his eyes that made Kirsty uneasy.

'The rent's five shillings a week and that's a bargain. You pay the first week in advance and an extra ten shillings key money.'

He wiped his grubby hands on his dungarees. 'When d'you want to move in?'

'Do you mind if I take a look at it first?'

He stared at her as if she were crazy. 'What d'you want to see it for? The rent's cheap, it's well furnished, and it has an inside stair with a cludgie on each landing. It's in a good class tenement, better than a lot of the other ones with their outside stairs and outside cludgies.'

It was a name she had not heard for years, and for a brief moment she blinked at him in puzzlement until she remembered. She just hoped this cludgie did not stink as much as the toilets she had already viewed.

'I suppose you can see it,' the landlord grumbled, 'although you're not going to get any better for the rent I'm asking.'

She followed him into the next tenement, up a creaking set

of stairs to the first landing and into the two-roomed flat that Dundee folks called a double-end.

Weak sunlight filtered through the dirty glass of the window, picking its way past the grimy sink. A greasy-looking gas cooker was situated to the left of the black fireplace while a gas jet on a swivel arm protruded from the dust-covered mantelpiece. A blue paisley-patterned oil-cloth covered the table in the middle of the room, and two wooden chairs sat close by. A sideboard, and an armchair sagging in the middle with what suspiciously looked like broken springs completed the room's contents.

A door in the rear wall led to the bedroom. It was sparsely furnished with a bed and a small chest of drawers on the top of which was a saucer with a candle stuck upright in its own grease. The bed looked solid enough, although the brass ends were badly in need of a polish and the blankets covering the mattress looked distinctly unsavoury.

'It's a new mattress,' the landlord grumbled when her eyes returned to the bed.

'Had to throw the last one out when the tenant left. Dirty bugger.'

Kirsty was tempted to tell him he should have thrown the blankets out as well but did not want to antagonize him. For, although she had hoped for something better, this was the best she was going to get for the price she was prepared to pay. At least there were no holes in the floor or walls, the door was intact, and the smells were only of dust and the lack of fresh air. With a good scrub, new bedding, whitewash and paint, it might not be too bad. Besides, she could easily afford the rent of this place out of her policewoman's pay of two pounds eight shillings a week.

'I'll take it,' she said. Although a moment after she spoke she realized the assistant chief constable had made no mention of how much she would be paid. She hoped it would be the same as she had been getting in London.

The landlord grabbed her hand and shook it. 'McKay's my name, Alfie McKay. You and me, we'll get on like a house on fire.'

Kirsty looked at him dubiously. She was going to have to watch out for this one.

Kirsty had paid for a week's stay in the Queens Hotel, so she thought she would use the next few days to make her new home liveable.

She found a stall at the Overgate market that had most of what she needed, and she bought a mop, washing cloths, large and small brushes, dusters, yellow soap, black-lead for the fireplace, matches to light the gas, and sweets to suck when the dust got too much for her.

It was late Friday morning when she finally finished shining the black fireplace, a job she had dreaded. Sitting back on her heels she admired her work.

But she was not finished yet. New bedding had to be bought, whitewash for the ceiling, and paint for the doors and wall-panelling. And, if she did not want to have to trudge downstairs to the cellar for coal every day, she would have to buy an oil heating stove.

Bundling up the dirty bedding that came with the flat, she hauled it downstairs and threw it into the coal cellar. With that done, she returned to the Overgate market to buy the rest of what she needed.

4

Friday night, 31 October 1919

Thoughts of witches and banshees raced through the young constable's mind as he ran through the dark cemetery in the direction of the screams.

His lantern swung wildly, splashing light indiscriminately in front of him, illuminating trees, bushes and gravestones. The unearthly sound of the screaming grew louder, and he dreaded what he was going to find.

He swore softly under his breath, cursing the gent who had reported the screaming, and cursing his partner for not being with him. It had not seemed to matter when he had agreed to cover the beat on his own to give Harry time to go off with one of the Overgate girls. But now he bitterly regretted it.

A movement, over to his left, was caught briefly in the wavering beam and he turned, raising his lantern higher. The light flickered over a macabre tableau. The girl was crouched over something on the flat top of a gravestone. She pushed herself upwards, stopped screaming, and stared towards the light with glazed eyes. Her white gown was saturated with something dark. The same dark liquid dribbled down the knife she held and, in the silence, he could hear the drips plop onto the body spreadeagled on the gravestone.

He took two steps backward, fumbled for his whistle, raised it to his lips with shaking fingers, and blasted on it for all he was worth.

Detective Inspector Brewster should have been home several hours ago, but the riot at the Scouringburn had turned into a pitched battle between the mob and the police, and he hadn't been able to leave the scene until the bobbies had the crowd under control. So when he heard the police whistle he was tempted to ignore it and leave the beat bobbies to respond. But when he heard it again, four short blasts, the emergency signal, he shrugged off his exhaustion and turned in the direction of the sound.

The screaming, and the bobbing lights of several police lanterns guided him to the middle of the cemetery. By the time he got there, the girl's screams had subsided, and one of the constables was approaching her.

'It's all right, lass,' the constable said soothingly, reaching out a hand for the knife.

The girl whimpered and drew back.

The constable hesitated in his advance. 'I'm not going to hurt you,' he said.

Brewster held his breath and sidled nearer to the girl. Her attention was on the constable, so he might be able to disarm her if she swung the knife at him.

The girl's head turned, drawn to his movement.

Brewster froze.

The constable took another step towards her. 'Nobody's going to hurt you, lass.' He advanced some more.

Brewster took the opportunity to circle behind the girl, but he did not want to rush her because the constable was now too close. One wrong move and she might plunge the knife into him.

'You don't want that knife,' the constable murmured. 'You might hurt yourself with it.'

The girl whimpered and turned towards the body on the slab. She reached out a hand and touched it. Tears slid down her cheeks, and her shoulders shook.

'Give it to me, lass, before someone else gets hurt.'

Brewster held his breath and tensed his muscles, ready to pounce.

But the constable reached out and took the knife from her unresisting hand.

Brewster exhaled. The danger was past, and now there was only the clearing up to do.

He strode forward. 'Good work, Ramsay,' he said. 'It took a

lot of courage to take the knife away from her.' He turned to the others. 'Henderson, Dixon, take her down to the police station and see she's locked up. After that go and get Davvy to bring his barrow. Mathers, you go off and get the police doctor while Dempster and Mitchell stand guard.'

Brewster sat on an adjacent gravestone. What a bloody night this had been, first the riot and now this. He would be lucky if he saw his bed at all.

It was more than an hour before the doctor arrived. 'You didn't need me to tell you she's dead,' he grumbled after giving the body a cursory examination.

Brewster shrugged and nodded to Davvy to bring the coffin-shaped box on wheels over. 'She's ready for the barrow to take her to the morgue,' he said.

It was morning before everything was done, and Brewster was able to go to the female cell block to interrogate the prisoner. Annie Baxter, the turnkey, accompanied him.

The girl lay prostrate on the mattress-covered bench. But as soon as she saw Brewster, she drew her knees up under her chin and started to wail.

'It's no use, sir,' Annie said. 'She's been like this since they brought her in. When she's alone she's so quiet you'd think she was dead, but as soon as someone approaches her, she starts screaming.'

'I'll leave it for now,' Brewster said. He sighed wearily as he retraced his steps to the charge room. He needed to go home and get some sleep.

'Any luck with the prisoner, sir?' The desk sergeant looked up.

Brewster shook his head.

'D'you want my Marge to come in and question her? She's good with the female prisoners, and she's done it often enough before.'

'No, Hamish. The chief constable has arranged for one of these new-fangled policewomen from London to be our statement taker. She can do it when she starts work next week.'

The sergeant snorted. 'I suppose policemen's wives aren't good enough to take the statements anymore.'

Brewster shrugged. 'Who are we to question why?'

'I was on duty when she was interviewed.' Hamish frowned. 'I never seen anything like it in my life before. All dressed up in some sort of outlandish uniform, and real snippy she was.' He shook his head at the recollection. 'You wait until you see her,' he warned.

5

Kirsty had not allowed herself to cry for more than ten years, but when she woke in the hotel on Saturday morning her face and eyelashes were wet.

Several nights this past week she had dreamed of her mother, but the dreams had not been distressing, although they had left her with an empty feeling when she woke.

She had been a child again, loved and wanted, held close in her mother's embrace. But she could not remember last night's dream, only the faint sound of a baby crying somewhere in the hotel.

A vision of Ailsa arose unbidden into her mind, and she squeezed her eyes shut trying to eradicate it. Her insides churned with the pain of the memory. Ailsa had not been her child for thirteen years now. She had no right to think of her or to see her.

She had given up that right the day she handed her baby to her own mother to raise.

She shuddered. Coming back to Dundee was doing strange things to her, and awakening memories and emotions she had long suppressed.

Leaping out of bed she scrubbed herself with cold water until her skin tingled, but she could not scrub the thoughts and yearnings away.

Suddenly, she knew what she had to do. She had to go to Broughty Ferry and face her family. Make peace with them, if they would let her.

She had been putting it off long enough.

Ignoring her previous plan to paint and whitewash her flat, she marched purposefully out of the door, down the stairs, past the dining room and along the road to the railway station.

She had no stomach for breakfast and the painting could wait until tomorrow.

On arrival at her parents' house, Kirsty had expected the door to be answered by Mr James, her father's butler, but the woman answering her knock was a stranger.

Disconcerted, Kirsty said, 'Will you inform Mr and Mrs Campbell that Kirsty wishes to see them.'

'Mr and Mrs Campbell will not want to be disturbed at this early hour. You will have to come back later.'

The woman obviously did not know of her existence and Kirsty, unsure how her parents would react to her return, did not want to explain she was a daughter of the house.

Her shoulders slumped, and she turned away. The visit had been a terrible idea.

'Who is it, Parker? I heard voices.' The breakfast room door opened and her father strode into the hall.

'I did not want to disturb you, sir. But this young lady wishes to see you.'

Robert Campbell stopped suddenly. Only the ticking of the grandfather clock broke the silence before he said, 'It's all right, Parker, you can return to your duties.' As an afterthought, he added, 'This is my daughter, Kirsty.'

'Yes, sir.' The housekeeper retreated to the swing door at the rear of the hall.

Kirsty's heart thumped. Her eyes misted. The lump that rose into her throat, restricted her breathing and threatened to choke her.

'My, my,' he said, after the housekeeper left them. 'The prodigal returns.'

Robert Campbell's voice gave no clues to what he was feeling, and Kirsty could not work out whether she was welcome.

'Well, come in, come in,' he barked, 'don't stand dithering on the doorstep.'

His eyes flicked over her. 'Where's your luggage? At the station, I suppose. Never mind. I'll send my chauffeur for it later on.'

'You needn't bother,' Kirsty said. Her voice floated in the air between them, disembodied, and sounding as if it did not belong to her. 'I have a room at the Queens Hotel.'

Her father snorted. 'I'll send him to collect your luggage from there. It shouldn't take long.'

Kirsty cringed. She wanted her father to open his arms to her and accept her unconditionally, and already he was dictating where she had to live.

'I said you needn't bother.' Her voice hardened in an effort to be firm. 'I will be staying on at the Queens Hotel until I get rooms in the town.'

She did not tell him she already had a flat and intended to move as soon as she returned to Dundee.

'Still the same old Kirsty, I see,' Robert said, a note of bitterness in his voice, 'still up to the same old nonsense.'

All of a sudden he looked tired. Realizing she could never be what he wanted, compassion replaced Kirsty's anger. Her eyes softened as she looked at him and noticed the changes: his red hair, now streaked with grey; eyes, duller, no longer the vivid blue she remembered; frown lines, not quite masked by his shaggy eyebrows; and a slight tremor in his hands.

'I'm not your little girl anymore, father,' Kirsty said quietly. 'I'm twenty-nine. I'm a grown woman with a career. I have to live my own life.'

'Yes,' Robert said, the rancour in his voice mingled with defeat. 'I suppose after living your own life all these years it would be too much to expect you to change now.'

'Yes, father.'

She yearned to reach out to him and grasp his hands, but held back because she remembered how reserved her family were, and the difficulty they had expressing deep emotions. Her father's anger, which could erupt at the least provocation, probably arose from these inhibitions.

'Your mother is in the breakfast room. I am sure she will be glad to see you.' Robert reached out a hand as if to put it on her shoulder, but drew back at the last moment.

'I'll be glad to see her too.' Kirsty made a conscious effort to relax and be more approachable.

She followed Robert into the breakfast room.

Ellen Campbell folded the Dundee Courier and laid it on the table. She looked up, caught her breath, and removed her spectacles placing them on top of the newspaper.

'I don't believe it!' Ellen said, placing one hand on her chest. Her face paled, and her voice shook. 'After all these years!' She struggled for breath. 'I had given up hope of ever seeing you again. But here you are.' A smile lifted the corners of her mouth, and she rose from her chair.

Kirsty sucked in her breath. This was an older, greyer and plumper version of the mother she remembered. The other changes were more subtle, like the spectacles and her interest in the daily newspaper. The mother she had known had never taken any interest in what went on outside the walls of her home.

'After you left I read so much about what happened to suffragettes I feared you might be dead. But you're not, and you are here.' Ellen almost toppled the chair in her haste to greet her daughter. 'You have been away so long!' There was a hint of reproach in her voice. 'And look at you. So smart and so grown-up, but it doesn't matter how much you've changed, you will always be the same to me.'

Kirsty knew she was not the same person who had left ten years ago, but she accepted her mother's embrace and did not argue. They would find out in time how much she had changed, but now was not the time to disillusion them.

In the meantime, it felt good to have her mother's arms around her, and she regretted the loss of contact over the years.

'Come, sit at the table.' Ellen loosened her hold and released her. 'You are far too thin, you must have something to eat. You haven't breakfasted yet. Have you? Sit, sit. Oh goodness, listen to me, I'm babbling.' She slid a finger across her eyelashes trying to hide the tear glistening there.

Kirsty sat down.

'I didn't wait for breakfast this morning,' she mumbled, trying not to let her mother know she had witnessed the tear.

'You have come home to stay?' Ellen ladled some porridge

from the tureen into a plate and placed it on the table in front of her daughter.

'No,' she said. The muscles in her jaw stiffened. 'I have come to Dundee to work and will be living in the town.'

'What's this about work,' Robert growled. 'Do you think I can't support you? You are my daughter. You do not need to work. I will not hear of it.'

'I don't need your support,' Kirsty flared, rising from her chair. 'I've made my arrangements.'

Ellen put a restraining hand on her arm. 'Father,' she murmured. 'Kirsty has only just arrived. Give her a bit of peace until she settles in.'

The warmth of her mother's hand calmed Kirsty. 'I want to work,' she said softly. 'I've made a career for myself since I left home.'

Robert snorted.

Ellen frowned at him. 'You can't expect Kirsty to settle in as if she has never been away. It's been too long, and we have no idea what kind of life she has made for herself.'

Kirsty looked up in surprise. When she left home, her mother had stubbornly refused to comprehend her reasons. Now here she was showing a level of understanding Kirsty would never have thought possible. Maybe there was hope for their relationship after all.

Robert sat down in his chair. 'Yes, you have been away for a long time.' He broke off and stared out the window. 'We missed you.' His voice was little more than a murmur.

'I missed you too.' Kirsty blinked hard. She would not allow herself to cry. That was not what modern women did.

'Tell us what you have been doing since you left home.' Ellen poured tea into Kirsty's cup. 'You never wrote.'

Kirsty thought of all the letters she had half-written only to tear them to pieces. Always it had been the memory of the terrible rows and the bitterness they left behind that got in the way. And, of course, the guilt she carried with her, guilt which had never lessened over the past thirteen years since the day Ailsa was born.

'At least the suffragettes had the sense to stop protesting

when the war started,' Robert growled. 'The only good thing to come out of the war if you ask me.'

'Kirsty knows we never approved of her joining the suffragettes. But that is all in the past. Is that not so, Kirsty?'

'If you are asking me whether I still believe in women's suffrage, then the answer has to be yes.'

'Some of those suffragettes were so unfeminine.' Ellen adjusted her skirt. She was wearing the new shorter length, and it was obvious to Kirsty she was not comfortable with it.

'I was a suffragette right up until the start of the war. I never got to be an organizer, like Martha.' Her voice saddened as she thought of the diminutive woman with the glorious dark-gold hair. 'But I did get paid to assist other organizers.'

Robert snorted.

'Robert, let Kirsty tell her story. I want to know what she has been doing since she stopped being a suffragette.'

Kirsty sighed. She had never stopped being one in her heart, but she was not going to argue with her mother. It would end up in bitterness again.

'When the war started, a women's police service was set up. I became one of the first recruits.'

Kirsty ignored Ellen's gasp of surprise.

'I trained and worked in London and then went to Gretna to be a munitions policewoman. I joined the Metropolitan Police last year, and now I've been sent to work with the Dundee force.' She stared defiantly at her parents. 'It's a probationary period, but if I like it I might stay on. I don't know yet,' she ended lamely. She decided not to mention her reception by the assistant chief constable and the likelihood the Dundee force might not want her to stay on.

'Working with the police? But you can't. It wouldn't be proper.' Ellen looked towards her husband.

He thumped the table with his fist. 'I will not allow it.'

'You can't stop me. And if you try I will leave this house right now and never return.'

'There is no need for that.' Ellen, always the pacifist in the family, put an arm round her daughter. 'You are home now, and we don't want to lose you again.'

'Then you have to let me live my life.'

'I think I have heard as much as I want to hear.' Robert pulled the bell cord. 'Tell the chauffeur I am ready to go to the mill,' he told Parker when she appeared.

He glared at his daughter and left the room, slamming the door behind him.

6

'You must understand,' Ellen said, plucking loose threads from the edge of the tablecloth, 'it's exceedingly difficult for him. He wanted so much for you. But then so did I.'

'I know,' Kirsty said. 'The problem was, what you both wanted for me wasn't what I wanted. I've chosen my life, and I like what I do.'

Ellen sighed. 'It seems so strange,' she murmured. 'People like us never have anything to do with the police. But now, it seems, we have a policewoman in the family. Heavens knows how I'll explain it to my friends.'

Relief swept through Kirsty, relaxing her muscles and lightening her heart. Although her mother was struggling with the idea of her daughter as a policewoman, she was clearly on the way to accepting it.

'I'm sure you'll think of something.'

'It would be lovely if you could live at home while you are in Dundee.' Ellen's voice was wistful. 'We kept your bedroom for you.'

Kirsty leaned over and grasped her mother's hand. 'I appreciate the offer,' she said, 'but I have to live near my work.'

'At least stay tonight and come to church with us tomorrow.'

A sigh trembled on Kirsty's lips. Although she was glad she had come to make amends with her parents this was no longer her home, and she could not sleep in the house, even for one night.

'I'm not sure that's such a good idea. Once I've said hello to Ailsa . . .' her voice shook as she said the name. 'I'll need to go back to Dundee.'

'In that case you will have to stay. Ailsa's not here. She wanted to see a moving-picture show, so Aunt Bea offered to take her to see the new Charlie Chaplin film, *Sunnyside*, which was showing yesterday at the La Scala. And then tonight they are going to the Kings Theatre, so she is staying at Aunt Bea's. But she will be back for church tomorrow.'

'I can't leave without seeing Ailsa.'

'That's settled then. You will be staying. I'll get Parker to air your bed.' Before Kirsty could object, she added, 'You will need something to wear, of course. But that won't be a problem because I kept all the clothes you left behind and you are bound to find something amongst them that is not too old-fashioned. If not you can borrow something from me.'

Kirsty was not sure, but she thought she detected a note of triumph in her mother's voice.

Ellen Campbell had always been adept at manipulation, and it was obvious she was going to use Ailsa to bind Kirsty to her family.

The next morning Kirsty hid in the gazebo until her parents left for church. Once the car rolled down the drive she emerged and returned to the house.

Curling up in a chair, in the library, she opened a book and gazed sightlessly at the words until the car returned.

Ailsa, she thought, when she heard the engine stop. Ailsa is here.

She hurried to the door and opened it, standing uncertainly on the top step, wondering if Ailsa would recognize her and whether her parents had told the child that Kirsty was home.

Robert was first out of the car. He glared at her. 'Where were you? Why weren't you at church with us?'

'I told mother yesterday I would not be attending church with you.'

'Why not?'

'I haven't been to church since I left home. It would be hypocritical to go now.'

'You're an atheist now as well as everything else,' he growled, pushing past her and entering the house.

Kirsty hardly heard him. Her eyes were fixed on the girl running towards her. She was small for her age, and she looked

37

younger than thirteen. Her wavy red hair reached her waist, and Kirsty suspected that when wet it would spring into curls, just as her own hair had done at the same age.

'You're Kirsty,' Ailsa said, her eyes sparkling with curiosity and a hint of mischief. 'Mother told me you lived here until I was three, but I don't remember you.'

Two sets of hazel eyes examined each other.

'Your hair's the same colour as mine, but it's short.'

'Yes, but my hair used to be long and curly like yours.' Kirsty stretched her hand out and stroked her child's auburn curls. 'It became even curlier when I was misbehaving. Does yours do that?'

'Yes.' Ailsa turned and ran back to Ellen. 'Has Kirsty come back to stay?'

'Of course she has, dear.' Ellen patted Ailsa's head. 'Go and be ever so nice to her and I'm sure she'll stay.'

'Oh no, I won't,' Kirsty muttered through gritted teeth, but her heart lurched when she looked at Ailsa.

After lunch, Ailsa sidled up to Kirsty. 'Come to the stables with me and I'll show you Betsy. She's my horse,' she added proudly.

'I used to have a horse too, he was called Velvet.' She turned to her mother. 'What happened to Velvet?'

'No one was left to look after or ride him after Sandy went off to the war, so we had to sell him.'

'Come on.' Ailsa grabbed Kirsty's hand. 'You'll like Betsy. You can ride her if you want.'

The kitchen was empty when they passed through it on their shortcut to the rear of the house. Ailsa darted into the pantry to grab a handful of sugar lumps. 'Cook won't mind. Sometimes she pretends to be cross, but she isn't really.'

Kirsty grinned. She remembered doing the same when she was Ailsa's age.

Betsy snuffled the sugar lumps out of Ailsa's hand.

'Are you happy?' Kirsty was not sure why she asked nor what she would do if Ailsa admitted to being miserable. A fleeting moment of yearning overtook her and she visualized the two of them running off together. But the moment passed. She had very little money, an uncertain career, and her living accommodation left a lot to be desired, so how on earth could she look after her child.

She waited for Ailsa's answer, remembering how unsettled she had been when she lived at home, how resentful she had been when her parents tried to make her into a young lady and how miserable that had made her.

'Oh yes.' Ailsa looked at her with glowing eyes.

'You don't find it lonely living here?'

The girl laughed. 'Lonely? I'm too busy to be lonely. I've got Betsy and sometimes Sarah May, my friend, comes to visit after school.'

'You attend school?' Kirsty thought of her own succession of tutors and governesses.

'Oh yes. I'm at Dundee High School. The lessons are difficult, but I have to study hard because I want to be a doctor, and you have to go to university for that.' She stroked Betsy's nose. 'Maybe I'll be an animal doctor instead.'

'But, Mother and Father, will they allow you to do that?'

'Oh yes, Mother talked Daddy round. She says I can do it as long as I don't leave home.'

Kirsty shook her head in amazement. Her parents had blocked her from any kind of career, and university had been out of the question. But she was glad things were going to be better for Ailsa.

Kirsty and Ailsa were inseparable for the rest of the day. They walked in the gardens, played hide-and-seek in the woods, read books in the library, and investigated Ailsa's room and the old nursery which had been turned into a playroom for her and her friends.

'It's time I went back to Dundee,' Kirsty announced after dinner. She had stayed later than she had intended.

'I fail to understand why you do not want to stay here.' Her mother's voice was filled with disappointment. 'We would not interfere with your life.'

Ailsa looked at her. 'Please stay.'

For a moment Kirsty was tempted, but she did not believe her mother would be able to stop herself from interfering. And as for her father, he would dictate how she was to live her life.

'It's too far from the police station.' She looked away from Ailsa's pleading eyes. 'I have to be available. I may have to work in the evening or even during the night if need be. So I have to live nearby.'

'Why you have to work I will never know. All our friends will think we are not able support you. In any case, it is time you found yourself a husband and settled down to married life. It is what any normal young woman would do. But, of course, you are no longer young so it might be difficult to find a match for you.'

'I'm only twenty-nine, mother, and I don't want a husband.' I don't want to be normal either, she thought bitterly, not if it means tying myself down to some man.

Her father, seemingly engrossed in the book he was reading, grunted his displeasure. 'Ridiculous,' he said. 'You will end up an old maid.' He slammed his book shut and stood up. 'What's more, you are a bad influence on your sister.' He patted Ailsa on the head. 'You must not pay any heed to Kirsty's modern ideas, my pet. We don't want you corrupted by them.'

'You see, you have upset your father now,' Kirsty's mother complained as her husband slammed the door behind him.

Now Robert was gone, Ailsa ran over to Kirsty's side. 'Can I come and see you in your lodgings, Kirsty?' Ailsa's eyes were large and enquiring. 'I've never seen lodgings before.'

'We'll see.' Kirsty's heart was heavy as she looked at her daughter.

She reached out and hugged Ailsa so the child would not see the pain reflected in her eyes.

Tears threatened, and she turned her head to prevent her mother and Ailsa seeing them.

'I'll get my coat and bag,' she said, and left the room to run upstairs. At the top, she stopped to wipe tears from her eyes with a handkerchief. She shrugged her coat on, grabbed her bag, and ran down again only to find Robert waiting for her at the bottom.

'In there,' he said angrily, pointing to the library.

Kirsty stalked into the room and, ignoring the chairs, turned round to face him.

'I was just leaving,' she said.

'Your mother wants you to stay.'

'I can't help that, I have to go.'

'No, you don't.' He glared at her. 'What is more, I do not approve of your choice of job. You will never fit in, and the policemen will soon let you know that.'

'You forgot to say that it's no job for a woman.' Kirsty's voice reflected the resentment she felt as they glared at each other.

'It isn't.'

'I have been a policewoman for the past five years. I have no intention of giving up because you do not think it's an appropriate career for your daughter.'

Robert's face reddened and anger flashed from his eyes.

'I will not have you coming here and upsetting your mother and Ailsa. Either you stay here and give up all notion of being a policewoman or you leave and never come back.'

'If that is what you want, father.'

Kirsty turned and stalked out of the door and out of the house, refusing to allow the tears to flow until the door slammed behind her.

7

Kirsty moved from the Queens Hotel to her flat on Sunday evening, and was glad to tumble into bed. She fell asleep with her father's angry words imprinted on her mind, 'leave and never return', the same ones which had prevented her from returning home ten years ago. And now, it was happening again.

Sleep was slow in coming. She tossed and turned most of the night until she woke to the room shaking as the first tram of the day rumbled past, its wheels clanking and grinding on the iron rails, in the street below. Kirsty forced her eyelids open and, for a moment, could not remember where she was.

She would have liked to stay at the Queens Hotel for another week, but the expense was draining her savings. In any case, starting her new job from her own home would be best, even though there had not been time to freshen it up with whitewash, paint and new curtains.

Ignoring the suspicious rustling behind the skirting boards, she lit the candle, padded through to the living room, filled the kettle with water and placed it on the gas ring. When she turned the tap she could not hear any hiss of gas, and realized she had forgotten to get pennies for the gas meter. Sighing, she washed herself with cold water, combed her hair and pulled her uniform on.

A cat yowled in the darkness as she left her flat. Further along the landing a door opened, and something solid whipped past her face, to land with a clatter behind her.

'Sorry.' A pyjama-clad figure hopped past her. 'I didn't know anyone was here.' He bent and retrieved the boot which he slid back onto his foot. 'It's these damned tomcats. They're after our mouser, wee Blackie, she's in heat the now. I wouldn't mind so much, but their howling wakes the bairn.' He hobbled back along the landing. 'Could have sworn she was a he when we got her,' he mumbled as the door slammed shut.

Kirsty, alone again in the darkness, put a hand on the wall to feel her way along the landing and down the stairs. A faint smell of rubbish mingling with the acrid smell of cats hung in the air, growing stronger as she descended. Holding her breath, she stumbled downward but, despite her attempts to be quiet, her boots clattered on the steps. She imagined restless sleepers turning in their beds and cursing quietly, and heaved a sigh of relief when she emerged into the early morning half-light.

She hesitated on the pavement in front of the tenement which was part of a long row of buildings stretching the length of the street, blocking the light, turning the road into a gloomy tunnel.

Adjusting her collar, she smoothed her hands down the rough serge of her uniform jacket, tightened her belt, pulled at her skirt so it hung straight, and checked her boots were polished and properly laced up. Then, taking a deep breath to calm her nerves, she turned in the direction of Dundee Central Police Office.

Echoes of her interview with the assistant chief constable plagued her and slowed her feet as she drew near. She had been through this so many times over the past five years – the suspicion, hostility and aggression of men who felt threatened by women invading their territory. She should be used to it by now, but going into a new situation, where she was not known, always affected her.

Pausing at the entrance to the office, she took a deep breath, braced her shoulders, and marched through the archway into the courtyard and through the main door. It was time, she told herself, to quell her nerves. Whatever else happened today, she must remain professional, or she would never be accepted by Dundee policemen as anything other than a silly woman.

Since the murder in the Howff on Halloween, sleep had eluded Jamie Brewster and he had been unable to settle. He was not sure why that was because he had the murderer in custody, locked up in one of the cells. But he had not been able to get her to talk. She shrank from him, curling into a foetal position on the bench in her cell, or clasping her knees and rocking back and forth with a deranged look on her face. Every time he approached her she reacted violently, banging her head on the wall with such force he had to leave before she knocked herself senseless. Not that she appeared to have much in the way of sense, and it was possible she was insane.

Returning from another fruitless attempt to interview her, he slumped onto the bench and closed his eyes. It looked as if he was going to have to admit defeat with this one, and he was not used to doing that. He prided himself on being able to get information out of the most reluctant suspect, but this time, he had failed.

The teapot simmering on the hob spurted tea onto the hot coals, where it sizzled and formed droplets. He grabbed his tin mug from the table, leaned forward and poured the dark liquid into it. No wonder the lads referred to canteen tea as tar. It certainly resembled it. He swirled the black liquid round the mug, decided he did not want it after all, and replaced the mug on the table.

He had been on duty since 6 o'clock that morning, and he was bone tired. He knew Maggie would quiz him about what he had eaten today, but the thought of food made him feel queasy, and he would have to lie to her again. It was getting to be a habit.

Flames flickered round the coals on the fire, and his eyes were gritty with lack of sleep. The place was quiet, and Jamie knew the lads would not be using the canteen for an hour or two, so he shrugged his jacket off, threw it below the bench, and leaned back against the wall. Stretching his legs out along the bench, he closed his eyes again, allowing the tiredness to take over.

It seemed as if the desk sergeant had never moved since Kirsty's last visit to the office. He stood at the high desk which formed part of the long, polished-wood counter stretching the length of the charge room. At his side of the counter, a pot-bellied stove sat in a corner near the window, and a large noticeboard covered most of the other wall.

Kirsty tried to attract his attention but, ignoring her, he continued to write in his ledger.

The nervous tension churning her stomach was turning to anger. She was tempted to bang her fists on the counter to make him look up, but thought better of it, and coughed.

Sighing, he laid his pen in the groove of the desk lid, blotted the page and closed the ledger. He pushed his spectacles up until they lodged at his hairline while a frown displayed his displeasure at being interrupted.

'Is there something you want?'

Kirsty refused to rise to the bait and met his glare with an even expression.

'The assistant chief constable told me to report to Inspector Brewster this morning.'

'Oh, he did, did he? And I suppose Inspector Brewster will be expecting you?'

'That is correct.' She breathed deeply to suppress her annoyance.

He smiled maliciously. 'Well, if he's expecting you, you'll find him in the canteen.'

He turned back to his ledger.

'And where, pray, is the canteen?'

The desk sergeant grunted, lifted his head and nodded towards a door behind him. 'Through there, first door on the right.' His eyes gleamed with spite. 'Don't bother to knock, just go right in.' He pulled his spectacles down again and returned to studying the papers on his desk, leaving Kirsty to find her own way.

The man she found in the canteen was lounging on a bench with his legs stretched along the length of it and his back against the wall. In his shirt sleeves and braces he looked more like a janitor than a policeman.

'Can you inform me where to find Inspector Brewster?'

The man blinked, and his eyes ranged over her disbelievingly. 'Don't tell me. You must be Miss Campbell.' He yawned widely. 'The chief constable did say you would be joining us. He's a bu . . . great one for new ideas.'

He swung his legs off the bench and reached below it for his jacket.

'Nobody told me you were starting today, but now you're here you'd better sit down and have a cup of tea.' He gestured to where a teapot simmered on the black hob of the open fire. 'It's probably stewed by now, but it's tolerable.'

Kirsty clenched her teeth. It was as she had expected. Dundee policemen were not going to take a policewoman seriously. This was obvious because the inspector had not taken the trouble to receive her professionally nor to dress properly.

'No thank you, sir, maybe later after you have briefed me on my duties. The assistant chief constable was not specific.' Kirsty was smarting after her recent interview, and her voice was sharper than she intended.

'Ah yes, your duties. What exactly did the assistant chief constable say?'

'He impressed on me I was to be a statement taker, sir. However, when Chief Constable Carmichael recruited me, he led me to believe my duties were to be that of a policewoman. I would not have come to Dundee for anything less.'

'I take it you do not want to work as a statement taker?'

'That is correct, sir. In London, there is only one statement taker, and she is a civilian.' Her anger boiled over. 'I am a policewoman and proud of it, sir. If I have been brought here on false pretences, I have no wish to stay.'

'You told the assistant chief constable this?'

'He did not give me the opportunity,' Kirsty said.

'I see.' His eyes were flat, grey and inscrutable. They travelled over her again, taking in every detail of her uniform.

Kirsty squirmed under his gaze.

'I will, of course, have to include your views in my report to Chief Constable Carmichael, as well as my belief they will lead to the failure of his experiment to integrate a woman into the police force.'

'Yes, sir.' Suddenly she wanted to take back all she had said. She did not want to leave Dundee. She wanted to promote the cause of women police in Scotland, to live up to the expectations of Superintendent Stanley and Commandant Damer Dawson and all the women police who fought for recognition.

And now, because of stupid pride over her official title, she would have to return to London and admit her defeat.

How would she ever be able to face her friends and colleagues?

8

'There have never been policewomen in Scotland.' Brewster's eyes narrowed, boring into her, making her cringe.

'Prior to the formation of the Women's Police Volunteers in 1914 there were no policewomen in England either.' Kirsty said coldly. 'But times change, sir, and last year the Metropolitan Police at Scotland Yard started accepting women.'

'This is not London.'

Kirsty knew she had already wrecked any chance she had of working in Dundee and her fiery temper was now in full flow. 'No, it is obvious to me, Scotland is still in the dark ages, sir.'

She caught her breath in horror. Momentarily forgetting she was addressing a senior officer she had vented her pent-up anger on him. What had happened to her professionalism, her self-control? Never before had she given way to her feelings in the workplace. But her anger had been increasing for several days, a reaction to all the disapproval and mockery she had suffered since arriving in Dundee. It might have subsided but, fuelled by her father and the assistant chief constable, it had flared into anger.

He stiffened. 'If this is how policewomen behave, I am thankful we are still in the dark ages, as you so nicely put it.'

She fought for composure. 'You have no way of knowing how policewomen behave if you have never had any. Nor could you have any conception of how useful they can be to the police. In an investigation, children and women will never tell a male officer the things they will tell a woman officer.'

He shrugged his jacket on and fastened the buttons. 'This is no place to discuss the worth or otherwise of women in the police. We will continue our talk in my office.'

Suppressing her surprise that she had not instantly been sent away, Kirsty followed him along the narrow corridor. He opened a door and ushered her in.

'Sit down,' he ordered, lifting a stack of files from a chair. He stood for a moment holding them in his hands as if wondering where he could put them. Eventually, he shrugged and added them to one of the heaps of papers on the floor of the office which, although fairly large, was crammed with books and files. There hardly seemed enough space for him to reach his chair, which was the only uncluttered thing in the room.

'That's better.' He collapsed into the seat and rummaged through an untidy bundle of papers in a wire tray perched on the end of his desk.

Kirsty sat on the edge of the chair, knees and feet pressed together as if this would protect her from the chaos the room represented.

Now that her anger was fading, and she no longer had a future in Dundee, she looked at him curiously. He was the strangest policeman she had ever encountered. He looked untidy, did not wear a uniform, his suit was in need of an iron, and the stiff collar on his white shirt was clearly on its second wearing. His rumpled brown hair stuck up in unruly tufts, and his grey eyes, which initially had been bleary with sleep, were now sharp and piercing.

He was younger than the police inspectors she had encountered in London, and would have been passably good-looking if it had not been for his crooked nose, which looked as if it might have been broken at some time or another.

He found the paper he was looking for and laid it on the desk in front of him.

'It is unfortunate Chief Constable Carmichael was unable to be here when you arrived since he is the one with the grasp of what he wants from a statement taker. However, now you are here, I can brief you on what would be expected of you. After that, you can decide whether you wish to remain and work with Dundee City Police Force.'

Kirsty barely suppressed the gasp that involuntarily rose to her lips. Surely he would not want her to stay after her outburst. But, if she was the chief constable's new 'experiment' as he had termed it, perhaps he would not relish explaining her return to

London.

He smoothed the sheet of paper flat. 'As I explained earlier, there are no policewomen in Scotland.' He held up a hand to silence any protest she might make. 'There is, however, a statement taker in Glasgow who performs the duties of a policewoman. In view of this, the chief constable, having no desire to create a precedent, decided to apply the name "statement taker" to your position.'

Kirsty opened her mouth to object, but he held up his hand again.

'As the position is a new one, we are in the process of formulating the duties it would be appropriate to attach to it. Initially we would expect you to deal with any enquiries relating to women and children. That would include taking any necessary statements during the course of an enquiry – and also taking part in investigations. Once you have settled in, we would come to some decisions in respect of patrolling duties. It is anticipated your patrols would cover any public place which presented a moral risk to women and children. This would include public houses, cinemas, ice-cream parlours and dancehalls, where your main duty would be to ensure the safety of any women or children frequenting these places. Obviously you would have to be accompanied by one of the men when you were checking public houses, although this may not always be possible on a patrol where the risk element to a woman is less.'

Kirsty tightened her lips. She wanted to tell him policewomen were accustomed to working in areas where there were considerable risks to them. But she decided to bide her time.

'The brief sounds far broader than the assistant chief constable led me to believe, sir.'

'It is an experimental post, however,' he said, folding the sheet of paper and replacing it in the wire basket, 'and the chief constable will require me to monitor it and provide a report as to the effectiveness of a policewoman. My first report will include the views you expressed earlier.'

Kirsty's pulse quickened when he said, 'policewoman' instead of 'statement taker', but she resisted the impulse to comment. She had done enough damage already.

'That is acceptable, sir.'

He looked up and smiled at her for the first time. 'I am glad that is settled.'

'Not quite, sir,' Kirsty said. 'The assistant chief constable did not provide any information on working conditions.'

He looked at her blankly.

'All he told me was that you would be my superior officer. In view of that, I assume I will be based in this office, but that has not been stated.' She wriggled uncomfortably in her chair. 'And there is the question of remuneration, sir.' She should not have had to bring this up, it was so embarrassing, but she had already started to use her savings, and she needed to know what her financial position was.

'I see.' He rustled in the wire basket for another piece of paper. 'I thought that had all been discussed.'

'No, sir,' she said, trying to hide her embarrassment.

'Here we are. The pay agreed by Chief Constable Carmichael when he appointed you was two pounds eight shillings a week, based on your London earnings. While your post remains probationary you will not have a clothing allowance. You will be attached to the criminal investigation department and come under my command . . .'

Kirsty gasped. In London, the CID was a male bastion not yet infiltrated by women.

He looked up.

'I'm sorry, sir. I had not realized I would be working with the CID.'

'I take it Dundee has, at last, compared favourably with London.' His voice was sardonic.

Kirsty lowered her eyes, knowing she deserved it.

'To continue,' he said. 'This is not a job where you will have regular hours. Although a work rota will be drawn up it may not always be adhered to, and you will be required to work as and when you are needed. Is there anything else you are unclear about?'

'Will I be sworn in, sir, and will I have the power of arrest?'

'No to both of those questions. Even in London women do

not have the power of arrest so that will be no different in Dundee. As for swearing in, the male constables in Dundee are not sworn in, so you will be on the same footing as them.'

'That seems satisfactory, sir.' Kirsty struggled to keep her face blank.

'I am glad to see you have brought your own uniform.' The faintest expression of distaste flickered over his face. 'That is something we would be unable to provide. However, you will only be required to wear it on patrols.'

'Yes, sir,' she said, wondering if her sparse selection of clothes would be sufficient if she was to wear them most of the time.

'I will arrange somewhere for you to work, but in the meantime, there is a girl in the cells I would like you to interview. She is in the female cell block. We have tried to take a statement from her, but she is not talking. So we thought a woman might have more success.'

'What has she been arrested for, sir?'

'Murder. Constable Henderson found her in the Howff graveyard beside the body. Her wailing drew him into the Howff to investigate. She had the knife in her hand and was bent over her victim's body. From the evidence available there does not seem to be any doubt she did it, but we do not know who she is, nor do we know who the murdered girl is. It is imperative you obtain her statement in order to find out who they both are and where they come from.'

'Yes, sir,' Kirsty said, picking up the notebook and pencil he tossed across the desk at her. Mentally she prepared herself to meet her first murderess.

9

Kirsty and Brewster strode down the corridor towards the female cell area, the staccato rhythm of their feet on the stone floor sending an eerie echo bouncing around the corridor, like an army on the march. The corridor, intersected by various other corridors, twisted and turned seeming to go on forever. Kirsty soon lost her bearings and, although she would have cut her tongue out before voicing it, thankful Brewster was with her.

'This is it,' Brewster said as they reached a short flight of stone stairs leading to a barred iron door. 'I will leave you once I get you through the door.'

He peered through the grille, muttering, 'Where is that dratted turnkey?' and rattled the iron bars until the door shook in its frame.

At the other side, the women's prison corridor seemed narrower than the ones they had already traversed. One side was tiled, and the other was lined with cell doors. A warren of other passages seemed to link with the corridor, making it difficult to gain any indication of size or number of cells.

The sound of footsteps and the jangle of keys heralded the arrival of the turnkey. She was a large woman, dressed in a navy blue dress. Around her waist was a leather belt from which hung several iron rings with large iron keys dangling almost to her knees. Her cheeks were flushed from hurrying, and a wisp of grey hair had escaped from the tight bun scraped to the back of her head.

'Miss Campbell to interview the prisoner,' Brewster announced and, giving Kirsty a conspiratorial grin, added, 'I will leave you to Mrs Baxter's tender mercies.'

The turnkey glared at him, then at Kirsty. 'What authority does Miss Campbell have to see the prisoner?'

'Now, now, Annie, Miss Campbell's our new statement

taker. You could almost say she is a policewoman.' Brewster grinned cheekily at the turnkey before turning back down the corridor. The disembodied sound of his whistling could be heard long after he was out of their sight, adding to the desolation of the empty passage.

Kirsty shivered. But she suppressed the feeling of hopelessness that had risen in her, and she gathered her resolve for the task ahead.

'Cheeky bugger,' the turnkey said. She swung the barred door open. 'You'd better come in.'

Kirsty entered the corridor behind the iron gate. The flaking, lumpy whitewashed ceiling, and the white tiled wall along one side lined with ugly pipes and wires, looked similar to the one she had left. But even more depressing was the other side of the passage, a row of studded iron doors fitted with peepholes shielded by iron flaps, so the turnkey could view the prisoners inside. No wonder Mrs Baxter was irritable having to work in this area. Kirsty could not think of anything more disheartening.

The turnkey suddenly grinned and stuck out a massive hand. 'The men call me Annie, although I never gave them permission to, but I don't mind you calling me Annie. We women have to stick together.'

Annie's smile softened the severity of her features and she no longer appeared intimidating.

Kirsty shook the hand offered. 'I'm Kirsty,' she said. 'It's nice to see a friendly face.' She was going to like this woman who seemed to share the same tough streak Kirsty had cultivated within herself.

'Keep the men in their place. Don't let them take advantage of you and you'll be all right.' Annie led Kirsty along the corridor. 'They're not a bad bunch.'

They stopped in front of a heavy iron door. Annie turned the cover of the peephole round so she could peer in. 'Poor wee soul, you'll be safe enough with her.' She pulled the door open. 'I'll be at the end of the passage. Bang on the door when you want out.'

Kirsty stepped into the cell. The door shut behind her with a metallic clang that jarred her nerves.

Standing for a moment with her back against the iron door, she fought the irrational feeling of panic that rose in her when the key grated in the lock. But she had no reason to panic because Annie would return to release her. She would not have to remain locked up like the girl sitting cross-legged on the narrow, mattress-covered bench.

The cell was bleak, an oblong, white-tiled room with a scrubbed stone floor that retained the stains left behind by previous occupants. Daylight filtered in through a small, barred window high up in the wall – too high for a prisoner to reach.

Kirsty forced herself away from the door and walked across the cell to where the girl sat.

The girl's arms were clasped tightly round her body. She rocked backwards and forwards, not looking up, showing no awareness anyone had entered her cell.

'Hello,' Kirsty said. 'I'm Kirsty Campbell. Do you mind if I talk to you?'

The girl continued to rock. Back and forth, back and forth.

Kirsty looked round the bare cell. It had no chair, no furniture, and only the tin pail in the corner. She wrinkled her nose, trying unsuccessfully to ignore the stench.

The only place for her to sit was the bench, but as soon as Kirsty sat on it, the girl's rocking increased in intensity. She waited, hoping for some further response, but the girl seemed oblivious to her presence. Watching her, Kirsty felt a growing sense of despair and helplessness as if she were picking up and mirroring the feelings of the girl in front of her. This was a sensation she had experienced many times before, in similar situations, when she was at a loss about what to do next.

'Will you tell me your name? I don't know what to call you?'

But the silence dragged on and on, seeming to fill the room like a sticky fog.

The girl was little more than a child, no older than fourteen or fifteen. Her aura of vulnerability fired up Kirsty's protective instincts, making her want to wrap her arms round the frail body to comfort her. She looked unkempt, uncared-for, with blonde hair tangled and straggling, and a trace of blood on her forehead from an open wound under her hairline.

'How did you cut your forehead?' Kirsty asked. She reached out to touch it, but the girl shrank away. As Kirsty drew back, the girl started to rock again.

'I won't hurt you,' Kirsty said. 'I'd like to help you.'

The girl continued to rock, but the tempo changed – and she saw the girl glance sideways at her.

'Nobody can help me,' she whispered, her voice almost inaudible.

'I'd like to try.'

Kirsty smiled encouragingly.

The girl began a tuneless humming, and the sound reverberated eerily round the cell. Still rocking, she glanced again at Kirsty, her eyes looking bleak and lost.

'What about your mother?' Kirsty kept her voice calm and gentle. 'Do you have a mother?'

The rocking halted briefly, and then increased again. A tear trickled down the girl's cheek and Kirsty reached over and grasped one of her hands. The cold fingers fluttered briefly like a captured butterfly, and then they went still within the warmth of Kirsty's hand.

The girl looked at the hand holding hers then peered up through her eyelashes.

'What is your pleasure, sir?' she asked in a husky voice. Her eyes seemed oddly glazed as if she had entered another time and place, looking at someone who was not there.

Kirsty, realizing the girl had lapsed into some event from the past, saw her chance. 'My pleasure is for you to tell me your name,' she said.

'Why would you want to know my name, kind sir? It is of no importance.'

'I have to know what to call you.'

A shadow moved behind the girl's eyes. 'You may call me Angel, kind sir.'

But then suddenly her fingers fluttered within Kirsty's hand, her expression went blank, and she started to hum and rock again.

Kirsty persisted, with more careful, gentle questions, but the girl did not respond. For some reason, she had slipped back into the empty place where Kirsty did not exist. So, in the end, Kirsty had to admit defeat, knowing the spell had broken, and she would get no more from the girl. She stood up and banged on the door.

'Goodbye for now, Angel,' she said before she left the cell. 'Maybe you'll feel better the next time I come to see you.' But the rocking figure did not seem to hear.

10

Brewster turned at the end of the passage, in time to see Kirsty pass through the iron gate into the cell corridor. The murder suspect she was on her way to interview was a strange one. Brewster recalled the girl rocking on the prison bench, with her arms clasped round her middle. So young, so vulnerable, he found it hard to visualize her wielding the knife that killed the child in the graveyard. And yet, he could not dispute the fact she had been found blood-stained, and leaning over the body with a knife in her hand. It could not be more obvious this girl had murdered the child. But he could not get the vision, of this ethereal girl, out of his mind.

Suppressing his thoughts about the girl in the cell, he turned away and continued walking to his office. He had no qualms about sending Miss Campbell to interview the murder suspect who, so far, had not presented any threat to her jailers. In any case, Annie would keep an eye on Kirsty, for despite her brusque manner the turnkey had a soft heart.

He slumped into his chair and fingered the file on his desk, a symbol of his failure. The new policewoman would be interviewing the girl now, and he wondered if she would have any more success than he'd had.

Instead of studying the file, Brewster's thoughts turned to the policewoman. Kirsty Campbell, that was her name, and apparently she had Dundee connections. She claimed to have experience, but Brewster had never met a policewoman before, so he had no idea what that experience might be. No doubt she would tell him because one thing he had noted, was how quickly she retorted to negative comments. It made him wonder how she would get on with the constables. There might be trouble, and he would have to contain it.

Despite that, he felt a grudging respect for her, and her

ability to stand up for herself, although he suspected she might be like Annie, hard on the outside with a soft inner core. Time would tell, and if the chief constable's experiment was to be a success, the two of them needed to work together. He hoped there would not be too many fireworks along the way.

His stomach rumbled. It might have been a reaction to thinking about Kirsty, but was more likely to be hunger pangs because he hadn't eaten anything since the slice of toast he swallowed at half-past-five this morning.

'If you're not careful, you'll end up with an ulcer,' Maggie had said as he'd kissed her goodbye. No doubt she was right.

He thrust the file into an overflowing tray, pushed his chair back, and headed for the canteen.

Following Annie along the passage, Kirsty felt an ache that seemed to permeate her whole body.

'Poor wee soul,' Annie said. 'Did ye get her to tell you anything?'

'Not really. But I wondered how she damaged her forehead.'

'Ah. That would be when her solicitor visited her earlier this morning. She got in a dreadful state and started banging her head against the wall.' Annie looked back over her shoulder towards the cell. 'It seemed to me she was terrified of him. I wondered about it at the time, but maybe it's because he's a man.'

'She has a solicitor?'

'Aye. The sheriff appointed one for her. Though I don't know what good it'll do her.'

'She's been in court already?'

Kirsty knew all prisoners had to appear before a magistrate on the first court day after the crime. She was still struggling to adapt to the differences between Scottish and English law, but she knew there were no magistrates in Scotland, and the equivalent here was a sheriff. However, it was still Monday morning, there hardly seemed to have been enough time.

'Aye, the sheriff heard her case at nine o'clock before the business of the day started. He does that sometimes with the difficult ones.'

Kirsty was thoughtful as she left the women's cell block.

'Like as not I'll be seeing ye again.' Annie slammed the gate behind her.

Kirsty found Brewster in the canteen. He glanced at her, placing his half-eaten meat pie on a paper bag lying on the rough wooden table. 'Well,' he said through a mouthful of pie. 'Did she tell you anything?'

Kirsty held herself erect, clasping her hands behind her back. 'Not much, sir,' she said. 'I think she's on the game, though. She says she's called Angel, but I doubt if that's her real name.' As an afterthought, she said, 'Sir.'

Brewster sighed. 'You don't have to call me sir all the time, and certainly not when we are in plain clothes. That would be a real giveaway if we were out on an investigation where we didn't want it known we were police officers. And, while I'm thinking about it, I'd better remind you the criminal investigation department is a plain-clothes force, and we do not wear uniform most of the time. Make sure you are wearing something different before you report for duty tomorrow.'

Kirsty had intended to tell Brewster about Angel's apparent fear of her solicitor. But his comment, which sounded like a reprimand, annoyed her, so instead she snapped, 'Yes, sir,' and bit her tongue to prevent her following it up with, 'you told me that earlier this morning.'

'Don't call me sir,' he repeated wearily. 'And for goodness sake sit down. You make me tired just looking at you.'

He crossed the room to the fireplace. Lifting the teapot from the dull black hob, he poured dark liquid into a mug and took it back to her. 'Get this down you. It might relax you before I take you to see the scene of the crime.'

Kirsty's hand tightened on the handle of the mug. Although she did not want his tea, she swallowed it.

The damp, fresh quality to the air that met them when they left the police office, was a relief. Kirsty lifted her head and breathed deeply, to clear herself of the sour stench of the cell.

The pavements were wet, and rivulets of water dribbled between the road cobbles on their way to the gutters. Spatters of water splashed up their legs as Brewster set off at a fast pace. Kirsty struggled to keep up with him, trying not to run. In this fashion, they went along the cobbled roads until they reached Barrack Street.

'Side gate,' Brewster said, pointing. 'That's where Constable Henderson first heard the screaming.'

Questions she would have liked to ask whirled round in her mind, but she was too out of breath to voice them. The tall building on one side of the narrow cobbled road and the high cemetery wall on the other side loomed over them, increasing Kirsty's sense of unease as she followed Brewster to the gate.

'Locked, as I expected,' he muttered. 'As it was on the night of the murder, so Henderson had to walk to the main gate.' He looked at his pocket watch before turning away, along the cemetery wall. 'Henderson said the screaming continued until he found the girl in the middle of the cemetery and even then she didn't stop.'

Reaching the top of Barrack Street, Brewster led Kirsty round the corner to the main gate in Ward Road. 'And it's unlocked. Just as Henderson found it.'

Checking his watch again, he muttered, 'Six minutes.'

He pushed the gate, and they entered the graveyard which had an unkempt, overgrown look, and seemed to be several degrees colder inside than it had been on the street. The bushes and trees overhanging the twisting paths made a whispering noise as a sudden wind rustled through them. The gravestones leaned towards her. She shivered. Why did she have a feeling this was an evil place, when surely this must be sanctified ground?

Convinced she was being foolish, she gave herself a mental shake. It was only a graveyard after all, even if it had been the scene of a murder.

Brewster stopped so suddenly she almost collided with his back.

'This is it,' he said, bending over the flat gravestone balanced on two stone struts like a table top. 'Look, you can see the bloodstains.' He got down on his hands and knees to crawl around the stone.

Kirsty, feeling slightly hysterical, nearly giggled. 'What are you looking for, sir?'

He did not raise his head. 'Clues,' he muttered.

'Why do you need clues if you're convinced you know who did it?'

'Because I'm a detective, that's why, and nothing is ever that simple. If she has a good solicitor and we do not have enough evidence, she could get off. Or maybe be given a nice, cosy bed in the lunatic asylum.' He leaned back on his heels. 'I've seen it happen before. You think you have it all sorted out and in walks someone like Simon Harvey, and before you know it, the person in the dock is the victim. And the policeman is the one to blame.'

'Who's Simon Harvey?'

'Only the sharpest solicitor in Dundee. He takes on charity cases in between his other well-paid work. It seems to give him some sort of thrill, but we could all do without his interference.' Brewster stood up and brushed dirt from his knees. 'Waste of time, there is nothing here anyway.'

Kirsty leaned over to study the inscription on the gravestone. 'Until we meet on the other side.' Her voice faltered when she saw the name, and she had to grab the stone to prevent herself falling as an unexpected nausea and faintness swept over her. A memory long forgotten rose to torment her – the summer house, a faraway band playing, couples dancing, chatting, drinking, eating, and not one of them heard her cries as the nice young man, of whom her parents approved, tore at her dress.

Brewster turned towards her. 'What did you say?'

Kirsty returned to the present with a jolt. Her legs were so weak they barely held her up, and she was damp with perspiration. 'Nothing,' she mumbled. She pushed herself up from the gravestone and further away from Brewster, for she knew if he were to brush against her at that moment, she would scream. 'I was reading the epitaph on the stone,' she said, in as normal a voice as she could manage.

'Mmh, Jonathan Bogue . . . strange that it should be his

grave.'

'What's strange about it?' She tried to keep her voice calm despite the thumping of her heart. Surely he could not know of her connection with the Bogue family.

'Jonathan Bogue's name has a certain notoriety in Dundee. They say he dabbled in necromancy. All sorts of strange rumours circulated about him, but the Bogue family keep it quiet. They would have preferred it if his reputation had died with him. The Bogues are a strait-laced family.'

A shiver crept up Kirsty's spine. The cemetery seemed to have grown darker and more silent. 'Do you think it might have any connection with the murder?'

Brewster laughed. 'I doubt it, Bogue's been dead for over sixty-five years, so this is one crime he can't be involved with.' He turned away from the gravestone. 'Come on,' he said over his shoulder, 'I'll take you for a tour of the morgue, providing it will not upset you.'

Kirsty shuddered. She had never seen a dead body. Morgue tours had been included in her training, but the morgue attendants had been given strict instructions to ensure the ladies were not allowed to see any corpses. Commandant Damer Dawson had done her best to overturn this decision, but Scotland Yard's Commissioner of Police had been adamant. 'Ladies, even though they are women police, should not be subject to such sights,' he had said, and so the matter was closed.

The epitaph on Jonathan Bogue's tomb wavered in front of her eyes, and she tore her gaze from it with difficulty. Brewster had already reached the path leading out of the cemetery, so she had to hurry to catch up.

'I've seen morgues before,' she said, trying to breathe normally so he would not guess how she felt. But the shiver creeping up her spine intensified, and goose pimples erupted on her skin.

11

Kirsty followed Brewster down the steep, winding stairway leading to the underground morgue. Her eyes had not yet adjusted to the gloom of the unlit stairs, and the smooth leather soles of her boots slithered on stone steps ground down with the passage of many feet. She lost her balance and grabbed the handrail to prevent herself from falling forward on to Brewster's back.

He did not even notice.

The railing was cold, damp and slimy. The hand she clamped round it, stung. Pain lanced through her arm, and her shoulder felt as if it might have been wrenched from its socket. The stillness closed in on her, suffocating in its intensity. Fetid air, drifting upwards, caught the back of her throat and she struggled for breath. Yet, she forced herself on, determined to maintain her outward appearance of calm.

The sound of their footsteps bounced upwards with a metallic echo which gave the impression they were being followed and added to the eerie atmosphere. The deeper they went the more disjointed the echo became. When they reached the bottom passage, they turned to the right and went through an unlocked iron-barred gate into a narrow dimly-lit corridor. Brewster led her to a door set in the wall.

'She'll be in the ice-room, I expect,' he said, holding the door open for her.

A blast of cold air and the sickly, sweet smell of embalming fluid mingled with disinfectant, rushed out to meet them. She shivered. This morgue, with its rows of white-sheeted trolleys lining the whitewashed walls, was even more primitive than the ones she had toured during her training.

Thankfully, most of the trolleys lacked occupants – although an air of expectancy hung over them, like hospital beds made up in readiness for their next patients.

Oil lamps hanging from hooks in the ceiling provided some patchy light. Shadows shifted and moved in a macabre slow dance, and the light failed to reach the furthest corners of the basement. Kirsty was sure she heard faint rustling and movement, although when she concentrated, trying to detect where this was coming from, there was nothing but silence, shifting shadows, and Brewster fidgeting beside her.

Her only consolation was that he seemed to be as unnerved as she was, although she hoped she was making a better job of hiding it.

The silence was broken by the slurping sound of rubber boots on the glistening-wet floor tiles. Kirsty's fingers curled into a fist, and she peered into the darkness in an attempt to see what was making the noise. But she was unable to see anything, although the sound slurped nearer and nearer.

Shivers raced along her spine, and the irrational feeling she was about to take part in some horrific ritual threatened to overcome her. She dug her fingernails into the palms of her hands as a reminder that her reaction could be an effect of the creepy atmosphere, and her imagination was taking over. But, although she knew she was being foolish, she could not rid herself of the feeling of foreboding.

Suddenly he was there, standing in front of her, a small, stooped man with longish hair whose skin had a yellowish tinge as if he had spent all his life in these subterranean chambers. A sharp-pointed nose and chin gave him the appearance of a malevolent gnome while the squint in his eye created an unsettling effect.

'Don't mind him,' Brewster whispered. 'He's a bit simple.'

Kirsty moved nearer to Brewster. Despite her bravado she would not like to be left alone with the morgue attendant.

'Let's see the new one, Davvy.' Brewster patted the man on the shoulder. 'You know the one I mean. The body brought in on Friday night.'

'Aye, sir. That'll be the lassie, sir.' He shrugged the shoulder Brewster had touched while his hands flapped aimlessly.

Kirsty sensed Davvy watching her. Her skin prickled. But

when she looked at him his eyes were elsewhere. She stared at him, daring him to look at her again, but he studiously avoided her gaze.

'Will ye be wanting the young lassie to see the body too?' Davvy asked. 'S'not a pretty sight, ye know.'

'That's all right, Davvy, the lady's seen bodies before.'

She shuddered. Now was not the time to tell him he had been misled.

'If you say so, sir.' Davvy shuffled to the back of the room, his wellington boots squelching. Finally, he stopped beside a white-sheeted trolley. 'This's her. D'ye want me to stay?'

'No, that's all right, Davvy. Miss Campbell and I will manage now, so you can go back to your work.' Brewster gripped the sheet between his thumb and fingers while he waited for Davvy to move away.

'Are you sure you want to see this?'

Kirsty glared at him, convinced he was either trying to protect her or shock and belittle her. It only made her more determined to prove herself to him.

'It's part of the job.' Kirsty, already aware of the pungent smell of rotting flesh, steeled herself. But when Brewster pulled the sheet off to expose the body an involuntary gasp escaped her lips, despite her attempts to suppress it.

The child, for that's all she was, lay naked on the table. Her face and the skin on her arms and legs were translucently pale, although underneath, where her body rested on the trolley, the skin was pinkish-red. The knife wounds stretched, raw and gaping, from her neck to her abdomen and from side to side over her waist. It looked as if someone had split her open, laying bare all her internal organs in the process.

The lamp, dangling above them, swung slowly on its hook and the shadows beyond the trolley deepened. The room shrank. The walls pressed inwards. The roof seemed lower than it had a few moments ago. Pressure gathered in her chest. Her vision blurred. Bile rose in her throat.

'I told you it wasn't a pretty sight,' Brewster said. Kirsty noticed he was also looking pale, and it gave her grim satisfaction to think he was not as tough as he made himself out to be.

Kirsty bit her lip hard, swallowing to quell the nausea. 'It looks like an upside-down cross. Do you think it might be something religious?'

'Whatever the killer was trying to do, it was vile.' Brewster covered the body up again. 'You see now why I don't want her to get away with it.'

'You're sure it was Angel then?'

Visualizing Angel rocking back and forth in her cell, Kirsty could not imagine her doing something like this.

'Of course I am. The body was warm when we found it, and I saw her myself, standing over it with the bloody knife in her hand. She was the only one there. Who else could it be?'

Kirsty had no answer for him.

Brewster was silent as they walked back to the stairs, and there was no sign of the attendant as they left. But as Kirsty climbed the stairs from the morgue, the shiver tingling her spine told her Davvy's eyes were following her.

'We might have taken the underground passage back to the office,' Inspector Brewster said as they emerged into the daylight. 'Only you looked as if you needed some air.'

Kirsty breathed deeply, enjoying the bite of cold air hitting her lungs. 'Underground passage, sir?'

'There's a tangle of them underneath the police station. One leads to the morgue, others go to the court and the prison.' He grinned. 'They say a person could wander in them forever if they don't know their way around.'

'And you do, of course.'

'I'll take you through them and show you – when you're not so green about the gills.' He grinned at her.

Kirsty bristled. 'You seem glad enough of the fresh air yourself, sir.'

He laughed. 'You're a strange one. But never mind, we'll just have to get used to each other.' Turning, he strode over the cobbles, leading the way down the narrow lane. At the corner, he paused. 'Do you know where you are now?' he said. 'The police station is along the road and through the arch, so I'll leave you here.'

She had thought he would be with her for the rest of the day. If he had been more explicit about her duties, and what he wanted her to do, it would not have mattered. But all she had done was tag along behind him.

'What am I supposed to do when I get there?' She had visions of sitting on the wooden bench in the charge room, twiddling her thumbs until he chose to return from wherever he was going. 'I could continue with the murder investigation,' she added.

'No,' he said, abruptly. 'You've done your part, trying to get the girl's statement. You can leave the investigation to me. In the meantime, I have left you some files on missing children. Study them and work out a plan of investigation for me to pursue. We can discuss it when I return.'

'Where are you going?' Kirsty asked before she could stop herself.

The crinkles at the side of his eyes seemed to sag. 'I have to go home. I won't be long,' he said.

Kirsty watched him go, thinking his shoulders seemed to have a droop that had not been there before.

12

Brewster pushed past an elderly couple, muttering, 'Sorry,' when they glared at him.

He was in a hurry to get home to Maggie. He had left her on her own far too long, and he worried she might need something when he was not there.

She always laughed at him and said he worried too much, but he could not help it.

The cottage was one of a row of similar cottages, and Brewster was proud of it. Maggie would never have been able to cope in a tenement flat. At least here she could get out, provided she had someone to push the wheelchair.

The gate opened with its usual creak. He would have to find time to oil the hinges, another of those jobs that remained undone and added to his feelings of failure.

He strode along the concrete path, ignoring the small overgrown garden at each side of it, and up the wooden ramp to the front door.

'Is that you, Jamie?'

The living room door opened, and Maggie guided her wheelchair through it, scraping the paint on the skirting board when she turned it to face him.

'Who else would it be?' Brewster leaned over and kissed her on the cheek. 'Now, let's see what we have in the kitchen.'

'I could have managed, you know.'

'I know, but I need to eat as well, and I know you would make do with a sandwich if I didn't come home.'

Brewster placed a pan of water on the stove, threw some potatoes in the sink and started to peel them. 'What else do we have?' He deposited the last potato in the pan of water which was now boiling.

'There's some left over stew from yesterday.' Maggie turned

her chair and reached into a cupboard, bringing out a pot.

'Excellent.' Brewster placed it on the cooker. 'It can heat on low until the potatoes are ready.'

Maggie smiled. 'You spoil me.'

'Nonsense.'

Brewster pulled out a kitchen chair and sat. He grasped her hands and said, 'How has your day been?'

She laughed. 'I've been fine. I made myself some porridge earlier on as well as a cup of tea. So you see, I'm managing to look after myself.'

'But you shouldn't be handling kettles of boiling water, I can't bear to think what would happen if you scalded yourself.'

'I'm careful,' she said. 'So you don't need to worry about me. But what about you. Tell me about your day.'

'You remember I told you we were getting a policewoman? Well, she started today.'

Maggie leaned forward. 'What's she like? Is she very formidable.'

'She's younger than I thought she'd be, but efficient and quite prickly. She has a no nonsense attitude that might annoy the men.'

'Is she pretty?'

'I didn't notice. I suppose she's attractive, but she doesn't make the most of it.'

'Do you like her?'

'I'm not sure. She keeps wanting to assert herself, and it makes me want to take her down a peg or two.'

What he didn't say, was how guilty he felt about taking Kirsty to the morgue and subjecting her to the horrors it contained. There had been no need for it, and it had backfired because even he had not been prepared for the sight of the child's mutilated body. In some ways, Kirsty had coped with it better, although he had seen her sway when the sheet had been pulled away from the body, and she had changed colour. However, he had been fighting his own nausea, and when he looked at her again she seemed composed.

'Oh, Jamie, that's not like you.'

Jamie pushed thoughts of Kirsty out of his mind and stood

up. Removing the potato pot from the cooker, he held it over the sink and strained the water off. He placed two plates on the table and ladled potatoes and stew onto them.

When Kirsty opened the outer door to the police station, someone at the other side forced it back, almost hitting her in the face.

Instinctively she thrust her foot between the door and its frame to prevent it closing. Heaving with her shoulder, she squeezed herself through the opening into the charge room.

Two uniformed constables were wrestling with a large woman who seemed determined to climb over the counter to get at the desk sergeant.

Freeing one arm, the woman thumped her fist on the wooden top, demanding, 'What right have these idiots got to hold me? I'm a citizen, amn't I? I pays my taxes, don't I?'

She stopped for breath, and scowled at the constables trying to restrain her.

The desk sergeant grabbed his opportunity. 'Paying taxes doesn't give you the right to cause a commotion, Aggie. And we only have your word about the taxes. Personally I'd have my doubts about it.'

The woman took a huge breath, and seemed to grow larger while her eyes bulged until Kirsty thought they would explode. She shook the constables from her, like a dog would shake fleas from its coat and, colliding with each other, they staggered across the room landing on the bench.

'That's all the thanks I get for trying to do someone a good turn,' the woman shouted. 'Well, you take the brats and do what you like with them.'

The posters on the large wall notice-board flapped, the pencils on the sergeant's desk rolled onto the floor, and the door of the pot-bellied stove swung open to let out a spiral of sooty smoke as she slammed out the door.

Kirsty thrust herself away from the wall. 'What was that all about?'

The desk sergeant wiped his brow with a large, red

handkerchief, and looked at Kirsty with unfriendly eyes.

He tucked the handkerchief into his pocket, and turned to the constables who were now standing up and muttering to each other, as they stared at two children huddled on the bench. 'Henderson, Wells,' he snapped, 'the answer to your prayers is here. Meet Miss Campbell, our new statement taker. She should be capable of handling this wee problem so you can get on with something more important.'

'Thank God. I don't fancy this job at all.' The taller of the two constables stood up. 'Pleased to meet you, Miss Campbell,' he said, staring at her with curiosity. 'I'm Constable Henderson, but I don't mind if you call me Joe. And this is just the job for a woman, so you're welcome to take over.'

'Constable Wells, Miss Campbell.' His partner had the broad, squat figure of the native Dundonian, in direct contrast to the lanky Constable Henderson.

Kirsty flexed her fingers, numb and crushed from the constables' enthusiastic handshakes, which she suspected had been deliberately over-firm.

'Why am I the answer to your prayers? And what am I supposed to take over?' Kirsty guessed it had something to do with the two children, but she was not in the mood to make it easy for them. Surreptitiously massaging her hand, she waited for them to explain.

The desk sergeant smirked at her. 'Move yourselves, lads. Let Miss Campbell have a better look at what you have tucked away on the bench behind you.'

'Gladly, sarge,' Constable Henderson said, standing aside. 'Miss Campbell, I'd like you to meet the problem of the day. Two toerags with nowhere to go, wee Bert and his big sister Nora.'

The girl was dirty and ragged, with hair straggling down her back and brown eyes that glared defiance. She looked about ten, although Kirsty thought she could be older because many Dundee children were small for their age. Her arm was around a smaller boy of five or six who was just as dirty and ragged, and her expression seemed to defy anyone to touch him.

Kirsty turned to the desk sergeant. 'How did they get here?'

she asked.

'Henderson and Wells can tell you that, missy.' He turned away from her and strolled back to his high desk. 'I've paperwork to do, so I'll leave you to them.'

'Never pay heed to him, Miss Campbell,' Henderson said. 'He doesn't like children.'

Kirsty ignored the insolence in his voice. 'Tell me about them, then. How did they get here? And what am I supposed to do with them?'

Henderson shrugged his narrow shoulders. Glancing at his partner, he said, 'It's like this, miss. Harry and me were out on the beat, just walking past the Howff graveyard, when we came across Big Aggie taking the children down Barrack Street. It looked like she was coming from the Overgate. So I said to Harry, "Some funny business going on here," I said. That's right, isn't it, Harry?'

'Aye, that's right, Joe. Seemed like funny business, right enough.'

'So I apprehended Big Aggie, and said to her, "Where you taking the children, Aggie?" But Big Aggie's not daft. "Why, lads, I was just taking them to the police station. The poor wee mites are fair lost," she said to me.' Henderson snorted. 'Taking them to one of her bawdy houses, more like, and nobody'd ever hear of them again. So I turned to her and said, "Well then, you won't mind if we escort you." She wasn't pleased – you never saw anybody able to scowl the way she did. But she came along with us, quiet-like, and it was only when we got here all hell broke loose. Mind you, he didn't help.' Henderson nodded in the direction of the desk sergeant.

'I heard that, Henderson. Watch your tongue else it'll be worse for you.' The desk sergeant glowered over the top of his desk.

'Yes, sarge. No harm meant.' Henderson winked at Kirsty.

'What about their parents?'

'Big Aggie says, they haven't got any?'

'Relatives then?'

'Same thing. According to Aggie, they're wee lost souls.'

'If that's true, what do we do with them now?' Kirsty asked.

'You mean what do you do with them?' Henderson grinned at her. 'Sarge said you were the answer to our prayers, so they're all yours.'

'Fair enough,' Kirsty said, 'but they can't stay here. I'll have to take them somewhere. Any suggestions?'

Henderson's grin widened. 'The Children's Refuge is just along the road. You can't miss it. It's the big three-storey building on the corner of West Bell Street and Constitution Road. Ask for Edward Gordon, he'll see you all right.'

Kirsty held a hand out to the girl. 'Come on, then, Nora. We'd best get you and your brother settled somewhere.'

The girl slid along the bench. 'Don't bloody well think you can take us to the Refuge, 'cause we're not going.' Her voice was loud and shrill, full of bravado. She glared at Kirsty, and her arm tightened around her brother.

'Is there somewhere else you can go?' Kirsty smiled at the children, hoping it would calm them down. 'If you tell me where you come from? Or where your mum and dad live? I could take you home.'

'Ain't got no home.' Nora's glare intensified.

'What about other relatives, maybe an auntie or uncle?'

'Ain't got nobody.'

'You must come from somewhere.' Desperation made Kirsty's voice sound sharper than she meant.

Nora glared at her.

Sniggering, the two constables left the charge room. As the door slammed shut behind them, Kirsty heard one of them say, 'Why'd you tell her to take them to the Refuge?'

'Why not,' the other said, his laugh echoing up the corridor.

Bert cowered away from Kirsty as she sat down beside him. 'You've got to go somewhere,' she said, 'but it's early yet, so I can wait until you're ready.'

The girl slid further along the bench pulling Bert with her. Kirsty moved at the same time, to stay close to him. So close she could feel his legs trembling.

Although Nora was hostile, Kirsty thought Bert might respond to her. She wanted to touch him, to reassure him she meant him no harm. But she did not want to rush her approach in case she frightened him even further.

After a few minutes, Kirsty said, 'You know, you won't be able to slide much further up the bench because the wall's going to stop you.' She put her hand in her pocket, searching for the paper bag of sweets she had bought in the Overgate. Pulling out a boiled sweet she offered it to Nora, but the girl ignored it. 'What about you, Bert, d'you want a sweetie?'

Bert took the sweet, but as he was aiming it for his mouth, Nora grabbed it and threw it across the room. 'Bert don't want your bloody sweeties.' Her voice was a low hiss, full of hate.

'But I did want it.' Large tears trembled on the end of his long, dark lashes, before sliding down his face, drawing two light stripes on his grimy cheeks.

Kirsty resisted an urge to put her arm around Bert and instead offered him her handkerchief. He took it, and while he rubbed his face, she could see Nora wriggling on the bench as if her seat had become more uncomfortable. Her brother's crying clearly upset her.

'Don't cry,' Kirsty said. 'I've got plenty more sweeties, and you can have one now if Nora will allow it.'

'Please, Nora.' Bert's voice trembled.

'All right,' Nora said grudgingly.

Kirsty took the paper bag of sweets out of her pocket, and as she did so she smiled at Nora, but the girl turned her head away and refused to look at her.

As soon as Bert popped the sweet in his mouth, Kirsty took hold of his hand. 'Come along, Bert. We'll get you settled in a safe place with a nice, cosy bed, and something to eat. And when we get there you can have the whole bag of sweeties all to yourself.'

'She's telling lies, Bert. She won't give you no more sweeties. She wants to take you away from me.'

Bert glanced uncertainly at his sister but rose from the bench, clutching Kirsty's hand tightly. 'All of them? Just for me?'

'Yes, Bert. All of them, but you can give some to your sister if you want to.'

'Don't go with her, Bert, you don't need her sweeties. Stay

here with me,' Nora wailed.

Kirsty glanced over her shoulder as she walked towards the door with him. 'You can come with us if you want,' she said to Nora, 'but if you're coming you'd better come now.'

The girl gave Kirsty a baleful look but followed her out the door.

13

The age-blackened stone edifice, facing onto West Bell Street and continuing round the corner into Constitution Road, loomed over Kirsty and the two children. The building looked neglected and decayed with its grime-streaked windows, rotting window frames, and sills splattered with bird droppings. A seagull, screeching defiance from the rooftop high above her, sounded like an omen of disaster.

Dismayed, she stared up at the building. What was she taking the children into? She had a sudden urge to turn back to the police station. But then what would she do with them? Despite her increasing reluctance, she knew she had no other choice but to take Bert and Nora into the Refuge.

In any case, the two police constables had said this was the place to take abandoned children. Although, remembering their laughter when they left the charge room, she was less sure now.

'Here we are, then,' she said with a cheerfulness she did not feel. 'We'll soon have you settled now.' Bert's hand, warm and moist, tightened in her grasp. Her heart went out to the child looking up at her with worry reflected in his eyes. Pushing her doubts aside, she smiled down at him. 'It's all right, Bert. I wouldn't take you anywhere you wouldn't be safe.'

One half of the large double door stood partly open. Kirsty pushed it wider, allowing daylight to penetrate the building far enough to show up the dirt and decay. A smell of sweat and unwashed bodies seeped out. Kirsty's throat contracted as the doubts at the back of her mind grew larger. She must be in the wrong building.

She turned to leave, but found her way blocked by a stooped figure dressed in rags.

'I'm sorry,' she said, 'but I think I've come to the wrong place. I'm looking for the Children's Refuge.'

The tramp's face collapsed in a toothless grin. 'Ye're in the right place, m'dear,' he slurred. 'Childrens is upstairs and us big folks is here on the ground floor.' He shuffled nearer to her. 'The Salvation Army's always been good to us old folks.' His confusion about her uniform was understandable as he would never have seen a policewoman before.

Kirsty pulled the children close to her as the tramp moved nearer. She smelled the sourness of him as well as the alcohol on his breath and saw his gaze fix menacingly on her pockets.

'Would ye have a few coppers to spare for a poor old man?' His voice assumed a whining sound and his hands reached towards the children.

Bert squealed with fright and, shaking his hand free from Kirsty's grasp, he dived up the stairs. Nora ran after him. 'Wait for me, Bert,' she shouted.

Kirsty whirled towards the stairs and ran after the children. She could hear their feet clattering on the broad, winding steps leading up out of the shadows of the entrance hall while the beggar's screeching laugh reverberated after them.

A stained-glass window, halfway up, allowed daylight into the stairwell and set dust motes swirling in the stale air. Jesus looked down from the glass onto the dirty stair, but Kirsty took little comfort from it.

'I told you we shouldn't have come here,' Nora said. The resentment in her voice was reflected in the look on her face, and in her eyes.

'Nonsense,' Kirsty replied with a confidence she did not feel, 'we'll be all right once we find Mr Gordon.' Heavy steps sounded on the stairs below them.

'Is he following us, miss?' Bert sounded scared.

'I told you we shouldn't have let her bring us here.'

'Keep on going up,' Kirsty urged. 'I expect we'll find Mr Gordon when we get to the top.' But Kirsty was no longer sure about Edward Gordon, or where he might be.

'What the hell are you doing on these stairs?' A voice soared up from down below. 'You know perfectly well you're not allowed beyond the first floor.'

Muttering and the sound of a scuffle echoed upwards. Then

the voice roared again. 'And stay down there or you'll answer to me, and believe me, you won't like that!'

Kirsty peered over the banister in an effort to see who was climbing the stairs. As a man rounded the bend in the stairwell, she drew back, not wanting the owner of the voice to see her looking. But he was looking up as if he had expected them to be there.

'I'm sorry. I hope I didn't startle you.' The voice was low and pleasant. 'I'm Edward Gordon. How can I help you?'

He was a tall man with a slight stoop, giving the impression he was embarrassed by his height. He had untidy brown hair that flopped forward over his face, eyes that reflected a gentle interest, and a slightly lop-sided smile.

His words and his appearance calmed Kirsty, and she found herself returning the smile. She also felt an unexpected warmth suffusing her body and, for the first time, she was acutely aware of the ugliness of her uniform.

'I've brought Bert and Nora. They need a bed and some feeding up until we find out what to do with them.' As Kirsty struggled against the unfamiliar surge of feeling, the words came out with a brusqueness she had not intended.

'And who would we be?' he asked gently. 'I'm not familiar with the uniform you're wearing.'

'Yes . . . I . . . sorry . . . I'm . . .' Kirsty's tongue seemed to be sticking to the roof of her mouth. She was not used to being flustered and could not understand why this was happening to her. Forcing herself to enunciate the words, she said, 'I'm Kirsty Campbell. I've just begun work with Dundee City Police, as a statement taker.'

'I'm pleased to meet you, Miss Campbell.' He enclosed her free hand with both of his, holding it for the briefest moment. Turning to Bert and Nora, he said, 'And what have we here? Two lost souls by the look of it.'

Nora glowered at him. 'I'm not a bloody lost soul, and I'm only here because she won't let go of Bert.' She nodded her head towards Kirsty. 'If she'd let us alone, me and Bert would have managed fine.'

Edward Gordon laughed. 'No doubt you would,' he said.

Turning to Kirsty he muttered, 'This little lass has spirit.' He extended his hand to Bert, 'D'you want to come with me, lad? I'm sure you must be hungry after your adventures, and I might be able to find you something to eat.'

Edward's feet were silent on the corridor floor, but Bert's shoes clattered on the linoleum as he trotted to keep up with him.

Kirsty held her hand out to Nora, but the girl slithered away from her to follow Edward and Bert along the passageway.

Edward led them into a large room that could only be the kitchen. He lifted Bert up onto a wooden chair and pulled it close to the table. 'Now let me see what we have here,' he muttered, lifting some pot lids and scrutinising the contents. 'Ah yes, I thought there would be some mince left. How does potatoes and mince sound, with maybe a doughball thrown in for good measure?'

'Yes, please.' Bert's face lit up at the mention of food. Even Nora showed some interest.

'Nora, if you want some you'd better sit down too.' Edward lit a match and held it to the hissing gas ring. 'The mince won't be long. It just needs heating up.' He took plates from a cupboard and laid one down in front of Bert and another in front of Nora. He stood balancing a third plate in his hand. 'What about you, Miss Campbell? I'd lay bets you haven't eaten yet.'

Kirsty could feel heat rising from her neck to her cheeks, and she was sure her face must look flushed. Something in the way he looked at her made her feel warm, but at the same time uncomfortable.

'I'm fine, thanks,' she said. 'If you'll see to the children, I'll be able to get back to the office.'

'Of course,' he said. 'But they won't be able to stay here, you know. This is The Working Boys' Home. We only take in older boys.'

Kirsty stared at him in dismay. 'But I thought this was a children's refuge? At least, that's what they said at the station.'

Edward laughed. 'I've no doubt they did. They've got too accustomed to me doing their job for them.' The mince pot started to steam, and he turned to stir it.

'What do you mean?'

'I have links with most of the charitable organizations and children's homes in Dundee. I can usually find somewhere to take children. So the constables bring them to me and then forget about them.'

Kirsty frowned. 'But, if a constable places children somewhere, aren't they supposed to know where they go and check they're all right?'

Edward spooned potatoes and mince onto three plates and placed one in front of each of them. 'I'm sure you're right. You'll know more about police procedures than I do. But I expect it's all a matter of trust. The constables know I'm reliable, and looking after children is what I'm good at. Now sit down and have some mince and potatoes.'

Bert bent his head over the plate and spooned the mince into his mouth, almost choking as he did so. Nora watched him for a moment and then she too started to eat.

'Won't you even taste it, Miss Campbell? I can guarantee the mince is good, and the children seem to be enjoying it.' He put the empty pot into a deep iron sink and, turning a tap, filled the pot with water.

Kirsty looked at the plate. The mince did look good, and the aroma reminded her she was hungry. 'I shouldn't,' she said as she dipped her fork into the food.

'Nonsense, it will be wasted if you don't eat it, and I can't abide waste.'

'That was most unprofessional, allowing you to feed me,' Kirsty said after she finished eating. But she had to admit to herself the meal had been excellent.

'Not at all. You looked hungry, and it's my job to take care of people. So are you going to allow me to take care of your waifs? Or are you going to take them away with you?' Edward stacked the dirty plates in a tub.

'I suppose I'd better leave them in your care.' Kirsty knew she should see them settled, but it made sense to allow Edward Gordon to help. He had the contacts and would know where to take the children. Apart from that, something about this man made her feel she could trust him. 'I'll want to know where they go, and I'll check up on them.'

'Don't worry, I'll come into the police station in the morning and let you know where they are.'

'You will keep them together, won't you?'

'I'll try.' Edward smiled apologetically. 'It depends where the vacancies are, and some of the homes take only boys or girls, but not both.'

Kirsty stood up. 'I'll find my own way out,' she said.

'You leaving us here, miss?' Bert looked at her with sleep-filled eyes.

'Course she is.' Nora's voice was scornful. 'What d'you expect. She don't care. She didn't even give you the sweeties she promised.'

The paper bag rustled as Kirsty pulled it out of her pocket. 'I wasn't forgetting,' she said, handing it to Bert. 'Do what the nice man says, and I'll see you tomorrow.'

She ran down the stairs without looking back, although part of her wanted to stay and look after the children. But she had been away from the police station too long already. Brewster would want to know what she intended to do about the missing girls.

And she had not read a word of the files he had left for her.

Edward listened to Kirsty's feet clattering on the stairs, then the thud of the door as she left the building. She was an interesting woman, attractive too, although the awful uniform did not do her any favours. But Edward felt drawn to her, and wanted to get to know her better. Meanwhile, the children needed somewhere to stay, and he had a good idea where to take them.

He poured water from a kettle into the tub, added some cold to it, and scrubbed the plates with a brush.

Bert had fallen asleep on his chair, and Nora stood between him and Edward.

'What you going to do with us mister?' Nora's voice was antagonistic.

'I think I know a place where you can be looked after. It's a big house, and there are lots of other children.'

Nora snorted. 'I'm not a child.' She scowled at him.

'Of course you're not,' Edward said. 'You must be at least twelve.'

He stacked the dishes to drip on the draining board. 'Come on, wake Bert up, and I'll take you there. I can guarantee you'll like it.'

Nora glared at him but did as she was told.

14

On her way back to the police station, Kirsty thought some more about what Edward Gordon had said about the constables dumping children at the Refuge.

It appeared they were in the habit of failing to check up on what happened to them afterwards. It worried her, and she decided to discuss the unorthodox nature of Dundee police procedures with Brewster.

'Has Inspector Brewster returned to the office yet?' she asked the section sergeant, who was now on duty behind the desk. The desk sergeant she had seen before was no longer there, and she supposed he had gone off duty.

'Inspector Brewster looked for you when he returned to the office. But he had to go out on a call without you because you weren't here.' The section sergeant's eyes glinted with malicious glee.

'But the other sergeant knew I had to take children to the Refuge,' Kirsty protested.

'The duty sergeant never mentioned it to me when we changed shifts.' He leaned over the counter with a mirthless smile. 'Unless you sign the log book when you leave the office, Miss Campbell, how do you expect anyone to know where you are?'

'No one told me about the log book!' Kirsty's annoyance was turning into anger.

'Not my responsibility.'

He wants me to lose my temper, Kirsty thought, but I will not give him the satisfaction. 'Is there anyone else in CID I could talk to?' she asked.

'There's Inspector McAllister, but he's on leave this week and won't be back until next Monday.'

'Then, if I can't talk to anyone can you tell me where my

desk is supposed to be? I have a report to write on the two children.'

The section sergeant pointed his pencil to the door at the end of the room. 'Go through there, past the canteen, and the door next to it is where the constables have their desks. The door next to that is the sergeants' room, and then the door after that is where you'll find your desk.' The smile vanished from his face. 'You're privileged,' he said sourly. 'You've got a room to yourself . . . Nobody lower than an inspector has their own office.'

Kirsty nodded glumly. That was something else the men would not like – but she could not see any way round it when she was the only woman in the force. Even in these enlightened times it was not considered appropriate for women to share their working space with men.

'I didn't ask for preferential treatment,' she said.

The sergeant's smile held less malice than it had earlier. 'The room's not much bigger than a cupboard, and it doesn't have a fireplace. Used to be a cloakroom.'

Kirsty set off down the gloomy corridor, counting the doors as she went. But she hesitated, at the door of the room she thought was hers, because the thought of working in a cloakroom dismayed her.

Suddenly she longed for the noise and bustle of the London office, and the support and companionship of the friends she had left behind.

The room was worse than she anticipated, small, narrow and gloomy with the strangest smell of dust, old boots, damp oilskins and floor wax. A row of coat-hooks lined one wall, and in the corner was an iron sink. A small window set high in the wall rationed the light that entered the room, and reminded her of Angel's cell.

Kirsty manoeuvred her way past the ancient desk that took up most of the space and sat on the wooden chair behind it. On the desk-top someone had arranged three files, several sheets of paper, a pen, a bottle of black ink, a couple of pencils, a notebook, and a ruler. Two narrow drawers on top of three wider drawers spread down one side of the desk, and the same again down the other, with a space in the middle for her knees. The empty drawers rattled as she pulled them out.

The feeling of suffocation Kirsty had experienced at the morgue came back to her. She could almost imagine she was imprisoned. She rose to prop the door open, but while this relieved her claustrophobia it did nothing for her dispirited state of mind.

She rolled one of the pencils between her fingers and contemplated the report she needed to write, but she could not concentrate.

Closing her eyes, she saw a girl sitting in a prison cell, rocking endlessly while she hugged her body with her arms. She saw a pale and mutilated corpse lying on a trolley in the morgue. She saw Nora's scornful look, and the tear that trembled on Bert's eyelashes.

A jumble of images swirled in her mind, overlapping, intermingling – along with the memory of the Howff graveyard.

She shivered. It was impossible for her to imagine Angel plunging a knife into the child lying in the morgue. And yet, Brewster said he had seen her, knife in hand, standing over her victim. What else could he have done but arrest her?

Her mind whirled. There must be another explanation. Maybe she should talk to the constable who had found Angel with the body.

Her brow furrowed as she tried to remember the constable's name. Harrison, Harris, Henderson? That was it, Constable Henderson. Her eyes widened as she remembered the two constables who had handed Bert and Nora over to her. One of them was named Henderson.

The walls of her room were closing in on her and she was glad of an excuse to leave it. She walked along the corridor to the constables' office and, hearing a rumble of sound from inside, pushed the door open.

The room was large, yet there seemed to be too many bodies for the space available. Desks covered most of the floor area. They were arranged in groups of three, and constables sat at them and on them, some chatting and some scribbling as they prepared their end-of-shift reports. Over everything there hung a cloud of smoke that drifted out to Kirsty's eyes and nose. Suppressing a cough she took two steps into the room.

A sudden hush fell as heads turned to look at her. Somewhere in the room a man sniggered.

Removing a pipe from his mouth, one of the constables grinned at her and asked. 'What can we do for you, love?'

Kirsty, flushing with annoyance at the familiarity, assumed her most formal voice. 'I'm looking for Constable Henderson.'

The constable continued to grin. 'He's on the early shift, love, and won't be back now until tomorrow morning. But if I can help, I'd be glad to.'

'No, thank you,' Kirsty replied in clipped tones as she backed out of the door. 'I'll see him tomorrow.'

Laughter followed her and she was relieved to get back to her cupboard. She kicked the door shut, preferring claustrophobia to the raucous sounds echoing in the corridor, and fought to keep her anger at bay. She sank into her chair.

Why on earth had she thought she could do this job? Being a policewoman in Dundee was far harder than anywhere else she had worked. At least in London there had been other women to support her and defend the policewoman's cause.

Gradually the beating of her heart slowed, and the insidious tide of despair threatening to overwhelm her was replaced by determination. She was not going to let this job beat her. She was not going to let them beat her.

Dipping her pen in the inkwell she started to write her report on Bert and Nora. It did not take her long, and with a sigh of relief she went up the corridor and laid it in the middle of Brewster's desk where he could not fail to see it.

Back in her own office she opened one of the files left by Brewster, and began to read. The file did not contain much. Rose McKinley, was twelve, almost the same age as Ailsa, but Rose did not have Ailsa's advantages. She lived at home with her parents, her mother a mill worker and her father unemployed. A kettle boiler as they called these men in Dundee where there were more jobs for women than for men. Rose was last seen two weeks ago at the travelling fair on Magdalen Green.

The second girl, Emily Tait, was a year younger and was last seen at the market in the Overgate. She had been gone for ten days.

Meg Strachan, the third girl, was the same age as Rose. She had been missing for a week after going to a moving picture show at the Odeon. She had been seen going in, but no one saw her come out.

Kirsty scribbled a few notes. She would take them home with her and try to figure out a plan of investigation she could give Brewster the next morning.

The building, where Kirsty rented her flat, was quiet when she pushed through the front door into the lobby.

She sidled past a bicycle and a dilapidated pram, and climbed upwards.

The wooden stairs echoed to the sound of her booted feet, and she expected a door to open at any moment. However, nothing stirred, although the nauseating smell of boiled cabbage which hung in the air indicated a human presence behind at least one of the doors.

The smell turned her stomach and took the edge off her hunger, and she was glad when she reached the door of her flat. But when she pushed the key into the lock it stuck. By the time she forced it to turn her hands were aching and still the door was reluctant to open. Gathering her strength, she heaved her shoulder into it, and it clattered open with a thud, making the hinges move in their sockets. Nevertheless, once she was inside she felt safe. this was her flat, and despite its shortcomings, it was her home.

After feeding some coins into the gas meter below the sink, she groped for matches on the mantelpiece. Striking one, she swung the swivel arm of the light fitment away from the wall, turned the gas tap on, and held the flame to the gas mantle taking care not to break it. When it burned down to her fingers she shook the match and dropped it into the grate. Striking another one she tilted the tubular top of the oil heating stove away from its base, adjusted the wick, and held the match to it until it caught. It would be a few minutes until even a little heat was generated, so she rummaged in the table drawer for a knife to tighten the screws in the door hinges.

Then, pulling a chair to the table, she spread out her notes and started to plan the investigation into the missing girls. Maybe when Brewster saw it he might feel confident enough to let her conduct the investigation on her own.

15

Tuesday, 4 November 1919
Kirsty was taller than most Dundee women and the bed was too
short. She dreamed she was locked in a cell and could not get
out. Her hands were sore from shaking the bars and banging on
the door, and she woke gripping the brass spars of the
headboard.

Her toes curled with the shock of the cold linoleum as her
feet hit the floor. She wanted to pull them back into the bed but
knew she had to get dressed in a hurry or she would be late for
work. Instinctively her hand reached for the skirt draped over
the back of a chair beside her bed, but then she remembered
Brewster's words. 'We are a plain clothes force so you will not
be required to wear the uniform except for patrols.' Never
before had she turned up for duty without it. But now, she
thought, suppressing her annoyance, she would have to look for
something else to wear.

She had forgotten to place matches beside the bedroom
candle. Tiptoeing into the living room and over to the fireplace,
she reached her fingers up to explore the mantelpiece. Matches
fell from the box when she opened it, but she rescued one,
struck it and held it first to the gas jet and then to the gas hob.
Lifting the kettle she gave it a shake. Water splashed inside, but
judging from the weight of the kettle it needed topping up. She
held it under the tap to fill, before placing it on top of the gas
ring.

Lighting the candle she padded to the bedroom. She pulled
aside the curtain hanging in front of the wall cupboard that was
her makeshift wardrobe, and inspected the contents. Settling for
a brown skirt and dark green woollen blouse, she pulled them
on. They were cold on her skin and did not have the same
comforting feel as her normal attire. The absence of the uniform

made her feel part of her identity had been lost. She missed the scratchy thickness of the blue serge skirt and jacket, and the formality of ensuring the buttons were polished and the belt drawn tight around her waist.

She lifted the simmering kettle from the gas hob, poured water into the tin basin, and washed her face. Grabbing a comb from the mantelpiece, she pulled it through her short, auburn hair. The length was one thing Brewster could not order her to change, she thought, with some satisfaction.

All Kirsty's friends wore their hair in the new bobbed style, and she never missed her waist length hair after she cut it off. The act of shearing her hair had given her strength and purpose. It had signified a rejection of childhood and femininity and symbolized acceptance of herself as a free woman, and a member of the police force.

She poured the water out of the basin, straightened her skirt and patted her hair before pulling on the brown coat and matching cloche hat. Unable to check her appearance because the room lacked a mirror did not worry her unduly. However, for the first time in several years, she wondered if she looked all right.

The streets, although dark, were busy with hurrying people when she left the tenement building. Women, with headscarves covering their hair, and coats and shawls pulled tightly across their bodies, scurried along the pavement, while a tram trundled past full of workers heading for the Lochee mills. A paper boy, eyes half-closed with sleep, a paper sack bouncing on his hip, almost collided with her. The clopping of hooves and the clank of empty milk churns, signalled the milkman taking his cart back to the depot, his milk deliveries completed for the day. No doubt he would go back to bed, getting up to work again when everyone else was asleep.

Kirsty walked through the arched entrance that formed a gateway separating the hurrying workers from the confines of the police yard. Early morning was never a favourite time for people to visit the police station, and the quadrangle felt like sanctuary. But the quietness of the yard was not reflected in the corridors and the constables' room which echoed with the noise of voices as the night shift came off duty and the day shift officers replaced them.

Kirsty welcomed the hubbub and the companionable banter even though she was not part of it. But it also made her homesick for the companionship of the female colleagues she had left behind.

The duty sergeant looked up from his paperwork and grinned at her from behind his polished counter. 'Hardly knew you, miss, without the uniform. Must say it's a big improvement. What you were wearing yesterday didn't do much for you.' He seemed friendlier this morning.

'Thanks,' Kirsty mumbled, despite her resentment at his comment. After all, how could he know how attached she was to her uniform?

She thought of her early days as a policewoman and her pride in wearing it. Neither she nor any of the other policewomen had cared that the uniform was unattractive. They had fought for a uniform, and they had a right to wear it, and now she was not allowed to wear it in Dundee.

'Has Inspector Brewster come in yet?' Kirsty asked the duty sergeant.

He leaned his elbows on the counter. 'Not yet, but then he's never early, especially if he's been working the night before.' He hesitated, looked away from her, and said, 'You know, miss, if you talk to him I'm sure he'd say it's not necessary for you to come in with the six o'clock shift.'

Heat crept up from her neck into her cheeks, and she did not have to look in a mirror to know her face had reddened. She did not like anyone making allowances for her because she was a woman, and Dundee policemen seemed determined to keep her in her place. She turned her face away so the duty sergeant could not see it, and said, 'That's all right, I've been used to shift work. It doesn't bother me, and I'd prefer stick to my working conditions.'

'I'm sure you know best, miss. CID don't work regular hours though, and he'll make you turn out at night as well as during the day.'

Kirsty was aware the men coming off the night shift knew

about her. It was apparent in their eyes and their demeanour towards her. Some of them glanced at her curiously as they left the office while others did not bother to disguise the boldness in their eyes, and yet others studiously ignored her. Kirsty waited until the last of them had left before making her way up the corridor towards the constables' room.

The sound of voices and laughter rumbled outwards, through the half-open door, into the corridor. Kirsty hesitated, tempted to scuttle down the corridor to her room rather than face their ridicule. But she had never shirked a confrontation before, and she did not intend to start now. Bracing herself, she stepped into the stale atmosphere of the room where the smell of sweat and smoke mixed together until one was almost indistinguishable from the other.

Trying not to let her distaste show, Kirsty raised her voice in order to make herself heard above the noise. 'I'm looking for Constable Henderson. Is he here?'

A momentary hush descended on the room before the voices started again.

'I say, Joe. There's a lady looking for you. Don't keep her waiting then.'

'Joe's no use, miss. Won't I do instead?'

'I'd be much more help than Joe. He's only a laddie.'

'That's right, Harry. Tell her she'd be better with a man.'

Henderson glared at the men as he hurried out of the room. 'Is there somewhere else we can go, miss? This lot's a bit rowdy. They don't know how to behave in a lady's presence.'

Rude comments echoed down the corridor after them as Kirsty led him towards her room.

'Is it about the children from yesterday?' Henderson perched himself on the edge of her desk and swung his legs back and forth.

'No, it's not that, Constable Henderson. I wanted to ask you about something else.'

Henderson kicked the door shut and then pulled a cigarette from the pack in his breast pocket. He tapped the end of it on her desk before flicking it up in the air and catching it in his mouth. Lighting it, he inhaled deeply before removing it and pointing the glowing end towards the door. 'Last fag before I go out on the beat,' he said. 'The sergeant doesn't mind if we smoke in our room as long as we don't make it too obvious.'

Kirsty looked at the lighted cigarette and was on the brink of pointing out he was in her room not his own, but she needed his help, so she said nothing.

She sat silently for a moment considering, and then stood up and opened the door. 'I think it best if we leave it open.'

A sly smile played around Constable Henderson's mouth, but he simply shrugged and exhaled smoke, allowing it to drift up round his nose and eyes.

'So what was it you wanted to ask me?' He inhaled again until the tip of the cigarette glowed.

'I understand you were the constable who found the body in the Howff last Friday night.'

'Yes, miss, that I was.'

'I had to interview the girl in the cells, Constable Henderson, and I'd be interested in your account of how you found her with the body.'

'You don't want to hear about that, miss. It's not nice. It's not for the ears of a lady like yourself,' he said, patronisingly.

Kirsty clenched her hands into fists but kept her voice low and pleasant. 'It's my job, constable. I don't have any choice. I've interviewed the girl, and I need to know everything about the case.'

'If you're sure, miss.' He studied the end of his cigarette before tapping the ash from the smouldering tip. 'I was out on the beat with Harry. He's my usual partner. But Harry got into this argument with one of the Overgate girls and I went on ahead. Well I had to, somebody had to keep the beat going, and it was better just me than nobody at all.' He glanced towards Kirsty. 'You won't tell on us will you?'

'Of course not.' Kirsty smiled at him.

'Well, as I turned the corner into Barrack Street I was accosted by a gent who said he thought he'd heard someone screaming in the graveyard. I continued up the road, and as I got level with the wall that circles the Howff, I heard this awful screeching. I never heard anything like it before. At first I thought it might be something supernatural, it being Halloween and all.' He smiled apologetically. 'But that was a foolish thing to think. Then I thought it was young folks mucking about and I went up to the side gate, but it was locked. I tried to see through it, but it was dark at that time of night. Although I did think I saw a flicker of light for a moment, but maybe I imagined it. I shouted, "Who's in there? And what are ye doing making such a racket?" but the screaming continued. Bloodcurdling it was, but nothing to be seen.'

Henderson rummaged in his pocket and, removing the packet, placed another cigarette between his lips, lighting it with the butt of the one he had finished smoking. 'Anyways,' he continued, 'that's when I decided it must be something serious, so I ran to the main gate, it's never locked.' He stopped speaking and looked at Kirsty. 'You don't want to hear the rest, miss. Really you don't.'

'But I do, Constable Henderson. I have to know it all.'

He shrugged his shoulders and looked away from her, seemingly fascinated by the little pile of ash gathering on the corner of her desk.

'The Howff was dark, miss, but I headed in the direction of the screaming, and it was her, miss. Her that's in the cells. Leaning over the body, almost lying on it she was, and she had this knife in her hand. All bloody it was. It gave me a fright, I can tell you. So I blew my whistle and all the time I'm scared she would turn on me before the other bobbies get there. But she didn't seem to hear it.'

He tapped the ash off the end of his cigarette before continuing. 'Her eyes were scary, all funny and glazed, but I knew I had to get the knife off her. So I went up to her, real slow and easy, and spoke as quiet as I knew how. "You don't need that knife," I said, "you'd be better to give it to me." Then I held my breath, but she handed it over no trouble at all. I couldn't get her to stop screeching though. Like a demented animal, she was. She didn't even stop when I put my arm round her.'

Kirsty had read the report and knew he was not the one who had disarmed Angel. But she made no comment on the embroidered account of his actions, and said, 'Why did you do that if you were frightened of her?'

'Only way I could get her to leave the body, miss. I couldn't leave her lying on top of it. Anyways I was glad to get out of the cemetery. Gave me the creeps it did.'

'What happened to the body? You didn't just walk away and leave it, did you?'

'Course not, miss. Harry had got there by that time, and other beat bobbies turned up. They'd heard my whistle, and we all likes to help each other. So I left them to deal with the body while I took the young missy to the station.'

'The body, constable. What did it look like?'

'I was more took up with the young missy who did it. Although from what I could see miss, the other one was a mess. She was lying on top of a slab and she'd been carved like a piece of mutton. It looked as if she'd been butchered good and proper.' He paused. 'Sorry, miss. I told you it wasn't nice.'

'Her clothes, constable. Where were her clothes?'

'I didn't see clothes, miss. She didn't have any on, and there was nothing lying beside her.'

'What about the girl you arrested, what was she wearing?'

'Didn't pay too much attention to her clothes, miss. I was too busy trying to get her to the station.'

'Think, constable. Did she have outdoor clothes on? You know, a coat or something.'

He scratched his head. 'Now you come to think of it she wasn't wearing much. Something thin it was, like a petticoat or a nightie, might have been white, but it was covered in blood, so it was hard to tell.' He hoisted himself off the desk. 'That's all I can tell you miss, and I've got to go now, it's time for my beat.' He flicked his lighted cigarette to the floor, ground it out with his heel and left the room.

Kirsty sat for a time brooding over Henderson's story, but all it had done was confirm Brewster's version. Despite that, Kirsty was convinced Angel could not have murdered the girl in the Howff cemetery, although she seemed to be the only one in the police force who believed in the girl's innocence.

She would have to find a way to prove Angel's innocence

and prevent her from meeting the hangman. Although how she was going to manage this without Brewster's help, she did not know, and she could not discuss it with him because he had made his views clear when he had forbidden her to investigate the murder.

16

It was mid-morning before Detective Inspector Brewster returned and by that time Kirsty had done a lot of thinking.

Looming in the doorway to her room, his height and broad shoulders effectively blocked the light from the corridor, and cast a shadow over her desk. 'Have you studied the reports on the missing girls,' he demanded, 'and worked out who you should question in order to ascertain where they've run off to?'

'Yes, sir,' she said, although he had not previously instructed her to see anyone.

'That's all right then.' He turned to leave.

'May I talk to you about something else, sir,' she said.

He eased himself back into the room. 'What's the matter, don't you have enough to do chasing up the runaway girls?' A smile flickered at the corner of his mouth.

'It's about the murder,' she said. 'I don't think she did it.'

'I take it you mean the murder in the Howff.' He raised an eyebrow as he studied her. 'The men who found the girl with the body thought she did it, and the sheriff agreed with them when she appeared at the court hearing yesterday, otherwise he would not have remanded her for trial.' He paused for a moment deep in thought. 'So, if all those involved think there's enough proof to commit her for trial, why would you think she is innocent?'

Kirsty's annoyance grew. It seemed obvious Brewster was not taking her suggestion seriously, and all he cared about was getting a conviction. But she stifled the thumping of her heart until she was able to speak again.

'What happened to the idea of someone being innocent until proved guilty?' Kirsty asked coldly.

Brewster laughed. 'Our job is to make sure the guilty don't get away with it. And that should be your job too. Anyway you haven't told me why you think she didn't do it.'

'The knife wounds were deep. Only someone strong would have been able to inflict them, and I don't think she has the strength to do that kind of damage.'

Brewster thought for a moment before saying, 'I'm not so sure about that. The girl is disturbed and sometimes deranged people gain strength through their insanity. The asylums are full of such people.'

Heat crept up Kirsty's neck into her face. Why would he not take her seriously? 'And there is the issue of the clothes, of course.'

'Clothes? What clothes?'

Kirsty had trouble stopping herself from exploding with exasperation. 'Exactly, sir. What clothes? There were none. The victim was naked and the alleged murderess was wearing some kind of thin shift and nothing else. Where were their clothes? Or did they walk through the streets in that condition and if so, why were they not noticed?'

'They probably disrobed in the graveyard.'

Kirsty thought she detected signs of irritation in him, but Brewster's voice remained calm and controlled, and this only increased her own exasperation. She wanted to shake him and make him see she was right.

'Did you find the clothes?' Yet again she had forgotten he was her senior officer in her anxiety to convince him, and her voice was as caustic as battery acid.

Brewster's face changed colour to a dull red. 'No, we didn't, but that doesn't mean they weren't left there.'

'Where are they then?'

'Any vagrant could have gone off with them. The cemetery is a regular gathering place for all sorts of riff-raff,' Brewster snapped. 'You'll need more of a case than that, Miss Campbell. Until you, or anyone else, can prove she's innocent she will have to stay where she is until her trial.'

'I have your permission to find the evidence, sir?'

'No,' he snapped. 'You are only a statement taker and you will concentrate on the cases allocated to you, the runaway girls, and leave the murder case to me.'

He glared at her, turned on his heels, and stamped up the corridor.

Kirsty's mouth twisted into a wry smile. She was convinced of Angel's innocence, and willing to fight to prove it despite Brewster's instructions to the contrary. And, if he thought she was going to allow him to leave Angel to rot in a prison cell until the law decided to hang her, then he was going to have to think again.

'And I'll prove it too,' she said to no one in particular, 'even if it means the end of my career.'

Kirsty spent the next half-hour locating and studying Angel's file. It contained signed reports from the constables who found the body, and details of Angel's arrest, including a description of her reactions and physical condition, as well as several photographs taken in the police station. The file told Kirsty no more than she already knew.

She lifted one of the photographs and traced the girl's features with the tip of her forefinger. It looked a reasonable likeness, and Kirsty wondered if Angel's eyes had always had a wild, haunted look, or if that had been the result of what she had experienced that night in the graveyard. Returning the photograph to the file, she closed it, before getting up and making her way to the cells.

The turnkey seemed preoccupied when she opened the gate to the female corridor and, as they walked along it, her keys jangled, cutting the silence.

When they reached Angel's cell, Annie selected one of the keys and inserted it into the lock. 'Just bang on the door when you're finished with the lass,' she said.

Kirsty nodded her thanks, and waited until the door slammed shut before she approached the girl huddled in the corner.

Angel did not look up, but Kirsty smiled, walked towards her, and sat on the edge of her mattress. 'You don't mind if I sit down, do you?'

The girl started to rock.

'I didn't think you would,' Kirsty said, although Angel refused to meet her eyes.

'I told you I'd come back, and here I am.' Kirsty hesitated, waiting and hoping for some response.

'I want to help you, but you have to help me too.'

Angel's shoulders hunched, her arms tightened round her body and the rocking continued.

Kirsty watched her, and the urge to take the girl into her arms was overwhelming. But she resisted it, knowing if she did so it would make Angel pull herself even further into the protective shell she had built around herself.

'You have to tell me what happened in the Howff so I can help you.'

At the mention of the Howff, Angel's rocking lost a beat, like a pendulum that had changed direction, and her head sank even lower onto her chest.

Kirsty was not sure whether she had struck a raw nerve and, hoping for a response, pushed her questioning even further.

'They say you killed the child. Did you, Angel? Did you kill her?'

The words sounded harsh and brutal, even to Kirsty, and she wondered if she had gone too far.

A low moan started somewhere deep within the girl, erupting upwards into a keening sound and she rocked faster and faster.

'Did you, Angel? You must answer me because I don't think you did it. But how can I help you if you won't tell me anything.'

The keening increased, the confines of the cell making it sound even louder.

'Who was she, Angel?'

The girl started to bang her head against the wall with such force Kirsty was afraid she would damage herself. And then the screaming started.

Putting her arms around her, Kirsty held her tightly. 'There, there,' she said, rocking with her. Gradually the girl quietened and lay passive in her arms. Kirsty continued to make soothing noises, and after a time she spoke to her, hoping the girl would tell her something. But Angel was far away, locked into her own mind.

Eventually Kirsty said, 'I have to go now, but remember, I'm here to help you.' She banged on the door for Annie to open it, and when she heard the key in the lock she turned for a final look at Angel. 'I'll come back again,' she said as the cell door swung open.

Brewster stamped up the corridor to his office. The woman was impossible. If any of the constables had spoken to him the way she did he would have put them on a charge, and it was only old-fashioned chivalry that prevented him treating Kirsty in a similar fashion.

He sat down in his chair with a thud and thumped the desk in front of him.

'Damned woman,' he muttered. 'This is not going to work. She's too damned full of herself and her own importance.'

But he was stuck with her, and the chief constable would not appreciate negative comments about the success of his experiment.

He sighed, and bent to pick up some files that had slid to the floor. What was he to do?

One thing he was sure about was that he needed some time to himself, away from this so-called policewoman, in order to regain some sense of equilibrium.

He stacked the files on the end of his desk, turning ideas over in his mind on how to keep her occupied and out of his hair. Coming to a decision, he rose, buttoned his jacket and left the office. A little bit of time with Maggie would calm him down.

The desk sergeant was busy with paperwork, and he lifted his head to nod to Brewster. 'How's it going, sir, with our new member of staff?'

Brewster wasn't sure, but he thought he detected a malicious gleam in the sergeant's eyes.

'It's early days,' he said, 'but I'll be taking her out on patrol tonight, so when you see her you can tell her to take some time off, and to report back here at 6 o'clock, sharp. Oh, and tell her to wear her uniform.'

'Yes, sir.'

The air outside the office was cold and fresh, but as Brewster walked down the street he felt as if a huge load had been lifted from his shoulders.

Kirsty was starting to get accustomed to the warren of passages leading to and from the women's cell area and no longer made wrong turns or hesitated over which way to go. However, as she made her way back along them, she found herself wondering about the other passages underneath the police station that Brewster had described to her. Maybe she would persuade him to take her down there.

His office was in its usual state of disarray, but Brewster was not in it, nor was he in the canteen, so she made her way to the charge room. The duty sergeant would know where he was.

The smell, reminiscent of the worst of London's docklands slums, hit her as soon as she left the corridor. She held her breath and sidled round the door, closing it quietly behind her.

The duty sergeant, engrossed in attending to an unkempt and extremely dirty man, did not look up. Kirsty hovered in the doorway wondering whether she should leave the sergeant to get on with what he was doing, but she was in now, so reckoned she had better stay.

The man, flanked by two police constables holding him under the armpits while he emptied his pockets, was younger than she had first thought, but the accumulated grime on his skin, the hopeless look in his eyes, and the tattered state of his clothes made him seem older.

'That's right, lad,' the duty sergeant said, 'empty it all out on the counter.' He scribbled in a ledger, muttering as he did so, 'One pocket knife, two pennies and a halfpenny, one comb, one handkerchief, dirty,' he held it by a corner and gingerly deposited it in the large envelope along with the other items. Looking up, he said, 'Is that all you've got, lad?'

The young man, who had been regarding his feet, nodded without looking up.

'Not much is it, lad?' The duty sergeant turned and nodded to the constables. 'All right men, take him down. He's too late for this morning's court session so he'll have to accept the hospitality of the establishment.' He chuckled at his own joke.

The two policemen, with their prisoner securely held between them, elbowed their way past Kirsty without looking at her.

She shrugged and smiled at the duty sergeant. 'I don't envy you having to attend to the charge desk all morning,' she said.

He considered her for a moment, then laying his ledger and pen on the desk top, he pushed his spectacles up into his hair and sighed. 'It's been hectic this morning. The dippers seem to be having a field day in the town, and if I've had one complaint about lost or stolen wallets I've had a dozen. God knows what it will be like by this afternoon.'

Kirsty's face felt stiff with smiling so much, but she was determined to get this man on her side. 'I suppose it must be the same all over. How do you handle it in Dundee?'

Lifting a pencil he scratched his head with it. 'The lads parade the beat in the most common places, like the Overgate or the High Street. Occasionally they catch someone, but the main purpose is to keep the dippers away. We don't want them in Dundee.'

'It was much the same in London, but it makes you wonder if there can't be a better way of working.' Kirsty leaned against the counter. 'I was looking for Detective Inspector Brewster, but he doesn't seem to be around.' Not that he is ever around when I need him, she thought, but did not voice.

'Oh, I almost forgot. He left a message for you. He said for you to take some time off, but he'll expect you to report back for duty at six o'clock tonight, and he said to wear your uniform.' The duty sergeant grinned at her.

Kirsty suspected the sergeant would not have sought her out to relay Brewster's message, but providence had brought her to the charge room when he was feeling more sympathetic towards her. Deciding it would not suit her purpose to provoke him, she said, 'And I'll bet you're the one who suggested the time off. I wouldn't expect Inspector Brewster to think of it.'

'You do him an injustice, missy. Anyway off you go while you've got the chance.'

'After I've tidied my desk,' she said.

Angel's file was still sitting there. She opened it and read it once more before returning it to Brewster's office. It did not make sense. Why would the girl murder a child? And why would she do it in such a vicious fashion? And why do it in the cemetery?

A vision of Angel, rocking manically in her prison cell, pushed its way into her consciousness. Rocking, clutching her body and screaming. Her mind tormented beyond reason.

17

As Kirsty left the police station thoughts of Angel continued to haunt her, and she could not help feeling that by taking time off as Brewster had directed, she was failing the girl. Discontented and restless, she crossed the quadrangle and hesitated outside the archway. Court House Square, which lay before her, was quiet except for the rumble and clank of trams as they trundled along Ward Road between the city centre and Lochee.

Reluctantly, she started to walk towards the two rooms she now called home. There was painting to be done and a ceiling to whitewash, and she would have to start sometime. But, as she passed the top of North Lindsay Street, something pulled her towards the Howff, and she changed direction.

Waiting until a coalman's horse and cart clattered past, she crossed over Ward Road, avoiding the heap of steaming dung lying in the middle. The high-pitched squall of a solitary bird, perching on the roof of a church, spiralled down to ground level. It sounded ominous and filled her with apprehension. Kirsty shivered, thinking maybe it was the same seagull that had screeched at her yesterday outside the Children's Refuge. But that was ridiculous.

She did not know why she had such a compulsion to return to the Howff, unless it was guilt for failing Angel, and her chest tightened with an inexplicable feeling of dread as she drew nearer. She tried to shake the feeling off by telling herself the graveyard had been investigated and nothing more was to be seen. Brewster had made that clear after his search for clues. But something was drawing her towards the place.

When she got to the graveyard it did not look so menacing in the pale November sunshine and, through the bars on top of the waist-high wall, she could see some people inside. She pushed the black, wrought-iron gate. It rasped open, the hinges making a screeching noise that set her nerves on edge.

Gravel scrunched under her feet as she followed one of the paths which wound its way between evergreen bushes and bare-branched trees. To her right and left were other paths between the gravestones. Kirsty passed a group of men, but avoided glancing towards them when she smelt the unmistakable aroma of methylated spirits.

She was not sure when the feeling of disquiet started, but by the time she reached the centre of the cemetery, it had grown to an almost unbearable level. Perhaps it was the drinkers, or the lengthening shadows made by the sun which had grown dim in the hazy sky, or maybe it was the lack of birdsong. The shadows deepened, and she looked up in time to see a black cloud pass over the sun. The cemetery darkened even more. The silence intensified, engulfing her. Her head swirled with the force of vague, unformed thoughts and a feeling of unreality swept over her. Reaching out for the nearest gravestone she leaned on it, ignoring the dank, clammy cold penetrating her clothes.

A sense of impending evil overwhelmed her. Something was going to happen, something terrible, and she was the only one who could stop it.

The feeling was so intense she wrenched her hand from the top of the gravestone and cried out, 'Stop, you must not do this. It is a sin before the eyes of God.'

The sun slipped out from behind the cloud and the darkness lifted, leaving only the path, the gravestones, and the overgrown grass of the cemetery.

A man straightened up from the flat stone over which he had been bending and stared at her. 'I beg your pardon,' he said.

Heat crept up Kirsty's neck into her face. What had come over her? And why had she cried out? She cringed with embarrassment.

A moment ago she had been convinced she was alone in this part of the cemetery, and now she stared in disbelief as the man, who seemed to emerge from the ground, rose from his stooping position over Jonathan Bogue's tomb.

'I'm sorry,' she said, turning to hurry away. She had seen the puzzlement on his face, and she did not want Johnnie Bogue to recognize her.

'Not so fast,' he said, blocking her path. 'I know you, don't I?' His hand gripped her arm. He was looking at her with a puzzled expression.

Kirsty stared back at him. Her breathing quickened. There were so many memories, so many awful memories. She pushed them away, just as she would have liked to push him away. And, with as much authority as she could muster, she said, 'Remove your hand from my arm, sir.'

It was obvious to Kirsty he did not remember her. She supposed this was not surprising, considering he had not seen her since that awful night fourteen years ago. She was no longer a child of fifteen and fashions had changed as well as her hair style. If he had remembered her at all, it would have been as a young girl with wavy hair that reached her waist, and who had looked at him with innocent eyes.

Later she had found out he had a weakness for pretty young girls. The younger they were, the more he liked them.

His grip did not slacken. 'What are you doing wandering around a cemetery on your own? This is no place for a lady.'

'I could ask you the same thing, sir.' Kirsty stared at him, not wanting him to see her aversion. 'You see, I am a policewoman, and you, sir, are behaving suspiciously at the scene of a crime.'

His grip slackened on her arm. 'There are no women police,' he said harshly.

'In that case you won't mind accompanying me to the police station, and I'll arrange for you to be questioned by a policeman.' Her heart thumped in an alarming fashion while she waited for his response, and she could imagine the duty sergeant's reaction if she brought a man in for questioning. 'Now, if you don't mind, you can either tell me what you are doing here or you can come along to the police station.'

'If you must know, my father sent me to check whether any damage had been done to my great-uncle's gravestone during the course of this crime you say you are investigating.'

'Very well, sir. I must ask you to go about your business and leave me to go about mine. I'll thank you to let go of my arm.'

Kirsty turned and walked towards the gate, leaving him standing in the cemetery. She never turned, but knew he stood looking after her with an expression of puzzlement on his face. Sooner or later, he would remember. She was sure of it.

Edward was heading for the Refuge when he saw Kirsty in the Howff cemetery. When he first noticed her he had been unsure because she was not in uniform. She was wearing a brown coat and matching cloche hat, and she looked stylish. He frowned when he observed a man with her. They seemed to be having an altercation, and the man had his hand on her arm. But the expression on her face convinced him this displeased her. He stood and watched for a moment, toying with the thought of intervening, but Miss Campbell was an independent young woman and might not appreciate his interference in what was possibly a private matter.

He hesitated, then walked back along the street, leaned against the railing at the corner, and waited to see what would happen. When she left the cemetery to walk along the road she looked distressed, and seemed to be in a daze.

Intrigued, he quickened his pace until he was behind her. Should he stop her? Or should he continue to the Refuge and let her go? As he debated, he was aware of the other man who seemed to be following her.

Maybe he should wait, and if she was accosted by the other man, he could come to her rescue. That appealed to him. He would like to get to know her better, and what better way than aiding her in a sticky situation.

On the other hand, she seemed like a woman well able to look after herself, and he doubted she would care for male heroics.

He quickened his pace.

Kirsty stumbled out of the gate and hurried along the road. She saw and heard nothing in her flight to get as far away from the cemetery as possible, and it made her oblivious to the curious stares cast in her direction.

Her meeting with Johnnie Bogue had been unexpected and disturbing. She had tried to remain calm in his presence, but memories of that night kept invading her mind, and she had struggled with the urge to remind him of the crime he had committed against her. Although she was sure he did not consider it a crime.

The sensation of impending evil she experienced in the graveyard had also upset her more than she would admit to herself.

Overactive imagination, her mother called it when she experienced these premonitions as a child, and when she grew up she had suppressed them. This was the first one for a long time, and she knew it must be because her mind was dwelling on the murder that had taken place at the Howff.

As she reached the corner of Barrack Street a hand grasped her shoulder, making her heart race. Dread filled her, and she turned, expecting to see Johnnie Bogue.

'I'm sorry, I did not mean to startle you, Miss Campbell, but you did not hear my shout.'

Kirsty stared up into the kindly eyes of Edward Gordon. Her heartbeat slowed, and she was so relieved she smiled at him. 'I was preoccupied, Mr Gordon. I met someone I once knew, and for a minute I thought he had followed me.'

'Am I a disappointment then?'

His expression had been serious when he looked at her at first. However, as he returned her smile it seemed to animate and light up his face.

'Oh no, I was relieved it wasn't him.'

'Ah,' he said.

'What I mean is . . . I'm glad it was you, Mr Gordon.' Kirsty looked away from his face. He was having a strange effect on her, making her say things better left unsaid, and she felt like a girl again, gauche and unsure of herself.

'I saw you in the Howff and waited for you to come out,' he said. 'It's a terrible business having a murder almost on your doorstep, everyone's talking about it. I expect you were investigating what happened.'

'Yes, we have the girl who was supposed to have done it in the cells.'

'You don't sound convinced you've got the correct person.' Edward seemed unaware that his hand lingered on her shoulder.

Kirsty frowned. 'I suppose you're right. But I seem to be the only one who thinks that.'

'I'll walk with you if I may, Miss Campbell,' Edward said, removing his hand. 'What does she say about it?'

Kirsty missed the warmth of it on her shoulder. But his presence was comforting, and she was glad of his company as they walked along the road. 'She doesn't say anything. She seems to have lost her mind.'

'But you don't think she committed the murder.'

If Kirsty had not been flustered or feeling so rejected by her police colleagues, she would never have considered responding to Edward's suggestion. But it was a relief for her to express her doubts to someone who was interested, and before she fully realized what she was doing, she explained why she thought Angel was innocent.

'But you don't even know who she is?'

'If I can find out who she is, then maybe I can prove she didn't do it.'

Kirsty looked up into Edward's face, and knew by his expression he was interested and sympathetic. She appreciated the opportunity to be taken seriously instead of being laughed at. But suddenly it struck her, she had told him more than she should have.

He smiled at her. 'If I can help I'll be glad to. I move around a lot in Dundee. I have connections with all the charitable organizations, and I can ask about to see who has gone missing lately.'

Kirsty pushed her discomfiture to the back of her mind. 'Oh would you, Mr Gordon? That would be so helpful.'

'In the meantime, I thought you wanted to check up on what happened to those two children you brought to me yesterday. That was why I was looking for you.'

Her eyes widened as she realized she had been so preoccupied with Angel she had not given Nora or Bert a second thought. She remembered Nora's anger and Bert's vulnerability, and her doubts about leaving them with this man whom she had met yesterday. She dreaded what he was going to tell her.

'I should have stayed with them,' she said, increasing the space between them as they walked along the street.

18

Edward walked beside Kirsty. She had not commented on what happened between her and the other man in the Howff, but he assumed it had not been a pleasant experience because of the aura of vulnerability she had briefly exhibited. He glanced at her, appreciating the softness and femininity in her bearing now she had dropped her authoritarian attitude, and his attraction to her increased. He was reluctant to let her go, and he wanted to keep her with him.

'I can take you to see Bert and Nora,' he said. 'You could see how settled they are, and it would set your mind at rest.'

Kirsty nodded. 'I'd like that.'

'We could get a tramcar from the Nethergate, it's not far. And that would take us to the front gate of the Orphan Institute.'

Edward sneaked glances at her as they walked along the road. He wanted to take her arm, but felt she might not like the familiarity.

'How were the children when you left them?' Kirsty kept pace with him.

'They felt strange, but the Orphan Institute is one of the better children's homes and I was lucky to get them places. They'll soon settle.'

'I hope so.'

When they reached the tram stop, they waited for five minutes before a tramcar came. Edward wanted to help Kirsty on, but she leapt on board before he had a chance.

Feeling awkward, he sat beside her. 'It's a short journey, we'll be there in no time at all.'

The tramcar clanked to a stop, and Edward, stepping from the platform, turned to offer Kirsty his hand to alight. Grasping it, she was surprised at the strength and the warm tingle of sensation which passed through her. She stepped down onto the pavement and quickly withdrew her hand in an attempt to conceal her confusion.

He stood for a moment looking down at her, and wondering what his thoughts were she nervously pulled her woollen coat more tightly round her body.

As if he could read her mind, he said, 'I was thinking how different you look out of uniform. As if you were another person. I like it.' Kirsty was not accustomed to compliments and did not know how to respond, but for the first time that day she stopped yearning for her uniform and started to feel comfortable in what she was wearing.

He turned abruptly as if he were embarrassed. 'The Orphan Institute is along the road. It used to be a jute baron's mansion but he moved to Broughty Ferry when Perth Road became less fashionable.'

Placing his hand on Kirsty's elbow he steered her towards a set of greenish-black, wrought-iron gates that opened onto a tree-lined drive.

Kirsty was aware of his hand on her elbow as they walked down the steep drive, past extensive lawns and gardens, towards the imposing house that rose bleakly in front of them. Even the sun shining behind it, dappling the uppermost part of the roof tiles with a rosy glow, could do nothing to alleviate the lifeless gloom of the age-darkened stonework of the building. If it had not been for the distant shouts of children at play, Kirsty would have thought the place was deserted.

Wind swirled round the house, and the chill of the cold November afternoon seeped into Kirsty's bones. She shivered.

'How were Bert and Nora when you left them here?' She could not keep the hint of anxiety out of her voice.

Edward turned his head to look at her in an enquiring manner. 'There's nothing to worry about, Miss Campbell. They are in excellent hands.'

Kirsty realized her anxiety must suggest she mistrusted him, and she turned her face away, afraid the heat spreading from her neck to her cheeks was obvious for him to see. Edward probably thought she was being silly, and that was the last thing she wanted.

'It's not that I doubted you, Mr Gordon,' she said. 'It's just that the house looks forbidding, and I had been worrying about them.'

'Bert and Nora were fine when I left them. My cousin, Maud Gordon, runs the place, and she treats the children well. It is not like some of the homes where they just feed and clothe them.' Edward stopped walking, and his hand tightened on her elbow. 'I am aware it looks intimidating from the outside but that's because it's large. The children like it here.'

Kirsty laughed, 'I have never known children who liked being in a children's home. But if you say they're all right then I'm sure they are.'

'Come on,' Edward said, letting go of her arm. 'I'll introduce you to my cousin, and then you will see everything is in order.'

Kirsty studied the brass plaque on the wall as Edward pulled the bell cord.

'Mr Gordon, the plaque says this is Bogue's Orphan Institute.' Kirsty's forehead tightened in a frown as her mind churned with unspoken thoughts. Surely Edward could not be involved with the Bogue family? And anyway, even if he were, he could not possibly know about her connection to them.

'Yes, that was the name of the jute baron who donated the house. Remember I said they moved to live in Broughty Ferry. The house was gifted, so the least that could be done was to retain his name and give him a seat on the board of governors. They like that, you know. It makes them feel immortal.'

A cloud drifted over the sun, and the cold intensified as Kirsty stared at the plaque. Painful memories overwhelmed her. 'Complain all you like,' Johnnie Bogue had said as he left her crying in the summer house. 'No one will believe you.' There had been a contemptuous expression in his eyes, and he had looked at her as if she were something dirty. 'I'll tell them how you led me on. And I'll tell them I wasn't the first.' He had left her then. Sobbing, she had pulled the fragments of her dress around her and, avoiding her chaperone, Aunt Bea, sitting in the ballroom, she had walked the two miles back home, thankful no one saw her.

'I didn't think the Bogues had a charitable bone in their bodies.' She was unable to keep the bitterness out of her voice.

Edward grinned at her. 'Everyone to their own opinion,' he said.

'If you knew Mr Bogue you would not say that. He is a fine, upstanding, charitable man anyone would be proud to know.'

Kirsty had not heard the door open, and she turned towards the speaker. The woman facing her was almost as tall as Edward but had neither the slight stoop nor the kindly expression of her cousin.

'I'm sure you are right, Maud. After all, you know him better than I do. But we didn't come here to discuss Mr Bogue.' Edward placed his hand on Kirsty's elbow again, drawing her towards the woman standing in the doorway. 'Miss Campbell, I want you to meet my cousin, Miss Maud Gordon.'

The woman's eyes narrowed. 'Why have you brought Miss Campbell here?'

Edward smiled. 'Miss Campbell has come to see the two scallywags I brought to you yesterday.'

'Of course, the policewoman you told me about.' A smile flickered at the corner of Maud's mouth, although her eyes retained a wary look. 'It's Nora and Bert you'll want to see.' She turned and retreated into the house. 'Follow me and I'll fetch them for you.'

Maud led the way into a large entrance hall with polished wooden floors. Closed doors lined the walls. Daylight, which filtered in through the large stained-glass windows overlooking the stairs, did not quite reach the shadowy pockets in the corners of the hall. A double staircase edged by intricate carved-wood banisters curved up to meet on the windowed landing, before separating and reaching upwards again. The house smelled of soap, disinfectant and wax polish. But the airless and stifling atmosphere, gave the impression no one lived there. And it struck Kirsty as strange that it lacked any indication of the presence of children. Although why she found this strange was unclear to her because most children's homes had a hushed atmosphere.

The stuffiness of the house pressed in on her, and an ache started to build behind her eyes. But the feeling of suffocation dispersed as soon as she followed Maud into the spacious, bright room at the rear of the house. Sunlight flooded through the two large windows, bathing the chintz covered sofas and easy chairs in a warm glow.

'Have a seat.' Maud pulled a bell rope at the side of the fireplace where a glowing fire sent flames flickering up the chimney.

Edward sat down on a sofa beside the fire, but Kirsty crossed the room to look out of the nearest window. Grass sloped down to where a row of trees almost hid the wall separating the property from the railway she could not see but knew must run behind it. A small building which looked like a church or chapel, nestled in the corner to the left of the building. It had a bleak unused look. Beyond the building and the boundary wall, the land sloped steeply to the railway line. And beyond that was the river flowing out to the North Sea.

The sharp sound of a whistle and distant shouting drew Kirsty's attention to the area of ground at the far right of the building. She leaned forward until she could glimpse the children who were taking turns to hit a ball with a bat before running in a circle and collapsing on the ground.

'Exercise is beneficial for growing children.' Maud had a propensity for moving quietly, and Kirsty had not heard her approach. 'The children are all outside, playing games. The boys play football, and the girls, rounders.' Maud turned as a young girl with a white apron and cap entered the room. 'Fetch a pot of tea and some sandwiches, Milly, we've got guests. And see if you can find out where Nora and Bert Lamb are. There's a good girl.'

'Yes, mum,' the maid bobbed a curtsy and left the room.

Maud turned back to Kirsty. 'You can't see the football pitch from here because it's round the corner at the far end of the house. But if you want I'll take you there after tea. You can have the grand tour and see all our facilities. We're proud of what we have here.'

'It's nice of you to offer, but I'm on duty tonight so I may not have time.' Kirsty thought she saw a flicker of disappointment on Maud's face and realized she had misjudged the woman. 'I could come back another time. That is, if it's all right with you.'

'Of course it is.' Maud leaned towards Kirsty, and taking her hand drew her towards the sofa in front of the fire. 'Tea will be with us in a moment, so make yourself comfortable, and I'll go see if Milly has found the children.'

'I told you Maud was a nice person,' Edward said when Kirsty sat down beside him. 'The children all adore her.'

Kirsty was acutely conscious of Edward sitting beside her and wondered why she had not resisted Maud and chosen another seat. She knew that since the war most modern young women were no longer bashful with men, but over the years she had avoided involvement with them. As a result, she was more innocent than her outward appearance suggested. Afraid of what her action might suggest to him she was tempted to move, but if she did so, it might appear too obvious she was uncomfortable.

The crackle of the fire and the ticking of the ormolu clock on the massive mantelpiece filled the silence between them. She watched the hypnotic dance of leaping flames propelling an array of fiery sparks up the chimney. It had a hypnotic effect on her, lulling her into a relaxed state of mind where the past and the present intermingled.

Edward leaned towards her with an expression of concern on his face and Kirsty could feel his nearness, the warmth of his body and the breath of his sigh. She was afraid to look at him and concentrated her gaze on his hands. He had pianist's fingers, long and slender, and as she watched them they reached towards her own hands. They hovered, then withdrew to his knees as Milly entered with the tea.

'Did you see Miss Gordon, Milly?' Edward helped her to lay the silver tray on the table at their side.

'Yes, sir.' Milly's eyes reminded Kirsty of those of an animal caught unawares. 'I told her I couldn't find Nora and Bert, so she's gone looking for them. I'd better go help her, sir, if you don't mind.' Milly turned and almost ran out the door.

Edward, using a napkin to protect his hand, lifted the silver teapot and carefully poured tea through the silver strainer into the china cup. Silently he handed it to Kirsty. She sensed his slight pause when she took the cup and saucer from him, but she kept her eyes looking downward. The silence between them intensified, and although Kirsty was not hungry she forced herself to eat one of the thinly cut sandwiches while she waited for Maud to return.

Kirsty struggled with the sandwich and with the lump in her throat. What was it about herself that made her draw back when Edward reached out? She liked him. He was kind and thoughtful and presented no threat to her, and even if he had she could take care of herself.

However, Johnnie Bogue's treatment of her, all those years ago, had led to a reluctance to get close to any man. She had her work and her independence, and up to now that had been enough for her. She had never felt the need for any relationship and had kept men at their distance. But Edward Gordon seemed different. Maybe it was his kindness, his concern for others, or maybe it was more than that. Whatever it was, an affinity had arisen between them, and yet, she had drawn back from his touch. Instinctively, she knew he would not approach her again unless she gave him a signal. She also knew she was incapable of giving that signal.

A scuffling noise and the sound of raised voices in the hall broke the awkward silence. Edward rose to open the door, and Kirsty followed him.

Maud stood outside holding onto Bert with one hand while she inspected the thumb-joint of the other. 'She bit me,' she said to Edward as he opened the door. 'The little besom bit me.'

'And I'll bite you again if you make me do something I don't want to do.' Nora grabbed Bert's other hand. 'Come on Bert. We don't have to do what she tells us.'

'Wait, Nora.' Kirsty took a step towards the two children.

Nora's angry young voice bounced and reverberated around the hall. 'Damn you to hell, it's your fault we're here. We didn't ask to come. Why didn't you leave us alone.' She glared at Kirsty. 'You made us come here,' she shouted, 'but you can't make us stay. We'll find a way out despite all the locked doors. Wait and see if we don't.' Pulling Bert with her, she ran off down the hall.

Kirsty caught her breath at the venom in Nora's voice. It confirmed all her doubts. She should never have allowed the children to be brought here. But where else could they go?

Maud's eyes glittered with an unknown emotion. 'Pay her no heed, Miss Campbell. It's all part of the settling in process. It's to be expected.'

'I expect you're right,' Kirsty said, suppressing her misgivings. Nora and Bert were better here than living rough on the streets.

19

As they sat on the tramcar taking them back to town, Kirsty was acutely aware of Edward's nearness. Out of the corner of her eye, she saw his long-fingered hand resting on his knee while the warmth of his leg next to hers aroused the strangest tingling sensation within her. She wanted to reach out to him and fought the urge to press her leg against his. Biting her lip, she kept her face turned away from him and looked sightlessly out of the window.

She forced herself to think of everything that had happened over the last couple of hours, and wondered whether the scene at the orphanage had disturbed Edward as much as it had her. But he gave no indication of how he was feeling.

The tram clanked to a stop in front of the City Churches, and they alighted in silence. She wanted to ask him to accompany her home, but was unable to speak the words. However, he did walk with her to her flat, hovering for a moment at the entrance to the tenement as if expecting an invitation inside. The temptation to ask him in was intense, but she could not do it, making the excuse to herself that she had her reputation to think about, although that was not the reason. So she just said, 'Goodnight, Mr Gordon.'

For a long time after Edward left her at the door, Kirsty sat quietly in her room. Their journey home had been silent and awkward, and she wondered if she would see him again or if he would think he had been rebuffed.

She turned the happenings of the day over and over in her mind, forcing herself to remember everything. Angel sitting in her cell rocking in despair, Edward reaching for Kirsty and her rejection of his approach, Nora screaming at her before she and Bert ran off. 'Damn you to hell, it's your fault we're here. We didn't ask to come. Why didn't you leave us alone.'

All of us in one way or another in a cage, she thought. Angel because she is locked up, me because I can't respond in a natural way to anyone, and Nora because she feels she is being kept against her will.

Dusk darkened the room as she sat, with the sound of the clock ticking on the mantelpiece, throbbing in her head. Each tick sounded louder than the last one, magnified by the silence of the room. The tempo seemed to pace itself to her pulse and her heartbeat, reminding her of the passage of time and the passing years.

Dark shadows gathered in the corners and with them came sadness. Not for the first time, she questioned the purpose of her life. What did she have and at the end of the day what was it all for? She had rejected her family and lost her daughter. Who among them could she care for? Who would care for her in return? She had nobody.

Eventually, she stirred and shook herself. Never in the past had she allowed these feelings to overcome her, and she did not intend to succumb now. She had a job to do, and she would do it well. Besides, if she was not there who would look out for Angel, or for that matter, Nora and Bert? And there would be many more like them.

Reaching her hand out to her uniform draped on the back of the chair, she was comforted by the feel of the familiar roughness of the serge material. At least she was being allowed to wear her uniform tonight. It would help her to regain her feeling of self-worth.

The police station was quiet when she entered. The dippers and scallywags who frequented Dundee streets during the daytime had all gone to ground, and it was too early for the night-time rogues.

The section sergeant, preparing for the end of his shift, looked up. 'Evening, miss,' he said. 'All prepared for duty, I see.' His manner was insolent, but a faint smile flickered at the corner of his mouth which made him seem friendlier than he had been yesterday.

Kirsty returned his smile with more warmth than she had previously shown him. She had already made some progress in winning over the duty sergeant and was now determined to cultivate the section sergeant.

'Yes, I've even got the awful uniform on. D'you think Inspector Brewster will approve?'

'I'm told he asked you to wear it tonight, so I don't see how he can do otherwise. He's probably going to take you out on patrol. Show you some of the sights, most like.'

'That's right, Geordie. It's time she saw some of Dundee's night life, and I don't mean a tea dance or a picture theatre either.'

Brewster lounged against the corridor door. He was in uniform, although his jacket was unbuttoned and his hair ruffled, giving the impression he had just wakened from sleep.

Kirsty had not heard him approach and wondered how long he had been there, watching and listening. She decided it did not matter, they had not been saying anything he should not hear.

'Aye, Inspector Brewster, and you're the man that'll be able to show her the sights. For I'm sure you've seen a few in your time.'

The section sergeant laughed, and Kirsty was not sure if he was being sarcastic or friendly.

'If you think I'll be shocked then I'm sorry to disappoint you,' she said tartly. 'I think I've seen a good share of the sights as you call it. You can't avoid it when you work in London, especially on Hyde Park patrol, which was what the policewomen were expected to do. You see, the men were too squeamish for it. They didn't know how to handle some of the things we disturbed happening in the bushes.'

Kirsty's lips twisted into a wry smile as she recalled some of the depravities that occurred in the park. She doubted if Brewster had seen as much in his entire career as she would have seen during the course of a week's work in London. Yet he persisted in treating her like a novice.

She saw his eyebrows rise and the glance he darted towards the section sergeant as if they shared a joke that was not suitable for her to hear, and she suspected they were laughing at her.

However, Brewster only smiled and beckoned her to follow him up the corridor.

He led the way towards his office. Lifting the ever-present files from a chair, he said, 'Have a seat.'

The chair creaked when Kirsty sat on it, and she perched nervously on the edge, expecting it to collapse under her. She wished he would start his briefing so she could stand up again, but he seemed to be in no hurry.

At last, he turned in his chair and selected one of the files from a heap on the floor.

'I've got Angel's file here.' He opened it and studied the contents. 'I take it things are the same, and you have had no further success obtaining information from her. So, as we do not appear to be any nearer knowing her identity, I thought we would make some enquiries tonight. We will take her photograph with us, maybe someone will recognize it.' He stopped talking for a moment as he rummaged on his desk. 'Ah yes, here it is.' He held out a photograph to her. 'This came in this afternoon so you won't have seen it yet. It's a photograph of the dead child, we'll take that with us as well, although I think these morgue photographs never look like the people they represent.'

Kirsty studied the photograph. The child's eyes were closed, and she looked as if she were sleeping, although Kirsty knew better. 'She looks so peaceful,' Kirsty commented. 'I suppose the photograph was taken shortly after her death.'

'Yes, we're lucky that Davvy is handy with the camera, so we don't have to wait until the next day when rigor would have set in.'

'Is Davvy always in the morgue? Doesn't he have time off?' Kirsty shivered as she remembered how Davvy's eyes had seemed to follow her every movement.

'He has a room at the back, so he's always there. He doesn't mind if we call him out, even in the middle of the night.'

'How gruesome,' Kirsty said, 'sleeping in a morgue.'

Brewster laughed. 'I suppose you're right. I never gave it a thought because he's been there ever since I can remember.'

He threw the file across the desk. It teetered on the edge for a moment before collapsing onto the floor. 'You'd better have another look at that before we go out, and remember to take the photographs with you.' He started to riffle through some papers. 'There's not much point in leaving before eight o'clock so that will be all for now. I'll come and get you when it's time to leave.'

Kirsty hesitated, wondering whether to mention something that had occurred to her.

'Well, what are you waiting for?' Brewster found the file he was looking for and laid it on the desktop.

'I just wondered . . .'

'Yes?'

'Those other missing girls,' she said. 'You don't suppose there's a connection, do you?'

'What makes you ask that?'

'We haven't been able to identify the murdered girl or Angel. And we have details of three missing girls. Maybe we've already found two of them.'

'I don't think so,' he said. 'I've already checked, and the descriptions don't match. But when you go out and interview the parents you can take the photographs with you.'

'Yes, sir.' She was unable to tell from his voice whether he had welcomed her suggestion, but his voice was less abrupt than usual.

Kirsty bent and rescued the file from the floor before leaving Brewster's office. She breathed in the cool air circulating in the corridor which seemed airy and spacious after the suffocating closeness of the room she had left, and once again wondered how Brewster could concentrate in such a cluttered environment.

Now she had got used to the lack of space, and stopped thinking of it as a broom cupboard, entering her own tiny office was like arriving at a sanctuary in the middle of a strange and unfamiliar world. She had arranged it to suit herself and the neatness and order made her feel comfortable. Sighing with contentment she sat behind her desk and opened the file. She already knew the contents off by heart, but maybe she might see something she had missed. Something to help her prove Angel's innocence and lead to the person who had mutilated the child.

Her eyes were drawn to the photograph of the murdered girl. The sepia tints hid any discoloration, and she looked young and pretty as if she did not have a care in the world. Kirsty shuddered, remembering the viciousness of the mutilation. Whoever had carved that cross on this child's body must have been deranged.

20

Kirsty read the file time and time again, convinced she must be missing something, but she knew no more now than she had earlier on. So she was feeling discouraged by the time Brewster came to her office.

'Ready to go, are you?' His eyes roved over her desk for evidence of what she had been doing. 'I'll bet you can't wait to compare the sights of Dundee with those of London. But I'm sure you won't be disappointed.'

'I'm as ready as I'll ever be, sir,' she retorted, standing up and reaching for her jacket and cap.

They swung right after leaving the police station, and after reaching North Tay Street they continued on towards the West Port. The street was almost noiseless except for the occasional tramcar which rumbled and clanked past them on the iron tramways set into the road. The quietness reminded Kirsty of Soho streets before trouble started, and it made her uneasy. In order to break the silence, she said, 'Is Dundee always as peaceful as this?'

Brewster laughed. 'Nothing much happens in this area after dark,' he said, 'but wait until we get to the Overgate. I'm sure you'll see a difference. Whether it matches up to London though, that's something else.'

Kirsty wished she had not spoken because he was laughing at her again. It seemed to her the more she tried to prove herself the more hilarious he found it.

Passing the quiet, staid Strathmore Arms, they turned left into the Overgate, and entered a different world. The street was packed with people, streams of them ebbing and flowing in all directions, creating a hum of activity in the tenement-shadowed, narrow streets.

Up until that moment Kirsty had only noticed the differences between patrolling in Dundee to the kind of duty she had been accustomed to. But now she could have been in any London back street, mixing with the crowds.

Young women paraded arm-in-arm on their way to a cinema or dance hall, while young men in their best jackets and flat caps, jostled each other, and tried to attract their attention. Older men wandered aimlessly, perhaps glad to escape the house and thankful for a moment of respite from their wives. Prostitutes, gaudily dressed, flaunted their charms at anyone who showed interest. In the public houses, rowdy drinkers attempted to consume as much as possible before they closed.

The sound of angry shouting, chattering voices, giggling girls, traders shouting their wares, and cartwheels rumbling over cobbles exploded round her and, like the crackle of lightning, she could feel tension in the air. The sense of excitement building within her was something she was familiar with, this waiting for something to happen and not knowing what it would be. This was the reason she liked policing, the thrill and the anticipation, the volatility of the crowd and the exhilaration of the unforeseen.

Brewster's stride never faltered, and she paced beside him with the slow measured tread she had been taught during her training. Both of them kept their eyes looking straight ahead, and the crowd parted to let them pass.

'Have you ever been inside a public house, Miss Campbell?' Brewster did not look at her as he asked the question.

'I am accustomed to entering public houses, sir.' Kirsty, struggled to keep her voice even. 'It was one of my duties when I was employed as a munitions policewoman in Gretna.'

'I understood you had only worked in London.' Kirsty thought she detected a note of interest in Brewster's voice but decided she must be mistaken.

'Yes, sir, I've worked in London, but I've also done munitions duties in Gretna and a place near Chester called Queensferry. It was a necessary part of policing during the war years.'

'You've moved around,' he said. 'You won't have any problems then if we visit a few pubs?'

'No, sir.'

'I'm not so sure about Dundee men though. They're not used to decent women visiting pubs.' He halted in a doorway. 'We'll start here. I'll ask the questions, but you have the photographs ready to show, and be ready to move out if trouble starts.'

'You don't have to worry about me. Policewomen are trained in self defence,' she said, resenting him because of his attitude towards her. If he thought she needed protection, he was mistaken.

'Really,' he said, then as an afterthought, 'how interesting. But I would appreciate it if you would be ready to move out should there be trouble.'

The public house was low-ceilinged and gloomy with the familiar smell of beer, smoke, sweat and urine that never failed to turn Kirsty's stomach into a queasy knot. She had an urge to gulp air, but resisted it and controlled her breathing into short, shallow inhalations designed to keep out most of the odours.

The floor was sawdust-covered with brass spittoons at each end of the bar. At the far end of the room, a fire glowed, sending out sparks and clouds of smoke in competition with the cigarette and pipe smokers. A fiddle player sitting on a stool in the corner of the room competed unsuccessfully with the shouted demands of the drinkers, the raucous sound of their laughter, and the clinking and clattering noises of glasses and jugs.

Brewster strode up to the bar, and leaning his arms on it, beckoned to the solitary bartender. The noise stopped. The fiddler laid his bow on the floor at his side. No one spoke, no glasses clinked. The silence descended so suddenly, it was like a wireless being switched off. Heads turned, and eyes focused on Kirsty and Brewster. The sense of menace in the air made the back of Kirsty's neck prickle with unease.

She stood, back straight, feet apart, hands clasped behind her, and stared back. Several men turned away and studied their glasses as if they had never seen the contents before while others glared at her.

The bartender polished the bar top with a dirty cloth. 'You wanted something?' His voice was surly, and his eyes seemed to look everywhere except at Brewster.

Brewster's voice was deceptively gentle. 'Why else would I be here? And you are going to help me, aren't you?' He paused and looked around the bar. 'I'm sure your customers would love to know how helpful you can be when you like.'

The hand polishing the bar stopped moving, and he glanced at Kirsty before staring into Brewster's eyes. 'That wouldn't be a threat, would it, Mr Brewster?'

'Of course it's not a threat, Jackie boy. You know I don't believe in threats.' Brewster leaned nearer to the barman. 'But it is a promise, and I always keep my promises.'

'Right you are, Mr Brewster. I've got the message. You didn't need to come here though, it's not good for trade.'

'We have some pictures we want you to look at.' Brewster nodded towards Kirsty, and she laid the photographs on the bar top. 'Take a close look and tell me if you've seen either of them before.' As the bartender shook his head, Brewster added, 'Show them to your customers. See if anyone else knows them.'

Brewster turned his back to the bar, watching the customers. Without looking at Kirsty, he said, 'Jackie Slater knows most of the working girls in this area, he keeps some rooms up the stairs and makes a reasonable living letting them out for an hour or two at a time.'

'Isn't that an offence?' Kirsty looked round the room but could not see a staircase.

'I suppose it is, but Jackie has his uses, and anyway, it's damned difficult to prove anything. Jackie says the girls sneak up the stairs when he's not looking. They're handy things, staircases which go up from the back yard.'

Kirsty watched the photographs being passed around the room. She could tell by the men's expressions that no one recognized the girls. 'I don't think we've had any success,' she said as Jackie returned to them and slid the pictures over the bar, shaking his head as he did so.

'The girls are a bit young for trade in this part of the town. Too many bobbies about. Maybe you'd have more luck if you spoke to Big Aggie.' Jackie looked away from them and started to polish the bar counter.

'What about Big Aggie, sir?' Kirsty asked as they left the

public bar. She remembered the large woman who had created so much havoc in the police station.

Brewster hesitated in the doorway. 'Yes, I suppose we'd better speak to her.' A hint of reluctance was evident in his voice. 'We'll try her after we've done the pubs. We can pick up reinforcements from the Western Police Station before we call on her. I wouldn't take you there on your own.'

Kirsty bristled with annoyance. He was implying, yet again, she needed to be protected. 'I don't need protection, sir. I've been in a lot of rough places in my time.'

Brewster laughed. 'It's not your protection I'm thinking about, it's mine. Big Aggie's been known to throw men off her plattie and she lives three storeys up. I have no wish to bounce off her back green.'

Kirsty smiled, despite herself. The thought of Brewster being thrown off the top floor landing, or plattie as it was termed in Dundee, at the rear of Big Aggie's tenement was too funny to resist. She could picture him flying through the air before thumping down on his back among the lank grass and the dog dirt in one of the overgrown back greens. It was probably a sight she would never see, which was a pity, because she would have enjoyed seeing him cut down to size.

'I doubt if she'd dare do that,' Kirsty said.

'Oh, she'd dare all right. There's no doubt about it. That's why we never go alone. Anyway we've got a fair amount of pubs to visit before we go to see Big Aggie.'

They worked their way up the Overgate entering pub after pub. There were fancy pubs, working men's pubs, hole in the wall pubs, pubs on the main street, and pubs up closes, pends and wynds. But in every establishment they were met with shaken heads and blank looks.

It was as if no one in Dundee had ever seen the two girls in the photographs.

'You'd think they'd never existed, sir,' Kirsty said, tucking the photographs into her pocket when they left the last establishment.

'I can't help wishing they hadn't. It would save us having to clear up this bloody mess.' He laughed, grimly. 'Come on, it's time we faced up to Big Aggie.'

Kirsty hesitated a moment before following him. She had wanted to say to him, 'Is that all it means to you? What about Angel? Is she worth so little she can be brushed aside as a mess to be cleared up?' But she compressed her lips and followed him.

21

The Western Police Station, a two-storey stone building at the west end of the Scouringburn, did not stand out from adjacent properties. But there were differences. Internally it was larger, occupying the same space that would house six families. The front door was much sturdier, and the two large ground-floor windows, one at each side, were non-opening. While a large, padlocked wooden gate protected the close at its side from intruders.

'Here we are,' Brewster said, shoving the door open and leaving Kirsty to follow him inside.

Kirsty had expected the charge room to be similar to the one at the central office; sometimes busy, sometimes not, but always orderly. But once inside they encountered chaos and disorder, making it difficult to tell whether they were in the charge room or a communal meeting place. The throng of bodies jostling for space seemed too large for the room to hold, and the clamour of voices was deafening. A police constable thumped the counter trying to attract the desk sergeant's attention.

The harassed sergeant was trying to answer several constables at the same time. At last, exasperated, he shouted, 'Ye'll all have to take your turn. I can only book one of them in at a time and if ye bring any more in ye'll have to take them home with ye for the cells are nearly all full up.'

'Aw, come on, sarge,' shouted one constable from the back of the room. 'Ye'll have to shove them in, for we must arrest them if they warrant it.'

Brewster pushed his way through the crowd. Kirsty, determined not to be left behind, followed him as closely as she could, but the assembled bodies closed in on her as they pressed and squeezed until she could hardly breathe. Several times she was sure she felt fumbling hands and was glad she had the protection of her thick, uniform skirt.

'Come on,' she heard Brewster's voice shouting above the racket, 'we don't have all night.'

She followed the sound of his voice. But by the time she reached the panelled wood door, which Brewster was holding partially open, she was gasping for breath. Someone in the crowd had tried to knock her cap off but had only succeeded in pushing it forward. It now perched precariously on the front of her head, so far forward it almost balanced on her nose, while her clothes strained tightly round her body in unfamiliar twists of material.

'I thought I'd lost you.' He grinned, seemingly enjoying some private joke. 'It's not quite the same as Central, is it?' He opened the door wider and beckoned her to follow him. 'Western gets a lot of drunkards, and riots are common. It's not unusual to have several stabbings every night. Central doesn't get so much of the rabble, but we handle the more serious crimes like the one I'm working on at the moment. However, I keep some CID men based here all the time, in case anything comes up that's more complicated than the usual.'

'I haven't met any other men in the CID,' Kirsty said. 'How many are there? I've only been told about the other inspector who is on leave.'

Brewster stopped in the corridor and turned to face her. 'I'm sorry,' he said. 'I hadn't realized you didn't know. I suppose I assumed you'd have found out for yourself by this time.'

'And how would I do that, sir?' Kirsty said drily. 'You were the one who briefed me.' Her already erect posture tightened, and she knew Brewster was studying her trying to figure out the degree of her annoyance.

He sighed and leaned against the wall, his limbs flopping into their habitual relaxed state. 'Well, I can't do justice to a briefing here, Miss Campbell, but just so you know. There are twelve of us, two inspectors, me and McAllister, four sergeants and six constables based at the different police stations. Three men are based here in Western, three in Eastern, two in Northern and two in Lochee. Between McAllister and me, we see the men regularly at their base, and we all meet at Central

Police Station once a month. You, Miss Campbell, are under my command. I trust that, at least, makes the staffing position clear. Now, if you follow me we'll go see the section sergeant and pick up our reinforcements.'

'Yes, sir,' Kirsty said through tight lips. Why was it that even when he was being reasonably nice, he had to assert his authority?

If Kirsty had been less disciplined, she would have whooped with delight when she left the Western Police Station. I should have known they wouldn't welcome me, she thought, remembering the section sergeant whose beady eyes raked over her, reflecting the disapproval he was so obviously feeling. She knew Brewster had noticed, but he had said nothing, and now he had lapsed into a quiet, thoughtful mood.

They moved through a labyrinth of similar looking back streets, each one darker than the last. Western had grudgingly supplied two constables to accompany them, but they seemed to be new recruits. It was obvious by the manner in which they fidgeted nervously with their batons and glanced repeatedly over their shoulders. Kirsty was tempted to say, 'Never mind lads, we've all had to go places that made us nervous. You'll get over it.' However, she restrained herself because she knew from experience two such burly policemen would never accept that from a woman, especially one claiming to be more experienced than they were.

As they went deeper into the Scouringburn, it grew quieter. Nothing stirred on the streets, giving the impression they were silent and deserted. But every now and again the shadows seemed to move and Kirsty sensed they were being watched. The back of her neck prickled with needles of uncertainty, and in imitation of the young policemen, she also started to glance over her shoulder.

'This is it.' Brewster stopped at the entrance to a close which looked like a dark tunnel carved into the body of the tenement. 'Big Aggie will know we are coming, so there's no point in creeping.' Brewster's voice seemed to have acquired an echoing quality.

He led the way into the close, penetrating the gloom with a confidence Kirsty was sure no one else was feeling. The darkness closed around them. Kirsty put her hand on the wall but cringed as her fingers met the sticky, greasy surface, and she quickly removed them, wiping them on her skirt before folding them into a fist. The smell of wood smoke mingled with the pungent stench of urine, and the distinctive odour of male cats on the scent of a receptive female, assaulted her nostrils, while the other smells too indefinable to distinguish, were far from pleasant.

Kirsty breathed more easily when she followed Brewster out of the close and saw the stars pricking holes of light in the night sky. But now they were in the enclosed space at the rear of the tenement. A place of wash-houses, coal-cellars, dustbins, and lank grass which rustled with the passage of something she could not see, and hoped was only cats.

Brewster turned right and entered the stairwell, a semi-circular, enclosed tower of stone steps jutting from the rear of the building and leading upwards.

The smell intensified. But they climbed up into the murky shadows, emerging into the fresh air each time they reached a landing. No one spoke, and only the sound of their laboured breathing disturbed the unnatural silence.

When they reached the third landing Brewster stopped and said, 'Big Aggie's house is on this plattie. The whole building is hers, she uses it for her girls. But she only admits to having her own house, and although she uses it as a shebeen we've never been able to catch her with the drink on the premises. She must have a devilishly good hiding place.'

'A shebeen?' The expression was new to Kirsty, and although she could take a guess at its meaning, she was not sure if she would be right.

'Aye, Miss Campbell. A shebeen. An illegal drinking den where you can drink all night and all day until your money runs out.'

'Do you think she'll be aggressive?' Kirsty followed Brewster, feeling her way along the plattie which was a stone landing, edged with iron railings about waist high. The plattie projected from the rear of the building and overhung the backlands below. She remembered Brewster's story of Big Aggie throwing men over it, and glanced over the railings. It was a long way down to the grassy area at the bottom.

'Don't worry, Aggie'll be all right provided she doesn't feel threatened.' Brewster stopped and turned to address the two constables. 'It might be better if you two remained in the stairwell. We don't want to give her the wrong idea. Miss Campbell will accompany me to the door. Come along, Miss Campbell.'

Kirsty suppressed a grin as the two young men scurried back along the landing. She could feel their relief because they would not have to face up to Big Aggie.

Brewster came to a sudden halt, but Kirsty had grown used to him doing this, so she stopped before she collided with his back. She had not heard the door open nor had she heard Big Aggie step out onto the landing. But the woman was there, larger than Kirsty remembered, and much more formidable at close quarters.

'Got rid of your two lap dogs, then?' Aggie folded her arms in front of her breasts, immediately increasing her girth.

Kirsty found it difficult to read the woman's expression and was not sure how to respond. Brewster saved her the trouble as he grinned up at Big Aggie. 'Ach, Aggie, they're just lads yet, and I didn't want to risk them being tempted by your girls' charms.'

'And ye think they'll be safe on the stairs, do ye?'

'I hope so, Aggie. For they're no use to me or to you if they do give way to that particular temptation.'

Aggie's laugh rumbled from deep inside her body. 'Ye're right, Jamie lad. I never knew a bobby yet with siller to spare, and the time hasn't come when I've needed to bribe one.'

From where she stood Kirsty could hear the gentle sound of air being expelled, and knew Brewster must have been holding his breath while he waited for Aggie's reaction.

'What d'ye want then, creeping up my stair at this time of night if it's not to see one of my girls. And I know it's not that because ye've brought one of your own.'

'I just wanted to ask you one or two questions, Aggie.'

'Questions?' The woman's body grew taller. 'Ye wouldn't be wanting to pry into my affairs, would ye?'

'No, no, Aggie, nothing like that, at least not tonight. I want you to look at a couple of photographs and tell me if you've ever seen the girls pictured in them. We're fair stuck, and you know so many girls.'

'Ye wouldn't be trying to be funny now, would ye?' Aggie's voice was abrasive.

'Not at all, Aggie. Just stating a fact.' Brewster turned. 'Show Aggie the photographs, Miss Campbell,' he said.

Kirsty already had the photographs out, and she handed them to Big Aggie.

'Miss Campbell is it?' Big Aggie held the photographs up to the light coming from her window. 'Never seen these two before, but I have seen you,' she said turning back to Kirsty. 'You were at the police station when I took those two brats in.' Her eyes gleamed in the darkness. 'Did ye get them settled then? In some nice cosy institution, I suppose? And they'll live happily ever after, I suppose?' She snorted and turned her back on them. 'Ye'd better go while ye still have time to get away in one piece,' she said.

The shadows moved in the dim lobby behind her and if it had not been for Aggie shaking her head Kirsty might have thought she imagined it.

'I think someone else was there,' she whispered to Brewster as they entered the stairwell.

'I know,' he said. 'Aggie always has minders.'

A rumble of laughter followed them down the stairs, but Kirsty restrained herself from rushing downward in as much of a hurry as the two young constables.

22

Midnight was long gone before they left the Scouringburn streets behind them, and Brewster insisted on escorting her home.

'You needn't come in early tomorrow, two o'clock will be soon enough,' he said, when they reached the outer door of her tenement.

Kirsty was on the point of thanking him when he added, 'You look tired.'

Her back stiffened. 'I'm all right, sir. I'm accustomed to long hours and hard nights.'

But his voice sounded weary and she wondered if her reaction to his comment had been too abrasive.

'I'm sure you are, Miss Campbell. I'm sure you are.'

She pushed the tenement door open, but as soon as it creaked shut, fatigue claimed her. She allowed her shoulders to slump, and it took all her time to pull herself up the stairs and into her flat. But it was not yet the haven she wanted it to be and was as dark and cold inside as it had been on the street. Without any hesitation, she shrugged off her clothes and leapt into bed, pulling the blankets up to her nose. The bed was not soft, but it soon warmed up, and she curled her body into a tight ball and slept.

She woke, with aching back and legs, when daylight crept into her room. Wriggling, she tried to get more comfortable, but she had lain too long in the same position in the unfamiliar bed, and the only cure was to get up. But she was reluctant to leave the warmth of her blankets for the chill atmosphere in the room.

She pulled the blankets down to her chin, and raised her head to look at the window to see what kind of day had dawned. Streaks of damp obliterated her view, and the puddles on the window sill dripped over the edge. Her uniform jacket and skirt lay in a heap on the chair where she had thrown them the night before. And a solitary spider investigated her underwear where it lay on the floor.

Reluctantly, she slid her legs from under the blanket. But, anticipating the coldness of the floor, she balanced on the edge of the bed for a moment before lowering her feet. When her soles made contact with the linoleum, she caught her breath, because it was colder than she expected. Her underwear would have shielded her feet from the floor's icy surface, and the temptation to stand on it was strong, but the spider had vanished from view, and she was afraid she would step on it. So, raising her heels, she tiptoed to the chest of drawers to get fresh undergarments and a clean pair of stockings. Once she had her clothes on she would shake it free.

Kirsty's fingers were still fumbling with the buttons at the side of her brown skirt when she left the bedroom and went into the front room. Spotting the note that had been pushed under the door, she quickly fastened the last button and crossed the room to pick it up.

The paper, a torn page from a diary, said – *I require to speak with you. Come and see me at the mill tomorrow. On no account do you speak to your mother first.* It was signed, *your father.*

Kirsty read the note twice over. What on earth had induced her father to hunt her out here? And why was he summoning her to see him? They had quarrelled after her last visit home, and he had made his disapproval of her present life obvious. Folding the note she placed it in her skirt pocket. She would go to the mill once she had eaten some breakfast.

The large wooden doors leading into the mill courtyard were closed. Kirsty turned the iron ring handle situated low down on one of them. A smaller door, inset into the larger one, opened, and the muted noise of machinery increased. Bowing her head she stepped up and over the rim of wood at the bottom, straightening up once she was in the cobbled courtyard.

She stood for a moment looking around. The gable ends of

three rows of stone buildings faced her at the other side of the square yard. The carding and roving sheds lay in the buildings to the left. Similarly, the spinning sheds stretched the length of the right hand side of the mill. And the middle building was for the weavers, who would not condescend to enter the sheds at either side of them. Nothing seemed to have changed, although she had not been inside the place for the past ten years.

Turning left she approached the lodge, a square stone built bothy inside the front gate. The heavy oak door swung open at her push, and as she stepped into the room, she also stepped back in time. Davie Paton sat on the hard backed chair in front of a glowing fire, puffing away at his pipe, just as he had been the last time she saw him.

He jumped up as she entered the room. 'Can I help you miss?' He lifted his flat cap in a deferential salute.

She grinned at him, and said, 'Aye, likes ye can, Davie Paton.'

He peered closer. 'Bless me, if it isn't Miss Kirsty. I hardly recognized ye, being all so grown up like. Mind ye, though, ye havenae changed much at all.'

'Neither have you, Davie.'

'I suppose ye'll be looking for your da.' Davie laid his pipe in the fender.

'That's all right, Davie. I can find my way to the office and he'll be expecting me.'

'But he won't be in his office, Miss Kirsty. That's what I was trying to tell ye. He always goes round the mill in the mornings, says it keeps the gaffers on their toes.' He looked up at the large clock hanging on the wall. 'Like as not, he'll be in the spinning sheds, probably number three, Sandy McNeill's room. I'll get a lad to fetch him for ye, but he'll not be pleased to come back up to the office.'

Kirsty smiled at Davie's discomfiture. 'Don't worry about it Davie. I'll go down to the sheds and find him. Sandy McNeill's room, you said?'

Kirsty left the lodge, although she could tell by Davie's expression he did not approve of her going in to the mill alone. However, she was familiar with the mill, having visited it often when she was younger. She remembered how she had dogged her father's footsteps as a young girl. And the many times he had taken her into the different areas of the mill to see the clattering machinery and watch the workers who tended them, some of them not much older than she was. 'Don't tell your mother now,' he would say to her as she followed him from one mill room to the next. 'She wouldn't like to think you'd seen this, but it will belong to you and your husband some day.' Kirsty sensed his desire for a son, so she had tried to think like a boy and be the son he never had, but she could never get over the feeling she had disappointed him in the end.

Reaching the spinning shed she pushed the door open. The room was large and long and had a claustrophobic feel because of the size and the amount of machinery it contained. Massive iron spinning frames were set in rows against the far wall extending both to the left and right of where Kirsty stood. The noise of engines and the spinning spindles beat on her ears, and the dry, musty smell of oily dust filtered into her nostrils.

A set of wooden stairs to the left of the door led up to a platform running the length of the room. By walking along it, the gaffer could oversee the entire work area. The glass windowed office at the top of the stairs was where he filled in his time sheets and kept a note of how many shifts each spinning frame did.

Kirsty knew this was where she would find her father, discussing production levels with the gaffer, and instructing him to boost production by increasing the speed of the machines. So she climbed the stairs to the office.

'Sit down a minute, Kirsty,' her father said as she entered, although he did not raise his eyes from the open ledger lying on the dusty, mahogany desk. He ran his finger down a column of figures. 'It's not good enough, McNeill. You'll have to get production up, or we'll all be out of a job. Times are getting hard, you know.'

'Yes, Mr Campbell. But the roves haven't been good lately. If you can get the roving sheds to improve the quality, I'm sure I could get an extra bit of speed on the frames. As it is, the extra speed just means more broken ends and more half-empty bobbins.'

'I'll speak to the gaffer in the roving shed. You see what you can do here. Now off you go and make sure those lazy girls aren't taking too long shifting their frames. While you're doing that, I'll stay here and have a word with my daughter.'

'Yes, Mr Campbell.' The door clicked shut, and Kirsty watched him walk along the platform, stopping now and then to shout to the workers below.

She turned her attention back to her father who was still frowning over the figures in the ledger. Smiling to herself she remembered previous occasions when she sat here watching him. He had not seemed so serious then and had always taken the time to look up at her and grin. He was not smiling today though, and the laughter lines on his face had been replaced by those of worry. Despite that, he was still a handsome man, even though his hair was now more grey than red. But his face had a weary look, and his eyes lacked sparkle. Funny, that had not been so noticeable when she had been home last week.

Her father snapped the ledger shut. He cleared his throat several times. Kirsty was tempted to say something, but her father was a forceful man, used to getting his own way. He did not take kindly to unwarranted interruptions, so she waited.

When he still did not speak she looked up at him, but he turned his eyes away. She had never thought him capable of embarrassment but that was how his actions seemed to her.

'You wanted to talk to me, father?'

He hesitated before he began to talk, and it seemed as if he were searching for the right words.

At last he started to speak. 'Kirsty, you have led your own life for some time now and although we don't approve we have never interfered.' His fingers tapped agitatedly on the ledger. 'However, events have overtaken us, and I must ask you to consider where your allegiance is, and I would hope it would be to your family.'

Kirsty's throat tightened. He had seen where she lived, and he did not think her flat good enough for his daughter. He was going to ask her to return home.

'I am sorry if you disapprove of my lifestyle, father. But I am happy, and I have no wish to change it.'

'Hear me out, Kirsty, before you get angry.' He cleared his throat again, before continuing, 'I have been approached about a merger. You know, the business hasn't been so good lately, and a merger could be the saving of the firm.' Pulling his shaggy eyebrows together in a frown, he paused and looked at her.

Her unease grew. He did not need to consult her about any merger he was considering. So why tell her?

'Surely that's a matter for you to decide,' she said.

'It's more than a business merger. It's also a family merger. Without it, we are finished.' He looked away from her. 'I need your support, Kirsty.'

'What for?' She kept her voice even, to conceal her anxiety.

'A family merger, Kirsty. A marriage.'

'Who?' she rasped, her throat closing even further.

'Mr Bogue approached me on behalf of his son.'

'Johnnie Bogue? I wouldn't marry him if he was the last man on earth, and you know the reason why.'

'It's because of the reason that you have to. Mr Bogue found out about his son's . . . indiscretion. He knows about Ailsa. He's taking the view she is his flesh and blood, and he wants her to be part of his family. He reminded me that, in law, a child's father can claim custody.'

'His son's indiscretion! That's an understatement.' Kirsty's voice was shrill with anger. 'His son raped me, father. Why won't you face up to it?'

Her father seemed to droop and become smaller. His face sagged, and he suddenly looked older. 'You never told me he raped you,' he said quietly. 'All these years I've thought you were just being stubborn.'

'The trouble with you, father, is you never listened to me. You thought I was a silly girl with modern ideas. Well I may have modern ideas, but I can assure you I have never been silly, or flighty, or immoral.' Kirsty gasped, unable to continue.

'I'm sorry, Kirsty. I didn't realize.'

'No, father, you didn't realize and you say you didn't know. But you didn't want to know. You preferred to think of me as a whore rather than believe Johnnie Bogue was anything other than a nice young boy.'

'I never thought any such thing.' Her father spluttered as he tried to regain his composure. 'Silly, yes, modern, yes, but never anything else.' He glared at her. 'If I'd thought you to have prostituted yourself, I would have disowned you.'

'But you did disown me. Didn't you, father? You've hardly spoken two civil words to me since that day,' Kirsty said bitterly. 'You have Ailsa now. My Ailsa.'

'Yes Kirsty. We have Ailsa, but that doesn't mean you were disowned. And it's because of Ailsa you must give the merger your consideration.'

'You can't mean that. Not after what I've told you.' Kirsty stared with disbelief at her father. How could he insist she marry Johnnie Bogue, when he knew how she had been violated by him?

'Yes, Kirsty. I do mean it. You must marry Johnnie Bogue or we lose everything, including Ailsa.'

The room whirled around her. Kirsty's chest heaved while tears scalded her cheeks. How dare her father suggest she marry Johnnie Bogue? He had no right to ask her to do that, even if his business were failing. 'I don't care what Mr Bogue has found out. I'll have nothing to do with Johnnie Bogue and that's final,' she screamed. 'But if he lays one finger on Ailsa I'll kill him, and you can tell him that from me.'

She slammed out of the office, clattering down the stairs, and out into the fresh air of the alley between the buildings. Her feet slipped on the cobbles as she ran towards the courtyard and the wooden gate that would release her from this monstrous building. She had to put as much space between herself and her father as she possibly could.

23

Kirsty continued to run, even after she left her father's mill far behind her. In her distress, she barely noticed her surroundings: narrow lanes, streets and wynds, where the daylight hardly penetrated; uneven cobbles that dug into her feet; high, windowless buildings; and the faint rumble of machinery. It seemed the whole of Dundee was one endless factory.

She had a mental picture of Johnnie Bogue in his dinner jacket, smiling at her, while underneath she knew the rottenness within him. She recalled the time when she told him she was to have his child. His response had been, 'Your bastard is nothing to do with me.'

Her father had never understood and had always thought she had let him down.

A tramcar clanked past, halting her flight. She stood, teetering on the edge of the pavement for a moment, confused and dazed, for she had no recollection of when she had left the back streets that led from the mill or how she had arrived in the Marketgait.

From where she stood she could see the prison looming at the other side of the road, the courthouse facing into Courthouse Square, and just out of sight, the police station which sat behind both. Further down to her right was the Salvation Army Home, and if she followed the road, she knew it would lead her to the centre of the town.

The tram halted at its stop with a squeal of iron wheels on iron rails. Two women, wearing headscarves and with shopping baskets dangling from their arms, boarded the tramcar which then trundled towards the town centre with a clanging of bells.

She hovered for a moment on the pavement's edge. Then, aware of how she must look, she pulled the brim of her hat forward hoping it would hide her tear-stained face. Without looking directly at any of the passers-by, she scurried over the road to Courthouse Square. A group of men, chattering, laughing and smoking cigarettes, jostled each other on the steps in front of the Sheriff Court, but they paid no attention to her as she hurried past.

She had an intense urge to talk. She considered Brewster, but she did not know him well enough and she thought he would be unsympathetic. Even if he were able to help her it would be too risky to confide in him because he would think she was weak, and it could affect her future in Dundee. The only other person she knew, apart from her family, was Edward Gordon, and she was not sure of him or his reaction to her since their visit to the Orphan Institute.

Nevertheless, her feet were leading her in the direction of the Refuge. The door was closed when she got there, but she pushed it open and ran up the stairs without registering the smells, the dust, or the dilapidation of the building.

Edward was waiting for her on the landing at the top of the stairs. 'I heard you coming.' He paused and stared at her. 'You're upset!' He grasped her hand in his and led her along the landing. 'Come into the kitchen, take your coat off, and I'll make you some tea. Then, if you like, you can tell me what's troubling you.'

Kirsty closed her hands round the warmth of the mug. She lifted it to her lips, and the steam mingled with her tears. Setting it on the table she turned her head away from Edward so he would not see the tears rolling silently down her cheeks.

'Don't cry,' he said, leaning towards her. 'I thought you were supposed to be an independent policewoman that nothing touches.' He offered her his handkerchief. 'Maybe if you tell me what it's about I could help. You can't keep whatever it is bottled up inside you.'

Kirsty wiped her face and turned to look at him. He put a tentative arm round her shoulders, and she leaned her head against him. The warmth seeping through the roughness of the tweed jacket he wore had a soothing effect on her. She relaxed and started telling him about Johnnie Bogue, about Ailsa and about her family. All of her frustration, misery and despair, flowed out in a torrent of words.

But when she finished talking, a sense of shame crept through her and made her wish she could take all the words back. But it was too late for that.

Edward sat down beside her and pulled her closer to him. 'I wondered why you were so against the Bogue family. But I can understand now, and I don't blame you for feeling as you do about them.' He cradled her head on his chest, and she forgot her shame as she relaxed into his arms.

'There, there,' he said as if he were soothing a distressed child. 'Nobody can force you to do anything against your will.' He rocked her in his arms. 'I'll take you to see a friend of mine, a solicitor, and he'll make sure the Bogues can't touch Ailsa. Everything will be all right, you'll see.'

Kirsty was not sure how long they sat like that, but she was becoming increasingly aware of his nearness. His tweed jacket scraped her cheek with its roughness, and the damp patch her tears had made was becoming uncomfortable. But over and above everything else his maleness overwhelmed her.

Feeling the flush creep up from her neck, her embarrassment grew. She had not meant to tell Edward everything, nor had she intended to allow him to get so close to her.

Pulling away from him, more abruptly than she meant to, she said, 'I'm sorry. I shouldn't have burdened you with my problems. I should never have come.'

'But you did come and I'd like to help if you'll let me.'

He drew her hand into his own, but she pulled it back again. She liked Edward, but she was not ready for this.

'Ah, well,' he sighed. 'At least I can introduce you to my solicitor friend.'

Edward did not expect to feel so bereft when Kirsty pulled away from him. Holding her had felt warm and comfortable, as if she belonged with him. He had wanted her to remain in his arms forever, and for the shortest time she had accepted his comfort. However, she was such an independent woman it had been foolish of him to think she would be willing to give that up. It would take more than this to win her over.

The level of her distress had been so great she confided in him. Telling him things she had never told anyone else, and now she was bound to be embarrassed. But she must have trusted him to tell him so much, and his urge to help her became overpowering.

To give her time to compose herself, he stood and picked up the mug. He rinsed it under the cold tap and placed it on the draining board. Without turning round, he said, 'Simon, my solicitor friend, is one of the best in Dundee. If he can't help you, nobody can.'

'I'm not sure,' she said.

'I'll take you to meet him anyway. I think you'll find him helpful.'

He picked up her coat and held it out, noticing as he did so that her face was tear-stained and her hat askew, while the droop of her shoulders indicated the depth of her despair. He wanted to take her into his arms again and never let her go, but instead, he said, 'You'll find a mirror on the back wall if you want to tidy up.'

24

Kirsty followed Edward as he climbed the steps to the courthouse. 'I don't want to speak to a solicitor,' she protested, becoming more reluctant with each step she took, but he did not seem to hear her. She knew her father would not approve, and if he wanted a solicitor he would hire one. He certainly would not want her to brief one.

She should have been more forceful and insisted Edward leave her alone to make her own decisions, but the thought of what her father wanted her to do sapped her strength.

They reached the top of the stone steps, passed under the pillars and entered the courthouse. Kirsty braced herself. She knew, from experience, policewomen were not wanted in court and routinely ejected. But, she did not have her uniform on so who was to know. Immediately the thought entered her mind, she felt ashamed. What had happened to her pride in her career? She lifted her chin and squared her shoulders. She was still a policewoman, even without the uniform.

But still her anxiety grew, for she had no idea how the Dundee sheriffs would view her. She had bitter memories of some encounters with Frederick Mead, one of the most critical magistrates in London. He would not tolerate any woman in his court and considered policewomen were abnormal women masquerading in police uniform.

Placing her hand on Edward's arm, she said, 'I don't want to see a solicitor right now. Can't we make an appointment to see him in his office?'

'Nonsense!' He covered her hand with his own and drew her through the courthouse doors. 'You need help, and you need it right away. I know Simon's in court in the mornings, so we'll wait until he's free. He's the finest solicitor in Dundee, and I'm determined to see you get the best legal help available.'

Kirsty frowned. 'You don't understand. If he's as good as you say, he will be expensive, and I can't afford to pay him.'

'You have no need to worry about that. Simon owes me a favour, and I'm sure we can come to an arrangement.'

'As long as he understands I have limited means. I wouldn't want him to waste his time due to any misunderstanding.'

The large open hall buzzed with the noise of a multitude of voices and was thronged with people, mostly men. Some of the men were well dressed in suits and ties while others looked decidedly scruffy. Kirsty had no difficulty distinguishing the clients from the solicitors. It struck her that she also was a client, and she wondered if that made her the same as everyone else who stood around waiting to be called into whichever courtroom their case was scheduled.

Maybe she too would be called to a courtroom if the Bogues got their way and tried to take Ailsa. They might try to prove she had abandoned Ailsa, and she could not deny that. How could she defend herself? She had allowed her parents to take her child from her. Who would listen if she said there was no other option? Who would believe her if she told them about the pain and guilt she had been living with ever since? And who would protect Ailsa from the agony of the truth? The truth Kirsty was determined the child must never know.

Shaking with emotion she decided she could not allow any of that to happen and became aware she would do anything, even murder, to prevent anyone touching or harming Ailsa. She shuddered, realizing that in her own mind, she was as low as the lowest criminal in this courthouse.

Edward guided her through the throng of people, his fingers tightening on her arm, stopping her from turning back. 'He should be around here somewhere,' he muttered. 'He's always in court in the morning.'

'Maybe he doesn't have any clients to represent today.' Kirsty hoped she was right because then she would have more time to collect her thoughts and decide what to do.

'That wouldn't matter to him, he would be here looking for someone to represent, whether or not they had money to pay him. He has a charitable nature has Simon, as well as a kindred feeling for those less fortunate than himself. Seems to me he's always trying to make up for his own good fortune, for he wasn't always so well off.'

A court usher approached a group of men standing near the wall. 'You're next for Court Two, so you can go into the witness room now,' he said, pointing down one of the corridors.

Edward waited until the men passed and then tapped the usher on the shoulder. 'I'm looking for Simon Harvey. Do you know where he might be?'

'Court Three,' the man replied without looking up. 'They should be finishing up about now because I'm getting ready to show the witnesses for the next case into the witness room.'

'I'm not sure I want to see Mr Harvey.' Kirsty turned to face the door leading out to the square.'

'Nonsense.' Edward led her further along the hall. 'We'll wait at the end of the corridor to Courtroom Three and catch him as he comes out. There's no better solicitor in Dundee than Simon, and you want to get him before the Bogues do.'

Kirsty was close to tears. Angry because of this sudden weakness she turned her head away from Edward and stared at the doors that must lead into Courtroom Three. She concentrated on breathing. Long slow breaths that drew air into her lungs and calmed her down. The threat of tears subsided, and gradually she regained her composure until she was calm enough to face Edward again.

'All right, I'll talk to him. But I don't want all of Dundee to know Ailsa is my daughter, least of all Ailsa. It would turn her life upside down.'

Edward gave her arm a comforting squeeze, and said, 'Simon will respect your confidences. And if it has to come to court he's sharp, and he's clever. You couldn't have anyone better on your side.'

The sound of hurrying footsteps on the polished wooden floor of the corridor drew Kirsty's attention. She had not heard the courtroom door open or shut, but the man walking towards them could not have come from anywhere else. She looked towards Edward for confirmation this might be Simon Harvey, but Edward was already moving towards the approaching figure.

'Good to see you again, Simon.' He gripped the man's hand, shaking it energetically.

'You too,' Simon said. 'It seems an age since we've seen each other.'

'I want you to meet a friend of mine.' Edward turned to Kirsty. 'Simon, this is Miss Campbell, and she has a problem she would like to discuss. I have persuaded her to consult you, but she is somewhat reluctant because she is of limited means.'

'Miss Campbell.' Simon extended his hand to her.

She mumbled something in reply and turned away in confusion, trying to avoid his penetrating stare. She had the feeling if she were to lie to this man he would know immediately.

His hand was cool and his grip stronger than she had expected, and he held her hand slightly longer than he needed to.

'If it's business then we can use one of the interview rooms at the back of the court.' Simon placed his hand on her elbow and steered her through the crowd, leaving Edward to follow.

He walked at a brisk pace. However he was only a little taller than Kirsty, so she had no problem matching her steps to his. Throwing open the door of a small room he ushered her in and pulled a chair out for her to sit on. He sat himself at the opposite side of the table and left Edward to stand awkwardly at their side.

Pulling a notebook from the briefcase he had laid on the table beside him, he said, 'Start wherever you want, but you have to tell me everything or I will not be able to help you.'

Kirsty had composed herself sufficiently to look into his eyes, and she wondered what effect they would have on whoever he was cross-examining in court. She imagined that icy stare could make a person reveal all their secrets, even if they did not want to, and she instantly decided she would prefer to have him act for her than against her. His businesslike attitude helped her to tell her story, and she did so in a flat, emotionless tone. She found it easier when she detached herself from the whole thing, so it was like speaking about someone else.

He made no comment while she talked, but when she finally drew breath and subsided into silence, he laid his hands flat on the table and leaned towards her. 'Do you want me to apply for guardianship or custody of Ailsa, either for yourself or your parents?'

Kirsty's thoughts were in turmoil, and she did not know what she wanted him to do.

She did not know if the Bogues would carry out their threat, although her father seemed to believe them capable of doing so. She did not know what her parents' reaction would be to her briefing a solicitor. And above all she did not want Ailsa to know Kirsty was her mother.

Kirsty looked directly into Simon Harvey's eyes. 'No! I don't want you to do that because Ailsa would be bound to find out, particularly if it resulted in a court case.'

'What do you want me to do then?'

'Nothing.' Kirsty stood up. 'It was a mistake coming to you. I should never have allowed Mr Gordon to persuade me.'

'Wait.' He grasped her arm. 'Who else, apart from your parents, knows that Ailsa is Johnnie Bogue's daughter?'

'No one, except you and Mr Gordon.'

'If you denied he was the father who could contradict you?'

'No one.'

'Could you, under oath, deny that Johnnie Bogue is Ailsa's father?'

'I would do anything to protect Ailsa.'

'Could you, under oath, deny you are Ailsa's mother?'

Kirsty looked at him. Deny her own daughter. She had been doing that for years. A pain, unlike anything else she had ever experienced, rose and sat like a stone in her chest. 'I could,' she said, and the stone twisted inside her like a razor sharp flint.

'That is all I wanted to know. I will act for you, and will contact you once I have made arrangements to discuss this with Mr Bogue. Hopefully it will not even get the length of coming to court, therefore it will attract no fees.' Suddenly he smiled at her, and the ice vanished from his eyes.

25

Every step Kirsty took drained more and more energy out of her but, she plodded on, putting one foot in front of the other, for she could not allow herself to stop. She should have accepted Edward's offer to walk her home. But her mind had been in too much of a turmoil, and she had wanted peace to think. Now she felt empty, like an old woman whose life force was in decline, even though her nerves were taut and her mind buzzed with activity.

Eventually, she reached the front door to the tenement and the stairs loomed in front of her. Up through the building where the smell of boiled cabbage and rutting cats never seemed to leave the air. She emptied her mind and concentrated on the climb until at last she inserted her key in the lock. And yet, tired though she was, she knew the two long hours before she would be on duty again would be intolerable.

The door thudded shut behind her. Hardly noticing, she staggered to the sink to splash her face with cold water. It did not revive her. She collapsed into the sagging armchair, but the broken spring dug into her thigh. Too tired to care she closed her eyes, but the jabbing pain of the spring became too much to bear. Sighing wearily, she got up, went into the bedroom and lay on the bed. Stretching full length she poked her feet between the brass spars at the end and dangled them in midair.

Her mind surged with thoughts. She went over the events of the day, again and again, trying to determine whether she could have handled things differently. Remembering the secrets she had shared, first with Edward Gordon and then Simon Harvey, she grew warm with embarrassment. What would they think of her? She stared at the lumpy, whitewashed ceiling as if it would provide her with the answers.

Thinking over what had happened between her and her

father was difficult. She had considered herself strong and yet it had taken very little for her to feel helpless and vulnerable. She did not like that. She preferred to be in control, both of the situation and her feelings. And this morning, she had been in control of neither.

A groan escaped her lips when she thought of how foolish she had been to unburden herself to Edward Gordon. He now knew more about her than any other person in her life, apart from her mother and father. She had crossed a line with him that she would never be able to retrieve. And now this solicitor, this Simon Harvey who was supposed to be so smart, knew about her as well. Her muscles tightened. The secret she had kept for so many years was now known to more than herself and her family.

Pent up emotion surged through her body. It forced her to turn over and bury her face in the pillow. But she could not let the misery she was feeling swamp her. For, although she was a woman uncomfortable in a man's world, she was still, after all, Kirsty Campbell who prided herself on her confidence, her strength of character, and her ability to help others.

It had been easier for her to be strong when she lived in London because she had only herself to consider, and she had deliberately avoided emotional entanglements. Here, in Dundee, she was too close to her family. So all the emotions she had suppressed over the years were surfacing. It had been a mistake to return to Dundee. She should have remained in London.

She rose a few minutes later, thinking she would be better at work than lying in bed feeling sorry for herself. After splashing some more cold water on her face, she searched for the face powder her mother had given her as a present. 'You should make yourself look more attractive,' her mother had said. Kirsty had replied, 'Yes mother,' although she never had any intention of using it. Now she was glad she had kept it because it would help disguise her reddened eyes and nose.

Kirsty hurried through the charge room. It was midday and the beat bobbies were out on the streets. The duty sergeant had his head down engrossed in some paper work. He looked up as she entered.

'You're early,' he grunted, scowling at her briefly before returning to the papers on his desk.

Kirsty smiled wryly at his unwelcoming comment, but as he did not seem to want a reply she did not bother to give one.

She had barely settled in her office when she heard the sound of running footsteps outside in the corridor, followed by the noise of a scuffle.

'But I want to see the missy.' The child's voice echoed, high and plaintive, on the verge of tears. 'I saw her come in. She has to be here somewhere.'

'Ouch! You wee brat. I'll get you for that.'

Kirsty opened the door and peered out. The duty sergeant held his leg with one hand while the other had the child's collar firmly in his grip. He had pulled him up until his toes barely touched the ground.

'Ye're hurting me,' the child squealed.

'What's going on, sergeant?'

Kirsty walked towards them.

'Miss! Miss! I have to see ye.' The child burst into tears.

'Why, it's Bert, isn't it?'

Kirsty peered at him in the gloom of the passageway and then turned to the sergeant. 'It's all right, sergeant. I'll see to him now.'

Reluctantly the sergeant released his hold on Bert's collar and the child dropped down onto his feet again, almost overbalancing so that he had to save himself by grabbing Kirsty's skirt.

'Come on, Bert. Into my office and I might be able to find a sweetie for you.'

Bert burst into tears. 'Don't want no sweetie. Want Nora. She said she'd come back, but she didn't.'

Kirsty sat Bert on a chair and, kneeling down, put her arm round him, but his sobs intensified. He shivered in his despair.

Kirsty held him to her body. She could feel his small frame shudder with sobs, and the stream of tears seemed never ending. His misery was so complete it took her all her time not to cry with him, and she felt the anguish within him as if it were part of herself.

'Where did Nora go, Bert?' She held him away from her body so she could see his face.

'Don't know. She said she wouldn't leave me, but she's went away.' His eyes filled up with tears until they brimmed over.

Kirsty remembered Nora's protective arms round Bert and the fierceness of her glare when she thought Kirsty was trying to take him from her. 'I'm sure Nora wouldn't leave you, Bert. She's your sister.'

'Said she wouldn't, but she did.' Bert had stopped crying, but his voice was sullen.

'Has she ever left you before?' Kirsty's arms tightened on the boy's small frame.

'No.' He looked up at her with despair in his eyes. 'D'you think Nora will come back, miss?'

'I'm sure she will, Bert. But if she's going to come back she's going to have to know where to find you.'

Bert thought for a moment. 'Don't want to go back to that place.' His voice was stubborn.

'Didn't you like it there?'

'It weren't too bad, but Nora didn't like it. Maybe that's why she went away.' He shivered.

'Will you go back if I take you?' Kirsty paused. What on earth would she do with him if he said no? 'Nora won't know where you are otherwise.'

'I suppose,' he muttered.

A half sob bubbled up in his throat. 'Will you look for Nora, miss?' His eyes had a pleading look. 'You know what she looks like, and she might come with you. She'd run from any of the other bobbies.'

Kirsty hugged him. 'Of course I'll look for her.'

'D'you promise, miss?'

'Yes, Bert. I promise.'

The boy shuddered. He pressed his face into her body, and Kirsty was sure he did not want her to see him crying.

Her thoughts were troubled. It seemed strange that Nora

would leave Bert alone in a place new to him. The girl had seemed so devoted to her brother and they were always together.

Kirsty's arms tightened on Bert's body. She hoped she would be able to keep her promise, but she had a horrible feeling Nora's name was about to be added to her list of missing girls, and she had not even started to look for the others yet.

26

'I have to take Bert to the Orphan Institute,' Kirsty said as she passed through the charge room. 'If Inspector Brewster comes in, tell him I'll be back as soon as I can.'

The duty sergeant grunted but did not look up.

Bert's small hand gripped Kirsty's, transmitting his anxiety to her. But he did not object to getting on the tram or alighting outside the Orphan Institute. Once they passed through the gate, however, his feet dragged on the gravel of the drive.

'We're almost there,' Kirsty said, with a cheerfulness she did not feel. She glanced down at Bert who was becoming increasingly agitated, and then up at the house that evoked such reluctance in him. Unlike her last visit, no sun lightened the sombreness of the building, and Kirsty shivered with a sudden premonition all might not be right here.

She stopped in the middle of the drive. 'You're sure you want to come back here?' She knew by his demeanour that he did not.

'Yes, miss,' Bert said. 'Cause Nora'll come back for me. Won't she?' He gave her a fleeting smile but the sadness did not leave his eyes.

Kirsty sighed. 'Yes, I suppose you're right. But if you need me you know where to come.'

'Yes, miss.' His hand moved nervously within her grasp as they started to walk down the drive again.

The door opened, and Maud came out onto the doorstep to watch their approach. 'I saw you coming,' she said. 'We've been worried about the lad since he vanished after breakfast.'

Bert's small fingers tightened round Kirsty's hand. He looked up at Maud, and it seemed as if he were trying to gather the courage to speak to her, but no words emerged.

'What is it, Bert?' Kirsty bent over until her face was level with his eyes.

Bert gulped. 'I just wanted to ask if Nora'd come back.' His eyes were wet, and Kirsty thought he was going to start crying again, but he did not.

Maud leaned forward. 'No, lad.' She put a hand on his shoulder. 'Nora's still missing.' She looked at Kirsty and shook her head before turning to shout into the interior of the house, 'Milly, come and see to Bert, he's come back.'

The little maid scurried out of the shadows of the hall and smiled at Bert. 'Come on then,' she said. 'You'll be hungry. Let's go and find something for you to eat.'

Bert looked up at Kirsty as if asking for permission. 'It's all right Bert. Off you go with Milly.' Kirsty smiled her encouragement, although a little area of doubt worried away in her brain. However, when Bert dropped her hand and went to Milly, she could see he liked the girl.

Milly stopped as she reached the rear of the hall and bent down to whisper to Bert. He smiled up at her and both of them vanished out of sight through one of the rear doors, leaving the hall empty except for Kirsty and Maud. The swinging door and the far off chant of children reciting their lessons did nothing to dissipate the feeling of emptiness the building seemed to have.

'I noticed you made no mention of Nora's disappearance when you indicated your concern for Bert,' Kirsty said thoughtfully, turning to face Maud.

'Come into the parlour, Miss Campbell. We'll be private there.' Maud turned and led the way through the hall.

Kirsty seated herself on one of the sofas. 'Bert is worried about Nora,' she said. 'They've never been separated before.'

'Ah yes, Nora.' Maud sighed and stared into the flickering flames of the fire. 'Nora didn't settle here, you know. She was naughty and spiteful and constantly swearing. She said she wouldn't stay, and she didn't.'

'But why did she leave Bert behind?' Kirsty frowned, wondering if Nora had been chastised and maybe that was why she had gone, but it did not explain why she would leave her brother.

'Who knows? Maybe she felt she would get on better

without him. Maybe she got tired of always having to attend to him. He did hang around her skirts a lot.' Maud paused. 'We thought at first she might be hiding but we searched the premises and the grounds, and found no sign of her. We had to conclude she had run away.'

'What time did she leave?' Kirsty withdrew a notebook and pencil from her handbag. 'I'd better take notes. After all, I have to consider Nora a missing child.'

Maud turned to stare at Kirsty and then turned away again before Kirsty could interpret the expression in her eyes. 'Nora left sometime last night. She went to bed at the usual time, eight o'clock, and was still there when the night warden made her rounds of inspection at ten o'clock. However, at the twelve o'clock inspection she was gone.'

'Did anyone see or hear her leave?' Kirsty moistened the point of her pencil with her tongue, a habit she had acquired in London.

'No. No one saw or heard her leave. The back door was unlocked, so we assume she must have left through that.'

'Do you mind if I take a look at the back door?' Kirsty was already standing up.

'Not at all,' Maud said. 'If you'll follow me I'll show you.' She led the way to the rear of the hall, past a kitchen area and then down a short flight of stone steps to a smaller hall where coats hung on hooks, and an elephant's foot umbrella stand stood in the corner. 'The children come in through this door after playing outside,' Maud explained as they passed a row of muddy boots lined up against the wall.

The door was locked, but the key rested in the keyhole and Maud turned it to reveal the grassy area behind the house.

'The key, is it always in the door?' Kirsty asked as she stepped outside.

'Yes, we see no reason to remove it. Locked doors are to keep intruders out, not to lock anyone in.' Maud's voice held a note of reproof.

Kirsty wandered over the grass. 'What's that building over there?' She pointed to the small stone edifice in the corner of the grassy area which reminded her of a small church. However, it had been built at an odd angle with its frontage facing along the garden, making her think someone had deliberately tried to conceal the entrance from visitors to the house.

'Oh that. That's the old chapel. I believe the Bogue family used it when they lived in the house. No one's been inside for years. The place is locked up and the windows boarded over.'

'You don't think she might be in there?' Kirsty approached the building and tried the door, but it was solid and did not look as if it had moved for a long time.

Maud snorted. 'I told you, no one's ever been inside. There's no key, and the rumour is the Bogues had the chapel sealed for some reason known only to them.' She clasped her arms round her body. 'In any case, the building is in a dangerous condition. The slates regularly fall off the roof, so I don't encourage the children to play here. I wouldn't want any of them hurt.'

'Yes, I'm sure,' Kirsty murmured, uncertain what she was sure about.

'Have you seen enough?' Maud asked. 'It's cold out here, and I'd like to get back inside to the fire.'

Kirsty could think of no reason to stay outside so she agreed and the two women returned to the comfort of the parlour.

Pushing the door open, Kirsty was surprised to see Edward standing in front of the fire warming his hands.

He hurried over to her, grasped her hands and pulled her into the room. 'I've just heard,' he said. 'I met Milly in the hall, and she told me Nora had run off and that you were here.'

'The child never settled,' Maud said as she followed them in. 'I've explained that to Miss Campbell, but she has some idea Nora would not have left without her brother.'

'Bert is distraught.' Kirsty wriggled her hands free from Edward's grasp. 'You saw them together, Edward. Do you think Nora would run away and leave him?'

Edward glanced towards his cousin, 'I know you think Nora has run off, but there is something in what Kirsty says. Nora is very attached to her brother.' He rubbed his chin. 'Maybe she's gone to the town centre and means to come back.'

Maud snorted. 'Unlikely, I'd say. I've seen girls like her before. Once they get the idea there are more exciting things beyond these walls you never see them again.'

'Maybe you're right,' Edward said. 'But then again, maybe not.' He turned to Kirsty, 'If she's gone to the town she'll probably be in the Overgate area. Maybe that's where the search should start.' He paused. Looking directly into Kirsty's eyes, he said, 'I'll help you look if you think it would be helpful.'

Kirsty looked away, not sure how to respond to him. She wanted his help, but he was having a strange effect on her again. Her skin tingled as if all her nerves were on the surface, warmth crept up from her neck to her cheeks. The heat of the fire became unbearable and she found it difficult to breathe. All she wanted to do was to escape from the stifling closeness of the room and Maud's disapproving stare.

'That would be nice,' she said her cheeks burning under the intensity of his gaze.

27

By late afternoon they reached the narrow cobbled lanes of the Overgate. Kirsty and Edward pushed into the crowd which closed round them in a heaving mass of bodies. The heat and smell was stifling in its intensity, and they were swept along with the tide of people, all hurrying somewhere up ahead. To her left, people surged in the opposite direction and, here and there, brave individuals struggled through the streaming masses, to reach a shop on the other side of the road. She could not help wondering how, even if Nora was here, they would ever find her.

Kirsty strained her eyes, constantly searching the throng of people, and her forehead tightened with the beginnings of a headache. The smell of horse dung, unwashed bodies, and rotten drains turned her stomach while the clatter of boots striking off the cobbles, and the gabble of countless tongues was deafening. A horse and cart pushed through the crowd, the iron-rimmed wheels adding to the din.

The crowds did not open up in front of her like they did when she was in uniform and, buffeted by passers-by, she had to fight her way through. Edward was more at ease, hailing many of them to ask if they had seen Nora, but they shook their heads and hurried on.

Most of the shops they passed were small and poky. Each one not much more than one dark room set below pavement level, in buildings that appeared to be on the point of collapse.

She stumbled on stone steps leading down into the first shop they entered. Once her eyes became accustomed to the gloom, she saw it was little more than a cellar. Racks of used clothes lined one wall. Coats, dresses, blouses and skirts hung limply in the stagnant atmosphere of the room. A mountain of shoes, piled precariously against the back wall, gave off an odour of sweat and mould while the fusty smell of old linen made Kirsty want to sneeze. The desire to leave as soon as possible was overwhelming.

'I don't think Nora would come into this kind of shop,' she whispered to Edward.

He laid a restraining hand on her arm. 'Maybe not, but Mags here sees most of what's going on in the Overgate. There's not much goes past her. Isn't that right?' He turned to the old woman behind the counter.

'Aye lad, that's right. There's not much as goes past me, and there's not much as I don't know what's a-happening.'

However, she shook her head when Edward described Nora. 'Saw a girl like that a couple of days back. She were hanging about the street with a young lad. Last I saw of them they were with Big Aggie. I worried about that, but then they all went off with a couple of bobbies. I mind thinking they'd be all right if the bobbies had them in tow. Never saw her again after that.'

'This is a waste of time,' Kirsty said several shops later. Her feet were aching from walking on the cobbles and she was tired of stumbling in and out of dingy shops.

'We'll go as far as the square. Everyone coming to the Overgate winds up there sooner or later.' He grinned at her. 'Only two more shops, I promise.'

'All right,' Kirsty said following him down the steps of the next hole-in-the-wall shop. The now familiar mouldy smell assailed her nostrils, but this time it was old books. She fingered a pile of second-hand comics heaped on a chair, ran her fingers along the spines of books stacked on a shelf. Everything was higgledy-piggledy with no order, and she saw copies of Shakespeare, Dickens and Annie S. Swan side by side, along with some historical works and an atlas. She promised herself she would return for a closer inspection once she had some free time.

'I see that shop was more to your taste,' Edward said as they emerged out of the gloom. 'Maybe this next one will be even better. It should appeal to your taste buds anyway.'

A distinctive smell of cloves, nutmeg and cinnamon met them before they entered the shop and, despite the darkness of the interior, Kirsty could see a fascinating array of confectionery. Jars of multicoloured sweets sat on the shelves, and trays under the counter contained horehound drops, striped balls, and humbugs, as well as some Kirsty had never seen before. 'Now this,' she said, 'is a shop Nora might be attracted to.'

However, the woman behind the counter shook her head in response to Edward's queries, and Kirsty's heart, which had lightened when she entered the shop, grew heavy with despair.

'Never mind.' Edward patted her hand. He turned back to the shop assistant. 'Give me two separate quarters of your humbugs,' he said. 'I think we need cheering up.'

'Here.' He thrust a bag of sweets into her hand as they left the shop. 'I doubt if you've ever tasted anything as good as Alice's home made humbugs.'

Kirsty mumbled her thanks and pushed the sweets into her handbag. 'I'll keep them for later,' she said, 'I'm not in the mood just now.'

'You don't think we're going to find Nora.' Edward, his voice low and sad, did not look at her.

'No. I don't think we are.' Kirsty was silent for a moment. 'I keep thinking something terrible has happened to her, and I don't know what to do.'

He reached out and squeezed her fingers reassuringly. 'We'll have a look around the market square and then I'll walk with you to the police station.'

The square was a piece of open ground, unpaved and lined with market stalls. It seemed as if the entire population of Dundee had crammed itself into all the available space. Kirsty closed her hand firmly around her handbag because she recognized a dippers' paradise when she saw one.

The stallholders all had their own individual brand of patter and the knack of talking without having to draw breath. Engaging their attention was difficult.

Kirsty and Edward stood on the edge of a crowd of people who were watching one stallholder with good-natured gullibility. He claimed to be able to turn base metal into silver with a special polish. Next to him was a juggler of plates and cups, enticing the crowd with details of the fineness of his china tea-sets, and telling them how cheap they were. No doubt the ones already packaged were less fine and of even cheaper quality. The crowd roared their approval as one cup fell to the ground and broke.

Edward seized his opportunity, but the stallholder shook his head. 'How d'you think I'd notice in a crowd like this, guvnor. I only clock the buyers.' Turning back to the gathered crowd, he complained, 'That's all my profit gone for today, mates.' He looked forlornly at the broken cup. 'Won't someone buy a set of china, so it's not a complete loss?'

Kirsty and Edward moved on, passing groups of people delving their fingers into twisted cones of paper to prise out chipped potatoes. They elbowed their way past the buster stall where the smell of frying chips, vinegar, hot fat and peas, hung in the air. But Edward did not stop until they reached the edge of the square.

'I don't like admitting defeat, Kirsty,' he said, turning towards her. 'But this lot wouldn't have noticed Nora if she'd been standing in front of them.'

Kirsty nodded her agreement. 'You're right,' she said. 'I think it's a waste of time to look any further because wherever Nora is, it's obvious she's not here.'

'If you need me, you know where I'll be,' Edward said, leaving her at the door of the police station.

Kirsty smiled her thanks and watched him walk away in the direction of the Refuge. Turning, she almost bumped into Brewster coming out of the door. She saw him frown as he glanced towards the retreating figure of Edward.

'What was all that about?' His voice was abrupt. 'And where have you been all afternoon?'

The rebuke and his obvious disapproval annoyed Kirsty. She knew she should hold her tongue and accept his criticism of her, but it had been a trying day and she did not have much patience left. 'I was not aware I was to be kept to a desk when I took this job, or that I needed permission to go out on an investigation, sir.'

'Perhaps not,' he said, icily. 'But that does not include going out with men friends when you are supposed to be working.'

'What are you insinuating, sir? I told you I was out on an investigation.'

A policeman scrutinized them as he pushed past to enter the station. He stopped in the doorway, to look back, before letting the door swing shut behind him.

'We are attracting attention here. I'll speak to you in my office. Inside, please.' He held the door open for her. She stalked in without looking at him, marching through the charge room with her head held high.

'Now, you'd better explain.' Brewster closed his office door behind her. 'You said you were on an investigation. What investigation?'

Kirsty flushed with indignation. He did not believe her and was forcing her into justifying her actions. Her anger grew. He was unwilling to recognize she was a professional policewoman who could be trusted. That had been evident when he had taken her to view the scene of the crime in the Howff, and afterwards at the morgue. He had spent a large part of his time trying to protect her, and treating her like some silly woman who might faint on him at any moment. What kind of picture did he have of her in his mind?

'I was investigating the disappearance of a child, sir.' She clasped her hands behind her back as she stood in front of him. 'Nora, the girl I took to the Refuge yesterday, has gone missing. Her brother reported it earlier today.' She stared straight at him, her posture and expression calm, although her insides were in turmoil. 'I left my report concerning the two children on your desk yesterday, sir.'

'But you did not sign the log book, and you told no one you were going on a further investigation.' Brewster fingered a pencil on his desk.

Kirsty bit her lip, she had forgotten about the log book. 'The duty sergeant knew, sir. He was here when Bert arrived at twelve o'clock.' She hoped Brewster would notice this was two hours before her duty started, but he did not. 'I thought I would have time to take him back and return to the office before the start of my shift at two o'clock.'

He ignored her reference to times. 'The duty sergeant informed me you had left the station with a child but did not tell him where you were going or when you would be back. It is important I know where you are at all times.' He glared at her. 'You do realize it puts me in an impossible position.'

'But . . .' Kirsty protested, angry because the sergeant knew where she had gone. Then she thought better of it and instead of continuing, mumbled, 'Yes, sir.'

'And this investigation, what exactly did you do?'

'I took Bert back to the Orphan Institute . . .'

'I thought you said you took them to the Refuge.'

'I did, sir. But Edward Gordon, the warden at the Refuge, placed them in the Orphan Institute.' Kirsty felt the heat rise from her body to suffuse her face. She realized, with a feeling of despair, how unorthodox it had been to leave the children with Edward.

'I see.' Brewster's voice sounded icy. 'And do you think that was the proper thing to do?'

'Probably not, sir,' she said, hating him because he was right. 'But he knew the children's homes in Dundee and I did not. Besides, he said the policemen habitually used him in that way because they trusted him and it saved them a lot of trouble.'

'I see.' Brewster sucked the end of the pencil. 'Go on then. You went to the Orphan Institute. What then?'

'I questioned the warden, Maud Gordon, and then I viewed the property.'

'Go on.'

Kirsty's voice faltered. 'I met Edward Gordon at the Orphan Institute, and he offered to help me look for Nora in the city centre. He accompanied me, and we questioned various people in the Overgate area.'

'You took a civilian on an investigation?' His eyes and voice expressed their disbelief.

'Yes, sir,' Kirsty mumbled. 'You see, Mr Gordon is more familiar with Dundee than I am.'

Brewster snorted and tapped the pencil angrily on his desk.

'And did you find the child?'

'No, sir. The warden at the Orphan Institute thinks she has run away, but I'm not so sure.'

'And Mr Gordon. What does Mr Gordon think?' Brewster's fingers tightened on the pencil which he now held in both hands.

'Mr Gordon concurs with her, sir.'

'I bet he does,' Brewster muttered below his breath. The pencil snapped. He sat and looked at the two halves as if he could not understand why it had broken.

Kirsty gripped her hands behind her back. She wanted to change position but did not. She too stared at the broken pencil and wondered what Brewster was thinking. There was something she did not understand here. Something Brewster was not going to tell her.

After what seemed an age he looked up at her with an inscrutable expression. 'I want to make something absolutely clear,' he said with a note of savagery in his voice she had not heard before. 'I am your supervising senior. You will work the way I want you to work. You will report everything you do, to me. If you leave the station, you will sign in and out of the log book which the duty sergeant holds. If I am not here you will leave a note of what you are engaged on and where you are, on my desk. Is that clear?' His voice had gradually risen as he spoke until he was almost shouting. 'And above all you will not involve any member of the public in your investigations. Especially not Edward Gordon.'

'Yes, sir,' she said, trying not to squirm under his furious glare.

'Write your report and leave it on my desk and then you may finish up for today.' He started to riffle through some papers in his in-tray and, without looking up, added, 'Tomorrow morning I will accompany you to the Orphan Institute to check if the child has returned. Wear your uniform.'

'Yes, sir,' Kirsty said, resisting an urge to slam the door as she left the room.

28

Kirsty woke after a restless night. In her nightmares she had confronted Brewster over and over again and his voice echoed in her mind, 'You have no place in the police force.' She shuddered, hoping this was not a premonition of things to come, but she had angered Brewster so often now she would not be surprised if it came to that. None of this showed as she walked briskly at his side that morning.

The Orphan Institute loomed in front of them at the end of a drive bordered with frost-silvered bushes and grass. Their footsteps, crunching on the gravel, announced their arrival. As they grew nearer Kirsty shivered, not sure whether her reaction was from the cold or her own feelings of apprehension.

Brewster wore his uniform today. He looked impressive, displaying an air of officialdom and authority unlike his more casual appearance when he was in plain clothes.

'I don't like the feel of this place,' he said as they approached the front door. 'It doesn't smell right.' He banged on the knocker with a hard authoritative action. 'If I were a child I wouldn't want to be here. No wonder they get runaways.'

Milly opened the door. Her eyes widened, and she hovered with her mouth open as if uncertain what to do. She shifted from foot to foot, her expression flitting between anxiety and fear.

'Tell Miss Gordon the police wish a word with her.' Brewster was at his most official.

'Yes, sir,' she squeaked, turning to run indoors.

Brewster pushed the door and stepped inside. Kirsty followed closely behind.

'It's not much better inside,' Brewster commented. 'And

where are all the children?'

'They are at breakfast, sir. And I can assure you the children are well looked after here. We attend to their physical and their spiritual needs, which is more than can be said for some other establishments.'

Kirsty had not heard Maud come up behind them, and she turned at the sound of her voice. She was dressed all in black and had a large bunch of keys dangling from her belt.

'I see you have returned to visit us, Miss Campbell. And you have not come alone.' Her tone was as forbidding as her expression.

'I am Detective Inspector Brewster, Miss Gordon. I am Miss Campbell's superior officer and we have come to make further enquiries regarding the disappearance of a female child named Nora.'

'Follow me.' Maud gave a heavy sigh that was almost theatrical. 'That girl has been more trouble than she's worth.' She opened the parlour door. 'All this fuss over a runaway, there are always runaways from children's homes. Sometimes they come back, and sometimes they don't.'

'I take it Nora has not returned?' Brewster strode to the window and stared out.

'No, and good riddance, I say. She was trouble that one.' Maud began to fidget with the keys at her waist.

'You've had runaways before, you said?' Brewster turned and looked at her.

'It's a common occurrence among the children brought here against their will.' Maud looked over at Kirsty as if indicating it was her fault.

Brewster's voice was deceptively quiet. 'Funny, I don't recall any reports of missing children filed by this establishment.'

Maud turned an ugly shade of red. 'Oh, we don't bother reporting them, sir. We reckon they'll turn up again or go somewhere else. You can't hold a runaway for long, sir. Bring them back and they'll run again.'

'I see.' Brewster turned to the window and studied the garden for a few seconds before walking over to Maud.

Standing right in front of her, he said, 'Well, this is one child that is on record as missing so we will be required to follow established procedures.'

Maud stepped back. 'What do you mean, procedures?'

'Procedures,' he mused. 'You won't have experienced them before if you never report anyone missing. Well, the first thing we have to do is make sure the child is not hiding on the premises, or locked in a cupboard or something like that. So I'll be sending some policemen to conduct a thorough search of the premises. We'll do it with a search warrant, so there are no complaints afterwards.'

'But . . . but the staff have searched the entire building.' Maud's voice heightened and her cheeks burned scarlet.

'Ah yes, but you might have missed something, mightn't you?' Brewster held out his hand towards her. 'We'll say good day then, Miss Gordon. Perhaps you'll get the wee maid to show us out.'

'Something decidedly strange about that place,' Brewster muttered to Kirsty as they left.

Brewster took Kirsty with him to the Sheriff Court to acquire a warrant to search the Orphan Institute. Obtaining search warrants was not always easy, and some sheriffs needed a lot of convincing. He was in luck, because it was one of the more amenable sheriffs on the bench, so it did not take him long to describe the situation, and why the search warrant was needed.

'It's important to do things properly,' he said to Kirsty as they walked the short distance to the police station.

She nodded, but he thought he detected a flicker of amusement in her eyes. She thinks I'm a pompous prat, he thought, but she brings out the official side of me, and I can't help wanting to put her in her place.

The charge room sergeant was studying a piece of paper and entering figures into a ledger.

'How many constables do we have spare?' Brewster could feel Kirsty's eyes on him. He gritted his teeth, aware he was at his most officious.

The sergeant looked up from his ledger and, as usual, scratched his head with the end of his pencil, before looking at the movements board attached to the wall.

'Most of them are out on patrol, sir. But Wells, Dixon, Ramsay and Henderson are in the constables' office writing up reports.'

'Send them to my office,' Brewster instructed.

He noticed Kirsty's disbelieving look, although she said nothing. But he could guess what she was thinking, and he had a sudden vision of his room crammed with four constables, as well as himself and the policewoman.

'On the other hand, I'll go to their room, it's bigger.' He strode through the connecting door. 'Well, are you coming?' He did not wait to see whether she was following him.

The rumble of voices emanating from the constables' office ceased when Brewster opened the door, but the cloud of tobacco smoke remained, hanging in the air in a hazy mist which nipped his eyes. He made no comment, knowing the men's smokes were sacrosanct.

'I want a complete search of the building,' Brewster instructed after describing the task in hand. 'While you are searching, Miss Campbell will question the staff. Any questions?'

The men shook their heads while they scrambled into their jackets and got ready to leave.

'Miss Campbell. You will present the search warrant to Miss Gordon and gain her co-operation. If you have any problems, call on one of the constables.'

He smiled grimly as he noticed the sidelong, resentful glances being directed at Kirsty, and he suppressed a tiny feeling of guilt at having put her in this position with the men. They would not like her being in charge of the search.

'I'll leave you to get on with it. Report to me when you get back.'

Later in the morning Kirsty returned to the Orphan Institute with four policemen and a search warrant.

'Leave the men to do the searching,' Brewster had instructed her, 'and while they're doing that I want you to interview all the staff and take their statements.'

'I don't know why you have to question my staff.' Maud's voice was sharp with displeasure. 'It will unsettle them, and it's so difficult to get good staff nowadays. It's not as if I haven't told you everything already.'

'It's all part of the procedure,' Kirsty said, trying to soothe Maud. 'And, you never know, they might know something of which you are unaware.'

'Hmph!' Maud snorted. 'You and your procedures. Coming here upsetting everyone.' Nevertheless, she settled Kirsty in the dining room and lined the staff up in the hall.

Kirsty walked past the scrubbed pine tables, which were obviously meant for children, and sat at the polished oak table in front of the window. She placed her notebook on the table with a pencil beside it before she walked over to the door.

'I'll see the first person now,' she said.

A thin acidic looking woman, who turned out to be the cook, entered the room first. Her answers to Kirsty's questions were short and to the point. 'I stay in my kitchen. The children aren't allowed in there unless I say so and, no, I don't know anything.'

The handyman was not much better. 'Oh, I sees the bairns all right. Little buggers, beg pardon for the language, miss, they're always in my way. Can't get the grass cut for them, and they runs over my vegetable garden. Good kick up the backside is what most of them need. But I don't know one from t'other. They all look the same to me.'

Next to be interviewed were members of the daily staff, and Kirsty interrogated two teachers, two wardens, a kitchen assistant and three cleaners. However, none of them lived in, so they had nothing to tell.

Then the night warden came in, bleary eyed and untidy. 'I don't know why I need to be pulled out of my bed to answer questions about a runaway,' she complained.

'I just want to check with you what happened on the night Nora went missing,' Kirsty explained.

'It's like I told Miss Gordon, She was there when I checked

the beds at ten o'clock, but she was gone at twelve o'clock. I checked the house and the back door was unlocked. I reckon she must have sneaked out that way sometime between ten and twelve o'clock.'

'Did you search the rest of the house?'

'There wasn't any need. The back door was open, and it's always locked when the children go to bed, so I assumed she'd run off.'

Kirsty scribbled in her notebook. 'Where do you go between bed checks?'

'The parlour,' the night warden replied. 'It's nice and quiet in there, and there's usually a good fire.'

'So you would not have heard anyone moving about the house.'

'No, it's a heavy door, and not much sound penetrates it.'

'Thank you,' Kirsty said, scribbling again in her notebook. She looked up. 'Who else is waiting?'

'Just Milly, miss.'

'Will you ask her to come in as you leave?'

Milly crept through the door, and her eyes seemed to look everywhere except at Kirsty as she walked across the room to stand before the table. Her fingers plucked at her apron, which was several sizes too large for her, and Kirsty thought she saw fear in the girl's eyes.

Cold air gathered in the room, and she shivered as a feeling of foreboding took possession of her. Shaking it off, she straightened her shoulders and studied the girl. She had a job to do.

'Sit down, Milly. You have nothing to be afraid of, I just want to ask you some questions.' Kirsty patted a chair; however, the girl remained standing.

'But I don't know nothing, miss.' Milly scrunched her apron between her fingers.

'How old are you, Milly?' Kirsty leaned her chin on her hands and looked closely at the girl.

'Fifteen, miss.'

'What kind of work do you do here?'

'I do most things. I wait tables, light the fires, do the

cleaning, scrubbing, polishing, dusting, laundry, that sort of thing.'

'But you don't look after the children.'

'No miss. That's Miss Gordon and the wardens as do that. There's some teachers as well to give them their lessons, but they don't live in.'

'You live in?'

'Yes miss, but I goes home to see Ma and Da on my day off.'

'I see,' said Kirsty. 'And how long have you worked here?'

'Since the summer miss.' Milly gulped. 'They've been good to me miss. If it weren't for this job I'd be in the mills, and that'd kill me miss. Got a bad chest see.'

'You like working here then?'

'It's all right miss. Got to work somewhere, don't I?'

'Tell me about Nora. Was she happy here?'

'Oh no, miss, Nora didn't like it at all. She were a right scallywag though, effing and blinding all over the place. Didn't think she'd leave without Bert though. Still, you never can tell.'

'Do the other children like it here, Milly?'

'Some does and some don't. Strange though, the boys seem to stick it better than the girls do.'

'What do you mean?'

'Well, the ones that run are all girls, so stands to reason they don't like it as much.'

'You have a lot of runaways then, do you?'

'Quite a lot, miss.' Milly's hands worked with the material of her apron scrunching and pulling at it until Kirsty was afraid it would tear.

On an impulse, Kirsty pulled out the photograph of Angel, the girl in the police cell. 'This girl, Milly. Have you ever seen her before?'

Milly's eyes widened. 'No, miss.' She gasped. 'I don't know her. I've never seen her before and will that be all miss?'

'Look again. Are you sure you haven't seen her before?'

'No, miss! No! I'm sure as sure can be.' The girl looked ready to collapse.

'Please, miss. I don't know nothing, miss. Can I go now,

miss? Please?'

Kirsty would have preferred to question her further, but Milly was so agitated she would be unlikely to give coherent answers, so she said, 'Yes, Milly, that will be all for the moment.'

Kirsty sat for a long time looking at the closed door, wondering why the girl was so scared. Was it the questioning, or a more sinister reason?

29

Brewster was preoccupied when Kirsty and the constables returned to the police station to make their report. His eyes, with their faraway look, seemed to reflect sadness buried deep within him. Not for the first time, Kirsty wondered about him. He seemed so full of contradictions.

It took him a few minutes to gather his thoughts before he asked them, 'How did the search go, did you find anything?'

The four constables shifted in their seats, obviously uncomfortable sitting round the conference table in the committee room. They purposefully kept their elbows and hands off the polished wood surface and looked to one another for support before answering.

'Well,' Brewster prompted. 'We don't have all day to sit here.'

'Nothing in the attics and the loft space except for old junk, cobwebs and spiders,' Constable Harry Wells reported. 'I moved things around, but there wasn't anywhere to hide. The dust was thick, hadn't been disturbed for years by the look of it.'

'What about you, Dixon?' Brewster sounded almost absentminded.

'I was with Constable Ramsay. We searched all of the upstairs and apart from one of the bairns who kept getting in our way there's nothing to report. The bairn wanted to look in all the rooms with us and was frightened we'd miss something, he even insisted we check every cupboard. He was all right though and showed us some places to look we'd never have thought of.'

'That would be Bert,' Kirsty explained. 'He's the missing child's brother.'

'Aye miss, he did say he was her brother,' Ian Dixon agreed.

Brewster rose and walked to the window. 'And you, Henderson? How did you get on?' he asked without looking round.

'Well sir, I searched all of downstairs and outside in the grounds but didn't find anything. Wasn't anything in the cellars either, except for the usual load of old rubbish. It was a regular jumble sale, everything under the sun but no young lassies.' Joe Henderson shivered.

'Spooky those cellars were, wouldn't want to go back down there in a hurry.'

'What about the old chapel? Did you have a look at that?' Kirsty asked.

Brewster glared his displeasure at her interruption but said nothing.

'Strange that.' Joe Henderson said. 'We managed to find a key, but it's been bricked up behind the door. And it's the same with the windows. Cook told us a funny story though. She seemed to think it had been used for black magic in the past, and that's why they had it bricked up.'

'Mmm,' Kirsty muttered. Cook had evidently been more forthcoming with the men than she had with her.

Brewster dismissed the constables and turned to Kirsty. 'What about you? Did you talk to all the staff?'

'Yes sir, but they don't seem to know anything. Not anything they want to tell me anyway. But I got the strangest feeling young Milly knew more than she was saying. I showed her the photograph of Angel, and I could swear she recognized her, although she denied it.'

The faraway look in Brewster's eyes intensified, but all he said was, 'That's interesting.'

'I could show the photograph to the other staff members. Do you want me to follow it up, sir?'

Kirsty bit down on her lip as she fought against her frustration. She wanted to shake him so he would pay attention.

'All in good time, Miss Campbell, all in good time.'

'But sir, it's a lead,' she protested.

'It's an instinct, Miss Campbell. It's not evidence.'

He gathered up the papers in front of him, and added them to the stack of files on the side of his desk. 'I have to go out. We'll discuss this later after you've written your report.'

Brewster toyed with his pencil. The Orphan Institute struck him as strange, but he couldn't put his finger on what was worrying him. Odd they had so many runaways though, and even odder they did not report the children as missing. If nothing else, it indicated negligence and a lack of care.

He fingered the reports on his desk. Nothing he had heard or seen had dissipated his concerns, and he was even more worried now. The place warranted further investigation and he decided to allocate this to one of the detectives on his team as a matter of priority. But first he needed to discourage Kirsty from further follow up because his gut was telling him danger lurked there.

He had seen how crushed she was when he dismissed her suggestions, and watched her flounce out of his office. But he did not want her returning to that place. The problem, however, was that she was like a terrier with a bone. She got an idea, and she would not give up on it. The only thing he could do was keep her busy with other things while he and his team did the investigating.

He shrugged, he had done what he could to discourage her, and he hoped she wouldn't get up to much mischief while he was out of the office.

An ink-blot splattered onto the paper as Kirsty wrote the last word of her report.

'Damn,' she muttered, she'd been trying to avoid that.

She reached for the blotting paper, but the report was readable, and she had no intention of writing it again. Brewster would have to accept it. He had been so offhand about the investigation he might not look at it anyway, which would be a pity because she had put a lot of effort into getting the facts right.

She mulled over the contents as she walked up the corridor to Brewster's office. If she left the report on his desk, and he did go to the trouble of reading it, he could not fail to see how her suspicions of the Orphan Institute had increased. She thought of all the girls who had gone missing from that place. Waifs and strays missed by no one other than those who lived or worked at the Orphan Institute. She thought of Angel, suspecting she had been one of those girls. She thought of the murdered girl and her suspicions crystallized into a horrific certainty.

She had to speak to someone. But who? Brewster did not want to listen to her and, when he did, he was dismissive of her ideas. She wondered if he had an ulterior motive for discouraging her interest in this case. Talking to the constables would be useless as well, because they would refer to Brewster. That left Edward. And Brewster had told her, in no uncertain terms she should not involve him, although he had not given any reason other than saying Edward was a member of the public. But Kirsty knew the police sometimes involved members of the public when it was felt they could help, so what was different about talking to Edward?

Kirsty made up her mind. Brewster could not choose her friends for her. Moreover, she did not think it right for him to dictate that Edward should be excluded from the investigation when he was already involved. Edward had placed Nora and Bert in the Orphan Institute, and he might take more children there. That gave him a right to know if there were suspicions about the establishment.

'I'm going outside for some fresh air,' she said as she passed through the charge room. She ignored the log book because she did not want the sergeant to know she was going to the Refuge. 'I've got the beginnings of a headache.' She did not bother to tell him the headache had a name and that it was Brewster.

Kirsty found Edward in the kitchen at the Refuge. He was slumped over the table, sound asleep. The evenness of his breathing was so soft it could hardly be heard floating out of his lips in fast, shallow puffs of air. And he had a vulnerable look which she found appealing. She stood for a moment looking at him before approaching and laying her hand on his shoulder. He woke immediately sitting up with a start and looking at her through sleepy eyes.

'You're tired,' she said gently. 'And yet you still found time to help me.' She sat down on the bench beside him and, daringly, because he reminded her of a sleepy child, she laid her hand on his. It felt warm and soft, and lay motionless beneath her fingers as if he was afraid to move it.

'I would always have time to help you, Miss Campbell. You only have to ask.' He placed his other hand on top of hers in a hesitant manner.

Now her hand was entrapped in his hands, she became uncomfortably aware of his closeness. She hesitated for a moment and then withdrew it from his grasp.

'I didn't mean . . .'

'I know you didn't, Kirsty. But I'll always be here for you.' His voice was low and warm.

It was one of the things she liked about him, the musical quality of his voice, which left her feeling cared for. That, and the humour radiating from his eyes and face. He was looking at her now in a good-natured quizzical way.

'But you haven't come up here to tell me I'm tired, I can tell. Has something else happened?'

Kirsty hesitated. The Orphan Institute was run by his cousin. 'How close are you to Maud?' she asked.

'She's my cousin, that's all. She came to Dundee last year, and before that we hadn't seen each other since we were children. Why do you ask?'

Kirsty studied his face, but it only showed curiosity. 'I don't know how to tell you this Edward, but I suspect something funny is going on at the Orphan Institute, and it's possible Maud might be involved.'

He looked mystified. 'I'm not sure what you mean.'

'It seems that a number of girls have gone missing from the Orphan Institute over the last six months.'

'But there are always runaways from children's homes and institutions, you should know that.'

'Yes, Edward,' she said gently. 'But that's not all. I showed one of the staff the photograph of Angel. You know, the mystery girl in the cells I told you about. And I could swear she recognized her.'

'That's interesting. Did she say she recognized her?'

'No, but I could tell from her expression. She looked stunned. That's the only way I can describe it. Stunned.'

'Well, I don't know what to say, Kirsty, but if this staff member did recognize the girl, then you need to ask Inspector Brewster to question her.'

'Brewster doesn't believe anything I say. He thinks I'm imagining everything.'

'I see. But surely if Inspector Brewster thinks there's nothing in it . . .' his voice tapered off and a look of embarrassment crept over his face.

'It's not imagination. I can feel it in my bones.' Kirsty realized as soon as she said it, how foolish it must have sounded.

'I'm sorry, Kirsty, but this is all very difficult to take in, and I'm finding it difficult to think Maud would be involved in anything underhand.'

Kirsty stood up. 'I can see this has been a shock and perhaps I was wrong to confide in you. I'll leave now.'

'Fool! Fool! Fool!' she muttered, clattering down the stairs. Of course he would have trouble believing me, she thought. I should have remembered earlier Maud was his cousin. Well, I'll just have to do this on my own.

30

On Kirsty's return to the police station, she slumped onto her chair and stared moodily at the desk. The files on the missing girls lay undisturbed where she had left them. She pulled one of them over and opened it. Emily Tait, she read, aged eleven years, last seen at the Overgate market. Lives in the Hilltown, mother a millworker, father unemployed. There would not be much point in going to see Emily's mother until the evening, she thought, and little hope of anyone at the market being able to provide information if yesterday's debacle was any example.

Discontentedly she pushed Emily's file away. What she wanted was to examine Angel's file, although she knew every detail off by heart. She looked for it on her desk, but could not find it. Brewster must have retrieved the file. Pushing her chair back she got up. It would be in his office, and surely he could not object to her having it again.

His office was in its usual disarray, but logic told her the file could not be far from the desk because the case was active. She riffled through his in-tray, his out-tray, and prodded the files balancing precariously on the end of his desk. Eventually, she found it on the floor behind his chair. Picking it up she returned to her own orderly office to study its contents. But, despite reading everything again, she could not find anything significant.

She rested her chin in her hands, remembering Milly's reaction to Angel's photograph. She wished now she had asked the rest of the staff at the Orphan Institute if they recognized Angel. However, Milly had been the last person she interviewed, and it had been pure instinct that made her produce the photograph. Even now she was not sure what caused Milly's reaction. Maybe it was just the girl's habitual state of anxiety. But Kirsty could have sworn it was more than that. Damn

Brewster for not allowing her to follow it up.

Her thoughts turned to Angel rocking backwards and forwards, enclosed in her own small world of unimaginable horrors. She wanted so desperately to help the girl. If only she could break through Angel's protective shell, the case might be solved.

Closing the file, Kirsty rose and entered the corridors leading to the female cells. Arriving at the iron gate, she rattled it to attract the turnkey's attention.

'How are you getting on?' Annie asked, unlocking the gate to let her into the cell area.

Kirsty shrugged. 'Not too badly I suppose. But I never know where I am with Inspector Brewster, half the time he's picking fault with me and the other half he's never there.'

'Aye, poor Jamie. I wouldn't want his life. He has a hard cross to bear has our Jamie.' Annie unlocked the cell door and, swinging it open, looked in. 'The poor lamb's much the same. Fair out of her mind she is.'

Kirsty passed through the door wondering what Annie had meant when she said Brewster had a hard cross to bear, but as she approached Angel she pushed the thought out of her mind to concentrate on the girl.

'Hello, Angel. I've come back to see you, just as I promised.'

The girl looked at her from underneath lashes so fair they were almost invisible. She looked cleaner, her hair had been brushed, and she sat on the edge of her mattress, although she was so still she could have been a statue.

'Are they looking after you all right?'

Kirsty approached the mattress-covered bench.

'Do you mind if I sit down?'

The mattress moved when she sat on it. She leaned towards the girl, wanting to hold her, take her hand, anything that might provide some comfort.

Angel moved further away, pressing herself into the wall.

She tried to make eye contact with Angel, but the girl refused to meet her gaze, and Kirsty was overwhelmed with the feeling of desolation surrounding her.

'You seem quieter today,' she said, 'so maybe you won't mind if I ask you a question.'

The girl remained motionless.

'Remember you told me your name was Angel.'

She did not respond.

'Well, Angel, you don't seem to remember much, but I think I know where you lived. Would you like me to tell you?'

Kirsty thought she saw a flicker of something in the girl's eyes, but was not sure.

'I think you lived at the Orphan Institute, in the Perth Road.'

A keening sound escaped from the girl's lips.

'Am I right, Angel? Is that where you lived?'

The keening sound stopped. The girl turned her face away from Kirsty, refusing to look at her.

'I talked to Milly, Angel. Do you know Milly?

Angel stared at the wall and did not move.

'You must have family somewhere, Angel.'

Silence.

'Your mother, Angel. Where is your mother?'

Silence.

'Your father?'

Silence.

'Aunts, uncles?'

Silence.

'Someone? Anyone? Please tell me.'

The girl's face remained fixed on the wall. Angel had retreated into her silent hell.

Unable to penetrate the wall the girl had erected between them Kirsty had to give up and hammered the cell door to be let out.

'I'll come back and see you again, Angel. I'm not giving up on you,' she said as she left the cell.

Angel continued to occupy Kirsty's thoughts, and she forgot to ask Annie about Brewster. She was sitting at her desk when she remembered.

Picking up a pencil she rolled it between her fingers. She wondered how it would appear if she returned to the cell area to ask Annie what she meant. Reluctantly she decided this would not be a good idea as it might lead to speculation about an interest in Brewster which did not exist.

A light tap on the door interrupted her thoughts, and she called, 'Come in!'

The duty sergeant poked his head round the door. 'There is a gentleman to see you, miss, and I said I'd ask if you would see him.'

'Did he give his name?' Kirsty asked, her thoughts immediately turning to Edward Gordon.

'No, miss. But I know him. He's that solicitor fellow, Simon Harvey. He's probably come to talk to you about the girl in the cells.'

'What do you mean? Why would he want to ask me about Angel?'

'Solicitors often want to discuss their clients, miss.'

'You mean Simon Harvey is Angel's solicitor?'

Kirsty thought of Angel with the blood trickling down her forehead after her solicitor's visit, and wondering at the time how he could have upset her so much she had banged her head with such force.

'Yes. Didn't you know?'

Kirsty shrugged her shoulders. 'No, I didn't.'

'He's in the charge room if you want to see him now, miss.'

Kirsty stood up, but then she thought about what she and Simon Harvey had been discussing. Maybe Simon Harvey had come to talk about Angel, but it was more likely he was here to discuss her problem and it would not do for the duty sergeant to know she had seen the solicitor on a professional basis.

'I'd prefer to see him here, sergeant.'

The duty sergeant frowned his disapproval.

'Don't worry,' Kirsty said, tartly. 'I'll leave my office door open.'

'I'll show him along then, miss. Will I?'

Kirsty suppressed a laugh as she watched the duty sergeant march along the corridor. The poor man was more hidebound by convention than she was.

A few moments later Simon Harvey followed the duty sergeant to Kirsty's office. He waited until the sergeant left and then sat down in front of her desk.

She looked at him accusingly. 'You didn't tell me you were Angel's solicitor.'

He studied his finger nails. 'You didn't ask. Besides, I didn't know you were involved.'

'The turnkey told me she was terrified of you. Why would that be?'

Simon laughed without humour. 'Probably because I'm a man. In any case from what I can see she's terrified of everyone.'

'Does that mean you won't be able to help her?'

'I can help anyone, but that's not why I'm here. I came to tell you I've arranged an appointment with the elder Mr Bogue for this afternoon. I wondered if you would like to accompany me?'

He studied his finger nails again. 'You don't have to come if you don't want to.'

Kirsty pushed her doubts about Simon Harvey to the back of her mind and thought for a moment. She was not keen to meet Mr Bogue, but he had to understand she wanted nothing to do with him or his family, and she was prepared to do anything to get this message across to him.

However, getting away from the office without divulging the reason would be problematic. Brewster had been adamant about signing the log book, but if he was not in the office then he was unlikely to find out. The appointment with Mr Bogue would be unlikely to exceed half an hour, and surely no questions would be asked if she were away for that length of time. If Brewster did happen to be in the office she could combine it with a visit to Emily Tait's home, even though she knew the girl's mother would be at work. She felt guilty about the intended deception, but could see no other way.

'How will you handle the meeting?'

She remembered her earlier interview with Simon. 'I thought we were going to deny Ailsa is my daughter so won't it be an admission that she is?'

'I do not intend to mention Ailsa at all. I will say you have been giving consideration to his offer of a family merger and you are not interested. If Ailsa is mentioned, we will handle that in the most appropriate manner we can.'

The Bogue factory was larger than her father's mill and concentrated more on weaving than it did on spinning. Kirsty could hear the staccato clack of the looms as the gateman led them across the cobbled quadrangle towards the office block.

'Mr Bogue will see you in the boardroom,' he said, opening a door and leading them into an oak-lined corridor. A large stained glass window reflected a myriad of colours onto the gleaming linoleum and lustrous wood.

The gateman tapped at a panelled door at the end of the corridor before opening it and beckoning them to go in.

The boardroom they entered was dominated by a massive mahogany table, the polished wooden surface glowed red in the reflected light while high backed leather chairs surrounded it.

Mr Bogue stood at the end of the table. His hand grasped the silver knob of a walking stick which he leaned on for support. 'Good afternoon,' he said, staring curiously at Kirsty's uniform. 'Sit down!' He gestured to two of the leather chairs. He remained standing whilst they seated themselves.

'You wanted to see me? Something to do with Miss Campbell I understand.' He eased himself into a chair at the head of the table. 'Well, now you are here what can I do for you, Simon?' His voice held an easy familiarity.

Kirsty stared at her hands. They were clasped loosely in front of her, and she could see the faint misting on the table where they rested. Simon had not told her he was acquainted with Mr Bogue. She wondered how well they knew each other.

'Miss Campbell understands from her father that you are interested in a business merger with him.'

'That is correct. I had suggested a merger with William. His mills have not been doing so well lately, and I thought he might be receptive to the offer.' His forefinger drummed on the silver top of his cane.

'I'm not sure I understand, sir. Why would you want to merge with a less profitable business?' Simon's full concentration was on Mr Bogue. He had hardly looked at Kirsty since they had entered the room.

'I don't know how much you know about the textile industry, Simon, although I'm sure Miss Campbell will have an understanding of the business.'

He glanced towards Kirsty who met his gaze without blinking.

'William Campbell's mills concentrate heavily on spinning, but his weaving sheds are small and inadequate and his looms are old and out-of-date. My factory, on the other hand, has the latest machinery and the best weavers in the business. I did have a spinning mill up in Lochee, but it burnt down last year, and it's not worth the time and money to rebuild. A merger is the sensible option.'

'I see,' Simon paused. 'Therefore what you are proposing is a business merger.'

'Of course.' Mr Bogue smiled stiffly.

'Therefore, this merger would not be dependent on the family merger you also proposed.'

Mr Bogue's eyebrows angled downward in a frown and his eyes narrowed. 'A family merger would make sense. My son has wasted enough of his life on frivolities, it is time he settled down, and I understand Miss Campbell is unattached.' He pursed his lips and stared at Kirsty. 'From what I can see it would be an excellent match. William was agreed on that.'

Kirsty clamped her teeth together to prevent herself from shouting at him. Who did this man think he was with his mergers that didn't include any discussion with the parties involved? Unable to contain herself any longer she opened her mouth to speak. Simon laid a restraining hand on her arm, and she pressed her lips closed on the anger threatening to spill out of her.

'My client asked for this appointment to put forward her point of view.' Simon's voice was deceptively quiet.

'You wish to draw up an agreement. That can easily be arranged.'

'Not quite, sir. My client wishes you to know she is not interested in a family merger, however, from what you say this will not prevent your business merger from going ahead. I wish you luck with it and I also wish you luck in finding an alternative merger for your son. Good day, sir.'

Simon rose and helped Kirsty out of her chair. Together they left the room.

'What good did that do?' Kirsty muttered as they walked along the corridor. 'How will that protect Ailsa?'

'What it did, Kirsty, was to let Mr Bogue know I am acting for you and that whatever he tries will be contested by me. You might find that will be enough.'

Kirsty stared at him with disbelief. 'Are you sure you know this man and what he's capable of?'

Simon's voice as he answered her was clipped and professional. 'I know Mr Bogue as well as anybody in Dundee. I've had dealings with him before.'

'Is that so. Well I've had dealings with the Bogue family as well and I'm not as convinced as you are.' Kirsty's eyes sparked with all her pent up anger, and she had difficulty curbing her tongue with this cocky young lawyer who seemed so sure of himself. 'But then, if you're such great friends with him maybe I've made a mistake putting my business in your hands.'

'I can assure you, Miss Campbell, you have not made a mistake.'

The silky-soft tone of Simon Harvey's voice did nothing to quell the distrust taking root in Kirsty's mind. She could not shake off the feeling that he was Bogue's man.

31

'I'll be in touch,' Simon Harvey said when they parted company outside the courthouse.

Kirsty nodded and hurried towards the police station. She had been gone longer than she had anticipated and she hoped Brewster was not waiting for her, scowling his displeasure.

'Has Inspector Brewster returned?'

The duty sergeant shook his head.

Recalling her decision to revisit the Orphan Institute, she added, 'Do you think he will return to the office this afternoon?'

'I doubt it, miss,' the sergeant said, 'the afternoon shift's almost over. Shouldn't you be thinking of going home yourself?'

Kirsty glanced at the wooden clock hanging on the wall, and was surprised to see the time was later than she thought. 'I've one or two things to do first,' she said.

The sergeant nodded, showing no interest. He showed even less interest when she left a short time later.

At home, she scooped a spoonful of tea-leaves into the brown earthenware teapot and covered them with boiling water. The meat pie she had bought on her way home was still warm, and taking it out of its paper bag she took a bite out of it while she changed from her uniform into a brown skirt and woollen blouse – she would be less conspicuous in plain clothes. She washed the pie down with gulps of hot tea. Pulling on her tweed coat, she fastened the buttons, filled her pockets with coins for the tram fare, grabbed her cloche hat from the hook behind the door, and left without a backward glance.

She got off the tram one stop before the Institute and strode up the road. There were no street lamps this far from the town centre and the moon was masked by clouds. Glancing around to ensure no one else was in the street she slipped through the

Orphan Institute's iron gates, thankful for the darkness which would conceal her arrival and allow her to look around without being seen.

Gravel crunched under her feet. Rising to her tiptoes she headed for the bushes lining the drive, stumbled over one of the boulders bordering it, and merged into the shadows of the shrubbery.

The dampness of the grass penetrated her shoes, and a light breeze riffled through the leaves bringing with it a chill which seeped through her clothes and numbed her skin. She knew silence was essential, and clamped her teeth together to stop their chattering.

The building, even more forbidding in the darkness, loomed in front of her increasing her sense of foreboding. Drawing nearer she could discern the black shapes of several cars parked haphazardly in the drive, and a light gleaming from the dining room windows. Kirsty, keeping to the shadows, crept up to one of the windows and, standing on tiptoe, peered in. However, all she could see were the backs of the men present.

As she watched, one of the men turned and Kirsty recognized Simon Harvey. She suppressed a gasp of surprise. What was he doing in the Orphan Institute? If, as she suspected, something evil was going on, was he part of it?

Her fingers slipped on the cold stone of the window sill, and she sank back on her heels. If the window had been lower, she might have been able to hear what they were saying. Leaning her back against the wall she wondered what she should do next. Brewster would have known, but he was not here, and he would not approve in any case.

She did not hear the approach of the motor car until its headlights flashed across the ground in front of her. In the split second before the place where she had been standing was illuminated, she threw herself under a bush. Peering out from behind the shrubbery, she watched as a chauffeur got out of the car and opened one of the rear doors. Several seconds later the occupant emerged, and as he stood up something about his tall frame and his stance reminded her of someone. He leaned into the car and helped an older man out. A man with a silver-handled cane.

The two men approached the front door. The younger one turned briefly to say something to the chauffeur, and as he did so his features were illuminated by the car headlights. Kirsty drew in her breath with a hiss. It was Johnnie Bogue. The older man was unmistakably his father.

Her suspicions about the Orphan Institute increased even more. Why were all these men meeting here? What were they up to?

She waited until the chauffeur parked the car, only then did she think it safe enough to leave the shelter of the bush. She stood up and turned to peer into the window, but someone had closed the curtains and there was nothing to be seen but a sliver of light where they met in the middle. The chink was too small to see anything through, and the murmur of voices indistinct. Disappointed, she turned away, there was nothing to be gained by remaining.

The pressure of kneeling on the soggy earth had left her knees damp and muddy, and her fingers were grazed where they had scraped the wall when she dived for cover. But she did not care about that, for now she had something to take back to Brewster. However, remembering his scepticism she knew it might not be enough to convince him. She needed more, but how to get it was a problem. She had failed to find out why these men were gathering here on such a dark and dismal night, and could not help thinking that if their business was innocent they would have met during the daytime.

Wind rustled through the bushes, and she shivered. It was time to leave, but she could see the glowing tip of the chauffeur's cigarette in the car blocking her exit up the drive. However, if she went round the house he would have his back to her and she could escape unseen.

It seemed to take forever to circle the house, avoiding obstacles and bushes that might rustle, but she could not afford to hurry in case she made a noise. Instinctively she knew she would be in danger should her presence be revealed to those men meeting inside.

Reaching the back door she was tempted to enter the

building to find out more, so she turned the door knob. The door was locked. Beyond it were lighted windows, and she guessed it must be the warden's parlour. She crept below one of the window ledges and reached up. She had to see who was in the room.

Through an opening in the curtain, she saw Maud pacing in front of the fire, seemingly alone in the room. After a moment, she stopped and faced one of the armchairs. 'We can't go on like this, you must know that.'

Kirsty was unable to see who was sitting in the chair, so she moved to the next window hoping to get a better look. Unlike the first window the second one was tightly closed, muffling the voices, and with the wings and high back of the chair effectively obstructing her line of sight she returned to her original viewpoint.

'It's easy for you to say we have to.' Maud's voice sounded bitter. 'You're not the one taking all the risks. We have to go before it's too late.'

She paced some more and then collapsed on the sofa sitting at right angles to the chair. Reaching over she grasped the man's hand, but all Kirsty could see was the sleeve of his jacket. 'Please, please, you must let me go. Haven't I done everything you asked of me? What more do you want?'

'It's too soon. Besides, I have another game organized for tomorrow that should prove lucrative.' The man's voice was harsh, but despite the unusual accent it sounded strangely familiar to Kirsty.

'The new game is too dangerous. I said that at the time but you wouldn't listen. You never listen.'

'It's all arranged. So you will do as you are told as you always do.' He shook off her hand.

Maud rose, and grasping one of the chair wings she leaned over him.

'But you don't understand. The police were here today. And the policewoman, she's getting too close to the truth. She managed to get something out of Milly.'

'Milly doesn't know anything. She just serves.'

'But the policewoman suspects something. I'm sure of it.

You'll have to take care of her before she spoils everything.'

The man laughed, a menacing, guttural laugh. 'Oh, I'll take care of her all right. I know just what to do about our Miss Campbell.'

Maud turned and walked to the window.

Kirsty gasped, ducking down below the window ledge.

Pulling the curtains shut, Maud turned and addressed the man in the chair. 'See and make a good job of it then. Otherwise we'll all regret it.'

Kirsty pulled herself up but, as her face drew level with the window, the curtains opened, and Maud placed her hands on the window frame to push it closed.

Kirsty had no opportunity to avoid Maud's startled eyes. She dropped down below the window again and scuttled to the edge of the building.

She stopped, and looked wildly around for an avenue of escape. But running to the drive was out of the question because she would have to return to the front of the house where everyone was meeting. That only left the wall separating the property from the railway track.

Her feet made no sound as she ran over the grass. Reaching the wall she hoisted herself up onto it. But when she looked over the other side, the drop looked much too steep. Momentarily she balanced on the top of the wall wondering if she should risk it anyway, but commonsense prevailed and she lowered herself back into the garden.

Creeping along the wall until she reached the old chapel she squeezed herself into the narrow space behind it. When the back door opened and light illuminated the garden, she was well hidden.

Kirsty found it difficult to breathe, clamped as she was between the boundary wall and the chapel. Her breathing became shallower, and everything seemed distant. But she continued to press herself firmly into the restricted space.

She listened to her heart thump. It seemed to combine with a strange singing noise in her ears and a feeling the chapel wall was vibrating in time with her heartbeat. She tried to decipher where the singing was coming from, and could not make up her mind if it was inside or outside her head.

Darkness enfolded her, and she became disconnected from reality, experiencing the strangest sensation of floating upwards while her body remained on the ground.

Even in that unreal state she gasped for breath before the darkness could claim her forever.

But the chapel walls were unyielding, and she was unable to draw air into her lungs.

32

Desperately she struggled for breath, knowing once she slipped into unconsciousness she was finished. But her chest was held in a vice leaving no room for the intake of air. Her arms dangled uselessly at her side but, with a superhuman effort, she forced the palms of her hands against the wall and pushed. She slid a few inches sideways and was able to grasp the corner of the chapel and heave herself free. She collapsed onto the grass and, oblivious to the noise she made, pulled air into her lungs in excruciating mouthfuls. Gradually the singing noise in her ears faded. The darkness lifted, and she could see and hear again.

Maud's voice floated in the distance sounding strange and disembodied. 'I wasn't imagining it. I'm sure I saw someone in the garden.'

The far off voices faded, a door slammed and she heard the crunch of someone's feet walking up the drive. Kirsty waited, until all sounds died away and the silence had lasted several minutes, before she moved. It was time to make her escape.

Her legs felt too weak to support her after her ordeal but, digging her fingers into the rough stone of the boundary wall, she pulled herself upright. While she gathered her strength, she looked curiously at the chapel but avoided touching it. She knew it was crazy, but she had a premonition the building had tried to claim and hold her, and she had been lucky to escape.

'Imagination can be a dangerous thing.' She heard her mother's voice echoing over the years and felt as foolish now as she had done all those years ago. But she could hear the singing noise again as the blood rushed to her head.

'This is ridiculous,' she said to herself, and to prove it she placed her hand on the chapel wall. It was only cold, damp stone.

Turning away from the building she walked towards the road

making sure she stayed in the shadows, close to the shrubbery and trees at the side of the drive.

When she reached the gate, Kirsty heaved a sigh of relief. However, her nerves were taut, and if anyone was pursuing her she would be in clear view as she left the drive. Nervously she looked back, but no one seemed to be following and the house was quiet, so she walked through the gates.

She walked straight into Edward. Her heart gave a thud as she looked up at him. Surely it had not been his footsteps she had heard walking up the drive? He could not be involved with what was going on at the Orphan Institute, she could not be so wrong about him, could she?

And yet, Edward introduced her to Simon Harvey, and Simon was obviously involved because she had seen him at the meeting in the Orphan Institute.

'Why, Miss Campbell, what has happened to you?'

'What do you mean?' she said, through stiff lips.

'You are all muddy and dishevelled. You look as if you've had an accident.'

Kirsty looked down at herself. Her coat was covered in caked mud as were her shoes, and her knees poked through the holes in her stockings. Her hands were dirty and grazed, and she dreaded to think what her face and hair looked like.

'Have you just come from the Orphan Institute?' She had to know. She had to be sure.

He shook his head. 'No, I was on my way there. Do you want to come with me? You could get yourself cleaned up. I'm sure Maud wouldn't mind.'

'No! No! I can't go back.' Kirsty looked up at him. 'And I can't tell you why because you won't believe me.'

'I would believe anything you said.' Edward put his arm round her shoulders. 'Now tell me what it's all about.'

'I can't. You didn't believe me this afternoon.'

'I found it hard to take in what you were telling me this afternoon. It was, shall we say, a shock. That's why I've come up here tonight. To confront Maud and see what she has to say. She is my cousin after all, even if I don't know her all that well.'

'You believe me?'

'Well, let's say I'll suspend my disbelief for the time being. But you have to tell me what is going on.'

Kirsty leaned into him. 'Take me away from here, Mr Gordon, before someone from the house comes.'

They walked down the road towards the town centre and Kirsty told him all that had happened. When she had finished talking, Edward tightened his arm around her shoulder. 'I wish I'd been with you. If I hadn't been so stubborn this afternoon, I would have been.'

He was silent for a moment. 'I don't know what's happening there, but I can answer one of your mysteries. The meeting would be the Board of Governors of the Orphan Institute. They meet in the evening, and that would explain why Simon, Mr Bogue and his son were there. However, I don't know what to make of what you overheard in Maud's room, and I don't much like the sound of it. Are you going to get Detective Inspector Brewster onto it in the morning?'

Kirsty gave a harsh laugh. 'What's the point? He doesn't believe me now. He thinks I'm a silly female who imagines things so if I tell him he'll think I'm being hysterical.'

'If you're sure that's the right thing,' Edward said, although his voice sounded uncertain. 'Promise me something then. You won't go to the Institute again without me, will you?'

Kirsty shivered. 'I'll never go there on my own again.'

'I think that's wise,' he said. 'Now I'd better get you home so you can get cleaned up.'

'Would you like to wait for a tram?' Edward tightened his arm on her shoulder. 'The only thing is you're muddy, it might be better if we walk to the town, it's not far?'

Kirsty nodded, and as she seemed to have no objection to his arm, he kept it on her shoulder while they walked along the road.

'You know, I think you should tell Inspector Brewster. I'm sure he would investigate your concerns.'

Kirsty laughed. 'There is no way on this earth I'm going to

involve him.'

'Well, as long as you don't come back on your own, I suppose that will have to do.'

'But, Nora. We haven't found her yet, and I'm sure the answer lies inside the Orphan Institute.'

Edward sighed. He did not want Kirsty to return to the Orphan Institute. But she was a determined woman, and he was afraid she would return, and from what she had said that might be dangerous.

'Leave it to me,' Edward said. 'I will return tomorrow and have it out with Maud. If she knows anything, I'll get it out of her.'

He glanced at Kirsty, but she seemed lost in thought.

'You have to trust me,' he said. 'Will you do that?'

She nodded.

33

Friday, 7 November 1919

The dream had come to Kirsty every night that week. Always the same, she was stumbling around in the cemetery bumping into gravestones and feeling damp tendrils of grass and weeds clutch at her legs like clammy fingers.

The night was dark and neither stars nor moon provided any illumination. She panicked, thinking she might be blind. But then she saw lights like fireflies, dancing and flickering and drawing ever nearer to her.

She wanted to run, but her feet would not move because fingers of grass bound her to the ground. She reached out her hand and laid it on the flat surface of the stone. And she knew it was the tomb of Jonathan Bogue because her finger was tracing the outline of his name.

Fascinated, she watched the lights draw ever closer, and still she could not move. Dropping to her knees she tried to pray, but no words came. Mud oozed between her toes, and the earth was wet and cold on her knees for she wore no shoes or stockings.

The lights were now so near she could almost touch them and she saw they were candles. She strained her eyes to see who carried the lights, but they had no faces and their clothes were as black as the candles under the flickering flames.

Once again Kirsty heard the harsh voice as it chanted, 'I know what to do with you, Miss Campbell.'

She tried to stand up, but her legs would not bear her weight and the chanting group encircled both her and the tomb. The child lay in front of her, spreadeagled on the flat gravestone. She was dressed all in white, and she had no face.

Kirsty's mind screamed, 'You cannot do this. She is a child.' But no words came.

The blade of the knife reflected light from the candles,

gleaming like a constellation of stars. The knife descended. The child screamed. And Kirsty woke with a start.

Her nightgown was damp with perspiration and the sheet was knotted round her body. She struggled free, reached down to pick up the blankets from the floor, wrapped them around herself and shivered on the edge of her bed in the gloom of the early morning.

The gleam of the descending knife remained vivid in her mind, filling her with horror.

Never before had the dream gone so far. Always she had awakened as the lights gathered in front of the gravestone.

She rose and fumbled for matches. Striking one, she lit the candle at the side of her bed. Shadows danced around the room, but now the darkness had dispersed they no longer seemed so menacing.

Carrying the candle through to the front room she lit the gas jet, filled the empty kettle with water, and placed it on the gas ring. She had not been eating properly this week, but she was not hungry and only wanted a cup of tea.

While she waited for the kettle to boil, she thought about the dream. She supposed it could be a logical follow-on from her worries about Angel, Nora, the other missing girls, and her daughter, Ailsa. But it made Kirsty wonder whether her dreams were a warning or a premonition, or whether they were the result of her confused emotions.

She did not know.

Brewster was waiting for her when she arrived at the police station. He was wearing his official face and manner. 'Something's happened,' was all he said as he ushered her through to his office.

Kirsty followed him, the first tentacles of unease entwining themselves around her heart and mind. She had not followed up the other cases and the files remained unopened. She had kept putting them off because of her obsession with Angel and the Orphan Institute. And now something had happened, maybe another murder. Why else would he be so grim?

Something was wrong.

'Sit down,' he said pulling the chair forward. He looked at her from under frowning brows as if uncertain how to begin.

Kirsty's stomach churned. She knew instinctively that whatever he was going to say, concerned her. She had not done what he ordered. She had defied him. Was it the end of her career in Dundee?

She forced herself to sit still, but her fingernails dug into the palms of her hands as she clasped them in her lap. 'You said something had happened, sir,' she said. Her anxiety masked by the calmness of her voice.

'Yes,' he said. 'I have your mother and father in an interview room.' He paused. 'I'll take you to them, but I wanted to prepare you first.'

'My mother and father?' Whatever Kirsty had expected, it was not this, and she was unable to hide her surprise.

Although she had anticipated they might interfere with her life, she had never thought they would take it as far as this. She was confused as to why they would appear at her place of work and anger rose up within her.

How dare he? Just because she would not agree to her father's plans, it did not give him the right to meddle in her life.

'What are they doing here, sir?' she asked in as calm a tone as she could manage. 'They've never taken an interest in the police force before.'

'I hardly think it's an interest, Miss Campbell.' Brewster's voice was gentle as he perched himself on the end of the desk. Leaning forward he took her hands into his own and looked into her eyes.

Kirsty moistened her lips. He had never touched her before, but his hands were warm and gentle on her own.

'What is it?' she demanded.

His hands tightened on hers. 'I don't know how to break it to you,' he said. Then heaving a deep, ragged sigh, he continued, 'It's your . . . sister, Ailsa, Miss Campbell. She's missing. She vanished from school yesterday, and your parents are distraught. They seem to think she may have been snatched by the Bogue family.'

Kirsty thought of Johnnie Bogue, with his hands on Ailsa, and shuddered. Then she thought of the elder Mr Bogue, and his connections with the Orphan Institute. She remembered Nora and all the missing girls. She thought of Angel sitting in the police cell on a murder charge. And the unknown murdered girl. And she thought of her Ailsa who was now missing as well. Had she been abducted by Mr Bogue or his son, Johnnie, or had she gone to join all the other missing girls, wherever they were?

A pain coursed through her stomach. She wanted to moan but did not. 'Why didn't they come and tell me? Why did they come to you first?' Her voice was angry and accusing.

'They're worried, Miss Campbell. The first thing they thought of was to report it to the police. They didn't know you were under my command, and I didn't know they were your parents.'

Brewster slid off the desk and stood in front of her. 'You have to understand, Miss Campbell, they are sick with worry.'

His hands still held hers, and she looked at them as if she could not understand why they were there. 'Why? Why?' she moaned, more to herself than Brewster.

'Your parents have explained why, Miss Campbell,' he said, and his hands tightened even more on her own. 'I have two men standing by, and I'll take them with me when I go to interview Mr Bogue.'

'I'm coming as well.' She looked into his face but could see no confirmation that he agreed. 'I have to come,' she said stubbornly. 'Can't you see that?'

'No, Miss Campbell.' His voice was gentle. 'You can't, because you're personally involved. It would not be correct procedure.'

She knew he was right but, she still wanted to go. 'But I have to do something, and I have to know. You must understand that.'

'I understand it Miss Campbell, but you cannot go. I'll take you through to your parents. They need you.' He withdrew his hands from hers. 'Try to get them to go home. They cannot do any good by staying here. Go with them and I'll get word to you as soon as I know anything.'

'You need me to help find Ailsa,' Kirsty protested. 'How can you find her without me?'

'We'll turn Dundee upside down to find her. Now go home with your parents and allow me to get on with my job.'

'Yes, sir,' Kirsty said bitterly, knowing it would not matter what she said, Brewster would never change his mind once he had made a decision.

Kirsty hesitated at the half-open door of the interview room. She did not want to see her parents' misery because it would mean facing up to the past, and admitting they had feelings and could be hurt.

It would also mean having to recognize how much pain they must have suffered when she left, as well as acknowledge the pain they were now feeling at the loss of another daughter. No matter that Ailsa was Kirsty's daughter, as far as they were concerned Ailsa was theirs. How could Kirsty help them cope, when she was not coping herself?

Robert and Ellen Campbell sat at one side of the square oak table dominating the interview room. Kirsty could not help noticing that her father's normally erect frame had wilted. He sat with his arm around her mother whose head was buried on his shoulder. He was not paying her any attention, and seemed lost in his own thoughts.

They did not notice her when she entered. Standing there, looking at them, Kirsty struggled to find the correct words to say. After what seemed an age, she coughed gently, and he looked up at her.

'Ah, Kirsty,' he said, straightening. 'At last you've arrived.' His brows furrowed and for a moment she thought he was going to cry. 'I presume Mr Brewster has informed you what has happened?'

'Yes, father. He has told me.' Kirsty paused, not knowing what to say to him. It had been a long time since she had been able to talk to him about anything.

'Ellen, my dear. Kirsty is here,' he said in a gentler tone stroking her mother's hair.

'Kirsty?' she said as if not knowing where she was. She looked at her husband with dazed eyes. 'Have they found Ailsa yet?'

'No my dear, but we will find her and Inspector Brewster has put his best constables on to looking for her. They are searching Dundee as we speak. And now Kirsty has come.' He looked up at his daughter. 'Your mother has had a shock, Kirsty. I was fool enough to tell her about Bogue's threat. It distressed her so much I thought it was going to be the end of her.'

Kirsty crossed the room and sat down beside her mother. 'Inspector Brewster will find Ailsa, mother. You just have to be patient.' She reached over and grasped her mother's hand. It felt cold and limp, like holding the hand of a corpse.

Her mother seemed hardly aware of anyone in the room. She glanced at her hand which rested in Kirsty's, and looked up with a curious expression in her eyes. Then clutching at her, she whispered, 'He will find my Ailsa, won't he?'

Despite the plaintiveness of her mother's voice Kirsty had to suppress a spurt of resentment. She had no right to be angry. She knew, better than anybody, that when her mother took over Ailsa's care the child became hers in every sense, and it had effectively negated any role Kirsty had to play. It was too late now to start feeling resentment.

'Of course he'll find Ailsa.' Kirsty was not convinced but made her voice sound confident and reassuring. 'He wants you to go home now. You'll be much more comfortable waiting there.' Kirsty looked at her father and nodded her head. 'It's for the best.' She tucked her arm through her mother's, and said, 'Let's go home.' She did not release her hold until they were outside.

34

Brewster heard Kirsty and her parents leave the interview room, and he followed them down the corridor. Their distress was obvious and he wanted to reach out and help, but did not know what to say other than he would do his best to find Ailsa. Kirsty, in particular, looked defeated, her normal ebullience missing. She seemed a different person altogether.

He was surprised to find he preferred the tough and challenging Kirsty, and that he had grown to like the policewoman.

Their car was waiting outside, and the chauffeur hurried to open one of the doors. Mr Campbell helped his wife into the back seat and tucked a rug round her knees. Kirsty did not look at Brewster as she got in beside her mother, and she seemed oblivious to his presence. But he watched them get into the car, and stood at the pavement's edge long after it was gone.

Eventually he returned to his office, his thoughts in turmoil. He had seen a different side to Kirsty due to what had happened, and he now knew far more about her than he wanted. A sensitive young girl lurked under that hard exterior, and he knew she was suffering. The best place for her while the search for Ailsa went on, was at home with her parents, and he hoped she would stay there, although, from what he already knew about Kirsty, he doubted this.

No one spoke on the journey home, and Kirsty was sure they were all praying Brewster would find Ailsa unharmed. She stared at the back of her father's head and the droop of his shoulders. He was obviously worried about Ailsa but, she was painfully aware, that was not the only worry he had at the moment, and his posture reflected his current level of stress. His mill business was in a bad way, and she wondered if her mother knew, although she could not imagine her father discussing business concerns with her.

Kirsty also recalled Brewster saying that her father had expressed a suspicion the Bogues might be involved in Ailsa's disappearance, and she wondered if her father had changed his mind about wanting her to marry into the Bogue family.

The wind increased and whistled in and around the car once they left the city streets. She pulled the rug firmly round her mother and tucked it in, although her mother did not seem to be aware of the cold. Sitting, with her hands clasped firmly in her lap, she seemed frail and vulnerable. Kirsty wanted to hug her and hold her close but did not know how to overcome the barrier between them owing to her prolonged absence from their lives.

They were all cold and windblown by the time they reached the house where Kirsty had grown up. And, even before the car stopped rolling up the drive, the front door opened. The familiar figure of Meggie, her old nanny, appeared.

She bustled over to the motor car as it drew to a halt in front of the house. 'The wee lass. Have ye brought her back with ye?' Her smiling face saddened as she looked into the car. 'I see ye havenae, does that mean she's still missing?'

Kirsty wanted to jump from the car and cry on Meggie's shoulder, wanted to feel her arms around her body, soothing her, just as she used to do when Kirsty was a child. But she was unable to move. A great weight seemed to press on her, holding her fast in the back seat of the car.

The screams and wails Kirsty found it so difficult to give vent to ripped through her head as her mother burst into tears. 'Hush now, Ellen. Inspector Brewster's taking care of it.' Her father leaned into the back seat and awkwardly patted his wife's hand, oblivious to his daughter's distress.

'I know,' she mumbled through her tears, 'but what if he can't find her. What if she never comes home again? It will be like it was when we lost Kirsty. All those years wondering and worrying, not knowing if she were alive or dead. Is it going to be the same with Ailsa?'

Kirsty cringed. Guilt gripped her for having subjected her mother to distress. And her despair, at the loss of her daughter, increased.

'Meggie,' her father said. 'Help Mrs Campbell in and take her upstairs so she can lie down. I think it will help if she gets some rest.'

'Yes, Mr Campbell.' Meggie led an unprotesting Ellen towards the house.

'Come inside, Kirsty. This is still your home, you know.' Her father's voice was stiff and formal. Kirsty recognized in him the characteristic they shared. An inability to express feelings, and realized he was as distressed and uncomfortable as she was.

Kirsty's restlessness would not allow her to settle in one place. She wandered through the house, not sure where she wanted to be or what she wanted to do. Even the library, which was her favourite room, had no attraction for her. She drew first one book from the shelf only to replace it and finger another and another. The sitting room was empty and bleak while the kitchen, which was the heart of the house, seemed lifeless. Kirsty guessed Meggie was with her mother, and she hesitated at the foot of the stairs. But, not wanting to face her mother yet, she turned away without putting her foot on a single step. Instead, she went into the parlour, to join her father.

She wanted to sit beside him, take his hand into hers and cry on his shoulder, but could not. They had never been that kind of family, although she remembered Ailsa sitting with him on her last visit home. Maybe her father had mellowed, or maybe he was only like that with Ailsa. Misery enveloped her and she felt the slightest tinge of envy because he loved her child more than he had ever loved her.

Like a caged animal she paced backwards and forwards in the parlour, until her father snapped, 'For goodness sake, Kirsty, sit down.' But he was no better, and before long he marched outside. 'Going to get some fresh air,' he said, gruffly.

Kirsty watched him walking over the grass to the gazebo.

His shoulders were hunched, and he looked like an old man.

On an impulse, she ran outside and followed him. Sitting on the bench beside him she looked with blank eyes towards the River Tay.

The sun glittered on the water, and several small boats bobbed up and down with the tide, but neither Kirsty nor her father paid any attention to them.

The silence between them was endless and awkward. Kirsty wondered whether her father was aware of her presence. She had an urge to reach out to him and wondered if he felt the same. But she did nothing.

Eventually, her father cleared his throat. 'Brewster? Is he a capable policeman?' He did not look at her.

'He's one of the best.'

Kirsty was not sure if she believed that, but her father needed the reassurance.

'If anyone can find Ailsa, he will.' The silence stretched between them again.

'Where do you think she might be?'

'I don't know, father.' She paused. 'You told me Mr Bogue was interested in her. Do you think he might have taken her?'

Her father's eyes were fixed on the horizon. 'That was my first thought because I couldn't think of anything else. But I've known Bogue for a long time, and I can't believe he would do anything like that. And young Johnnie doesn't seem to be interested in anything except having a good time.'

'I went to Mr Bogue, you know.' She paused. 'With my solicitor. I told him I wasn't interested in marrying Johnnie.'

Her father turned to look at her. 'You have a solicitor?'

'Yes, father. I briefed Simon Harvey because I was afraid Mr Bogue would try to take Ailsa.' She returned his gaze. 'You're not angry, are you?'

He sighed. 'Disappointed maybe,' he said. 'But not angry. Bogue wouldn't have done anything, you know.'

'That may be,' she replied. 'But Ailsa's not here. Is she?'

They sat in silence for a few more moments. 'I think I'll go back to the house now.' Kirsty told her father.

Her steps were heavy as she walked over the grass. She was

not sure what she had expected from her father, but it was obvious he did not have anything to give her. Nor did she have anything she could give him.

They were like strangers to each other, and she did not know how to make it any different.

35

Brewster came to the Broughty Ferry house just before lunch. She had been watching for him and opened the door before he reached it. Dashing down the steps, she demanded, 'Have you found Ailsa?'

He did not answer her directly but, looking around, asked if her parents were present.

Kirsty froze. She felt as if she had been turned to stone, and inside her was emptiness where there should have been feelings. But, like an automaton, she invited him in and said, 'You can wait in here,' before turning to do what he asked.

She did not need him to tell her there was no news, she could see it in his face. She had always known they would not find her. If the Bogues had Ailsa, they would never admit it to Brewster.

Hurrying into the parlour with an expression of hope on his face, her father said, 'Well, have you found her? Have you brought her home?' His eyes searched the room. 'She's not here, does that mean . . .?'

'I'm sorry sir, but we have not found her yet. I have interviewed Mr John Bogue, but he assures me he has never seen the girl and is not interested in her. Apparently he was with a lady friend at the time the child went missing, and he is sure she will vouch for him. Likewise, the elder Mr Bogue told me he was at his factory yesterday afternoon, then had dinner at his club and went on from there to a committee meeting in the evening. The servants say that no child has been to the house since last Christmas. And, I'm afraid, that's all.'

Kirsty's stomach knotted. Although she had known before Brewster started to speak the news would not be good, she could see her father had been hopeful. He loved Ailsa and was suffering, unable to understand what was happening and why he could do nothing to help. Crossing the room, she put her arm round his shoulders, expecting him to rebuff her. But he did not. 'It's early yet. Mr Brewster will find her.'

Her father looked at Brewster. 'What now?' He sounded like a little boy who was lost, instead of the forceful, authoritative man Kirsty thought she knew.

'We will go back to the school, sir. Someone might have seen something. And we will put all our missing persons procedures into operation. In the meantime, I suggest you all get some rest.'

Kirsty followed Brewster out. 'I need to do something,' she said. 'I can't just sit here.'

'I have told you before, Miss Campbell, there is nothing you can do. You cannot be part of the investigation because it is personal to you.'

She noticed a peculiar expression in his eyes. Maybe he was holding something back, something he was not telling her.

'I can't stay here anyway. I'll go back to the office after lunch. I have to find something to do.'

'If you must, Miss Campbell. I am sure you can find things to do, but one thing you must not do is become involved in this investigation.'

Brewster placed a hand on Kirsty's shoulder. She swayed under his touch. He wanted to console her, assure her he would find Ailsa, although the search so far had been fruitless and he did not like to make promises he could not keep.

Kirsty's body tensed, and he removed his hand. He had no right to touch her, and their closeness did not feel right. He sensed she felt the same.

He cleared his throat, and his voice was more brusque than he intended. 'I would have preferred you to stay here, Miss Campbell, but if you insist on coming in I'll leave some files on your desk, but remember what I said, you must not become involved in this investigation.'

'Yes, sir.'

She sounded unusually submissive. Brewster stared at her,

and wondered what she was planning, but her demeanour gave nothing away.

'I meant it, Miss Campbell. Stay out of the investigation.' However, he knew deep within himself he could not trust her to do that.

Lunch was a tense affair with only Kirsty and her father at the table. Ellen was sleeping a drug-induced sleep in her bedroom, and Meggie had vanished to the old nursery.

'I need to return to Dundee.' Kirsty pushed the meat on her plate from one side to the other. 'I'm not doing any good here, and at least I can help look for Ailsa if I go back.'

'Do you have to?' He reached across the table and grasped her hands.

She stared at them for a moment. How often had she wanted to feel the touch of her father's hands? And now, the only thing between them was embarrassment. 'Yes, I have to,' she whispered.

Refusing his offer of the car, because she could not bear to be cooped up anymore, she walked down the road to Broughty Ferry Railway Station.

The empty southbound platform was windy and cold. Flying dust and sand swirled along the platform, peppering her face with needle-sharp grains and almost blinding her. Kirsty turned her face away from the wind, thrust her hands inside her pockets, and pulled her tweed coat tighter round her body.

She perched on the end of a bench, but the hard wooden spars dug painfully into the back of her legs. The pressure was nothing, however, compared to the ache in her heart.

Unseeing, she stared at the crowds on the platform. Her thoughts focused on her father. He was a confident if somewhat overbearing man, more likely to force his opinions on others rather than listen. Kirsty was accustomed to him expecting her to do his bidding, and her continued refusals had been the cause of much of the trouble between them.

Ailsa's disappearance had changed him. Suddenly he did not know what to do. He had not wanted Kirsty to leave, clinging on to her as if her presence would make things all right. But despite years of quarrels and disagreements Kirsty preferred him as he had been, blustery and argumentative, rather than dependent.

A young woman sat down on the bench beside her, and Kirsty's eyes were irresistibly drawn to the baby cradled in her arms. Normally the sight of a baby would have left her unmoved, but as she watched the young mother she recalled her first glimpse of Ailsa.

'It's a wee girl,' the young nun had said as she placed the baby in Kirsty's arms. 'What will you name her?'

Kirsty had not thought about names. She had never had any motherly thoughts or feelings when she had been carrying the baby, and waiting for the birth had been a chore. 'I'll be glad when it's over,' she had confided in her mother. So, when she looked down at the tiny baby, the love surging up within her, suffocating in its strength, took her by surprise.

'I never knew babies were so tiny,' she said to the novice as she looked at the baby's red wrinkled face and inspected her fingers and toes. 'I'll call her Ailsa.' When her mother finally came and claimed the baby from her, Kirsty, for the first time in her life, had been firm with her and would not allow her to change the name.

During the first few weeks when Kirsty nursed Ailsa she grew to love her more and more. It could not last though, and she had to let her mother take over the care of the baby when they returned to Dundee from the west coast nursing home.

'You have no choice in the matter,' her mother said. 'Everyone must believe the baby is mine otherwise you will be unable to remain at home. The disgrace would be too much.' Kirsty knew her mother was right in what she said, and anyway she was young and had no choice but to accept the situation. So she deliberately blocked her feelings for her daughter. She hardened and convinced herself she did not care. But now, as she listened to this baby crying, she could feel herself filling up with the tears of a lifetime.

A tear escaped and trickled down her face. Dashing it away with her hand, she stood up and walked to the furthest end of the platform, so she would not have to hear or see the baby. She peered up the railway line in the hope she might see the approaching train, but there was no sight nor sound of it.

Unable to remain still, she paced back and forth, stopping every now and then for another look until at last the train roared into the station, belching steam and cinders and smelling of smoke. Kirsty climbed into a carriage and slammed the door behind her. Minutes later she left the train at Dundee, moving rapidly away from the locomotive, hissing and steaming loudly in the enclosed space.

Emerging into the fresh air she stood for a moment, undecided whether to return to the police station or walk the streets in the vain hope of seeing Ailsa. A young girl ran past, hair flying out behind her, and a sudden pain probed her heart. Thoughts of Ailsa filled her mind, and she knew she had to make some attempt to look for the child who might, even now, be somewhere in Dundee.

She strode out in the direction of the Green Market where there were stalls and fairground rides.

Men, women and children jostled and closed in on Kirsty. Raucous music blared from the roundabouts and shrieks of laughter echoed from the swing-boats. Smells of fish, meat, putrid vegetables, and sweat, rancid and overpowering, caught at her throat until she was gasping for breath. Young girls with long hair seemed to be everywhere. But no Ailsa.

Finally, she gave up and left the market. She walked along street after street, peering up closes and pends. She stopped passers-by describing Ailsa to them and asking if they had seen her. She dropped coins into the hats of several beggars, and ran towards the screams and laughter of children playing. All with no result.

A war veteran, perched precariously on a slab of wood with four wheels attached, caught her eye when she turned into the Seagate. The stumps where his legs should have been protruded grotesquely over the edge of his home made cart.

He shook his head when she questioned him. 'I'm sorry miss, but the bairns are scared of me, so they don't come near. I'll keep an eye out though.' She tossed a copper in the cap balanced on his upper legs, and he saluted her with one hand touching his forehead. Placing his other hand on the pavement to propel himself along, he trundled out of sight.

Eventually, she reached the Wellgate and in the distance saw some children playing on the steps leading up to Victoria Road. One child ran to the top of the steps and swung from the railings. The girl's hair swung out behind her. Kirsty's heart gave a lurch and her mouth dried up in expectation as she hurried towards her.

She stopped when she was within calling distance. 'Ailsa?' She was afraid to breathe.

The girl turned and stared at her with large, frightened eyes. 'I didnae do it. It wasnae me.' She turned and ran off up Victoria Road, the hair that was so similar to Ailsa's, streaming out behind her.

Breathing deeply, Kirsty retraced her footsteps down the Wellgate, into the Murraygate and from there into the High Street. She continued to scan the crowds, even though it seemed to be a waste of time. Ailsa was not helpless, she was thirteen. If she were anywhere in Dundee, she would have found some way to ask for help. Kirsty knew she had to accept Ailsa was not on these streets, neither was Nora, nor any of the other missing girls.

But even knowing the search was hopeless she still bypassed the end of Reform Street which would have taken her to the police station, and instead, entered the narrow lanes of the Overgate.

She instantly regretted it. The cobbles dug into her already aching feet, and she was in no mood to push through the crowds of people, crowds that did not include Ailsa. So she left the Overgate and took the shortcut back to the office.

Barrack Street was deserted. She reached the first gate to the Howff and realized this must have been the beat the constables had been covering on the night of the murder. She stood for a moment, looking through the iron spars. A vault to the left of the gate effectively masked part of the graveyard, but she could still see some considerable distance inside.

Further up the road she came to a double gate with black,

heavy-looking iron spars held firmly closed by a large padlock. She had a clearer view of the cemetery from this gate and she was convinced if anything unusual had been happening that night it should have been possible to detect from this angle.

Following the line of the wall she reached the railings bordering the front of the graveyard. Her hands gripped the cold metal, and she thought how ordinary it looked. Secluded paths meandered between the gravestones, while grass, bushes and trees bordered the walls and paths. It looked like any other burial ground.

A shiver crept up her spine. Despite the innocuous look of the graveyard, she could not forget this was where a brutal murder had taken place. With a distinct feeling of unease she turned her back on the cemetery, and changing her mind about going directly to the office she made her way home to change into her uniform. She needed the reassurance it would give her.

36

'I didn't expect to see you back here today,' the duty sergeant said, glancing at her over the top of his polished counter. 'Are you feeling all right?'

He did not expect a reply, and she did not give one, instead, she said, 'Inspector Brewster hasn't returned yet, has he?'

'I've not seen him since he left this morning.' He looked at her over the top of his spectacles. 'He's a good man is the inspector. If anyone can find your sister I'm sure he will.'

'Thanks,' she murmured. 'I'm sure you're right.' But she was not sure at all because she had the feeling that Ailsa's disappearance was linked to Angel and Nora and the other missing girls.

What was it the strange harsh voice had said? That he would take care of her, and he knew just how to do it. Did that mean he would do it through Ailsa? She shivered at the remembrance of the menace in that voice, and although she accepted her job could be dangerous, it had struck a chord of fear within her.

The clack of her heels sounded unnaturally loud as she hurried down the corridor. Reaching her cupboard of an office she pushed the door open, and collapsed into the chair behind her desk. Her brain was buzzing, jumping from one thought to the next, trying to work out where Ailsa might be. Everything seemed to link back to the other missing girls. White slavery kept surfacing in her mind, but this was Dundee, not London. Still, her thoughts fixated on it. And, if it were a white slavery operation, there was little time to be lost before the girls were shipped out to some foreign brothel. The answers had to be in Angel's tormented mind, but she had not yet found a way of unlocking it.

She lowered her head to the desk and groaned. Nothing inside the file was of any use, and she had read it so many times her brain felt as if it would burst. What else could she do to get Angel to talk?

Was there anything she had missed? She raised her head, pulled Angel's file out of her desk drawer and stared at it, but the file would not be any help because she could have recited everything in it, word for word. But what about the files on the other missing girls? Maybe if she compared all the files there might be a common factor. She would do it now, it was better than doing nothing.

It took a few moments for her to realize the other files were no longer where she had left them. She stared at the wooden desktop. The files contained all her notes and observations and now Brewster must have removed them. She groaned again. He could not even trust her with the files now.

A sense of failure and uselessness swept over her, and she stared bleakly at the wall. What was she to do? How could she find Ailsa and all the other missing girls if they sent her packing, back to London? Well, she would not let that happen to her without a fight. Maybe Dundee did not want her, but before she left she had to find out where the girls were, as well as solve the mystery of Angel and the body in the cemetery, and if Brewster did not like it, well, that was too bad.

She tried to ignore the tight band circling her head, and the ache behind her eyes. She rubbed her forehead with her knuckles, sure she would be able to find the answer, if only she could concentrate.

Lifting a pen she began to write her report on the previous evening's events. Brewster would not like it because he had not known she had returned to the Orphan Institute, and would never have sanctioned it in any case. But she no longer cared what he thought. Writing furiously, she attempted to put all her suspicions on paper as well as the facts, but her words were disjointed, and all she was able to think of was the strange, harsh voice, and the fear. The answer was in that building, and she was convinced Maud was involved.

Laying the pen on the desk she leaned back in her chair and tried to sort out her thoughts, put the puzzle together. Something strange was definitely going on at the Institute. But what? If

Nora was still in the building, where was she? And if she found Nora, would she also find Ailsa?

The building had been searched and nothing found, although the strangeness of the bricked up chapel continued to worry her. She remembered hiding behind it and sensing a vibration through the walls and a strange singing noise in her ears, like a religious chant of some sort. She had put it down to her imagination at the time because she had been overwrought.

But what if it had not been her imagination? What if there had been chanting and singing?

Shaking her head at the absurdity of the thought she closed her eyes. But then she remembered her dream of the night before and how the lights had flickered towards her as if coming from nowhere, rising out of the ground as if from some awful tunnel leading straight out of Hell. Her mind drifted, seeing the lights, watching the advance of the faceless ones, feeling the fear again. A fear generated by her growing realization the missing children could be in great danger. A chill spread through her body, and she shivered involuntarily.

Her limbs stiffened in a paralytic spasm held fast by her fear. But, instinctively, she knew if she did nothing, more children would end up in the morgue like the nameless child she had seen on Monday. She could not allow that to happen.

Closing her eyes yet again she visualized those horrific knife cuts, and the child's vacant lifeless eyes. And she could hear Davvy's voice echoing, 'Will ye be wanting the lassie to see the body too?'

Her skin prickled remembering how Davvy's eyes watched her when she was climbing out of the subterranean depths of the morgue, and Brewster's voice telling her about the underground corridors linking that place and the police station.

Kirsty's eyes snapped open. That was it. Tunnels. Underground corridors.

The Orphan Institute was previously Jonathan Bogue's house. Jonathan, whose grave was in the Howff. Jonathan who, as the story went, had been involved in necromancy. If the chapel had been used for anything other than religious services, he would not have wanted his secrets to be discovered accidentally. Therefore, he would have had it bricked up and gained access by other means.

That was it. She had to be right.

She remembered Constable Henderson saying the cellars were eerie. So, the entrance to any secret passage was bound to be there. And where better to hide anything or anybody than a bricked up chapel.

She knew she had to investigate further, and she did not want to waste time. Briefly scribbling a note for Brewster she attached it to her report, which she then left on his desk.

Recalling her promise to Edward Gordon that she would not return to the Institute without him, she hurried out of the police station and ran along the road to the Refuge. But the place was deserted with no sign of Edward.

The empty kitchen looked bleak and unfriendly without his presence, and she wondered where he could be. Crossing to the window she looked out. Down below the street was busy, but none of the small figures was Edward. Further down the street where it merged with Ward Road and Barrack Street, she could see the Howff. But the only people inside the cemetery were the usual meths drinkers.

Turning, she went on an exploration of the rest of the rooms. Several doors led off the top landing. Three of those doors opened into dormitories, lined with beds but little else. She found nothing to suggest that boys lived there, no clothes, books or personal possessions of any kind. Other doors led to a small study with desk, chair and filing cabinet; a cupboard with mops, brushes and a bucket; a tiny windowless room with a truckle bed; and finally a door that was locked.

Devoid of any life the rooms had a deserted and abandoned air as if no one had ever been there. Looking around, Kirsty could sense nothing of Edward at all.

Sitting on the top step of the stairs deep in thought, she watched the dust motes swirl in their relentless passage down the light rays filtering through the stained glass window. Last week she had never been inside this building, and now she was more familiar with it than her own flat. And yet, without Edward, it lost its friendly atmosphere and was only a building.

Strange how much she had come to rely on Edward over the past week. And yet she knew so little about him. She knew he was good and kind and cared about others. But what else did she know about him? She did not know where he came from, how old he was, how long he had lived in Dundee. He certainly was not local because his speech did not reflect the long drawn out vowels of the Dundee dialect. And what about Maud? She was his cousin, but he had said he did not know her well, and that she had only recently come to Dundee.

But Kirsty did not know anything about his family or the strength of feelings he might have towards them, even ones he did not know well. Was he a person who considered blood more important than anything else? She did not know. Initially he had been reluctant to believe her when she told him of her suspicions about his cousin. But when she met him last night he had indicated a willingness to question Maud.

Kirsty acknowledged it must be hard for him to accept his cousin might not be all she seemed to be, so maybe it was as well he was not here today because she might have involved him in something he would find difficult.

Kirsty stood up and slowly made her way downstairs, suddenly hoping Edward would not appear.

But her determination to investigate the Orphan Institute was undiminished. She could not give up now even if the building held unknown dangers for her.

37

Kirsty sped back to the police station, although she would have preferred to go directly to the Orphan Institute. But she needed to find someone to accompany her. She could not explore the cellars on her own.

The door slammed behind her, making the duty sergeant look up in astonishment. 'Has Detective Inspector Brewster come back yet?' she demanded, knowing the answer before he answered.

'No miss, not yet.' The sergeant shook his head. 'Has something happened?'

'Not really,' she muttered through gritted teeth. 'I needed to discuss something with him.'

'I'm sure he'll be in later on. Won't it wait?'

'It doesn't matter,' she said, turning away. Brewster was never around when she needed him. She was halfway to the corridor door when she whirled round. 'What about Constable Henderson?' She remembered him saying the cook had told him a strange tale about the chapel. At the time, Brewster had only been interested in the outcome of the search and dismissed him before he could go into details.

The duty sergeant pulled a watch from his pocket. Glancing at it, he said, 'He's out on the beat, but he should be back in about ten minutes. I'll send him along to your office if you want.' Holding the edge of his pocket with one hand he swung the watch on its chain. It landed neatly inside.

Kirsty forced a smile. 'Nice trick,' she said as she left the charge room for her cubby hole of an office.

Joe Henderson tapped on her door several minutes later. 'You wanted to see me, miss?'

'Yes, Constable Henderson.' Kirsty looked up at him and smiled. 'Sit down,' she said, pulling a blank sheet of paper

227

towards her. 'I want you to tell me about your search of the cellars at the Orphan Institute, and also what the cook told you about the chapel in the grounds.'

Ignoring the chair, he perched himself on the end of her desk where he sat swinging one of his legs.

'What d'you want first, miss?'

Kirsty thought for a moment before replying. 'Cook's story, constable. What was it she told you about Jonathan Bogue and the chapel?'

Joe fidgeted. 'Mind if I light up a fag, miss.' Without waiting for an answer he took the pack of cigarettes from his pocket, shook one out and placed it between his lips. Striking a match on the sole of his boot he held it to the end of the cigarette and inhaled until it glowed strongly. 'Ah, that's better.' He stared at the spent match before tossing it onto the floor.

'You know, Jonathan Bogue's only a legend,' he said. 'He's been dead so long nobody knows what he was like. Dundee folks use him to make their children behave, like the bogeyman. They tell them, "Jonathan Bogue's coming to get you!" That's why I didn't pay too much heed to the cook's story.'

'Never mind that.' Kirsty leaned forward. 'Tell me the story.'

'The cook said her granny told her. She said her granny wouldn't have liked her working in Bogue's house, but granny couldn't interfere now she's dead and gone.' Joe blew a smoke ring and watched it spiral upwards.

'What she told me, miss, was that Jonathan Bogue practised devil worship and some thought he was the devil. He had the chapel special built and used to hold his devil worshipping services there, black masses and the like. She told me some folks said he used to make sacrifices on an altar that was covered with a black cloth and there wasn't a cat or a dog to be found in the whole of the Perth Road, and it was whispered there might have been human sacrifices. But nobody was brave enough to try and find out.'

Joe's voice dropped to a whisper. 'Folks were scared of Bogue in those days, but it seems a child went missing, and a crowd ganged up on him. They would've lynched him if they'd got him, but he hid in the chapel and when they knocked the door down he wasn't there. That scared folks. They thought he'd called on the devil, to protect him. Anyway the folks in the crowd got scared and, after wrecking the chapel, they all went home. After that Bogue had the chapel bricked up and no one ever used it again.'

'What about the child who went missing?' Kirsty looked up from the paper where she was jotting down everything Joe said.

'Well, it seems it was all a storm in a teacup miss, for the child turned up safe and sound soon after. Seems she wandered off and got lost. Didn't seem to know where she'd been.'

'And Bogue?'

'The cook said he was never seen again. Some said he vanished, and others said he became a recluse. She'd also heard tell his body was never found, and all that's in the Howff is an empty lair.'

Kirsty was silent. The story was a strange one, and she was not sure how much of it had been told to Joe by the cook, or whether he had exaggerated the story with snippets of Dundee folklore.

'What about the house, constable? Could access be gained to the chapel from the house?'

'I don't see how, miss. The chapel's away at the end of the garden and I've seen for myself it's all bricked up behind the doors. Strange, though, you'd almost think it had been bricked up from the inside.' Joe paused to think for a moment. 'You don't think Jonathan Bogue bricked himself in, do you?' He took a long drag on his cigarette as if the thought worried him. 'It would explain why he was never seen again. Wouldn't it?'

'I suppose it would, constable. But it seems unlikely he would do that if he didn't have an escape route.' Kirsty paused for a moment, but Joe was silent and deep in thought. 'What about the cellars, constable? Did you think they might have any hidden rooms or secret passages or anything?'

'Not that I could see, miss. They were big though, and creepy. Lucky I'd seen fit to take my lamp with me because I needed it.'

'Describe the cellars to me.'

'Well, you get down to them from a door in the corridor between the kitchen and the back door. There's a deal of stone steps goes down to a long passage at the bottom. Masses of rooms lead off the passage, but they didn't have doors which made them seem more like caves than rooms. You can only see into one at a time, that's what makes it so spooky, and as you move from one to the other you feel something might jump out at you.' Joe gave a shiver. 'I'm not a great one for imagination, miss, but I can tell you mine was working hell for leather when I was down there.'

'You're sure you looked in every part of the cellar?' Kirsty tried not to show the doubts bubbling up in her mind, but she could imagine what the cellars were like and understand why the constable might not want to explore them.

'Oh yes, miss. I shone my flashlight into every room and corner, and there was nothing but a lot of old junk. You know, discarded furniture and such like.'

'What about other doors or anything that might have led somewhere else?'

Joe dropped his cigarette onto the floor and ground his foot on it. 'You think there might be tunnels or a secret passage or some such?' He thought for a moment. 'I didn't see anything that would measure up to that, miss. Still, the cellars were so big I suppose anything's possible.'

'Yes, constable. Anything is possible.' Kirsty's skin prickled with excitement. She wanted to test out her theories but did not relish going back to the Orphan Institute on her own. But Henderson was here, right in front of her. If she took him with her, she would not be on her own.

She looked up from her scribbled sheet of paper and smiled at the young constable. 'Constable Henderson,' she said. 'You know how Detective Inspector Brewster said you were to help me with this investigation.' She held her breath, hoping he would not notice her slight distortion of the truth.

'Yes, miss,' Joe said.

Kirsty exhaled. 'Well, I want you to come with me to the Orphan Institute so I can take a look at those cellars.'

Joe shrugged his shoulders. 'If you're sure that's what you

want, miss. But you won't find any more than I've already seen.'

Kirsty smiled at him. 'Yes constable, that's what I want.' It had been easier than she had anticipated.

The light was starting to fade when they arrived, and it would be dark before long. But Kirsty's enthusiasm for the search ahead overcame any worries she might have had.

Milly answered the door to their knock. 'The mistress isn't in,' she said. 'You'll have to come back.'

Kirsty was already halfway through the door.

'That's all right, Milly. We don't need to see the mistress this time. We only want another look at the cellars.'

'I'm not going nowhere near them cellars.' Milly glanced over her shoulder as if expecting someone to be standing behind her. 'No one goes down the cellars.'

'Why not, Milly?' Kirsty was in the hall now with Joe at her heels. Milly had no option but to stand back for them.

'I don't know, miss. But I'd be afrighted to go down there. Besides, Mistress Maud says we don't have to go there if we don't want.' Milly's voice rose. 'And I don't want to.'

'That's all right. You don't have to go down into the cellars.' Kirsty soothed. 'We'll go ourselves. You can stay here.'

'But what if something awful happens? How'm I supposed to tell Mistress Maud?' Milly was almost crying.

'Nothing awful is going to happen,' Kirsty reassured her. 'You tell your mistress you couldn't stop us from going into the cellars and that I had a policeman with me. I'm sure she'll understand.' Kirsty continued to walk through the hall. 'Constable, you'll need to show me where the cellars are.'

Joe turned to the maidservant. 'I'll come with you to get the key, and then I'll take Miss Campbell into the cellars.'

The two of them walked off towards a door almost level with the foot of the stairs while Kirsty wandered round the hall. She could hear Joe's voice tailing off. 'Now don't you worry about it, Miss Milly. I'll be there, and I'll make sure everything's taken care of.' A moment later, Joe returned with the key.

'I've persuaded Milly to go and see to the children while we investigate the cellars,' he said, leading the way to the corridor at the rear of the house.

The cellar door opened noiselessly, and Joe shone his lamp down the stone steps.

'D'you want me to go first?' He stepped down the stairs without waiting for an answer. When he reached the rough dirt floor of the cellar, he stood for a moment and shone his lamp around. The light bounced off vaulted openings that reminded Kirsty of a crypt.

Shadows flitted from one opening to the next casting weird images on and between the arches, making Kirsty think of dancing phantoms. She could see why the constable had thought the place was eerie.

'I suppose we'd better make a start.' She took a few tentative steps forward.

The first few vaulted rooms contained a collection of old furniture – beds, mattresses, tables, broken chairs and an assortment of odds and ends. Kirsty moved some of the smaller pieces and opened wardrobe doors, she poked mattresses and pulled on a pile of musty curtains sending up so much dust it left her spluttering and coughing.

She could hear the sounds of small scampering noises which she ignored. A policewoman had no right to be frightened of rats and mice, she thought, while at the same time hoping they would stay out of her way.

'Doesn't seem to be much in here.' Joe's voice sounded disembodied as it echoed back at him.

'Now we're here we'd better finish it though,' Kirsty said, although like Joe she had become dispirited.

Vault after vault seemed to be the same. Dust and cobwebs covered the assorted debris of generations past. Kirsty rubbed her hands on her skirt trying to get rid of the dirt and grit that seemed to be infiltrating every pore in her body. A musty smell hung over everything, turning her stomach and reminding her of morgues, and graveyards, and death and dying.

When they reached the vault at the end of the central passage Joe gave a grunt, and the lamp went spinning out of his grasp to shatter on the ground. The darkness was absolute, and Kirsty groped her way along the wall.

'Constable Henderson, where are you? What's happened?'

There was no answer. She could not even hear him breathing.

Her eyes tried to penetrate the darkness, but it was no use, and she had visions of Joe hurt and needing help. She had to get out of here and find help for him.

She followed the wall to find her way out of the vault she had entered, but it did not seem to lead anywhere. She turned a corner, and still with her hands on the wall, she followed it for a time. But it seemed endless. Surely the vault could not be that large, and if she were out in the passage there would not be a solid wall, it would be broken up by openings.

She sensed she was no longer in the cellars.

38

If she was not in the cellars, where was she?

Darkness enveloped her, and she groped her way forward like a blind person without a white stick. Her fingers slid along the damp, slime-covered wall, but she was afraid to remove her hands from it in case she lost her bearings.

Scurrying noises of small rodents sent shivers racing through her, and she gagged on the putrid smell of rot which had increased to an unbearable level. Her pulse rate accelerated. Her breathing quickened. The beat of her heart resounded in her ears and hammered through her head.

She shuddered, wondering what lay ahead of her in the darkness of the tunnel. An eerie place which seemed like an ancient catacomb from which she would never escape. The primitive fear of being buried alive set her heart thumping so hard the pulse-beat resounding in her ears increased its tempo.

Her foot hit something round and solid. It rolled away from her. She refused to think what it might be and the urge to turn back intensified. But, she was no longer sure what was forward and what was back.

All she craved now was to return to the surface, to daylight and normality. But how would she ever know what was at the end of the tunnel if she turned back? She had to continue, if only to satisfy herself the missing girls were not here. But deep within herself she knew they were here, and once she reached the tunnel's end she would find them.

Just when she thought the wall would continue for ever, her fingers slid round an angle, and her hands came into contact with a door. Turning the handle she pushed, expecting it to resist her. It opened effortlessly on well-oiled hinges.

A sudden urge to pull it shut, and run back, seized her. But where would she run? The dark passage which led to the cellars? She did not know what would be waiting for her there. On the other hand, she did not know what was on the other side of the door. What if the girls were there?

Every instinct she possessed screamed for her to back away, but having come this far she knew she would never be able to rationalize her actions to herself if she did not continue her exploration. She had no other choice but to go on. So, taking a deep breath, she stepped through the doorway.

It did not seem so dark on the other side, and she started to identify shapes in the gloom. She removed her hand from the door. It swung closed so gently and soundlessly she did not notice until she turned back to it.

She looked around for something to prop it open, but found nothing, so she removed her jacket intending to wedge it under the door. Rolling it into a ball she placed her hand on the iron door ring.

But the ring would not turn, and the door would not open. She rattled and shook the handle, but it made no difference and, although she could not be sure, she thought she heard a muffled laugh coming from the other side.

An icy draught whispered along the passage from somewhere up ahead. She shivered. Shaking her jacket, she thrust her arms into the sleeves. Something tinkled to the ground, but she could not see what it was or where it went.

Turning back to the door she moved her hands from one side of it to the other, feeling for the walls that told her she was still in a tunnel. She was. Again she turned and followed the passage and as she moved further along it, her eyes got used to the gloom, and she was able to detect the set of steps leading upwards before she reached them.

The steps were wooden planks jutting out from the earth wall to form a steep ladder. Grasping one of the boards at shoulder level she started to climb. Several times she stumbled on the uneven strips of wood, scraping her knees and knuckles as she struggled to save herself from slipping backwards. But she continued to climb up.

Scrambling up the last step and heaving her body into an upper passageway, she saw a faint ray of moonlight, and for a moment thought it might be a way of escape.

She was standing under a brick lined shaft which led up from the roof of the passage to a metal grille flanked by grass, and beyond that she could see small chinks of starlit sky.

Thinking she might be able to get finger and toeholds in the brick lining she stretched up towards the lower end of the shaft, but it was just out of her reach.

If Henderson had still been with her they would have managed it together, but she was on her own. Kirsty punched the wall and groaned with frustration. If she had been taller, or the shaft had been lower she would have had a chance.

A prayer formed on her lips, although she had not prayed for years. 'Dear Lord,' she begged, 'help me get out of here.' But, even as she recited the words, she knew it would take more than prayers to get her out of this mess. Her body shuddered with pent-up emotion. 'I'm no help to anybody like this,' she muttered, giving herself a shake. And, taking several deep breaths to calm her nerves, she continued along the upper passage until she came to a ladder that led to a trapdoor in the ceiling. She grasped the rungs and climbed up.

Pushing the trapdoor, which lifted easily, she found herself looking into a fairly large and opulent room. She pulled herself through the opening, letting the trapdoor fall shut behind her, and stood looking around.

Several oil lamps burned, sending off a faint vapour as well as a dim light. Red velvet curtains draped the walls, and various sofas and chaise longues were placed strategically in alcoves with erotic paintings hanging above them. A thick pile carpet, as red and luxurious as the velvet curtains, covered most of the floor. Large floor-standing mirrors were positioned at various points of the room. Ornate carved wooden beams, black with age, lined the vaulted roof. The carved faces of gremlins and ogres threw their sinister gaze on all who dared to walk beneath them, as if lying in wait, ready to pounce on her.

She walked round the room, fingering the drapes and the furniture. At the far end, two steps led up to a table. Kirsty lifted the black cloth covering it, and stared at it with a recognition that turned into horror. It was an altar.

She was in the chapel. Bogue's satanic chapel. It could not be anywhere else. But it did not look like a chapel. It looked like a high-class whore house. But, if it were a brothel, where were the girls? The place was empty.

Kirsty sat on the top step in front of the altar, thinking. Could this explain the missing girls? Were her suspicions confirmed and had she stumbled on a white slave operation? But if so, where were the girls kept? Or was she too late?

She stood up and walked round the room again until she came to the trapdoor. She lifted it and stared down the steps which led away from the chapel, and then she turned and looked at the room again, pondering the possibility of another trapdoor leading to a hidden cellar.

Walking round the room yet again she inspected the floor and found the second trapdoor behind the altar. She opened it to reveal a set of steps leading down. Easing herself through the opening she carefully lowered herself onto them, pulling the trapdoor closed behind her. Oil lamps hung from the walls lighting the passage below which was lined with doors. She descended the steps and walked along the passage. All the doors had circular iron handles, and she turned the handle on each door, but they were all locked. However, she heard soft movements and clinking noises behind them.

'Is anyone in there?' Her voice echoed loudly in the confined space. But, once the echoes died away, the only sound was her breathing.

She looked around for a key but could find nothing, so she decided to return to the upper room to search. Emerging through the trapdoor, she lowered it behind her to give her more room to move. It closed with a click, and that was when she heard voices, the sound of feet and the scrape of the other trapdoor opening.

39

Sliding behind the altar she lifted a corner of the black cloth and edged into the alcove beneath. For one horrible moment she thought there would not be enough room, but desperation forced her to think she might be able to get her body in if she clasped her knees to her chest. She wriggled into position and let the cloth fall back into place. Provided she could keep still and silent she should be able to remain hidden.

The footsteps approached. She held her breath as they paused in front of her hiding place.

'I thought you said the policewoman would be here,' one voice said.

'Evidently she's not, so she must be hiding in the cellars. Don't worry about it she won't get away, and we'll attend to her later.'

Kirsty recognized one of the voices as the man she had overheard talking to Maud.

He continued. 'We don't have time to look for her now. Not if you want to take part in the new game. But we'll lock the cellars when we leave and she'll keep.'

The edge of the cloth concealing Kirsty fluttered against her arms and shoulders as the trapdoor was lifted just inches away from her. She heard the voice saying as it descended the steps, 'The rest of the players will be coming to the Howff at midnight. So we'd better be quick.'

Kirsty was tempted to leave her cramped hiding place while they were at the bottom of the ladder, but she dare not. She would never have time to get down the passage before them, and she was bound to be caught. So she remained where she was.

Moments later the footsteps returned, and the trapdoor closed with a thump.

'This is a new one,' she heard a voice say. 'Never been touched. It should make the game more realistic.'

'Bit of a pity though, to waste a fresh one,' the other voice answered.

The sound of a harsh laugh sounded above her. 'The councillor insisted on a virgin to make it more realistic, and he's paying plenty, so we can afford it. A few more games like this and we'll be all right.'

She waited until the thump of the second trapdoor signalled the men's departure before she emerged.

Her brain whirled as she tried to make sense of what she had overheard. Overcome with fear for Ailsa and Nora, she pulled herself up too fast. Her legs buckled beneath her and the hard top of her boots bit into her knees. She loosened her laces and massaged the cramp from her legs while her mind flitted from one thought to the next. With a growing sense of horror, she realized if they were going to the Howff there would be another dead girl. And she was the only one who knew. She had to prevent the murder happening. But how?

The gargoyles grinned down at her with their fixed wooden smiles while their wooden eyes seemed to follow her every move. Silence enveloped the chapel, and all she could hear was her own breathing. This should have reassured her, but it did not, and she could sense the menace in the air. It hung, thick and cloying, mixing with the smoke and the vapour from the oil lamps until she could almost smell it.

After she finished lacing her boots Kirsty pulled herself up from her sitting position and opened the trapdoor. The soft movements she had heard earlier, behind the locked doors, had convinced her the lost girls were there. She peered down into the darkness. 'I'll come back,' she whispered.

Suppressing her guilt feelings, she closed the trapdoor and walked across the room to the other one, half expecting it to rise and a body to emerge. But her instinct told her the men had left, and she was alone with the gremlins, ogres and gargoyles.

Kirsty raised the trapdoor lid and peered down into the darkness. Maybe if she could loosen the ladder she might be able to use it to climb the shaft that led to the grass covered grid.

Easing herself over the edge she climbed down to the passage below. Once there, she gripped the ladder with both hands and shook it. But it did not move. She tried lifting it, kicking it, slamming her body against it and shaking it again. But still it would not move.

Despair gripped her, and she leaned her head against one of the rungs feeling as if she were being smothered by a blanket of darkness and evil.

'What am I going to do?' Her wail echoed down the passage. And yet, despite her despair, she knew she had to do something. She had to help the girl who had been taken from the chapel. Thoughts of Ailsa and Nora flashed into her mind, but she refused to allow herself to think the girl who was taken was either of them, in case she became overcome by an incapacitating horror.

Kirsty scurried down the passage until she arrived at the shaft. But, even though she tried to reach it, this attempt was no more successful than the last. She examined the wall and ran her hands over the slimy, dripping surface, but it was too smooth and she was unable to get the necessary grip to pull herself up.

She tried shouting upwards, hoping Milly or someone from the house would hear her, but the darkness swallowed her voice. Maybe if she blew her police whistle. Perhaps that would be shrill enough to be heard. The chain was still attached to her button, but there was no whistle on the end of it.

'Damn,' she said, remembering the slight tinkle of something falling when she rolled up her jacket in an attempt to prop open the door. It must have been her whistle.

Sighing, she returned to the chapel. She knew the doors and windows had been bricked up, but maybe she would be able to find one that was not. It was a faint hope, but better than no hope.

She found the bricked up door immediately and looked at it in dismay. The bricks were solid and well cemented, she would never be able to move them. Running round the room, she pulled at the velvet drapes until she found every window. But they were bricked up as well. Whoever had sealed this chapel had made an excellent job of it.

Breathing heavily, she examined the furniture. But the mirrors were attached to bases which were securely fastened to the floor, and the sofas and chaise longues were much too large to pass through the trapdoor. Desperately, she cast around for something smaller, but found nothing.

She sank to her knees on the blood-red carpet and stared wildly around. Was this to be her prison, this opulent room with its velvet furnishings, gilded mirrors, its gremlins and ogres and its black-draped altar? Was there no way out?

Staring down the open trapdoor into the claustrophobic gloom below she knew she had no other option but to try the passage again, even though she was sure she would never get through the door. She removed a lamp from the wall. At least she would have some light this time.

Once again she eased herself through the trapdoor and descended the ladder. The light made it easier to move back down the passage and the stairs, and a few minutes later she reached the door.

Kirsty was convinced it would not open, but she pulled at the door ring anyway. The door opened. She looked at it in disbelief. It could not be open. She must have fallen asleep and be in the middle of a dream. But dream or no dream, the door had opened.

She slipped through it, afraid it would slam on her and, as she did so, her foot hit something small that tinkled and rolled away.

Holding the lamp in front of her, Kirsty saw the tinkling object was her police whistle. It must have rolled into the space between the door and its frame when the two men left the passage. She picked the whistle up and, rubbing it on her skirt to remove the dirt, she kissed it before placing it in her pocket.

She half-ran and half-stumbled along the passage to the cellars her boots slithering on the slimy floor, and soon she was in one of the vaulted chambers. Despite her hurry, she realized she would have to find the opening again, so she moved two broken chairs to the front of the wardrobe which concealed the entrance. She arranged one chair on top of the other in a pattern she would recognize. Spotting Joe's broken police lamp, she placed it on the topmost chair.

Remorse clawed at her for bringing him here, and she swung the lamp in an arc, trying to see into every corner, expecting to see a body, either injured or dead. However, the constable was nowhere to be seen.

Ignoring the moving shadows conjured up by the swinging lamp, she hurried up the main passage between the vaults until she reached the cellar stairs. Standing at the bottom of them she remembered the man's guttural voice. 'We'll lock the cellars. She won't get out.'

But she climbed the stairs anyway. The door at the top was locked. She thumped on the oak panels. No one came. She shouted. There was no response. Her frustration mounted, and she kicked the door.

Someone must be around, she thought. But she knew she was fooling herself because the men had been so sure that if they locked the cellar she would not get out.

With mounting fury, she sank down behind the door and stared into the cellar that had become her new prison.

40

Fuelled by anger, Kirsty rose and stomped down the stairs into the cellar. 'I'm not going to be beaten,' she muttered to herself. 'Cellars are basements. And basements have some sort of ventilation otherwise the whole house would rot.' She was not entirely convinced by her own argument. The place was rotting, the diabolical smell was proof of that.

Kirsty went into each vault in turn, holding up the oil lamp to check for draughts. The flame flickered and bent towards her when she was in the third one. Moving to the back of it she examined the walls. And there, high up near the ceiling, was a small cobweb-covered window that looked hardly big enough for a pygmy to get through.

Placing the lamp on the floor she dragged an old sideboard over to the wall. Then she piled a table on top of it and a chair on top of that.

Leaving the lamp where it was she climbed onto the pyramid of furniture and, grabbing the window sill, pulled herself up to the window. It was bigger than it looked from down below, just large enough for her to squeeze through provided she could open it.

Her fingers grasped the window sill and jolts of pain shot through her arms and shoulders as she hung there. Taking a deep breath and summoning up all the energy she could, she hoisted herself further up until she was able to balance her forearms on the sill. The chair wobbled underneath her toes, and she willed the pyramid not to collapse. Carefully stretching one arm up to the window fastening, she tried to turn it. It would not move. But Kirsty gritted her teeth and pressed it as hard as she dared, turning it at the same time. She was on the point of giving up when it gave way, and she pushed the window open. Looking at the gap she knew she would need all her remaining strength to pull herself through it.

She did not hesitate. Gritting her teeth again she pulled herself up. The chair below her wobbled and crashed to the floor. Kirsty hung for a moment, her feet scrabbling against the wall, her arms aching and her shoulders feeling as if they were parting company with their sockets. She knew she could not give up. A girl's life depended on her.

Levering her arms against the frame of the window she pushed her hands through until they scraped on the stone wall outside. Putting pressure on her arms and shoulders she heaved herself up until her head was clear and her upper body balanced on the window's edge. Then digging her elbows into the framework she pushed out into the night air.

The pain in her shoulders was agonising. Her elbows and knees ached, but the cold, damp grass she fell into welcomed her with a wetness she found exhilarating after the clammy cellars. She rubbed her face in it, feeling the cold moisture gather on her skin. The wind ruffled her hair and she wondered, for a brief moment, where she had lost her cap but decided she did not care, it was enough she was out of the cellars and free. Rolling onto her back she looked up into the moonlit night, towards stars she never thought she would see again.

But she was not safe yet. What if she had been seen? She stared up at the house, waiting for the inevitable shouts that would signal disaster, but only the windows stared back at her, black empty eyes set into the dark and brooding structure hanging suspended above her in all its menacing grandeur.

She shivered, but not with the cold, even though the icy wind left a chilly dampness on her skin. Her breathing quickened, and her heart thumped. She felt an overwhelming urge to leave this place but found it difficult to move.

Pushing herself to her feet she wondered what time it was. It felt like an eternity since she had entered the Institute with Henderson, and the darkness of the sky indicated many hours had passed. Panic gripped her. Would she get to the Howff in time to prevent another murder, or was she already too late?

She forced her arms and fingers to move, and attempted to brush the tiny spears of grass from her skirt. It made her aware of the ache in the palms of her hands. Her elbows, rubbing against her jacket sleeve, stung with a raw and sticky wetness. Tentatively she prodded an elbow but decided to leave it alone when the pain increased.

Turning away from the house her thoughts focused on Constable Henderson and her fears about his fate. She should return to the house to investigate, but she was running out of time. So the choice about whether to look for him or leave this place was not too difficult to make, she had to rescue the child. The constable could look after himself.

The stones on the drive scrunched and scattered under her hurrying feet, but noise no longer mattered because she knew everyone involved in what was going on had already left for the Howff.

Reaching Perth Road she turned right and ran to the next set of gates which were closed. The house was in darkness, but she climbed over the wall and ran down the drive. She tried the front door and the back door. There was no response to her pounding knocks, and her knuckles were as raw as the palms of her hands before she gave up in despair.

She might have known better, this was the sort of area that attracted housebreakings. Anyone living here would be unlikely to open their door late at night.

Returning to the main road she started to run again, in the direction of the town until the breath squeezed out of her in painful gasps. Her legs faltered and, unable to continue without stopping for a rest, she leaned on a wall. Despair seized her and she could not see how she was going to get to the cemetery in time. Perth Road was too long, and she was too far away.

She would have given anything to see a tram come clanking and rocking down the road, but they did not run this late. So, to get there she would have to go on foot, and she forced her shaking legs to continue walking.

Perth Road was lined with large houses bordered with walls and heavy gates, and as she passed each gate Kirsty stopped and looked in vain for lights and signs of habitation. She had reached the sixth gate before she saw it. A bicycle propped up against the wall inside. It probably belonged to a servant's boyfriend, who was afraid to take it too close to the house.

Pushing the gate open she grasped the handlebars. 'Needs must,' she muttered to herself, and without further thought she pushed it out onto the road. Pulling her skirt up to her thighs she swung her leg over the bar and placed her feet on the pedals.

The bicycle was heavy, the crossbar made it difficult to pedal, and she was displaying a disgraceful amount of leg, but ignoring all that she careered down Perth Road in the direction of the town. Luckily it was downhill most of the way, so this gave her legs time to recover their power and by the time she had reached the Nethergate she was able to put all her strength into pedalling.

She wobbled to a stop outside the Queens Hotel, but the doors were locked, and the building was in darkness. Remounting, she continued on in the direction of the town centre, looking for someone she could ask to convey a message to the police station. She was disappointed, the streets were unusually quiet. The drinkers had probably gone to the various shebeens in the Scouringburn after the public bars closed, while those looking for company would have headed for the dock area where most of the prostitutes plied their trade.

She glanced at the church clock before turning off the Nethergate into one of the narrow pends leading to the Overgate, and was relieved to see the time was twenty minutes to midnight. For some unknown reason, her instinct told her nothing would happen before twelve o'clock. So she was still in time.

The pend was dark and shadowy with shapes shifting and moving on the periphery of her vision. Had there been more time to think about it, she would have regretted taking the short cut. However, she continued to pedal madly on.

When she reached the Overgate, she quickly crossed it to enter Barrack Street. Her legs were tiring now, and she needed more effort to push the pedals round. The bicycle slowed, and the wheels caught on the cobbles. Wobbling dangerously, she almost fell off. The street was in darkness, and tall buildings loomed at each side of her. But she was here, she was at the Howff, and she was in time.

Dismounting, she leaned the bicycle against the cemetery wall and peered through the first of the iron gates. The cemetery was in darkness, and no sound disturbed the silence.

Creeping up the road to the next gate she again tried to see into the cemetery, but nothing stirred. Nevertheless, an uneasy feeling was creeping over her. The silence was too intense and the darkness too black. It felt as if someone had thrown a black cloak over everything, muffling and hiding what was going on from curious eyes.

She should not be here. She knew that, just as she knew she should go to the police station for reinforcements. But she did not go because it would waste too much time, and time was crucial.

Her heart thumped. The beat of it echoed in her ears. Her breathing quickened. 'This is madness,' she muttered, simply to hear her own voice. She tiptoed towards the front entrance to the Howff, trying to control her breathing, afraid to break the silence.

The wall was lower at the front of the cemetery and lined with iron railings, but still she could see nothing within. Kirsty began to doubt herself. Surely she had not been mistaken when she had overheard the men say they were going to the Howff. Maybe she was too late, or maybe she was too early.

But one thing she was not imagining was the prickle of fear and apprehension attacking her neck muscles. Deep in thought, she turned into the front gate and walked straight into the man standing in the shadows.

41

She started, unable to stop the rapid intake of breath that hissed in and stuck at her throat. But the hand reaching out to grasp her arm and the voice were familiar and reassuring.

'You got my message, Miss Campbell,' Edward whispered.

'Your message?'

'The one I pushed under your door,' he said urgently. 'That is why you've come, isn't it?'

Kirsty suppressed a nervous laugh. She was glad he was here and she was not on her own anymore. But she did not want to go into explanations about what had happened to her tonight, so she merely murmured, 'Yes.'

'Nothing has happened so far,' Edward whispered. 'Maybe it would be better if we went into the cemetery. We could hide behind one of the grave stones so we could see what is going on.' He squeezed her arm in a friendly grip. 'You know, you were right. Maud's mixed up in this. I feel such a fool for trusting her.'

The cemetery paths were in darkness, and shadows flitted between the rustling bushes. But Edward did not hesitate, he walked quickly and confidently. His grip on Kirsty's arm tightened, his fingers pinched her skin. Kirsty tried to match her steps to his, but his stride was longer and she stumbled over rough pebbles and stones in her hurry to keep up.

The paths wound through the graveyard. Shrubbery and trees stretched out dank tendrils to stroke her face. She became disoriented and was no longer sure in which direction she was walking. But, despite the darkness, she could see the outline of Edward's tall figure as he strode along beside her. It reassured her and made her feel safe.

She guessed they must be in the centre of the graveyard when Edward suddenly stopped. 'Down,' he hissed. 'I saw a flicker of light over there. Do you see it?'

Kirsty knelt down behind the nearest gravestone. The damp earth seeped through the holes in her stockings, chilling her legs. She looked up. Flickering lights approached them looking like pinpricks in the enclosing darkness. She had been here before. She had seen this before. It was her dream come to life.

She leaned closer to Edward, taking comfort from his warmth. As long as he was with her she would be safe. 'Are you sure we won't be seen here?' she whispered.

'Trust me,' he said.

The lights drew nearer and nearer until Kirsty heard the wordless chanting. Strangely musical, but making no sense. The lights stopped right in front of the gravestone concealing Kirsty and Edward.

The hooded figures began to chant. 'Come to us, oh Master. Reveal yourself to us, oh Master, that we may perform the ceremony.'

Kirsty pressed herself down onto the earth. Mud squeezed through her fingers and clung to the top of her boots and her knees. She stretched a hand out to Edward, but he was no longer there.

The lights circled the gravestone now. Hooded black-robed figures were in front of her and behind her. She knew she was trapped, and anticipated what was going to happen next.

The figures in front of her parted and a child in a white flimsy robe was led forward. 'Oh Master, we bring you our gift,' they chanted.

A hooded figure, taller than the rest, joined the circle. 'Mother and daughter. Daughter and mother,' the harsh voice intoned.

'Mother and daughter. Daughter and mother,' the circle chanted in chorus.

Kirsty stared at the child. It was not Nora. It was Ailsa. The fears she had suppressed earlier rose up to choke her. She spat out the acrid bile and tried to scramble to her feet. But her knees gave way, and she sank back to the earth. She felt helpless but had to do something. She had to stop this.

'Ailsa,' she wailed. Her fingers were rapidly searching her

pockets for something she could use to stop this madness. But all she could find was her whistle. Pulling it out she blasted on it for all she was worth. She managed four whistle blasts before it was torn from her hands and thrown into the bushes.

'What do you expect?' The guttural voice addressed her. 'No one here will come to your rescue. No friendly beat bobbies tonight. I've taken care of that, haven't I, Joe?' He pulled the hood of the figure standing beside him so Kirsty could see the constable.

'What did you do that for?' Joe muttered. 'I thought the idea was that no one could identify us.'

'After tonight that won't matter, because there will be no one left to identify you.'

Kirsty struggled to her feet. She had to know the identity of this man. She had to see to whom the voice belonged, the voice she could not identify, although it sounded strangely familiar.

'And what about you?' she shouted, leaning forward to pull at the leader's cloak.

The hood fell back, and she stared into his face. A face, twisted with malevolence, retaining nothing of its former caring expression.

'You!' She stood motionless, with the strangest sensation time had stopped, and everything had gone into slow motion. 'And to think I trusted you.'

Edward seemed to have grown taller and more menacing. He glared at her, his eyes glittering with some unknown emotion. Flecks of white spittle gathered at the corners of his mouth.

'You should have joined us, Kirsty. The games we play are more exciting than the one you are playing, and they are more lucrative. You would have enjoyed our games, Kirsty.' His voice had risen, and his words seemed to pierce her brain until even the roots of her hair tingled.

She leaned forward to protect Ailsa and grabbed her wrist. 'I will not allow you to harm Ailsa.' Kirsty's strong and confident voice expressed a bravado she did not feel.

'The game begins, and you have no choice.' Edward held his arms aloft and started chanting.

'Oh, don't I!' Kirsty whirled around and grabbed Joe,

throwing him to the ground. She had excelled at jujitsu during her training, but this was the first time she had needed to use it. Gaining confidence in her abilities, she kicked Edward in the groin as hard as she could. He doubled over in pain, and she ran off into the darkness pulling Ailsa along with her.

Ailsa's eyes were glazed, her movements slow, and her body shivered with terror. She whimpered and clung tightly to Kirsty's hand.

Kirsty ducked and scuttled between the tombstones, dragging Ailsa with her.

'You're hurting me,' Ailsa moaned, wriggling her hand within Kirsty's grasping fingers.

Kirsty loosened her grip and turned to the child intending to put her arm around her and hug her. But as soon as Ailsa was free of her grasp she darted off into the darkness of the cemetery.

'Ailsa,' Kirsty called softly. But no answer came, and she could hear the calls of the group.

Lights flickered along the paths, and Kirsty darted between the gravestones hunting desperately for Ailsa while all the time the lights danced behind her.

She could see the faint glimmer of a lamp at the main entrance. Ailsa must have seen it as well and had probably headed for the safety of the street. Kirsty ran to the gate, only to be brought up short when she crashed into a man entering the cemetery.

It was all over, she might as well give up. But she could not because Ailsa was somewhere inside, and even if she had found a hiding place they were bound to find her sooner or later. Lashing out with her feet she tried to break free of the arms restraining her.

'Hold on.' The voice was familiar.

She looked up into Detective Inspector Brewster's face. 'You're in it as well are you?' she panted. 'I might have known.'

42

Brewster's arms held her fast while he signalled to the constables behind him. 'All right men, into the cemetery. It looks like we're going to catch that lot tonight.'

Kirsty stopped struggling. 'You mean you're not part of it?'

'No, Miss Campbell. I'm not part of that bunch,' he said, turning to face her. 'But you, Miss Campbell, have some explaining to do.'

She wrenched free from his grasp. 'Later,' she panted. 'Ailsa's in the cemetery I have to find her before they do.'

He grabbed her arm, holding her back. 'That's all right, Miss Campbell, we'll find her. I have men posted at every entrance to the cemetery. Edward Gordon and his little band won't escape.'

This time Kirsty was unable to shake him off. His fingers dug into her arm, her head hurt, and the group's singsong chant echoed in her brain. How did he know about Edward? She wanted to ask him, but time was too short. She panicked, thinking of Ailsa in the cemetery, scared and alone, so frightened she had even run away from Kirsty. How on earth did Brewster imagine his constables would find her without scaring her half to death?

'But I have to find her. I must find her. She'll be terrified,' Kirsty yelled at Brewster, expecting him to object.

His eyes reflected concern. 'All right, Miss Campbell. But you're in no state to be roaming around the Howff, so I'll come with you.' Releasing his grip on her arm, he clasped her hand within his own. 'So I know where you are,' he said.

The sounds of shouting, whistles and pounding feet echoed around the cemetery while Brewster and Kirsty hunted for Ailsa. Eventually, they found her, huddled behind a gravestone at the rear of the graveyard. Kirsty knelt down beside her, but the girl rolled herself into a ball, and whimpered like a wounded animal.

'Hush,' Kirsty said. 'You're all right now. You're safe.'

She put her arms round Ailsa and pulled the child's head onto her chest. Ailsa's tears, hot and wet, saturated her jacket. Kirsty rocked her and made hushing noises, but the girl continued to whimper, reminding her of Angel rocking and wailing in her cell.

She looked despairingly at Brewster.

'What have they done to her?' Her voice soared in the confines of the cemetery.

'Come on, Miss Campbell. We have to take her away from here.'

Brewster helped Kirsty up. She staggered as she rose because she refused to let go of Ailsa.

Brewster put his arms around the distressed child and tried to take her, but Kirsty resisted him.

'Let me have Ailsa,' he pleaded. 'She's too heavy for you.'

Reluctantly, she released her grip on the girl who had lapsed into a catatonic-like state. Then together, they made their way out of the cemetery. Kirsty stumbled once or twice, and Brewster put one arm around her shoulders while he held Ailsa close to him with the other.

'Where are we going?' Kirsty wanted to know as they turned in the opposite direction to the police station.

'I'm taking you to my home. You both need food and sleep.'

'But what about the others?'

'Others?'

'The other girls,' she said. 'I think I know where they're being held.'

He stopped and looked at her. 'And how would you know that, Miss Campbell?'

She squirmed. 'I heard them. At least I think it was the girls.' She remembered the soft, shifting noises behind the locked doors and hoped she was not wrong.

'You'd better tell me about it,' he said resignedly, and started walking again.

He was silent after she finished speaking.

'What are we going to do?' Kirsty said when she could bear the silence no longer.

'You are staying with Ailsa,' he said, his tone brooking no argument. 'I'll see to the rest. First, I have to make sure none of this gang escapes. Then I'll get a warrant and make arrangements to look for this secret passage of yours.'

Ailsa had fallen asleep on Brewster's shoulder, so they walked on in silence. But Kirsty's thoughts were churning. He might have taken the information she had given him about the Orphan Institute a bit more seriously. Instead, he had been almost dismissive. Oh, he would go and take a look all right, she had no doubts about that, but it would be in his own good time.

Maybe she should have been more adamant that the girls were there, but she had allowed doubt to creep into her voice when she was describing the chapel.

A sudden thought struck her. 'How did you know what was happening at the cemetery?'

'I've been investigating Edward Gordon for several weeks. I did try to warn you about him, you know.'

'Why didn't you tell me properly, then?'

'You appeared to know him quite well, and I thought you might tell him.'

'You didn't trust me because I'm a woman,' Kirsty said despairingly.

She thought of all the other things he had done that had sidelined her activities, and added, 'Well, in that case I don't see how I can continue to work in Dundee when I'm not trusted by the people I work with.'

'That's not fair, Miss Campbell. You're new, and we don't know each other properly yet, so how could I gauge. It's nothing to do with whether you're a woman or a man.'

But it is, she thought bitterly; otherwise he would listen to her, act on the information she gave him, and include her in the follow-up to the investigation.

She trudged silently beside him because she had no option. If Ailsa woke with no one familiar beside her, then Kirsty was afraid to think how the child would react. A vision of Angel, rocking dementedly in her cell, rose in Kirsty's mind. That was not going to happen to Ailsa.

Brewster's cottage was in a small side street that led off Constitution Road. The gate creaked as he pushed it open and they walked down a garden path and then up a wooden ramp to the front door. Light from the hallway spilled out into the darkness when he pushed the door open. Still carrying Ailsa he led the way in. The small, bare, spotlessly clean hall had paintwork that was chipped and scraped. Brewster opened one of the doors and gestured for them to go inside.

Following them, he knelt down beside the young woman in the wheelchair and grasped her hand. She was fair with the delicate features genuine blondes have. Her eyes were a faded blue colour, but they brightened to a more brilliant shade when she looked up at him, and her face lost its lacklustre appearance.

'I'm sorry, Maggie, my love. I never got back in time to help you to bed.' Brewster's voice was apologetic.

Kirsty fidgeted as she met the woman's eyes. She wished Brewster had not brought her here, where she had no right to be. It made her feel awkward and uneasy. She remembered all the vague references to Brewster having a hard life, and as understanding flooded through her so did embarrassment and guilt. She wanted to tell him she was sorry for all her uncharitable thoughts because he was never there when she wanted him. But she was too ashamed even to attempt it. And even if she did, this was not the right time or place.

Brewster stood up. 'Maggie, this is Kirsty Campbell and her sister Ailsa. They've had a difficult time tonight, and I thought they'd be better here than anywhere else. I knew you wouldn't mind.' His hand lingered on her shoulder.

Maggie smiled at them with her eyes and one side of her mouth. 'You know I don't mind, Jamie.' Her words were ever so slightly slurred. She turned to Kirsty. 'Jamie has told me about you, Miss Campbell. He has so much regard for you I suppose I should be jealous.' However there was no hint of jealousy in the way she said it.

'Maggie's an awful tease,' Brewster said, but his neck had reddened. He leant over and kissed Maggie's forehead. 'I'll settle them in the spare room with some cocoa and sandwiches, and then I'll come and help you to bed.'

Maggie reached out and clasped his hand as she looked up at him. 'I'm such a burden to you,' she said.

Embarrassed, Kirsty led Ailsa through to the hall, but not before she saw and heard Brewster's response.

'Nonsense, Maggie.' He kissed the tip of his fingers and laid them on her cheek. 'I'll always be here. Remember, it was for better or worse, so you're not getting rid of me that easily.'

Kirsty waited for him in the hall. 'You had no right to bring us here,' she said, 'we're intruding.'

'Nonsense,' he replied. 'The spare room is upstairs, first on the right. I'll bring you some cocoa in about ten minutes.'

'It would be best for Ailsa if she went home to Broughty Ferry,' she persisted.

'And how do you suggest we take her? On Davvy's barrow, perhaps?'

Kirsty flushed. 'You have no need to be sarcastic.'

'Miss, Campbell. The police force are not yet in a position to provide motorized transport, and I did not think it appropriate to use a cab. It will be best for everyone concerned if you stay here tonight.' He held up a hand to silence her. 'No more arguments, Miss Campbell. Do as you are told for once.'

Kirsty snapped her mouth shut, tightened her arm round Ailsa and climbed the stairs. But inside she was fuming.

43

Saturday, 8 November 1919

Ailsa fell asleep almost immediately, but Kirsty's mind was active, and she was too tense to do anything more than doze fitfully. But she must have slept eventually, for when she woke the fire was ash and the bedroom cold. Not that Kirsty cared, because waking up in the large double bed, with Ailsa enclosed in her arms was something she knew she would never forget. She lay, in the darkness of the room, enjoying the feel of Ailsa, tempted to remain snuggled down into the warmth of the bed with only the tip of her nose outside the blankets. But the clock on the mantel struck six times, and she knew morning had arrived.

Ailsa's body lay curled, close to her own, with an intimacy that was at once strange but pleasurable, sending a surge of warmth through her that could only have been generated by love. Afraid to disturb her, she watched the sleeping girl, enjoying the feel of her, and although her arm was numb where Ailsa lay on it, Kirsty would have cut it off before she would have moved.

The last time she had held Ailsa, and been this close to her, was just after her birth and she remembered how empty her arms had seemed after she had handed the baby over to her mother. Since that time, Kirsty's mother had been the one who had cuddled and comforted Ailsa in times of distress while all Kirsty could do was look on, and feel the ache in her heart intensify until finally she had been forced to leave the family home, or go mad.

Ailsa stirred and mumbled and a small bubble gathered on the corner of her mouth. Kirsty wiped it away with her free hand, and the child's eyes blinked open. Ailsa gave a small whimper, but when she saw who was beside her she threw her thin arms around Kirsty's waist and buried her face in her chest.

Tears gathered in Kirsty's eyes, and she leaned forward to kiss the top of Ailsa's head. It had a comforting smell and Kirsty fought the urge to bury her face in the tousled hair.

'You're safe now,' she said. She wanted to add, your mother is here, but did not. 'And you'll soon be back home.' She blinked away the tears pricking her eyes. Kirsty knew home was not with her, and Ailsa would return to the woman she thought was her mother.

'Maybe we should get up now,' Kirsty said. Wriggling her arms free she slid out of bed and padded over to the window. Frost, silvering the grass in the small, overgrown front garden, illuminated the darkness. But, although it was early, her father's car sat outside the gate. 'I think our father's here,' she said, turning to Ailsa. She watched with an ache that went right through her as the girl smiled her delight.

They dressed hurriedly, although Kirsty had to brush the worst of the dried mud off her uniform before she pulled it on. Ailsa, who only had the white shift she had been wearing the night before, moaned her dismay when she thrust her arms into it. The two then descended the stairs, hand in hand.

Hesitating for a moment, before she pushed the sitting room door open, she heard the faint clink of china and soft voices. Kirsty's mother and father were sitting in armchairs at either side of the fireplace with Maggie's wheelchair positioned between them. But as soon as Kirsty and Ailsa entered the room, her father laid his teacup on the floor and held out his arms. Ailsa ran straight to him. His expression softened, and he patted her back and made soothing noises before releasing her so she could go to her mother.

Kirsty stood awkwardly in the doorway. Her mother was openly crying while her father, fighting his emotions, cleared his throat several times.

At last he gained control of himself and, turning to Maggie, he said, 'You've been very kind, Mrs Brewster, but it's time we got Ailsa home.'

Maggie nodded.

'You'll be coming home with us as well,' he said, turning to

Kirsty. 'No more of this nonsense about being independent.' He hesitated before he continued less brusquely. 'We want you home with us, Kirsty. It's where you belong.'

Kirsty suppressed her annoyance because she recognized how difficult it must be for him to express that, and with a sense of surprise she understood he loved her.

She wrestled for a moment with her own feelings and was almost tempted to agree. But she knew it would not work, just as it had not worked ten years ago. They were Ailsa's parents now, and it hurt. She could never return to the family home.

Kirsty looked at her father. Her love for him had been buried for so long she had thought it lost forever. But, she realized with a sudden burst of insight, it was bubbling away under the surface. It had needed an emergency like this to reawaken.

'I'm sorry,' she said. Her voice was gentle, and she hoped he would not be hurt. 'But you must understand I have another life now. A life I'm proud of. But I'll visit, and things will be good again.' She walked over to him and kissed him on the cheek, then turning to her mother she did the same. She gave Ailsa a hug and said, 'I'll always be your big sister.' It had to be said, because it was her way of finally relinquishing her child. 'But now it's time to go home. I'll see you later.'

She watched the three of them walk down the path and get into the car. Ailsa had to be her sister from now on, never her daughter. Struggling to suppress the lump rising from her chest into her throat she raised her hand in a wave of farewell, and watched until they were out of sight.

'You love that child. Don't you?' Maggie said as she turned back into the room.

Kirsty nodded, unable to speak.

44

'Jamie said he'd see you at the office.' Maggie rolled her wheelchair down the corridor. 'But you'll take some breakfast first.'

Kirsty followed Maggie into the kitchen. 'I'm sorry, I won't have time.'

Now she no longer had to worry about Ailsa, the other girls were preying on her mind. Maybe if she hurried she could catch up with Brewster.

'When did he leave?'

Maggie laughed. 'He's been gone all night.'

She pushed a slice of bread onto the prongs of a toasting fork and held it to the fire until it browned, then turned it and did the other side.

'All night?'

'That's not unusual when he's working on a case.'

Maggie shook the toast off the fork onto a plate. 'Put some butter on that,' she said, 'you can eat it going along the road.'

'Thanks, Maggie.' Kirsty grabbed the toast and ran.

'You're just like Jamie,' Maggie shouted after her, 'always on duty.'

It was eight o'clock when she walked into the police station, still early, but not early enough to suit Kirsty.

The duty sergeant looked up. 'You had a busy night last night, I see. If you keep this up, we're going to need a bigger police station.'

He grinned at her, and Kirsty had a feeling the atmosphere had changed, become warmer, more accepting.

'It was a bit hectic,' she agreed. 'Where's Inspector Brewster? I need to find out what's happening.'

'He's interviewing the prisoners. He said if you were to come in you might want to talk to Angel, because after last night it looks as if we'll have to release her. Then you're to wait in his office.'

Kirsty almost ran down the corridors to Angel's cell. 'Angel's free,' she announced to Annie Baxter. Grasping hold of the woman's hands she did a jig in front of her. 'I always knew she didn't do it.'

'Ah, poor lass,' Annie said. 'What's to become of her, the wee lamb's got no wit left.'

Kirsty stopped dancing and let go of Annie's hands. In her anxiety to prove Angel's innocence, she had not given too much thought to what would happen to her. 'You're right, Annie. What are we to do with her?'

They paused outside the cell. 'Well now, I'm sure I don't know,' Annie said, before clanging the door shut behind Kirsty.

Angel did not look up from where she sat on the mattress covered bench, and Kirsty's pleasure at having saved her turned into sorrow. She had not thought the girl could look even frailer than she did the first time she had seen her. But her ethereal appearance had increased, and she now looked more like a ghost than a real person. A week had passed since she had been locked up but, given her condition at that time, she supposed the deterioration was to be expected.

Walking over to the bench, Kirsty sat down beside her. She wondered how much Angel remembered or understood, and whether the girl recognized her. She watched her for a moment as Angel plucked invisible threads from her prison dress. But her face was blank with no hint of recognition in her eyes.

'I've come back to see you, Angel,' she said. 'Like I promised.' Kirsty watched the girl's fingers. At least she was not rocking.

'We know you didn't commit the murder and the person responsible has been caught.' Kirsty hoped for a response, but was not surprised when she did not get one. She had known all along the girl was not shamming her condition.

'You have nothing to fear anymore, and if you could tell me where you come from you could be set free.'

Kirsty sat in silence for a time, but Angel never once looked at her. The girl sat immobile, although her fingers were in constant motion.

At last Kirsty rose. 'What are we to do with you?'

Her heart was heavy when she left the cell.

Kirsty went looking for Brewster, but his office was empty. She decided to wait for him and sat in his chair because it was the only one with nothing on it. His desk was cluttered with files and papers, and she examined them hoping to find some indication of what had happened since last night, but everything was in chaos. She fidgeted, wondering when he would return. To give herself something to do, she started to tidy the papers and files.

'What are you doing?'

She had not heard him come in. 'I was tidying up. Your desk is such a mess it's a wonder you ever find anything.'

'It may look like that to you, but the only time I can't find anything is when it's tidied. Everyone here knows that.'

'I'm sorry,' she said. 'I was restless, and when I'm like that I have to keep busy.'

'I know, Miss Campbell. I have noticed. But whatever you do to keep busy, never, and I mean never, tidy me up.'

'I'm sorry, sir,' she mumbled again.

'That's all right,' he said, smiling at her, and she knew he meant it.

Kirsty returned his smile. 'You've got your uniform on,' she said. 'It suits you.' She did not add he looked more like her idea of a policeman when he was wearing it.

'That's because I still have a job to do, but I was waiting for you,' he said. 'I've got a search warrant for the Orphan Institute. You said there might be some girls in the building, and I wanted a few more details about how to find them before I leave. In the meantime, you'll be pleased to know we have all the men involved under lock and key.'

'Is Mr Bogue involved?' Kirsty was anxious to go and look for the girls, but she had to know.

'No.'

'Simon Harvey?'

Brewster raised his eyebrows. 'No.'

'What about Edward Gordon?' Kirsty asked.

'He's well and truly locked up, as well as Maud, Constable Henderson and several other well known men including a couple of councillors. By the way, did you know Maud was not actually Edward's cousin, but his wife?'

Kirsty bit her lip. She did not want to think about Edward because she knew her feelings for him had become more than friendship. She had been sure he had similar feelings for her, and she found it difficult to grasp that he had meant her harm.

'When we come back from the Orphan Institute do you think I should see him? He might tell me things he wouldn't tell you.'

'No.' Brewster said decisively. 'That would not be a good idea. He's a nasty piece of work is our Edward Gordon. He was running a brothel for those men with, shall we say, certain tastes for the unusual. He calls it a games club. He'll organize any type of sexual game, for a price. The cemetery thing was one of his games.'

'You mean he wasn't performing some sort of satanic ritual?'

'Oh, it was a ritual all right. But it was a sexual ritual rather than a satanic one. Anyway I don't have time to waste. I have to find out whether there are girls in that chapel you told me about, so tell me what you know and I will take the Institute apart if I have to.'

'I'm coming with you,' Kirsty said.

'It would be best if you stayed here.'

'No!' It was Kirsty's turn to be decisive. 'I've been there, and I think I know exactly where the girls will be, but I can't tell you, I'll have to show you.'

Brewster's eyes glittered for a moment, and she thought he was going to argue, but after a slight pause, he said, 'All right, if you must, you must.'

The Orphan Institute did not seem so menacing under the harsh, brittle rays of the November sun, although it could never fully lose the forbidding look of its sombre architecture. An unseen train, chuffing past on the railway line beyond the garden, sent smoke from its engine wafting above the wall and the chapel in the far corner of the grounds.

Kirsty shivered as she remembered what the chapel contained.

Milly opened the front door when Kirsty, Brewster and the police constables were halfway down the drive. She seemed to have been watching for them, and stood in front of the house, her hands in their customary position screwing her apron into a tight bunch in front of her, while she shuffled her feet in an anxious dance.

The chauffeur, who had been watching from the corner of his eyes, concentrated on polishing the hood of the car as they drew nearer. He did not look up when they approached the door, but his hand slowed.

'Mr Bogue's waiting in the parlour,' Milly said anxiously.

'Wait here,' Brewster instructed the constables. 'Not you,' he said as Kirsty hung back. Together they followed Milly inside.

Scraping noises and whisperings sounded above them as they crossed the vast hall. Small heads and bodies scurried about the landing at the top of the staircase. One of them separated from the crowd and scrabbled noisily down the stairs. Milly grabbed him before he reached Kirsty.

He stretched out a hand in her direction, and in a woebegone voice said, 'Have you found her yet, Miss? Have you found our Nora?'

Kirsty moved to his side and gave him a hug, 'Not yet, Bert. But it won't be long now.' Doubts flitted through her mind. How sure was she the soft noises she had heard were what she thought they were? They could have been made by animals or even vermin. She shuddered. And even if it were the girls she had heard, it did not mean Nora was among them. She hoped she would not have to let him down.

Forcing a smile to her lips she said, 'Off you go and join the other children and I'll send Milly to get you when we find her.'

'If you're sure, miss.' He climbed the stairs with dragging footsteps, pausing every now and then to look back at her.

Milly watched Bert go, and then took Kirsty and Brewster to the parlour where Mr Bogue stood in front of the fire tapping his walking stick on the floor. Kirsty had assumed he needed the stick to walk, but realized he was fitter than he at first appeared as he turned towards them with the energy and posture of a younger man.

'Nasty business,' he said. 'Nasty business. To think I trusted the Gordons. Just goes to show you can't trust anyone.' He stared at Kirsty but addressed himself to Brewster. 'I understand you have some sort of warrant. So what happens now?'

'Yes, sir. We have a warrant to search the premises. I trust you will be agreeable to my men having a look around.'

'Of course. The sooner this . . . problem . . . is resolved. The best it will be all round.'

'What will happen to all the children here?' Kirsty forced herself to look at Mr Bogue.

'Cook and Milly will continue to look after them, and I'll send some extra staff from my house in the Ferry.' Bogue's brows gathered into a frown. 'I can't throw them out on the street.' He glared at her, but there was curiosity behind his gaze.

Bracing herself, Kirsty turned to Brewster. 'The investigation needs to start with the cellars. Follow me and I'll show you.' Her voice was a shade more brusque than she meant it to be, and she realized it sounded like a command rather than a suggestion. She knew she had no right to instruct her senior officer, but he said nothing, although she sensed his amusement as he summoned the constables to follow her.

Trying hard to maintain her confidence she strode in the direction of the cellars. But when she closed her hand around the doorknob fear gripped her, and it took all her willpower to open the door.

She hesitated momentarily at the top of the stone stairs before forcing herself to descend into the darkness below, to face the evil it contained.

45

Entering the cellar vaults, her anxiety mounted. But she swallowed hard and led the way to the rear where she looked for the wardrobe and the two broken chairs marking the entrance to the hidden passage. The broken lamp was still perched on the topmost chair and she remembered how it had fallen, leaving her in the dark. But this time several police lamps lighted the way, and Henderson was not there to sabotage her progress.

A constable led the way into the passage which, illuminated by his swinging lamp, now seemed shorter. Moments later they reached the inner door. Memories of being trapped when it swung shut made her falter, reluctant to go through to the inner passage. But she pushed her fears aside in the same way she always did.

'You'll have to prop the door open because if it swings shut it can't be opened from the other side, and we don't want to get trapped.' Her voice wavered, and she hoped no one noticed.

Brewster took his notebook from his pocket and, after wedging it beneath the door, turned to two of the policemen and said, 'Wells, Mitchell. You stay here and guard the door while we go on.'

'Yes, sir,' they chorused.

Kirsty, Brewster and the three remaining policemen continued down the passage. They climbed the steps set into the earth wall, passed below the shaft that led upward, and finally reached the ladder into the room above.

Brewster drew in his breath with a whistling noise as they entered the red draped chapel. He stood for a moment looking around and then said, 'What now? I don't see anything here.'

'Follow me,' Kirsty said, her eyes avoiding the gargoyles in the roof beams as she led him to the second trapdoor.

Brewster leaned over and opened it, revealing the ladder

which led down into the blackness of the passage below. The burning lamps when Kirsty had been here before were now extinguished, but a faint smell of oil and singed cloth hung in the air. It made Kirsty wonder if Ailsa had been the only one imprisoned below, and with her removal there was no further need for light.

'Come on lads, let's get some more light here,' Brewster shouted as he clambered down. 'You stay up here,' he told Kirsty, but he was too late to prevent her following him.

One of the doors in the lower passage stood ajar, and Brewster pushed it open with his foot. The room inside was bare with a bed opposite the door. A manacle rested on the bed, dangling from the end of a chain that hung from the wall above it. Kirsty walked in and examined it. She shivered. This must have been where they had kept Ailsa. She felt sick as she tried to imagine what it would have been like, and how frightened she must have been, shackled and imprisoned in the cell-like room. She dropped the manacle back on the bed.

'We'll have to batter the doors down,' Brewster was saying to the constables after they had unsuccessfully tried to force them.

Kirsty emerged into the passage and, as before, could hear rustlings behind the closed doors. The sounds were so slight they could have been made by rodents or wind wafting through a vent. But, if the evidence from the first room was anything to go by, it had to be more children.

Alarmed, she watched the men shouldering and kicking the doors. The noise resounded loudly in the narrow confines of the passage, and the vibrations travelled from the earth floor up into her feet and legs. If children were inside, they would be petrified.

'It's no use, guvnor,' one of the constables said. 'The doors are too solid. They won't give way.'

Brewster squeezed his chin between finger and thumb until Kirsty was sure he would leave a bruise. 'We have to find a way in,' he said. 'But I don't think we're going to do it by force.'

He stopped to think for a moment. 'Mathers, you go back up the passage and look around for something to lever the doors.

An iron rod, or something similar. There's bound to be something in that heap of junk in the cellar. While you're doing that, the rest of us will search the chapel.'

Kirsty removed an oil lamp from the wall and shook it, expecting it to be empty. However, she heard the slurp of the oil inside and called out, 'Maybe if we lit the oil lamps we'd see better.'

'Good idea, Miss Campbell.' Brewster turned to the remaining two constables. 'Dempster, you're a smoker. Dig out your matches and light the lamps, there's a good fellow. You can join us upstairs when that's done.'

Kirsty unhooked the lamps and laid them on the floor. Dempster lit them, replaced the glass chimneys, and hung them on the shoulder-height iron hooks in the wall. 'They'll be safer up there, miss,' he said before climbing the ladder to the chapel.

Kirsty remained in the lower passage and laid her hand on one of the doors as if she could reassure whoever was behind it. The sounds of Brewster and the two constables searching drifted down to her. She leaned on the door and closed her eyes, trying to think back to when Ailsa had been brought up to the chapel. Had the two men deposited a key anywhere? She had not been able to see them, but she was sure they had not stopped anywhere before the trapdoor clattered shut behind them. That meant the key was in their possession, or it was here in the lower passage.

She climbed the ladder until she was high enough to peer into the chapel.

'Did you find a key on any of the men, when you arrested them?'

Brewster walked over to her. 'There were no keys, Miss Campbell. I looked at their possessions myself.'

'Then the key must be down here,' she said.

She descended the ladder but, even though the oil lamps were lit, the passage was dark and shadowy. She stretched up to lift one from its iron hook. Holding it in front of her she started to inspect the passageway. She looked at the doors, the walls and eventually the ladder itself, and that was when she found them. Two keys: a large iron key and a smaller silver key, hanging on a nail behind the ladder.

'I've found the keys,' she shouted through the opening, and soon Brewster's familiar figure joined her in the corridor.

Taking them from her hand he opened the first cell door. The child on the bed cowered away from him. He made soothing noises, but it did not help.

Kirsty placed the oil lamp on the floor and entered the cell. 'The poor girl's terrified,' she said, shouldering past Brewster. 'It's all right, my love,' she said. 'We've come to help you and take you out of here.' She turned to Brewster. 'Hand me the smaller key, will you?' Taking it from Brewster she unfastened the manacle circling the child's ankle.

They went from cell to cell and found three more girls, all dazed and in a state of exhaustion, and then, in the last cell Kirsty found Nora.

'What took you so bloody long?' Nora asked as Kirsty released her.

Kirsty wanted to give her a hug, but she did not think Nora would accept that familiarity.

'I see you haven't lost your spirit,' she said. She thought of the chapel upstairs, the erotic paintings and Brewster's information about the sex games. 'Did they harm you?'

'Not bloody likely. Some dirty old man tried, but I kicked him in the balls and swore at him, so they stuck me down here again.'

Kirsty was so relieved she leaned over and, unable to stop herself, hugged the child.

Nora relaxed into Kirsty's arms for a moment before stiffening and pushing her away. 'Get off,' she said. 'What do ye think I am.'

But Kirsty was almost sure Nora was smiling. Grinning up at Brewster, Kirsty said, 'Let's get them out of here.'

Brewster smiled back at her. 'They seem to trust you more than me,' he said, 'so if I go up the ladder first, you can start sending them up.'

Kirsty turned to Nora. 'You're not frightened of Mr Brewster. Are you?'

'I'm not frightened of any bloody thing,' the girl said.

'All right then. You go up the ladder first, and I'll send the girls up to you. I don't think they like Mr Brewster.'

Nora scrambled up the ladder, and Kirsty persuaded first one girl then another and another, to climb up to Nora. But the last girl suddenly woke from her dazed state and, giving a squeal of fright, turned and ran back down the passage knocking over the oil lamp which sat on the floor outside the first cell they had opened. Oil spilled out, and flames licked towards the cell door and the bed beyond.

Kirsty ran after her and grabbed her round the waist. It took an effort to haul the struggling girl back to the ladder. 'Get Brewster down here,' she shouted up to Nora. 'I can't get her up the ladder on my own.'

The flames by this time had reached the bedding and were starting to flicker up the walls toward the wooden roof. Smoke was gathering in the confines of the underground passage.

'Hurry,' Kirsty said as Brewster descended the ladder. 'I don't think it's a good idea to linger down here.'

'I see what you mean,' he said, grabbing the girl and hoisting her upwards.

Brewster hauled Kirsty up the last few steps of the ladder, and she emerged into the chapel, coughing and spluttering. Grabbing Kirsty's hand Brewster ran to the other trapdoor that led to the way out.

'Where are the children?' Kirsty gasped.

'It's all right. Dempster and Ramsay have them. They'll be halfway down the passage by this time.' He pushed her through the trapdoor into the passage below, holding on to her hand so she would not fall. 'Keep your breath for running,' he panted. 'We don't know how quickly the chapel will burn.'

46

Smoke wisped through the trapdoor into the passageway and Kirsty, her throat raw and burning, collapsed against the wall coughing and gasping for breath.

Brewster slammed the trapdoor shut behind them, 'That should keep the fire contained in the chapel for the time being,' he muttered, grabbing Kirsty's hand again and starting to run.

If it had not been for Brewster hauling her along the passage, she would have fallen. But she stumbled behind him, each breath rasping painfully in her chest.

They reached the door where the two constables, Harry Wells and Dave Mitchell, stood guard. Brewster reached down and removed his notebook. 'The door's cast-iron, so even if the fire spreads to the passageway it won't be able to get any further,' he said, 'and it will keep the smoke back. We should be all right now.'

Milly was hovering at the cellar door when they emerged. Her eyes widened when she saw the girls. She walked up to them and, touching each in turn, she named them. 'Jeannie, Maggie, Nora, Sarah, and Ruthie.'

'You know them?'

Kirsty's brows furrowed. She had been hoping the missing girls, Rose, Emily and Meg had been found.

'Oh yes, miss. We thought they had run away. But here they all are safe and sound.'

She turned and ran into the kitchen, shouting, 'Cook, come and see who's here.'

Kirsty turned to Brewster. 'We still haven't found the missing girls we were looking for.'

'Perhaps not, but I'm certain these girls are glad you found them, although whether they are safe and sound is another matter altogether.'

271

Milly re-emerged from the kitchen door followed by the cook who smiled acidly at Kirsty and the men.

Cook wiped her floury hands on her apron. 'You'll have to excuse Milly, she's so excitable.' Then she saw the girls and her face softened.

'My, my,' she said, 'what have we here?'

'I think they might need something to eat,' Brewster said.

'You leave it to me, sir. I'll see they get fed.'

She turned to the maid. 'Come on, Milly. We've got a job to do.'

Cook led the children into the kitchen. 'Now don't think you're going to get into my kitchen all the time,' she scolded the girls, but her smile took the sting out of the words. 'It's a special occasion this is.' The door swung shut behind them.

But Milly was still hovering in the back lobby, twisting and pulling at her apron.

Kirsty stayed back as Brewster led his constables out.

'Was something bothering you, Milly?'

The scared look was back on Milly's face. 'I didn't know anything, miss. You do believe me, don't you?' Her voice was scared and timid.

'Why wouldn't I believe you?' Kirsty stared at her. Something was bothering the girl.

'Was there something else you maybe wanted to say?'

'I didn't know you was still in the cellars last night.' The girl's voice came out in a rush.

'Constable Henderson said you'd gone on in front of him.' She hesitated. 'I'm sorry, miss.'

'That's all right, Milly. You weren't to know.'

Kirsty patted the girl on the shoulder. 'Go on now and see to the children.'

'There's something else, miss.' Milly looked at her shoes, and her hands twisted faster.

'Something else?'

'Yes, miss. You know that picture you showed me? Well I knows the girl. She were called Angela and she had a sister called Cissy. They stayed here for a while, but they run away a long time ago.' A tear trickled down her cheek. 'I didn't know what to say when you showed me it, and I didn't want to lose me job.'

'That's all right, Milly, you've told me now.' Kirsty watched as Milly scuttled towards the kitchen.

Bogue was waiting for them in the parlour. 'Well, did you find anything?' He tapped his walking stick on the floor.

'Yes, sir. We found five more girls in the old chapel.'

'The chapel? But how can that be? It's been bricked up for all of my lifetime.'

'There were underground passages, sir.' Brewster walked over to the window and looked out. 'I don't think you're going to have a chapel for much longer, sir,' he said, turning back into the room. 'It's well alight now.'

Kirsty joined him at the window and looked out. The flames were bursting through the roof of the chapel sending sparks floating in the air. 'It's a shame the evidence will be destroyed,' she said, and as a policewoman she believed that. However, Kirsty, the woman, could not help but breathe a sigh of relief because the evil the chapel represented was burning and floating away with the sparks and flames, spiralling upwards in clouds of smoke.

She had not been aware Bogue was standing behind her. 'Good riddance,' he said. 'That place always gave me the creeps.'

Kirsty went to check on the girls while Brewster informed him what they had found in the chapel.

'I wouldn't have believed it.' She heard him say as she returned.

'What are we to do about the girls? They can't stay here, not after what they've been through.'

She looked at Brewster, but Bogue answered her question. 'I'll get in touch with the Barnhill Orphanage right away. The minister owes me a favour, and the matron is a motherly soul. After that I'll see if I can pull some strings, and get them boarded out.'

Kirsty was still unsure about Bogue, but he seemed genuine

enough this afternoon. 'There's Bert as well,' she said.

'Who is Bert?' The old man looked at her for the first time.

'Bert is Nora's brother,' she explained, 'and they don't like to be apart.'

'I'll see Bert and Nora stay together.' Bogue turned his attention back to Brewster, leaving Kirsty feeling she had been dismissed. But as she turned to go, Bogue called softly after her, 'It's a pity about that merger, Miss Campbell. I've a feeling you'd have been the making of my Johnnie.'

She paused with her hand on the doorknob. 'The answer's still no, Mr Bogue.'

'Pity. Such a pity,' he said.

Kirsty told Brewster she felt a responsibility for the girls and would escort them to the Barnhill Orphanage.

He looked at her, and she sensed he was aware of her distrust following what had happened at the Orphan Institute, but he nodded, and said, 'I'll see you at the police station once you've seen them settled.'

Bogue's car was large but by the time the five girls, one boy and Kirsty crammed themselves into it hardly an inch of breathing space was left, and they were all glad to spill out when they reached Barnhill.

'They'll be safe here,' the matron said as she bustled around. She was just as Bogue described her, a buxom, motherly person who immediately fussed over the girls. Kirsty noticed that even Nora responded to her warmth and good humour.

Kirsty finally left, but only after inspecting the house and gardens to make sure the girls would be comfortable, although she had doubts as to whether they would be happy. But maybe that was too much to expect after their experiences.

'Mind you bloody come and see Bert and me,' Nora told Kirsty before she left. 'I don't want no more adventures like that last one.'

'Of course I'll come,' Kirsty promised.

The afternoon sun was low in the sky before Kirsty got back to the police station. She found Brewster waiting in her small office.

'The men found your hat in the cellars when they went back down to make sure the fire was contained. I'm afraid it's dirty.'

'Thanks,' she said taking it from him.

His finger traced an ink-blot on her desk. 'I've been in touch with one of the hospitals, and they have a bed for Angel,' he said. 'Dr Perry, an old friend of mine, is coming to see her. He doesn't usually come out himself, so I suppose we should feel privileged.'

'What sort of hospital?' Kirsty knew before he said anything that it was the Lunatic Asylum. Where else did they take people who did not have all their wits.

Brewster grasped her hand. 'It will be all right Miss Campbell. Perry's a good man. He won't keep her locked up forever. He'll help her.'

Kirsty knew within herself Angel did not have any other option, but she still said, 'Are you sure?'

'I told you. Perry's a good man. If anyone can make it right for Angel, he can.' Brewster looked at her with a helpless expression in his eyes. 'Ah, Kirsty,' he said, 'you want to make the world a better place for everybody, don't you?'

She was conscious he had used her first name – he had never done that before – and of the warmth of his hand as it held hers. For a moment, they stood and looked at each other. His other hand rose and gently stroked her cheek. 'Don't ever change, Kirsty,' he said, turning away and dropping his hands to his sides. His eyes were suspiciously bright, and his shoulders had the droop that reminded Kirsty of a small boy caught doing something forbidden.

Resisting the urge to reach out and hold him as she might have done with Bert, she concentrated her thoughts on Maggie. Frail, beautiful Maggie, who loved and depended on this man standing beside her.

'Yes, sir,' Kirsty said softly before she turned her back to leave the room.

'Oh, Miss Campbell, one other thing.'

'Yes, sir?'

'The assistant chief constable has asked me to report on how you are fitting in with the Dundee City Police Force.'

She stared at him. No wonder he had been sympathetic towards her, he knew what was going to happen next. This is it then, she thought, this is the end. Well, it was no more than she expected. But all she said was, 'Yes, sir.'

47

Kirsty heard him leave his office, listened to the sound of his feet growing fainter as he penetrated the depths of the building and knew he was off to report to the assistant chief constable.

The report would not be favourable. How could it be? She had been insubordinate and disobeyed orders, and she had told Brewster she did not want to be a statement taker. She had not fitted in from the beginning, right from the start when the assistant chief constable told her he had not asked for a woman.

At least it would not take her long to empty her desk. Everything, except for her coat hanging on a hook on the wall and her hat perched on the end of the desk, belonged to Dundee City Police Force.

She sat, immobile, impervious to the clatter of feet, slamming of doors, and voices and laughter resounding in the corridor, signalling a shift changeover. No one ever talked, laughed or joked with her. No one stopped, at the door of her office, to ask how things were. She was a woman in male territory, and she was not welcome. The minutes ticked by as she waited for Brewster to return and tell her she was no longer wanted in Dundee.

The duty sergeant poked his head round her door. 'Inspector Brewster said for you to come to his office, Miss Campbell.'

'Thanks,' she said, dully. He had not even had the decency to come for her. He had summoned her through the sergeant.

She stood up, straightened her skirt and buttoned her jacket. Thank goodness she had worn it today. It would allow her to leave the force with some dignity, as a policewoman.

Dr Perry was waiting in Brewster's office.

'Jamie told me I should wait for you,' he said, when

Brewster introduced them. 'He told me you know Angel better than anyone.'

He was younger than Kirsty imagined a doctor should be, tall with darkish fair hair, blue eyes and eyebrows that were too neat to be natural. His suit was smart, a dark grey with a faint stripe. He also wore a white shirt and a large spotted bow tie. He clasped Kirsty's hand within his in a formal handshake, and although his skin was soft and nails manicured, his grip was firm and confident. He was the opposite of Brewster who never looked tidy.

'I'll take you to see Angel,' Kirsty said, feeling the gloom settle over her as all sorts of thoughts flitted through her brain. Momentarily she forgot her own problems. What were they going to do to Angel? Surely she had suffered enough. And yet, what else was there for her?

'Good. Do you think you could give the attendants a shout, Jamie? I think they are in your staff room. Knowing them, they will be drinking tea.'

'You're sure Angel will get the help she needs?' Kirsty said as they walked down the dingy corridor to her cell.

She bit her lip and kept her face turned away from the doctor to hide the tears of frustration and anger pricking at the back of her eyes. Angel deserved better than the Lunatic Asylum and now it was all over it should be made right for her. Kirsty had failed her, but then maybe she had been naive to think the girl would regain her senses once the crime was solved and she was no longer accused. Kirsty knew, and had always known, it could never have been as simple as that, although she had hoped for more.

'Of course she will get help. We have a lot of new treatments nowadays. However, the child has suffered a great deal of psychological damage and recovery can be a long, slow process.' He hesitated, and his fingers strayed towards his bow tie. 'From what I have been told she has blocked all memory of her suffering, and until she can open up and grieve for her sister recovery cannot commence. Even then it could take months, maybe even years for her sufferings to fade from her memory, and it is possible she will never entirely forget.' Dr Perry fingered his bow tie as he looked at her. 'We will have to ensure her safety during the treatment period. You do understand?' he finished lamely.

'Yes, I understand.' Kirsty's voice faltered. She knew it meant Angel would be locked up. She would not be allowed any freedom. She would have to be kept safe. 'But I'll be visiting her regularly,' Kirsty said defiantly, wanting to add, to make sure she is all right, but did not.

'Of course,' he said, 'that may aid her recovery.'

A pang of conscience hit Kirsty. She wanted desperately to honour her promise to visit Angel, but her future in Dundee was uncertain, and if she returned to London it would be impossible to keep. But, if that was the case, she would make sure to visit before she left.

Keeping her thoughts to herself, she said, 'Well, I'd better take you to her.'

Walking a few paces in front of Dr Perry she led him to the cell. The two white-coated attendants followed closely behind. When she reached the cell door she turned to Dr Perry. 'The attendants can wait outside.' Her voice was firm, and she was not prepared to give way if he argued. However, he nodded his agreement.

Angel was in her usual position, sitting on the mattress with her arms wrapped around her body. Her eyes were blank, and she did not turn her head in their direction as they entered the cell.

Kirsty walked over and sat beside her. 'I've come back to see you, Angel, like I promised. And I've brought a doctor with me. He's going to help you.'

Angel remained motionless, although Kirsty sensed she was listening.

'I want you to go with the doctor. He's got a bed for you in the hospital, and you can stay there until you feel better.' Kirsty paused. 'You won't have to come back here because you're not under arrest any longer. We know you are innocent. So you are free.'

Angel's eyes flickered, and her arms tightened around her body.

'We caught the murderer, Angel. We know it wasn't you.'

Angel started to rock, slowly at first, then faster and faster.

'We caught them all, Angel. The men who murdered Cissy, they won't be able to kill any more girls.'

Angel started to beat her head against the wall. Kirsty put her arms round her to prevent her from hurting herself. But even Kirsty was not prepared for Angel's response.

'Cissy! Cissy! Cissy!' The howl echoed around the cell sounding like an animal in pain, tearing at Kirsty's heart and making Dr Perry flinch.

Unable to stop the tears which streamed down her face, Kirsty tightened her arms around the girl. Why couldn't she make it all right for Angel? She wanted so badly to take the girl's pain away. She just hoped Dr Perry could do it.

Angel's howling intensified, and Kirsty, barely managing to restrain herself from joining in, clasped her tightly and rocked with her. The girl was only exchanging one cell for another, she thought bitterly, and it was doubtful she would ever be free.

Brewster was waiting in her office when she returned from the cells.

'How did it go?' He slid off the desk, took her elbow, and guided her to the chair.

Kirsty heaved a long, shuddering sigh. She wanted to ask him about his meeting with the assistant chief constable, but she said, 'Terrible, I can still hear Angel's screams in my head.'

'We have done all we could for her. You do see that, don't you? And you will find no better doctor than John Perry. He will do his best for her.'

'Yes,' she said. 'I don't doubt it.' She struggled to maintain her composure. 'It wasn't his fault. He was gentle with her, but I doubt if Angel can stand any man to be near her, no matter how kind they are. And I don't blame her, not after what she's been through.'

The duty sergeant knocked on the open door. 'I thought you might like a cup of tea, miss.' He entered the room and laid a cup and saucer on her desk. 'It's been a hard day.'

'Thank you,' Kirsty said, watching him go. 'Fancy,' she said to Brewster, 'at the beginning of the week he couldn't stand me, and now he's even managed to find a china cup and saucer instead of those horrible tin mugs in the canteen.'

'The men need time to adjust,' Brewster said. 'They've never had to work with a woman before. It's hard for them.'

'I suppose so.' Kirsty resisted the temptation to add it had been hard for him too. But it did not matter anymore. She would not be here much longer.

Her fingers hovered over the files on her desk, then she thrust them at him. 'These cases are still outstanding. I had hoped we would find these girls when we raided the Orphan Institute, but it wasn't to be.'

A guilty look passed over Brewster's face. 'I forgot to tell you,' he said, 'Rose McKinley's been found at St Andrews. She was with the travelling fair.'

'That leaves Emily Tait, and Meg Strachan for you to find.'

He handed the files back to her. 'You will need them,' he said, 'they are your cases, not mine. Oh, and Rose is waiting with her mother in the interview room. I will need you to take her statement.'

'Yes, sir,' Kirsty said.

Historical Note

Metropolitan Police Force
In 1919, the police service was not the professional body it is today. Indeed a properly constituted police service had not existed prior to the formation of the Metropolitan Police Force in 1829 which introduced the first official policemen. Prior to 1829, there had been the 'Parish Constables', the 'Watchmen', and finally the 'Bow Street Runners'.

In 1835, legislation required cities and boroughs to establish and maintain an adequate police force, but it was not until 1856 that England, with the exception of London, was policed by a paid professional force.

The first constables had been of poor quality but by 1919, things had improved somewhat, although the force still remained a working class organization. The main educational requirement for recruits was the ability to read and write. The men appointed to prominent positions never came from the rank and file; instead they often had legal or military backgrounds.

City of Dundee Police
The City of Dundee Police Force was established in 1824 after the introduction of the first Dundee Police Act. Prior to that, policing had been the responsibility of the 'Town Officers' and then the 'Nightly Watch'.

John Carmichael, a man with considerable police experience, was appointed chief constable in 1909 and he remained in that post until his death in 1931. He is described as a man who kept himself well abreast of the times and was associated with the many developments in the police service during his period of service.

The City of Dundee Police employed a woman, Mrs J. F. Thomson, in 1918. In various published documents, she is sometimes described as a police sister, a policewoman or a statement taker. Her duties were to work with wayward girls and women, erring children and young persons, and to escort female prisoners and reformatory children between various centres in Scotland and England. She gave evidence at the Baird Inquiry and described her duties in the subsequent report, in 1920.

Women Police

The first women police appeared in London in 1914. They were recruited, trained and employed by voluntary organizations and worked independently of the all-male police forces. Although the women police were not employed by the police authorities these organizations were given approval, by the Police Commissioner, Sir Edward Henry, to provide police women to patrol the streets of London, and they worked closely with the police forces in London and around the country.

There were two voluntary organizations providing a police service. The first of these was the Women's Police Volunteers (WPV), founded in 1914 by the two main suffragette societies, the Women's Social and Political Union (WSPU) and the Women's Freedom League (WFL). The second was the Voluntary Women Patrols, set up by the National Union of Women Workers (NUWW).

Women's Police Volunteers/Women's Police Service

Margaret Damer Dawson (WSPU), an anti-white slavery campaigner, was the chief of the WPV. Nina Boyle (WFL), a militant suffragette, the deputy. Many of the women they recruited were suffragettes and in September 1914, the first person to appear in WPV uniform was probably Edith Watson, suffragette and columnist.

One of the aims of the women's police service was to change the attitudes of the police towards women and to provide protection to other women who suffered at police hands, namely prostitutes.

When Damer Dawson and Nina Boyle parted company over a disagreement about the level of co-operation with the male police (Damer Dawson favoured co-operation with the men, Nina Boyle did not), Mary Allen was appointed deputy. Their titles were Commandant and Sub-Commandant. Mary Allen became Commandant in 1920 when Damer Dawson died. Mary Allen had been a militant suffragette who was imprisoned three times, one of these occasions was after throwing a brick through a Home Office window.

In 1915, the Women's Police Volunteers was renamed the Women's Police Service (WPS). Damer Dawson and Mary Allen were subsequently awarded the OBE for services to their country during wartime.

At the end of the war, Scotland Yard tried, unsuccessfully, to disband the Women's Police Service, and in 1920, it was renamed the Women's Auxiliary Service. It remained operational until 1940.

Voluntary Women Patrols/Special Patrols
The second voluntary police service set up during the war years was the Voluntary Women Patrols.

The women patrols wore armbands, and their main aim was to safeguard, influence, and if need be, restrain the behaviour of women and girls who congregated in the neighbourhood of army camps.

New Special Patrols were formulated in 1916, in an endeavour to check unseemly conduct in the Royal Parks, and to assist the police in making enquiries into the machinery for the sale of cocaine among women and soldiers. They still did not wear uniform, but their armlets were replaced by those of the regular police. They had no power of arrest, but they were allocated a constable to escort them through the streets.

Mrs Sofia Stanley was appointed Supervisor of the Special Patrols in March 1917. At the time of her appointment, there were 37 Special Patrols in central London and 29 in the suburbs, most of them working one or two nights a week.

This organization was made up of women who were mostly middle class. Members of the WPS, who prided themselves on their professionalism, thought they were do-gooders.

Women's Police Patrols

In 1918, the Commissioner of the Police, Sir Nevil Macready, set up an official body of women police, the Women's Police Patrols, and appointed Mrs Sofia Stanley as Superintendent.

The policewomen's pay was poor, and they were employed on a yearly basis. They wore uniforms but were neither sworn in nor given power of arrest, and one of their main duties included prostitute control. The first recruits were ex-Special Patrols, closely followed by women from the WPS.

Their training included instructions in police duty, education, first aid and foot drill. They were also taught jujitsu as a form of self-defence.

Their uniforms of high-necked tunics and long skirts were made by Harrods, and their footwear was hard knee-length boots of solid, unpolishable leather (old land-army issue considered too heavy for work). A heavy, shallow helmet completed their outfit.

Although the men resented them they found the women police useful for escorting lost children and dogs to the police station, and fetching the barrow for the conveyance of drunks.

In 1922, a decision was taken to disband the Women's Police Patrols, but this met with resistance and instead their numbers were reduced to 25. Mrs Sofia Stanley was one of those who lost their jobs. The threat of disbandment, however, was a prime factor in Sergeant Lilian Wyles' acceptance of an offer to be the statement taker for the CID. She became the first woman detective in the Metropolitan Police Force.

The Death Game was inspired by these early policewomen and those forward looking men who supported them. I have taken the liberty of assigning minor roles in the novel to some of these groundbreaking people. All other characters are fictional.

CHRIS LONGMUIR

Chris Longmuir was born in Wiltshire and now lives in Angus. Her family moved to Scotland when she was two. After leaving school at fifteen, Chris worked in shops, offices, mills and factories, and was a bus conductor for a spell, before working as a social worker for Angus Council (latterly serving as Assistant Principal Officer for Adoption and Fostering).

Chris is a member of the Society of Authors, the Crime Writers Association and the Scottish Association of Writers. She writes short stories, articles and crime novels, and has won numerous awards. Her first published book, Dead Wood, won the Dundee International Book Prize and was published by Polygon. She designed her own website and confesses to being a techno-geek who builds computers in her spare time.

www.chrislongmuir.co.uk